Cats, Chaos, & Condo Board Wars

Books by Nikki LeClair

STANDALONE NOVELS:

Cats, Chaos, and Condo Board Wars (Romantic Comedy)

EDIE EDWARDS COZY MYSTERY SERIES:

Haunting Me (Book 1)

Locking Up Santa (Book 2)

Busting the Bloodsucker (Book 3)

Cats, Chaos, & Condo Board Wars

NIKKI LECLAIR

KINDRED INK PRESS

About the Author

Nikki LeClair is a Canadian-born award-winning author and audio book producer. When she isn't sitting behind her laptop constructing new adventures, she's chasing her two little girls, brewing a pot of her current favorite tea, or admiring a fine glass of Pinot Noir.

She's a fan of nearly every genre out there, but her heart beats loudest for chick lit, cozy mysteries, thrillers, dramas, and biographies.

Connect with Nikki at http://nikkileclair.weebly.com/

To my darling friend Keelan,
the bravest person I know.

Chapter One

"I don't want *lilies*. I don't want *roses*. I want orchids and saffron crocus!"

What the bloody hell is a saffron crocus?

Sarah Graham blinks at me, her thin blonde eyebrows raising high over her green almond-shaped eyes. In her left hand is a long, light-blue lily that she swings violently before me. "Hello! Did you hear me?"

"Right, yes." I nod and quickly glance down at my cell phone. "But see… The thing is… You requested lilies and roses two months ago and again last week when Eli emailed to confirm—"

Towering over me in her six-inch pink heels, she puts a boney finger up in my face. "Am I not allowed to change my mind? Is that what you are telling me? Isn't changing my mind one of my civil rights?"

The thing with these types of clients is, well, they do anything they can at the last minute to get a discount. And I mean *anything*. I once had a client tell me they found out they were allergic to shrimp the day before their anniversary event in which they had hired a caterer who *specializes* in seafood. Sydney, my boss, approved the discount, and at the event, I found the client downing shrimp cocktail after shrimp cocktail.

Sarah sighs and slumps before me. "Is it that hard to ask for the flowers I want? Is it that difficult of a task for an event planner? I mean, you're acting as if I'm asking for a golden egg."

Why do I always get stuck with these clients? Oh, that's right. Because they ended up giving Sydney too many migraines so she took a seat back from planning. Now they come my way.

"Orchids and saffron crocus," Sarah repeats, locking eyes with me again. "Can you do it, or do I have to call another planner?"

I can hear Eli, my assistant and junior planner, in my head saying over and over again, *Don't be a pushover. Don't be a pushover.*

I force a smile onto my lips. "Ms. Graham, we are six hours away from your husband's birthday party. The decorations are on their way, and so are the ice sculptures. I doubt any event planner will come in blindly to finish the job."

"Are you challenging me?" She glares down at me. "Because I'll have you know that—"

"I'm not challenging you," I say quickly. "I'm simply stating the facts—"

"Well, this is *me* stating the facts. I want orchids and saffrons," Sarah snaps, adjusting her posture. "Make. It. Happen." She stomps away without another word.

My phone jingles in my hand, and I look down to see Sydney's name on the screen.

"Perfect timing," I mutter as I press the phone to my ear. "Hi, Sydney."

"Hilly, love, how's it going? Setup going as planned?"

I turn my back to the commotion in the room and walk toward the beautiful glass doors that lead to the hallway. "Not exactly. We've got a hiccup with the flowers."

"What kind of hiccup?"

"She's changed her mind about the roses and lilies."

Sydney lets out a long breath. "What does she want?"

"Orchids and saffron something."

"Well, the party's at the botanical gardens. It can't be that hard to find…"

I reach the doors and lift my shoulder to hold the phone in place as I reach for the handle. "I can't take flowers from here!"

"Why not? It's not like they'd notice…"

Once I'm out of the room and the noise is behind me, I hear a pop on Sydney's end followed by a gulp. "Migraine again?"

"Not yet, but I feel the throbbing. Just getting ahead of the pain," she answers. "So. Can we handle this, or do we need to throw the term 'breach of contract' at the client?"

By we, she means *me*.

"I can handle it." I exhale as I hurry down the empty grey hallway. "I mean, how hard can it be to find thirty orchids and saffron whatevers?"

Apparently, it's very hard.

Finding the saffron crocuses anyway.

The orchids were easy. I just had Eli run down to our favorite flower shop, Petals Forever. Turns out, saffrons are small, delicate purple flowers that are used in cooking.

Four o'clock rolls around, and I'm still at the botanical gardens awaiting Eli's arrival with the flowers.

Luckily, Sarah Graham is nowhere to be seen, and the room is coming together nicely. Round tables, each seating six guests, are dressed in white satin with black cloth napkins as accents. Twinkle lights hang above the tables and fan out to the glass walls. The only things missing are the orchid and saffron centerpieces and surrounding tea lights.

In the center of the room, two ice sculptures—the numbers five and zero, representing the birthday guest of honor's age—are kept cold on special ice tarmacs. The band is setting up in the back of the room underneath a chandelier of green leafy branches.

"Hils!"

I look over my shoulder to see Eli running toward me, the glass doors now propped open, glistening tulle hanging from the door frame.

Wide-eyed, he scans the room as he approaches me, his dark eyebrows arching high. "Hil, this place looks ah-mazing!"

I give him a quick smile. "Thanks. Let's hope the client thinks so as well."

He rolls his dark brown eyes and pats the top of his dark, wavy hair. Next to Eli, I always feel slightly less stylish. He's in a pair of dark jeans, a classic rock T-shirt, and an expensive brown leather jacket that he's paired with a taupe scarf. Meanwhile, I'm in a black knee-length skirt and a red short-sleeved blouse, my unruly dark hair pin straight down my back.

"Speaking of," Eli sighs as he looks into my eyes, "where is the she-bat anyway?"

"Probably at home getting ready," I say. "Flowers?"

Eli motions behind him. "Coming in as we speak. But Hil, I couldn't find those saffron things anywhere." His smile tightens. "Fresh, anyway…"

I frown. "What do you mean, exactly?"

His face twists in a bunch.

I feel my back straighten.

"Yo! Where do you want these stanky things?"

Eli spins, his hands on his waist, and I take a step to the side to look at the burly man who just entered the room, grunting a few times as he glances around. In his large arms, he holds a medium-sized barrel.

"Um, just set it down wherever," Eli orders with a wave of his hand. "Thanks."

The man drops the barrel onto the floor, the thud echoing throughout the room as he rushes back through the door.

I tug on my assistant's arm. "Eli! What the hell is that?"

"Those saffron things." He looks at me with huge eyes and cringes. "Dried."

"No! Eli!"

"It's the only kind I could find!"

I hurry toward the barrel and pull the heavy lid off. Eli and I both gasp when we look inside. There are no actual flowers—just dried, stringy red pieces. The smell is intense—sweet, kind of like honey, but there's a heavy, earthy aroma you can't miss.

"It looks like garbage," Eli says.

I'm so screwed. I place my hands on the edge of the barrel and look over at him. "Didn't you look at it before you bought it?"

Eli shakes his head. "No! Patricia at the flower shop said she knew of another shop that had it dried, which was probably the best we would get on such short notice. She said the smell was sweet and she was one hundred percent sure everyone would enjoy it!"

He reaches into the barrel and picks up a few strands of the flower. "People cook with this stuff?" He puts the red pieces into his mouth. A moment later, he coughs and gags it up, and I have to hold back a smile. He shudders as he looks at me. "This stuff… It tastes like hot garbage."

I groan and shove both of my hands into the dried flower mess. "What am I supposed to do with this?"

"Sprinkle it on the tables?" Eli gestures to a nearby table.

Before I can lose it on him again, I hear my phone ring in my bag. I withdraw my hands from the shredded flowers and pull out my phone. My screen flashes my roommate's name.

Next to me, Eli leans closer to the barrel.

I press the answer button on my phone and bring it to my ear.

"Luna? I can't talk right now. I'm having a bit of a work emergency."

"It's Glover!"

My toes curl.

"Oh, God." I swallow, forcing a lump down my throat. "Did she find out—"

"No! It's not about the washing machine. Stop being so paranoid!"

I can't help it. If she were to find out I bought a washer and dryer set without her permission—I can only imagine what she would do. I mean, I looked at the condo board rules, and it didn't say you aren't allowed to have them in your unit. It just said that some floors are "forbidden." The floor I live on is one of the forbidden ones, but I have a sneaking suspicion our neighbors down the hall have a set. They stopped doing laundry in the creepy basement a while ago.

"Glover just had animal control take Pax away!"

My heart drops to my feet. "What?"

Eli looks at me, frowning.

"She said he was the one that impregnated Mr. Spatola's show cat. She also slapped an orange notice on the door because she said he was the one who peed in the ficus trees in the lobby, and now you have to replace them. Last week, she said it was Mina's cat. You know the one, blind in one eye. They live on floor seven. I swear, she hates cats."

I stomp both feet, and Eli jumps at my reaction. "He never even leaves the apartment!"

"Well, sometimes I let him roam the hall when I go down to do laundry…"

"Luna!"

"I feel bad he's stuck in these three rooms! He's a cat. They're natural prowlers. They need the chance to explore, hunt, and… He's fixed anyway, you said! Glover just hates him because she hated your grandfather. You know she's been gunning to get rid of Pax for the last three years."

Pax isn't even my cat. He's my grandfather's. Pax came with the condo at Fairway Towers that I otherwise would not be able to afford. Actually, I still can't really afford it on my own, which is why I asked Luna to move in with me two years ago. My grandfather had paid off a large portion of the mortgage before he passed so I wasn't left with much to pay. He even paid for the mortgage transfer into my name, unbeknownst to me.

He was such a kind, loving man. When he passed on, almost everyone in the building came to his funeral, and when I moved in, they all came to greet me. Some brought me pies and casseroles. Glover brought me the condo rule book and warnings.

In hindsight, maybe I should have sold the place, but Fairway Towers is smack dab in the middle of downtown. It's in one of the trendiest neighborhoods, and it's also the fourth most sought-after condo building in the entire city. Plus, I work four blocks south of it.

The only problem with this exclusive building is Mrs. Glover, who lives in penthouse two on the top floor. She's been the president on the condo board since before I moved into the building. In short, she makes everyone's lives a living hell—except for three people who've mastered the art of sucking up to the tyrant.

"Hil?" Luna presses.

"What time does the animal control place close?"

"They said you have 'til six o'clock to come get him, and you have to pay a fine. Tomorrow morning, they're transporting him to another city because they have no room. It's the building on Queen and Mackle."

I moan. "That's all the way across town!"

"I'd go for you, but the guy said they won't release him to me because I'm not his owner."

Damnit.

I watch Eli push the barrel out of the way so the two men from Petals Forever can roll their trolley of orchids into the room. He then turns to me and mouths, *What's going on?*

I hold up my pointer finger. "Okay, thanks, Luna. I have to go. I'll see you in a bit."

"Sorry I couldn't be of any help."

"It's okay," I say softly, hanging up as Eli approaches.

"What's happening?"

"Glover sent my cat to animal control. I have until six today to pick him up."

Eli hisses through his teeth. "It's almost four thirty."

"I know." I sigh as I drop my phone into my purse.

Eli grabs my arms and leads me around the barrel toward the door. "Go get your cat."

"I can't leave, Eli. This party starts in an hour and a half." I almost laugh at his suggestion.

He shakes his head. "Leave it to me. I had no plans tonight anyway."

"This is a pretty big event, Eli—"

"Right, of course," he agrees, "but you've done all the major stuff already, and all that's left is to set up the flowers then make sure stuff runs smoothly." He smirks. "And we all know I'm better at handling the divas than you are anyway."

It's true. I don't have much of a backbone and suspect it's why Sydney made him my assistant.

I bite my bottom lip.

I can't let Pax be shipped off to some weird place. He was my grandfather's everything.

I give in. "Call me every thirty minutes with updates. I can come right back after I get Pax."

"Just go."

It took me an hour to get to animal control then thirty minutes to get Pax out. By the time I got home, it was already eight thirty, and according to Eli, the party was going great. Apparently, Sarah Graham had rung him out for producing dried saffron, but when several guests complimented the sweet smell of the subpar flower, she took full credit.

As I cross the lobby of Fairway Towers, I smile at our concierge, Mateo, and spot the dying ficus trees in each corner of the bright white lobby. I'm quickly distracted when a fellow tenant exits the elevator. Mrs. James is the newest member of the building and lives on the fifth floor directly beneath me. She's in her late sixties and sits on the board of the Royal Museum. Normally, I don't bother much with my neighbors, but when she found out I was an event planner with LaBeau and Gilde, she mentioned possibly hiring me for the museum events.

Which would be a massive contract. A *very* big deal. They have gala events almost monthly, and celebrities show up, and politicians, and… If I ever got her to sign with me, even just once, Sydney would flip out.

"Evening, Mrs. James."

"Hello, dear." She smiles at me, her straight teeth glowing as if recently bleached. She's also dyed her hair a beautiful dark blonde, getting rid of the ashy blonde she had last week, and twirled it up in a small beehive. She stops next to me and adjusts her purse. "You look lovely this evening. I wish I could chat, but I'm late for a patron's birthday party. Have a good night."

"You too! Don't party too hard now," I joke.

I'm so lame.

She chuckles and nods her head as she makes her way past the concierge.

I step up to the elevator doors and wait for them to open again then grab my phone and start an email to Sydney about the updates of the party. Pax meows at my feet from a cage the animal control center made me buy because I hadn't brought my own.

The elevator pings open in front of me, and a face I haven't seen in some time stares back at me. I have to blink because I think I'm seeing things. My heart must think so too because it starts to drum inside my chest.

Mr. Neal Turner.

Mr. Neal "I'm going to show you how to make the best homemade pizza on our date, kiss you then shove you out of my place like a jerk, disappear for three months and never call you again" Turner.

He looks equally surprised to see me, and as the elevator doors begin to slide shut again, he reaches out to stop them.

I bend over to pick up Pax then hurry into the elevator. "Thanks."

"No problem." He slides his hands into his jeans pockets and keeps his dark blue eyes on the doors as they close.

I make sure to stay close to the opposite side of the elevator with Pax's cage between us. I have to focus on my phone because it's hard not to look at his reflection in the mirrored elevator walls.

He's almost unrecognizable, sporting a goatee now, far from neat, and a tanned complexion that almost makes me envious. His light brown hair is short on the sides, longer on the front.

"Did he run away?"

I look over at him. "Sorry?"

He motions at Pax.

I shake my head. "Glover had him taken by animal control."

He nods, but from the corner of my eye, I can see him smirk, and it irks me.

I finish the email to Sydney and scroll through my inbox, pretending to be engrossed in an email. My left foot begins to tap slowly, nervously. How long does it take to get to the sixth friggin' floor? This elevator is such a hunk of junk.

"Going to the condo meeting tomorrow?"

"Nope, never do."

"It's mandatory, I think."

I mimic his voice in my head, like a child, *It's mandatory,* but say nothing out loud.

Finally, the elevator stops on six, and I pick Pax up. "That's never made me go before."

I hurry from the elevator before he can say anything else and don't ease up until I'm at the end of the hallway. The elevator doors have long closed, and I'm sure he's already at his floor by the time I reach my front door. I instantly see the orange note and snatch it off the door, crumpling it in my hand before stuffing it into the pocket of my suit jacket.

Glover.

Living at the end of the hallway on the sixth floor has been a godsend. That, and the luck of only having one next-door neighbor who's always traveling for work. I glance around the simple hallway with its black and grey geometric carpet, white walls, and black doors. A set of mirrors hangs on the wall right across from the shiny elevator doors.

Before I can slide my key into the lock, the door swings open.

Luna appears, her wild, short black hair held back by a leopard print headband. She's in a peasant skirt and matching brown blouse, a new white and blue gemmed mala hanging around her neck. She throws her arms up when she sees me and Pax, her gemstone bracelets falling to her elbows. "Baby Paxy!"

She reaches for Pax, and I hand him over as I hustle into the condo, which smells like patchouli, courtesy of Luna. Not that I mind it. It's sure better than when she burns that incense that smells like pee. She works at an herbal store down the block from the condo. It's where we met. I needed some catnip for Pax, and she talked me into signing up for one of her "Herbs in Cooking" classes that she does every Sunday night.

Before she moved in, my condo was pretty boring. An IKEA couch here, a round wooden dining table in front of the balcony windows, cheap canvas paintings on this wall or that. Within a day of Luna moving in, she'd thrown colorful pillows on the grey sectional, placed faded vintage carpets in the living room and dining room, hung tapestries of different colors on the walls, and set up a mini garden near our balcony with herbs and flowers.

She painted the bathroom a bright yellow and found lime green decor and wall hangings. That took some time getting used to. Everything with Luna takes some getting used to.

Luna kneels, gently placing the cage on the floor. "He looks absolutely terrified!"

I kick off my shoes as I shut the door behind me. "He should be. He owes me a hundred and seventy dollars."

"I thought it was a hundred to release him?" Luna asks as she fiddles with the cage lock.

"Plus seventy for that cage."

She shakes her head as the cage door swings open. "This cage is not even worth ten dollars. They stiffed you."

"I figured." I sigh as I hang my purse on the coat rack next to the door.

We watch as Pax strolls out of the cage, his long white and black tail swishing side to side. He meows once then waddles to the kitchen, his big belly swinging left to right.

Luna sets her hands on her knees and smiles up at me. "So! How did the work emergency go?" She jumps to her feet, and we head into the kitchen where I tell her the story. She's got all four burners on the stove going, and as she stirs, she shakes her head. "Where does your boss find these clients?"

I lean against the fridge.

Our kitchen is a small one, but the frosted glass cabinets, grey granite countertops, and tiny island with a wine rack on the side work just fine for two people.

"They find us! The worst part was finding the saffron whatevers at the last minute!"

Luna frowns. "Why didn't you just ask me? You know we sell them at the shop."

I push myself off the fridge and blink at her. "*What?*"

Luna smirks. "Where do you think I get our saffrons?"

"We have saffrons?"

I step out past the wall and look over at the mini plant farm near the balcony, instantly spotting the tiny purple flowers poking out from a big green pot. "How have I never noticed that?"

Luna lets out a chuckle just as something scrapes across the floor in the condo above us. "I thought subletters aren't allowed…"

I shake my head as I slink up to the island and retrieve a bottle of wine. "Not a subletter. Jerky McJerkface is back. I ran into him in the elevator."

Luna's dark eyes almost pop out of her head. "Nooo…"

"Yup, that was the best, most awkward ride ever," I quip sarcastically. I pull out a wine glass and set it down next to the bottle.

"I thought he was going to be gone for six months," Luna says. "How long has it been?"

"Three."

She raises her eyebrows at me.

"Not that I'm counting."

"Why'd he come back so early?"

I look at her as I twist open the bottle of wine. "Our conversation consisted of 'Thanks,' 'Did the cat run away?' and 'Mandatory condo meeting,' followed by me fleeing as soon as the doors opened."

"What are you going to do?" Luna asks, her eyes never leaving mine.

"I'm going to not do anything. It was one date—one *bad* date—and I'm over it."

Except it wasn't a bad date. It was a great date, it just ended…abruptly. And I'm not over it. I actually really liked him, and I thought I'd heard from another tenant that he'd had a crush on me for a while too.

Doesn't matter. It's ancient history.

Luna says nothing as I pour wine into my glass and take a long drink. Then she asks, "Think you'll see him at the condo board meeting?"

I let out a laugh. "I will not, for I am not going."

Luna whines at me. "Hil, you have to. I'm going to my parents' tomorrow."

"Can't you go Sunday?" I whine back.

"No! I have to drop off *Hidden Desires* for my mom's book club." Luna gestures with her chin toward a book resting against the backsplash near the sink. A black cover, two sets of legs entangled atop silk sheets. "It's about a sex club in the seventies. Really thought-provoking and endearing."

I make a face, and she chuckles. "Whatever, Grandma. Anyway, I won't be back 'til Sunday night, and the meeting is mandatory, so you have to go. I mean, maybe that's another reason Glover is coming after you. You've been to a total of, what, four meetings in three years? You don't take that stuff seriously."

"Nobody but Glover takes that stuff seriously, Luna." I reach into my coat pocket and retrieve the orange note. I uncrumple it and see that it's addressed to Luna, not me.

Tenants of 608. Cease with the burning of incense immediately, per condo code violation 36c.

Luna sets down her wooden spoon and reaches across the island for the note in my hand. "She can't stop me from burning incense! I've been doing it for two years!"

It's my turn to smirk. "According to the condo code, she can."

Luna crumples the paper in her hand. "This is all because I put Miracle Grow into the lobby trees."

"You what?"

"Earlier today, she caught me putting Miracle Grow into the trees downstairs and had a fit. Said she doesn't use mass produced fertilizers because you never know what's in them, and what I was doing was proof that Pax was peeing in them because I was trying to cover it up."

I can't help but chuckle, and Luna just gives me a sharp glare. "Okay, I'll tell you what I'll do. I'll bring her the basket of muffins she likes from the corner bakery. She'll back off of us for a while and put her crazy on someone else."

"You can't keep bribing her, Hil!"

"Why not?" I take a quick drink of my wine. "It's what everyone else does."

Luna shakes her head as she turns back to the stove. "Somebody needs to stand up to her."

"You do, all the time, and what good has it ever done?" She glares at me.

I shrug and lift my glass from the counter again. "Sometimes, with people like her, it's best to keep your head down. Let them have their little fits and bribe them to stay away from you."

"Avoidance, that's avoidance," Luna mutters. After a second, she adds, "You should go to the meeting tomorrow."

"No way. Saturday mornings I do my laundry," I remind her, and then I smile. "And tomorrow I'm looking forward to doing my laundry in *our* condo. Not in that creepy basement."

"What time are they getting here with the machines?"

Luna asks as she looks at the kitchen clock. "It's almost nine o'clock."

"Nine thirty." I grin. "I paid them extra to deliver after hours and to use the freight elevator so Glover wouldn't notice."

Chapter Two

Except the delivery never came.

I waited until eleven and couldn't even call the store to find out what happened.

Serves me right. This is what happens when you buy discounted machines from a shady appliance store that also serves cheap pizza.

It's now nine o'clock on Saturday morning. I've given up calling and have gone down to the basement to do my laundry. Usually it's full of tenants, but today, it's empty. That's when I remember the mandatory meeting that starts…now.

The laundry room isn't much to look at, just a long white room with fifteen washing machines against one wall and fifteen dryers against the other. Two couches sit in the middle of the room. A large coffee table with magazines stacked on top accompanies it. Right now, the table has election pamphlets covering it, promoting Mrs. Glover for condo board president—again.

I throw my laundry in and head back up to my condo where I call the store and finally get through.

"What do you mean I gave you the wrong address?" I'm in grey sweats and a white T-shirt, pacing in front of our couch, frazzled the machines will now be delivered in bright daylight.

"Sorry, lady, but nobody by the name of 'Hilary Brandt' lived there."

"What's the address you have on file then?"

"Fairway Towers, Unit 603."

"That's the right address!"

I hear the sales associate mutter something to someone and then return to me. "I'm trying to figure out what happened. I'll give you a call in a few minutes." She hangs up before I can respond.

I drop down on the couch.

Minutes later, I'm mindlessly flipping through morning sitcoms when my phone rings. I see Eli's name and answer the call.

"Major faux pas situation, Hil!"

"It's ten thirty in the morning. How can there be a situation?" I pull my legs off the couch. "We don't even have an event this weekend."

"I'm talking about last night! Sarah sent Sydney an email about the saffrons. Apparently, the flowers may or may not have stained some of the guests' dresses."

I gasp. "Eli!"

"How was I supposed to know it would stain?"

"What did Sydney say?"

"She said that she would be speaking to you when you come in Monday. Sarah's gunning for your dismissal. She said she was humiliated."

"It was an honest mistake!" I jump from the couch and put a hand on my forehead. "Sydney has to know that."

"I think she knows, but Sarah insisted on the meeting…"

"She's going to be *at* the meeting?"

"Apparently so." Eli sighs. "So sorry, Hil. I wanted to give you a heads up. Just know that I plan to fight fiercely at your side."

"That doesn't bring me much consolation."

"She's been walking all over you from the moment she hired you, and you know I'll be telling Sydney that." He pauses in his flustered state and lets out a sigh. "What are you doing? What are your plans for the day? Want to tag along to view some moving art pieces with me and Jacob later tonight?"

Jacob is Eli's boyfriend. They met when Jacob hired us to plan his art gallery's grand opening. He's the only son of a very famous contemporary art couple. I always find him to be a little bit…intellectually draining. Other than his obvious good looks, I don't see what Eli sees in him. "I thought you hate that stuff?"

"I do, but he gets all whiny if I don't go with him so I pay my dues. Want to join? You could meet a nice, hot artist to have a fling with!"

"Thanks, but I'm just going to stay in tonight, catch up on Netflix."

"Shhh!" Eli remarks hastily. "Did you hear that?"

"What?" I whisper back, completely on guard.

"It's the sound of your womanhood collapsing in on itself as you prematurely age it!"

"I'm not prematurely aging anything," I declare. "I'm just being patient as I wait for someone who deserves me."

"Pinterest?"

"Saw it on a coffee mug."

"You're thirty-two, not sixty-two. God, my nana gets

more action in her retirement village than you do. And she has dentures and uncontrollable gas."

"Ew, Eli."

"I'm just saying. You're in your prime. When's the last time you were on a date, huh? Or even had some noble gentlemen whisk you into a night of passion—"

"Two weeks ago. I went out with your accountant friend."

"That wasn't a date. That was coffee as he did your taxes."

I think back on the date with Leo the tax man. He was very touchy and winky for someone just having coffee with a potential client. "Well, it definitely didn't seem like that with all his winking—"

"He winks at everyone!" Eli interrupts. "Hil, honestly, you are a catch. Hard working, pretty, smart, kind—"

"I'm overqualified," I joke. "*That's* from Pinterest."

"Hil. I'm serious."

"I know, and I appreciate it, but honestly, I'm good." I get up from the couch and drag myself toward the condo door. "And I have to get back to my laundry right now, so if you don't mind…"

"Fine. Have a nice weekend, Grandma Brandt."

He hangs up, and I shake my head as I lock my door.

Once I'm downstairs, loading my wet clothes into the basket to move them into a dryer, I get a text message from Eli. It's a GIF of an old lady surrounded with cats, and underneath it, he's written "YOU" in all caps. It makes me smirk, and for a second, I think about telling him my little secret to get him off my back.

Although, it could also get him in such an upheaval, he'd make me join a convent.

I'm immediately filled with a rumble of regret, and I shudder when I think about sharing my secret with anyone. It's *so* humiliating.

"Ms. Brandt."

I freeze.

That voice has that kind of effect on people. I feel my toes curl in my sneakers as I shut my eyes and exhale softly. "Good morning, Mrs. Glover."

"So nice to see you're not suffering from some incurable disease which has left you bedridden. We were all concerned."

I roll my eyes and turn around to face her, opening my eyes and forcing the best smile I can muster. I raise my arms. "Nope! I'm just fine."

She stands in the doorway, her bright yellow dress suit making her stand out against the white walls. Diamond bracelets wrap around her thin wrists, and a string of pearls delicately hangs around her neck, perfectly in line with her dirty blonde shoulder-length bob. She runs her small, sharp blue eyes up and down my body. "I see. Perhaps you missed the memo about the condo board meeting I placed in everyone's mailbox?"

"Oh, um, I must have," I lie, my face bunching up. "I guess Luna forgot to mention it. She usually goes to those things and is gone for the day. I'm so sorry."

Mrs. Glover frowns as she enters the room and crosses her arms over her chest. "Okay, well, I suppose that's understandable."

I give her another smile then turn back around to finish unloading my clothes. "Won't happen again."

Please go away. Please, please, please…

She lets out a shrill laugh that echoes between us and

forces me to turn back around. "Although, it's funny because Neal Turner from 703, you know Neal, yes? He lives on the floor above you."

She knows I know who he is. Everyone knows who Neal is.

"I know him," I say carefully.

"Well, he said he saw you yesterday and that you knew about the meeting last night?"

Damn him to hell.

I nervously frown as I look up at the ceiling. "I don't recall if I said anything to him…"

"Don't frown, dear," she suddenly snaps. "It causes wrinkles."

I turn my head and set my eyes on her. The tightness of her face makes me swallow anxiously as she goes on.

"The meeting was mandatory. It was about the upcoming election, allocating voter polls, volunteer forms, and our budget overhaul."

"Well, maybe I can get the minutes from Bryson in 310."

Bryson I-don't-remember-his-last-name has been the minute taker for all the condo board meetings since day one, according to my grandfather. He works from home doing something with computers and doesn't have much of a social life. He's always been so nice to me and Luna. I don't know why he would ever work with Mrs. Glover on anything.

"I've already instructed him to email both you and Luna," she tells me, her eyes narrowing as she looks at my wet clothing. "Such an odd thing happened last evening. Did you hear?"

I slowly shake my head, preparing for another blindsided comment. "No."

"A pair of big, confused men showed up at the freight elevator doors out back and tried to deliver a clunky-looking washing machine and dryer. Thank goodness I caught them and sent them back to where they came from. Can you imagine?" She lets out a rattle of a laugh. "As if someone in this building would try to bring in non-approved appliances underneath my nose."

She—

She was the—

Argh!

"If I hadn't been out walking Sabeen, I would have missed it," she goes on, her arms uncrossing and dropping to her sides. Her eyes have yet to leave mine. "Right place at the right time, wouldn't you say, Ms. Brandt?"

I'm stunned into silence.

After a moment, she clasps her hands together and gives me a tight smile. "Well, you have a pleasant weekend. Do read that email the *moment* you receive it, will you?"

"She's insufferable! She's a mean, old tyrant with nothing to do all day but walk that dumb poodle of hers!" I suck in a breath. "I mean, really, a rich white woman with a poodle? How much more cliché can you get?"

"Not much more," Luna agrees.

"She's a disgrace to women her age, really. If you really, *really* think about it. She puts women in their…in their…how old is she?"

Luna's face scrunches up as she looks up from the cucumbers she's dicing. "I think she's sixty? Or maybe fifty-five?"

"Whatever. She puts a bad image on women her age."

I'm not sure I'm even right, but ever since Luna got home thirty minutes ago, I haven't been able to stop venting. I followed her from her bedroom to the bathroom, and now I'm sitting on a stool at the kitchen island, watching and stewing as she preps for her Sunday night cooking class.

"I take it the muffin peace basket idea is out the window?" Luna raises an eyebrow and laughs at my scowl, her bangs falling over her eyes. "What did the store say when you asked for your money back?"

"They don't do refunds." I slink onto a stool and watch her dice. "It was in the contract I signed, apparently. They gave me a store credit."

"That's not bad."

"What am I ever going to buy there if I can never have my own onsite washer and dryer? It's an appliance store!" I drop my head onto my hands. "I lost seven hundred bucks. All because of that stupid old cow in the penthouse!" I groan and kick the island a few times with my swinging feet. I look up and see Luna's sympathetic face. "I wish somebody would just knock her off her stupid pedestal. Then they could dish it back at her and she'd see how awful she has always been. She misuses her power as condo board president."

Luna gives me a quick look. "Nobody else is running against her."

I pull my elbows off the counter. "Yeah, well, somebody should."

Luna shrugs. "Everyone in the building is scared to."

I don't say anything because I know she's right.

"Want to join in on the class tonight?" She gives me a smile. "It's vegan Irish stew night."

I wrinkle my nose. "No thanks, I like my meat. But you have fun. I'll just sink into the bathtub and overthink my meeting tomorrow morning with Sydney and Sarah."

I hobble off the stool just as Luna says, "She may ring into you just to get Sarah off her back, but you know she won't fire you."

I groan as I drag myself toward the bathroom.

An hour later, I emerge into the dark condo. My robe is tied tight, my hair is wrapped in a towel, and I'm finally at ease about my run-in with Glover yesterday. There really is nothing I can do about it other than keep avoiding her as best as I can. Or maybe I could just sell the place?

I mean, my grandfather wouldn't really mind, would he? He only bought this place after my grandma died to be closer to my parents and me.

As I cross the living room, something glides against the balcony doors, and I let out a scream. I stumble into the wall against one of Luna's tapestries. It falls from the wall over my face and tears the towel off my head just as the lights go on in the living room. I hear a snort of laughter followed by giggling.

"Oh my God, Hil, are you okay?"

I yank the tapestry off and shove my long, wet hair out of my face so I can see. Luna stands a few feet away from me, her hands on either side of her face as she watches me drop the tapestry to the floor.

But it's not just her eyes on me.

It's five other pairs belonging to several of our neighbors.

In shock, I stand in place and look around the room.

Bryson, Glover's minute taker, stands behind Luna, giving me an awkward wave. His skater boy hair falls over his eyes as he averts his gaze. He's in jeans and a classic rock T-shirt.

On the couch sits Martin Tweed, who lives down the hall from us. He's a recent widower who spends his time playing chess at the local YMCA and in the park behind the condo building. He's always smiling. Even now, as awkward as the situation is, he smiles brightly at me, brushing his thinning grey hair to the left. He's wearing a plaid sweater and khakis, his cane rested against his legs.

Next to him are the Dorsts, a middle-aged couple who live with their teenage son a few floors below us. Mrs. Dorst has her legs crossed, her hands cupping her top knee. She's in a pair of Lulu's and a tight grey runner's top, her long brown hair pulled back into a ponytail. She gives me a fleeting smile as her legs begin to bounce. Mr. Dorst sits on her other side, one leg over the other, donning a dark, expensive-looking suit, his arm on the armrest, fingers tapping anxiously.

Paulette Robbins sits on the ground near our coffee table, patting Pax who's shown his belly for attention. She's hard to miss with her curly, bright blue hair pulled into two pigtails. If Luna is a hippie, Paulette is a hipster. She's rocking light high-waisted jeans paired with a vintage plaid shirt. Paulette works for a local radio station as their graphic designer.

I greet the crowd with a shaky voice as I clench my robe tighter against me. "Hell-lo. What's up?"

Luna draws in a breath and exchanges a look with Mrs. Dorst quickly before giving me a serious glare. "Hil, we need to talk."

I motion toward my bedroom door. "Can it wait until I get into some clothes?"

"No, we have to be quick," Paulette says, her voice becoming a whisper. "She could be on to us."

They look at each other, slowly and suspiciously.

"Who?" I whisper back, entranced by the designer's serious tone.

"Arlene," Luna says. Her eyes narrow, a sign of the severity of the person they speak of.

"Ohhh." I nod my head as the word comes out in a whisper again. I look from her to Paulette then back to Luna. "Who's Arlene?"

"Glover!" Mrs. Dorst exclaims, the lines around her mouth bunching up to show her annoyance. "Mrs. Glover, honestly…"

"Well, sorry," I throw her way. "I'm not on a first-name basis with the woman who hates me."

Luna takes a step back from me and joins Bryson at his side. "We've come to talk to you about something really important."

"Is this about the email?" I look from her to Bryson. "Because I did get it, I just didn't think I needed to respond to it."

"It's not about the email," Bryson replies, his New Jersey accent coming in thick.

They all sit up and stare at me with hard eyes.

Even Mr. Tweed.

I suppose it's his glare that puts me the most on edge. "Okay, then what?"

"Hil, there's no Sunday night cooking class anymore," Luna begins. "There hasn't been a cooking class in almost two years. I cook for everyone as a cover so nobody knows what we're really doing."

I frown at her. "What?"

"We've formed a new club," Paulette tells me. "A secret club, more intimate."

I look from the woman with blue hair back to my roommate. We lock eyes, and for a second, Luna seems nervous. Frown lines appear on her forehead. She's tapping her fingers against her legs. She's standing awfully close to Bryson, and he's glanced her way more than once in this short time.

Wait, this isn't…that book Luna read…does it have anything to do—

Ew!

Oh my God.

Gross.

My face twists, and I feel my mouth curve. "Is this a— Please don't tell me this is some kind of weird *Fifty Shades of Grey* sex club."

Mr. Tweed lets out a chuckle. Mr. Dorst scratches the back of his head as he laughs, and his wife's eyes widen at my suggestion.

"No judgement!" I immediately backtrack as I look from her to Bryson and Luna. They look just as stunned. "I think it's so awesome if you guys are into that. So very, er, courageous and free-spirited of you." I pump both of my fists into the air. "And I'm so honored you all thought of inviting me, and I know you all think I've turned into a hermit, but I assure you I've been having my own stupid office rumpus—"

Luna's hands fly in the air as she screams at me to stop. "Gross, Hil! What in the hell would give you the impression we were a sex club?"

I look from her to Mr. Dorst who's laughing into his hand as his wife elbows him in the side.

"I don't know! Paulette said the thing about it being intimate!" I cry back. "And you were reading that book about the 1970's sex club!

"When I said intimate, I meant small." Paulette snorts. "Jeez…"

I then gesture at Bryson and Luna. "Well, you two are standing so close together, and everyone here looks so uncomfortable and is acting weird, and I just thought—"

"Well, no, you thought wrong," Luna interrupts. She huffs and runs a hand through her hair. "Like, Jesus, Hil…"

"Okay, sorry, my bad." I throw my hands up apologetically.

Silence fills the room as everyone looks at each other.

"So, if that's not it then what is your little club about?"

Mr. Tweed stands and clears his throat. I watch Luna give him a nod, and the old man clasps both hands in front. "We're called 'the Resistance.' A small group of people that gather weekly, if we can, to discuss matters of great importance. We're working to change things, to take back the power, to make things better for the common folk. We're willing to do that at any cost, big or small."

"Last week, Glover changed our parking spaces for the sixth time this year," Mrs. Dorst states, her eyes glued on mine. "It's only May." She shakes her head slowly and looks at the floor. "All because she hates that we both drive Hummers."

Mr. Dorst sighs and plays with his tie. "She thinks they're ugly. She's had them towed three times since we got them last summer."

"Two days ago, she had me remove my new, vintage patio furniture," Paulette tells me. She twists a strand of her blue hair between her fingers. "She says the paint was full of lead and a danger if my balcony ever caught on fire. But I know it's because my balcony faces the front of the building and she thought the set was ugly."

"Same thing just happened to Hil," Luna informs her as she gives me a quick glance, "only it was a washer and dryer."

"You don't have an en suite washer and dryer?" Mrs. Dorst looks around the condo.

"You *do*?" My jaw drops.

She nods too proudly for my liking.

"I'm sick of taking minutes at her stupid meetings," Bryson admits. "She's the only board president that has meetings weekly or bi-weekly. Most condo board presidents have them once a month. She's awful if I miss a line or forget to email her the minutes right after the meeting. I know she was the one who turned off the power in my unit last month when I had a date over, all because I forgot to send her the minutes from that morning's meeting."

"Point is," Luna rushes in, "we've all had enough of Glover and her abuse of power. And we *have* to do something about it."

"We can't let her push anyone around anymore," Mr. Tweed adds. "We've been trying to figure out ways to bring her down for months."

"We've been brainstorming, making notes," Paulette says, "coming up with scenarios—"

"None of them will work against her," Bryson interjects. "She's too crafty, and she's proven that."

"Until now," Luna states, her eyes meeting mine. "We've finally come up with a way to knock her off her pedestal, as you said earlier today."

I frown. "Okay?"

Luna's hands come together like a gun, and she points at me. "We want *you* to run against her in the condo board election."

A laugh escapes me, and it trickles throughout the room. "You *must* be joking?"

"Dead serious," Mr. Tweed claims. "One hundred percent so."

"It was your idea," Luna reminds me as she steps closer. "An hour ago, you were telling me someone needs to finally run against her—"

I jerk my head toward her. "Not me! I meant someone else!"

"But you would be perfect for it." Luna gives me a small smile. "Glover wouldn't see it coming. And everyone likes you."

"Everyone likes me because I'm a pushover." I scoff and pretend not to see Mr. and Mrs. Dorst nod in agreement. "A pushover can't run for president of a condo board!"

Luna shakes her head at me. "You're not a pushover! You're just…too nice. But I've seen you get fed up and handle things when you need to. And besides, we'd all help you! Right, guys?"

They all nod and mutter, but only Mr. Tweed sounds enthusiastic.

This is insane.

Ridiculous.

"No, no thank you." I shut my eyes as I shake my head. "No way."

"Come on, Hil," Luna begs. "I seriously think you'd—"

"Even if I wanted to run, which I don't, do you actually think I have time?" I look around the room. "You know how busy work can get. Especially in the summer. Sometimes I'm not home 'til well after nine p.m.! And I work most weekends!"

"We can be your election team!" Bryson jumps on the enthusiastic train with Mr. Tweed and gives me a small smile. "It'll be fun. Luna can be your campaign manager."

"And I can do your flyers or posters," Paulette offers.

Mrs. Dorst raises a hand. "I suppose I could bake for any events we do to promote you running."

I put my hands up in front of me. I need to stop them before they get any more ideas. "No, sorry. It's not happening." I see Luna's face fall. "I'm sorry, I really am, but I'm not into this idea. You run, Luna. Enough people like you, and I bet you'll win."

"Not true." Mrs. Dorst leans back into the couch. "Glover has half the building thinking Luna grows weed."

Luna raises her eyebrows. "See?"

Mr. Tweed waves his cane in the air to get my attention. "I think you'd be a fine president. Your grandfather was on the board, as you know, and people always said he should run. You're exactly like him, kind and a hard worker. You care about people." He chuckles a bit. "He and Glover always bumped heads. Probably why she isn't your biggest fan. You remind her of the old man."

I appreciate his trip down memory lane for my benefit, and though it warms my heart, it also cautions me against what they want me to do. I have to deal with Glover enough as a regular tenant. Dealing with her as a campaign opponent would be a horrible thing altogether.

I bite my lip and feel my chest tighten uncomfortably as their stares become more pleading. "Sorry, answer is still no. You guys need to find someone else. Now if you'll excuse me, I need to get dressed."

Chapter Three

"Over seven hundred dollars in dry-cleaning bills, Sydney. Seven hundred dollars' worth of damage to designer dresses and suits. Not to mention my complete humiliation afterwards. My guests were just shocked at the lack of care shown by LaBeau and Gilde Event Planning. For the second most prestigious event planning company in this greater city, you really dropped the ball."

I can't even be bothered to roll my eyes. Instead, I keep them glued on Sydney, who sits across from us behind her giant oak desk, her dark arms folded on the marble desktop. She's giving Sarah her utmost attention and sympathetically nodding along with everything she has been saying.

When I first met Sydney two years ago, she intimidated me. She's almost six feet tall with a curvy but toned frame and is always dressed in something designed by Adeline Andre. Today, she's in a bright yellow and orange dress with black and blue ruffles at the bottom. It may be eccentric, but against her dark skin, it really is gorgeous. For a forty-five-year-old woman, she pulls it off.

Next to me, in a matching white leather armchair, sits

Sarah wearing a pair of bug-eyed sunglasses. Her giant pink Kate Spade bag rests on her tiny thighs.

"Honestly, I am just so devastated," Sarah tells Sydney. She shoots me a glance. "And to receive no sympathy by the planner hired for the event is just…" She turns her head from both of us, faking a trembling bottom lip.

I take a slow, quiet breath and turn to face her. "Mrs. Graham, I am sympathetic to what happened to you. One hundred percent."

"Well, you aren't acting like it!" she quips, keeping her back to me.

I look to Sydney, and she motions for me to go on. "I had no idea that the dried saffron would stain. Neither did my assistant when he ordered it. I can most certainly feel for you *and* your guests."

"What can we do to make this situation better for you?" Sydney jumps in, a kind smile appearing. "How about a discount on future planning services? I can offer you fifty percent off if you'd like."

I'm speechless by Sydney's offer, and when Sydney sees my jaw drop, she swats at me to remain silent. I turn from Sarah and slump back into the chair. Sydney and I both know I won't say anything.

"I suppose asking for your planner's dismissal is out of the question?"

I raise my eyebrows at Sydney.

She keeps her kind smile as Sarah finally turns to face her. "I cannot do that, Mrs. Graham. Hilary's one of our top planners with an approval rate of ninety-eight percent. I have clients who would be very upset to hear she had been let go."

Ha. Take that, She-Bat.

"A refund then," Sarah counters, lifting her chin.

Is she crazy?

Sydney's silent, but by the way she bites her bottom lip, I can tell she's thinking about it.

I don't believe this. I know Sydney hates confrontation as much as I do, but even *I* can put my foot down once in a while.

"I can't give you a refund, but I will pay the dry-cleaning bill and offer you fifty percent off on a future planning service. With a different planner."

Who is she going to give her? She's an A client. She won't get a junior planner. My deskmate, Susan, is on maternity leave, and I know Sydney won't give her Jasmine. She's a horror. Tramples on everyone, flirts with the male clients, is selfish… On second thought, maybe Jasmine would be a better fit for Sarah.

"I suppose that's the only option I have, isn't it?" Sarah mumbles as she adjusts her sunglasses. "Fine, I'll take it. I will be in touch via email with the exact cost of the dry cleaning." She rubs her temples before adding, "Also, I think maybe the dry-cleaning bill was near eight hundred…"

Sydney smiles at Sarah. "You just send me that bill when you can."

I lean back into my chair as Sarah rises to her feet. Sydney follows suit and they shake hands before Sarah leaves with a big smile on her face. I can't help but glare at her as she passes me, throwing shade with her high eyebrows.

Once she's gone, I push myself up from the chair and shake my head at Sydney. "I can't believe you did that for her."

"Oh, sometimes it's easier to give people like Sarah Graham what they want." Sydney moves around her desk to join me, and we stare through her glass office walls. Sarah walks toward the elevators at the very back of the floor, head down, eyes focused on her phone.

"She was a menace to work with," I tell her.

"I know. It's why you have Eli. You two are like yin and yang."

I look toward my desk on the left side of the floor. It's only thirty feet away from Sydney's office. We're on the sixth floor of a skyscraper downtown, and while the view on all sides consists of the neighboring skyscrapers, the actual office of LaBeau and Gilde is beautiful. Right outside of Sydney's office is a harvest table with a fancy coffee machine and basket of muffins and bagels. Industrial L-shaped desks with smooth dark wood surfaces sit neatly for everyone. Macramé pot holders hang from the ceiling, housing weeping ivy or air purifier plants. Diamond-shaped lights drop from between the pipes and vents in the exposed ceiling. Across from the elevators is our receptionist desk, and to the right of that are two meeting rooms. There's a man in one right now, phone to his ear and back to the door.

I can see Eli hovering near my desk. He's dressed in a denim outfit complete with a studded jean jacket, his eyebrows raised high as he flips through the latest issue of *CityDaily*, the local city business magazine.

"Oh, what about that woman in your building?" Sydney suddenly asks. "The one who runs the museum. Have you sealed the deal yet?"

"She's on the board. I don't know if she runs the whole

thing, but she is in charge of the events. And I haven't started pushing her yet, just buying my time."

"Perhaps you should step up the wooing? I heard there's some big exhibit coming up in the fall that is set to bring the city and museum millions." Sydney raises an eyebrow as she looks down at me. "That account could be big for us. I'd reward you with a nice bonus of course, or a spread in *CityDaily*."

Sydney's only been in *CityDaily* about a hundred times. They love her, and every time she has an article written about her, we get a slew of new clients. She even catered an event for Martha Stewart's people last time they were here.

I smile at her. "Would you?"

"If we get the account," Sydney says. "*If.*"

I have to get Mrs. James to hire me ASAP!

"Meanwhile, your ten o'clock is here." Sydney motions at the man in the meeting room. "It's for some corporate event. He said we came highly recommended."

"Jasmine specializes in corporate planning," I remind her.

"She declined it," Sydney says with a sigh. "Says her plate is full with the two clients she has right now. Eli says all you have right now is Mrs. Sarris's charity Bingo thing in a few weeks so you can take a last-minute client."

I cross my arms over my chest. Then we both look toward the back of the room where Jasmine's desk is. She's in her chair, headset over her chestnut smooth hair, chatting away as she occasionally picks at her nail beds. She dips her head in a laugh, and I can tell she's on a personal call.

I sigh and look up at Sydney. "All right, I'll take him."

I leave her office and walk over to Eli who is now standing upright, hands on his hips, shaking his head as he watches Jasmine at her desk.

I smirk. "Eli, you shake your head any faster, it'll roll off."

"My grandma tells better jokes than you," he retorts before giving me his attention. "How did it go with She-Bat?"

"Sydney's paying the dry-cleaning bill and offering her fifty percent off any future planning service." I reach for my phone on my desk to check my messages.

Three from Luna, all about the election. I don't respond to any.

"We have to work with that she-demon again?" Eli groans. "Are you serious?"

"Sydney will stick her with Jasmine."

Eli nods and leans against my desk. "Good. So, how did Grandma Brandt spend her weekend?"

I ignore his sarcasm. "If you *really* must know, I fought with my condo board president."

Jasmine lets out a loud, bulbous laugh, which draws our attention to her.

"Ugh, she's awful," Eli breathes out. "Just do me a favor and don't send one of your letters out, okay?"

"My letters?"

He frowns at me. "You know your letters— Wait. Didn't you hear what she's spinning through her rumor mill now?"

Damnit. Jasmine and her stupid rumor mill. She has this habit of spinning white lies about me, or other planners, to Debra in HR, and whenever she's confronted, she just denies it. Or states that she 'assumed' it were true or that she'd heard it 'through the grapevine.' She once started a rumor that I didn't give to charities because I hated giving to others. All because I wouldn't buy the last box of Girl Scouts dark chocolate cookies from our secretary's daughter. I'm allergic to dark chocolate. It gives me headaches! I had to email everyone a letter and explain how charitable I really am.

Whenever she starts a rumor about me, I just throw a letter back to her and everyone else.

"What's the rumor?" I regret asking already.

"That you intentionally embarrassed your last client because she yelled at you."

I roll my eyes and groan quietly. "Who heard it?"

"If she told Debra, everybody knows by now," Eli sighs.

"All right, I'll write a letter after this meeting. Who's the client?"

Eli shakes his head at me. "I said *don't* write a letter. It just makes things worse."

"People need to know the truth," I tell him harshly. "Now, what do we know about the client in the conference room?"

"Warren Redler, in his early forties, software engineer or something like that. Owns two companies, workaholic clearly, and he needs a last-minute planner for some anniversary party. His first one fell through."

I blink at him. "Thanks, Eli."

He shrugs, catching my tone. "That's all the information Sydney gave me. I Googled him, but it's all boring stuff. Big on charities though."

I check my reflection in my blank computer screen and pat down my wavy hair, just in case. I make sure my red blouse is tucked into my black skirt, then I motion for Eli to follow me. He grabs his clipboard and our planning binder and tags behind me.

I knock before entering the meeting room and smile as Mr. Redler turns around, quickly ending his call.

My heart jumps.

Holy. Hell.

"Oh, God," Eli whispers.

I elbow him sharply.

The man is a stone-cold fox.

Dark, wavy hair greying at the temples. A warm smile beaming from ear to ear. A set of piercing blue eyes. It's clear he takes care of his physique. His dark suit fits him *very* well. He approaches with a confident stride and extends his hand. "Hi. Warren. You must be my new planner?"

"She is, yes," Eli replies quickly. His face twists into a giddy smile. "Yup. Both of us. I'm her partner. Not in that sense, in the business sense."

I clear my throat and smile again as I take Mr. Redler's hand. I hope he doesn't notice how sweaty my palms have become. "Mr. Redler, I'm Hilary Brandt. Nice to meet you. I look forward to working with you and your company."

"Please, call me Warren." He shakes my hand for what feels like an eternity then lets go, much to my dismay. "Mr. Redler is my father."

Eli laughs a little too loudly at the joke, but Warren doesn't seem to notice. I motion for Warren to have a seat at the long glass table. As he does, I take my usual chair at the head of the table and wait for Eli to join me at my right side. But today, he sits on Warren's other side.

I place my hands on the table and give him my attention. "So, Mr. Redler—"

"I told you, call me Warren." He smiles again at me.

"Warren, right," I correct, holding my smile in place. His gaze is so laser-focused that I feel myself getting nervous, so I stare at his eyebrows instead. That way, it looks like I'm holding eye contact. "So, Eli tells me you need a planner for an anniversary party of some sort?"

"For my company. It turns ten years old in a few weeks, and I want to do something special for my employees. My clients as well. I run World Cube. I'm not sure if you've heard of it, but we specialize in gaming chips, software for computer companies, and..." He suddenly stops and lets out a laugh. It's loud but smooth. "It's boring stuff. Anyway, I want to make it a big event. From the morning to the evening. Maybe a company family picnic thing for the families during the day then a formal dinner for the adults."

"Oh, wow, how generous of you." Eli cocks his head to the side. "Your wife suggested this? Or girlfriend? Fiancé, perhaps? Would she like to be involved in the planning? Should we get her contact info?"

Warren shakes his head. "Oh, no. There's no wife. I'm single. It was my secretary's idea. She usually does this kind of thing, but she said she'd be out of her element with this big of an event."

Eli tosses me a sly look when Warren brings his attention back to me. If he thinks that I should make a pass at this man, he's insane.

"My secretary is old fashioned," Warren goes on. "She's in her sixties. Was really pushing for the dinner and dancing thing."

"We can definitely do that," I tell him. "As soon as you tell me the price point, the number of guests—"

"No price point," he interrupts. "No budget. I want to go all out for my people. And as for guests, I'd say there will be about five hundred for the family picnic during the day and maybe three hundred for the dinner and dancing. But I can get you definite numbers in a week—"

"Coffee anyone?"

We look over at the door, and Eli lets out a groan. Marco Tilcott stands in the doorway, his dark jeans and super tight T-shirt making his obnoxious muscles look even more ridiculous. A gold chain hangs around his thick neck, and his black hair is spiked up and highlighted.

Marco's our social media expert. I'm not even sure that's a real job. I think Sydney just hired him because he's her nephew through marriage.

"Nope, never," Eli declares as he turns his back to Marco.

"I'm okay," Warren answers. "Thank you."

I ignore Marco as he looks my way.

"How about you, Hil? Anything you *want*?"

Oh, God. I'm going to throw up a bit in my mouth.

See, Marco is my big secret.

If anyone in this office found out I had accidentally made out with him—not once but *twice*—I'd either be fired or have to quit from the insane amount of shame I would endure.

I mean, nobody would sympathize with me. Even if they found out that I had been in a bad place, reeling from Neal's rejection and drinking a bit too much—

Ugh, I can't even think about it.

"Nope, thank you, Marco." I look away from him, surprised at how well I've kept my composure.

He shrugs like he doesn't really care and leaves.

"Anyway," Eli says loudly, "how about themes? For the dinner and dancing portion, I mean. Is it a romantic theme?"

Warren frowns a bit. "I hadn't really thought—"

"We could do Romeo and Juliet?" Eli jumps in. "Or how about a Gatsby and Daisy prohibition theme? Maybe even Snow White and Prince Charming—"

Warren scoffs nervously, and his smile twitches. "I'm not sure if those themes are what I'm looking for—"

"Okay, Eli. This isn't a prom." I laugh a little bit with Warren then smile at Eli. "I think I have it from here. Could you head back and see if Mrs. Sarris has emailed back about the vendor applications?"

His eyes narrow briefly before he looks at Warren, smiles, then drags his fake glee my way. "Sure. Of course." He pushes the clipboard and binder toward me and stands from his chair.

I ignore the look he gives me as he leaves.

"Okay, Warren, so tell me what you're thinking right now?"

Our meeting lasts thirty minutes, and my nerves never really flutter away, but I think I played it pretty cool. I've never had a client this charming and attractive before, and it's thrown me.

It turns out that Warren has little idea what he actually wants, so I showed him the binder Eli brought in. It's a roster of our last few events, including pictures, price points, guest numbers, and press attendance if requested. In the end, he decided he wanted something fun and quirky for the family picnic portion and something classy but low key for the dinner and dance. His company logo colors are grey and silver, which he would like incorporated.

I walk him to the elevators when the meeting is over and wait until he's inside before I head back to my desk.

Eli is sitting in front of my computer, scrolling through my email inbox. "So, how did it go with your future husband?"

"Eli, stop. He's a client."

"Haven't you seen *The Wedding Planner*?"

"This is real life though, and I would never ever do that. Personal rule."

Eli sighs. "Grandma Brandt strikes again."

I drop the binder and clipboard full of notes down next to him. "I told him we would have a list of ideas for venues, decoration, caterers, the works by Friday."

"All right, and I'm just throwing this out there, but he seemed kind of into you." Eli finally glances my way.

I roll my eyes and reach down for my cell phone when I see the notification light blinking.

"He at least thought you were cute, I bet."

I check my phone to see another text from Luna, which I ignore again.

Eli gasps, and I look over at him. "What?"

"What," he begins to laugh, "is *this*?"

I step up behind him and lean over his shoulder.

He's opened an email sent from Paulette Robbins. It's a picture of my face plastered on a red and yellow checkered background under Comic Sans lettering that reads, "Vote for Hil, she's got the skills!"

It actually looks quite good. *I* look quite good.

I moan. "Delete it."

Eli laughs. "Hil, *what* are you running for?"

"Nothing. Luna and her group of secret fighters want me to run for condo board president."

"Wait, what?" Eli pushes the chair back and looks at me. "Group of secret fighters? Rewind and tell me from the beginning."

I fill him in on my crazy weekend, and he listens intently, albeit with dramatic facial expressions. When I'm done, he exhales, and a serious look appears on his face. "Okay, Hil, I'm sorry, but you *have* to run. You know this, yes?"

I lean on my desk. "Did you not hear my story?"

"It's exactly why you should run!" he proclaims. "You've told me nothing but horror stories about this woman. She would never see it coming, and I bet your roommate is right. Everyone likes you because you're such a pushover. You'll easily win."

"I'm not that much of a pushover," I snap.

His face drops. "That's not— I mean it in a good way, for the election. Everyone thinking you are a pushover will get you votes. When you do get elected, just be super assertive."

"I'm not running," I tell him. He opens his mouth to retort, but I'm faster. "No. Stop. I'm not running, Eli. End of story. Now did Mrs. Sarris email the vendor applications?"

Eli throws his hands up in frustration. "Fine, okay. And yes, she did. I will email them to our waiting vendors."

I thank him as he heaves himself from my chair and crosses the few feet to his desk. Once I sit down behind my computer, I delete Paulette's email.

It's not unusual for me to leave the office after six p.m. Tonight, I have to move fast since I don't have an umbrella and the sky is dark and full of rain clouds. I pop by the Indian restaurant around the corner from the condo and grab my usual order of Korma chicken and rice to go.

I'm not two feet into our lobby when I spot Neal by the mailboxes. I hold my takeout close to my chest and decide to check my mail tomorrow morning. I give our concierge a small smile as I walk past him toward the elevators.

They ping open, and Mrs. Glover exits, a black and white polka dotted umbrella under her arm. She stops when she sees me, and her eyes fall straight to the paper bag in my hands. Her tiny nose wiggles, and she inhales, her face twisting up a bit. "That wouldn't be from Taste of Tandoori, would it?"

"Uh, maybe."

"From the Indian place around the corner?" she clarifies, her eyebrows rising.

"Yes."

Taking the last few steps toward me, clearly exasperated, she asks, "Did you not receive my email? The one I sent last Tuesday?"

I frown as I try to recall it.

"I specifically asked all tenants on floors six and seven to refrain from bringing take out home from *any* Indian restaurant. Mrs. Powell on your floor keeps complaining of headaches and vomiting due to the horrid smell of that food. We've had to replace her carpets twice already."

She can't be serious.

"So, I'm forbidden to get takeout?"

Mrs. Glover reaches into her coat pocket. "Just that kind, yes."

There's no way she can control what I eat!

She produces a pad of her orange sticky notes and a pen. I watch as she scribbles on the paper, slowly shaking her head. "Honestly, Ms. Brandt, there is no need for you and your roommate to make things so difficult for yourselves. It'd be much easier if you followed the rules of the building. Isn't that right, Mr. Turner?"

I shift my gaze and see Neal behind her, standing at the elevators about to push the button, his mail tucked under his armpit. When he looks our way, he only gives me the briefest of glances.

She sticks the orange note onto the takeout bag and gives me a quick smile. "You'll have to throw it away."

"I'm not going to throw it away!" I retort, my voice getting whiny. I clear my throat. "I paid for it. I want to eat it."

"You could always eat it somewhere else?"

Glover glances over her shoulder.

I peek at Neal again.

His hands are in his pockets, and he just shrugs as his light blue eyes now hold mine.

To think I once gushed to Luna about how warm his eyes were. I'm such an idiot.

"Now isn't that a great idea?" Glover quirks her brows.

"And where exactly should I eat it?" I snip.

She suddenly smiles one of those tight, sarcastic grins that makes her eyes darken. "Why not our courtyard, Ms. Brandt? It's only a hop and a skip away, and it's such a lovely night too."

She knows very well that the courtyard is overrun by

weeds, and the stone table and bench are cracking under years of wear and tear. She was the one who practically condemned the place around the time Luna moved in, claiming every time she tried to remodel it, everything would just die from the horrible soil.

Glover sidesteps me. "Go on then. We wouldn't want your food to get cold now, would we?"

Twenty minutes later, I'm back at my condo, soaked, carrying the empty takeout bag and containers. I slam the door behind me and throw the bag into the kitchen with a frustrated cry as Luna exits her bedroom.

She gasps at me.

I'm shaking.

Partly from the cold rain, and partly from sheer anger.

I can only imagine how I look.

Five minutes into eating, the rain gushed down hard and cold, soaking me to my underwear. I ate as fast as I could, trying to cover my food with the paper bag.

Luna looks me over from my trembling legs up to my raccoon eyes. "What happened to you?"

I kick off my black heels. "*I hate her*. I hate that woman more than I've ever hated anyone else my entire life."

"What'd she do?" Luna asks. She picks up the red fleece blanket off the couch and approaches me.

"Did you know we are no longer allowed to eat Indian food on this floor?" I snap at her as she hands me the blanket. "Because what's-her-name down the hall throws up every time she smells it?"

"Yeah, I got that email last week," Luna sighs. "Ridiculous, I know."

I wrap the blanket around me and glare at Luna. "I was

forced to eat my supper in the rain! If I wasn't swatting away bugs, I was trying to eat fast enough so I wouldn't end up like," I look down at my shivering body, "this."

Her shoulders drop, and she gives me a sympathetic look.

For some reason, that just eggs me on more. I stomp my feet and walk around her. "She's a dictator! For the three years I've been here, it's been her way or the highway all the time. And have I ever been rude to her? No!"

Luna nods her head in agreement.

"Have I ever fought with her? No! Have I ever hounded her with demands like half of the tenants in this building? No! And she just pushes and pushes and pushes…"

I drop the blanket to my feet and try to run a hand through my wet, tangled hair. I turn around to face Luna. I point a finger at her, my chest still hot, rising with every sharp, deep breath. "You tell your little club that I'll run in this election. I'm going to knock that dictator off her throne."

Luna smiles, and her hands come together at her chin. She bounces toward me and grabs my damp hands in hers. "You are not going to regret this! This is going to be amazing. You are going to wipe the floor with her, and we'll help you every step of the way! We can—"

"Luna," I hold my hand up, "pause. I need to shower."

"Yes, okay, good." Luna lets go and nudges me toward the dark bathroom. "You go shower. I will handle everything. Don't you worry. We got this!"

Chapter Four

"So posters went up last night. Did you see them? Oh! And I stuck flyers in everyone's mailboxes. Well, almost everyone's. I avoided Neal's and the Tempermans' because, you know, they're BFFs with Glover. Then Paulette had this great idea that tomorrow morning, you give, like, free lattes or something in the lobby as incentive to vote for you. Bryson thinks you should make pins, so he's off at the printing press place now. Mrs. Toscano, the lady who sells Saucy Leggings, she wants you to come by her place in a week or so for this pants party she's having. What's the harm, I say? If you schmooze well enough, she and her six minions may end up voting for you. And their husbands. She has that cult-like sway over them all. Maybe we could have that other lady who sells Avon gather at our place with other tenants and—"

"A pants party? Schmoozing? Free lattes? This isn't high school. I'm not running for prom queen."

The elevator doors open, and I step into LaBeau and Gilde with my phone pressed against my ear.

"Exactly!" Luna squeals. "It's more important than high school elections!"

I'm starting to rethink this whole running for condo

board president thing. After a few nights of solid sleep, and Luna's growing excitement, I realized I may have spoken without really thinking.

"I'm at work. I have to go."

"Okay! The team is getting together tonight, so we'll see you later!"

I hang up as I reach my desk, my shoulders slumping.

"What's with the hunchback, Quasimodo?" Eli leans back in his chair.

I stand up straight and clear my throat. "Luna."

"Still all hyped up about the election, eh?" He stands up and makes his way toward me.

I sit down and look at him.

He's in a grey vest and matching trousers today, a bright yellow bowtie neatly clasped around his tanned, muscular neck.

"They're making me pins."

He puts a hand over his heart. "How cute...and high school. I love it."

My face scrunches up. "Don't you think it's kind of, I don't know, juvenile?"

He raises his dark eyebrows. "Actually, yeah. It's kind of sad if you think about it..."

"I have to give away free lattes on Saturday in the building," I say as I turn toward my computer.

"Starbucks?" Eli questions.

"I think I have to make it myself."

A tight-lipped smile appears on his face. "Ohh..."

"How do I even make lattes?"

He puts both hands up in the air. "You're asking the wrong fashionable gay man. Or used-to-be-fashionable gay man..." He drags himself back to his desk and lifts a black bag from his chair. It's a Prada purse, the upside-down triangle a dead giveaway. It's simple but sleek. "Jacob got it for me. He insists I carry it. His sister got it for him because she works at Prada corporate, that fancy designer boutique."

"She got you a woman's purse?"

"It's a 'man bag,'" Eli reports. Then he convulses before dropping it back down on the chair. "I hate it. It so…uninteresting."

"So don't use it." I shrug.

Eli sighs. "I have to, or Jacob's feelings will be hurt. It was still quite a bit of money."

I smirk and reach over to turn my computer on. "What do we have today?"

"Just a meeting with Warren in about an hour, and Mrs. Sarris in the afternoon." Slowly, Eli's eyes run up and down my outfit. "Although, I have a feeling you remembered about our meeting with Warren this morning…judging by that outfit, of course…"

I recoil. "I look perfectly normal, Eli."

I do. I'm in a dark red knee-length skirt, simple three-inch heels, which I have never worn before, and a black T-shirt.

He leans over and frowns. "Are you wearing a push-up bra under that super tight V-neck?"

I wrap my arms around my chest and gawk at him. "It's a regular bra!"

"It is not!" He giggles. "It's so obviously a push-up bra!"

Damnit. How the hell did he even know? The lady at Victoria's Secret said it's their most inconspicuous push-up bra ever, that it gives a natural looking lift.

"And dear God, since when do you wear heels that high?" Eli laughs as he looks down at my smooth legs. "They're sex-kitten heels!"

"They are not!" I hiss. "Jasmine wears these kinds of heels all the time!"

Eli frowns at me. "Yeah, *Jasmine*. What happened to your 'I would never do that, Eli, it's a personal rule' speech from Monday?"

I hate when he mimics me. It's always dead on.

"I'm not doing anything. I got new heels, and I wanted to wear them. End of story."

He's about to retort when someone springs up at his side.

Jasmine.

She folds her arms over her chest and gives me a tight smile. She's in a white bodycon dress and a slender black suit jacket. Her hair is back in a slick ponytail, and her signature smoky eye is perfect as usual.

Eli fakes a startled jump and looks over at Jasmine. "Oh, it's you. Sorry. From the energy, I thought it was maybe Satan. Or Rasputin."

She sneers at him and grunts. "Shouldn't you be busy trying to further tarnish LaBeau and Gilde's reputation?"

His jaw drops, and he points a finger in her face. "You little—"

"Eli," I interject loudly so he looks at me, "can you get everything ready for our meeting with Warren please?"

It takes him a second, but he pulls his finger from her face and smiles at me. "I will do just that."

He stomps to his desk, a cold shoulder thrown Jasmine's way, but she doesn't notice. Instead, she gives me a smile and steps up closer to my desk. "So, how's it going, Hil?"

"Fine, great." I nod. "And with you?"

"Oh, so fantastic." She cackles and shakes her head. "People keep calling in, requesting my planning skills ever since I nailed that New Year's gallery benefit. It's hard for me to keep up! I've had to turn down quite a few potential clients."

Eli leans back in his chair so he can see me. He mouths, *She's lying,* but the thing is, I'm not so sure she is. That gallery gig was a major account. Sydney told us it could open doors to bigger clients and corporations. We both wanted it, but we could never work together, so for all of October, we tried to best each other to nab the account. They chose Jasmine's plans over mine. I'm still a little sore about it, but I've learned to let her comments slide off my back.

Mostly.

"That's great." I nod, holding my own smile. "Anything I can do for you?"

"Well, I'm just so sorry to hear about what happened with Sarah Graham," she says, her faux concern barely shining through. "It must have been so humiliating for you. And Eli. Mostly Eli 'cause he dropped the ball. Such a rookie mistake."

Eli's middle finger quickly rises behind her back.

She gives me another small smile. "Anyway, I just wanted to tell you I heard that nasty rumor about you purposely ruining Sarah's event, and I read your letter reply." Her smile couldn't be faker if she tried. "And I totally believe you. You couldn't have known those saffrons would stain!"

I give her a small smile, hoping I don't choke on her bad acting. "Thanks. Anything else?"

"I really just came by to tell you that." She takes a step back then halts and laughs. "Oh, and to offer to take the Redler account off your hands. It's a big corporate account, and I know it's not really your forte. I feel bad passing it on to you. If you want, I can snap him right back up!" She even snaps her fingers.

I see Eli's wild gesture. He keeps mouthing, *No no no.*

I clear my throat and give Jasmine another small grin. "I appreciate it, Jasmine—"

"Great!" She grins. "So just email me the file and—"

"No, no," I frown at her and get up from my chair. "No, you misunderstood. I'm not giving you the Redler account."

Her smile remains, but her jaw tightens just a fraction. "You don't even do corporate accounts."

"I've done a few before."

"Three," Eli announces loudly. "She's done three. So we'll be fine, Jasmine. Off you go to your hive of hell in the corner."

She clears her throat before casting me a tight smile. "Fine. I'll be expecting your call or email for help then."

"Won't be necessary," Eli says.

Jasmine flips him off as she stalks away to her desk.

Eli wheels himself closer to where I stand and looks up at me. "She only wants the account 'cause she saw how gorgeous he is."

"I figured."

"Look at her seething with jealousy that she gave up an account." Eli grins as we watch Jasmine drop into her chair and struggle to hide her pout. "She won't be the one seducing him. Bet it's killing her!"

"I'm not going to seduce him."

He rolls his eyes. "Then what's the push-up bra for?"

"It's a regular bra!"

We're interrupted when the phone on Eli's desk rings, and he wheels over to pick it up. "LaBeau and Gilde, Hilary Brandt's desk." He looks up at me quickly, his eyes widening. "Mr. Redler, good morning."

I watch Eli nod as he takes the call. "Yup… It's no problem at all. We will see you there… Okay, bye-bye then." He hangs up quickly and gives me a sparkling smile. "His breakfast meeting ran late, and he wants us to meet him for a quick brunch at the restaurant."

"What restaurant?"

Eli clasps his hands together on his lap. "The Peacock."

❦

I've never eaten at The Peacock, and that's mostly because spending over thirty dollars on an entree always made me uncomfortable. Even approaching the glass doors right now with Eli, and knowing this is on Warren's dime, makes me unsettled.

Eli draws in a breath when we enter the restaurant. "This place is everything I read and more."

We step into a circular room with glass walls and exposed light brick. The square tables are made of dark wood, and succulent plants sit as centerpieces. The kitchen is visible through a glass wall, and even *that* is glamorous with its shiny steel ovens and large fridges. The chefs all stand out in black uniform.

Eli grabs my arm. "There he is!"

He points across the room, and I spot Warren instantly. He's at a small table, speaking to the waitress that hangs over him. The menu is in his hands, and he points down at it.

There goes my stomach and clammy hands.

"Warren!" Eli suddenly calls.

He and the waitress look our way, and with a smile, Warren waves us over.

"Behave, Eli," I find myself saying as I follow him. I know he hears me, but he ignores it, weaving around the table with the project binder in his hands.

"Good morning!" Eli's over-enthusiastic attitude is lost on Warren, who just thanks the waitress and stands up to shake his hand.

"Thank you so much for meeting me here." Warren moves to shake my hand. His eyes, if possible, look even clearer in the restaurant's lighting. He's in another dark suit, but the light blue shirt beneath works well with his eyes.

"Of course," I say as I take a seat across from him.

Eli nestles in between the two of us.

"I've ordered their charcuterie board and scallops benedict," he tells us. "No allergies, I hope?"

"Nope, none," Eli says. "You didn't eat at your meeting?"

"Oh, I did," Warren answers, "but meeting with my board always leaves me famished."

"Well, thank you for inviting us." I reach for the binder that Eli set on the table. "Per your schedule that you sent

Eli the other day, we've lined up a few caterers for you to try next week with us. Monday at one, we try Louis Girault. He's a well-known caterer in the city and specializes in seafood and appetizers—"

"I've had his food before," Warren shares. "It was good."

"He has a high approval rating by our clients, yes." I nod.

"Like Hil here," Eli declares giving me a soft smile. "She's got a ninety-eight percent approval rating at the agency. People are always asking for her. She's very popular."

"Is that so?" Warren asks. "That's pretty impressive."

My cheeks warm, and I have to look away, returning my attention to the binder. "There are a few of us with ratings that high."

"She's so modest," Eli laughs, grazing my arm with his fingers. "Nobody else has that kind of high rating. Not even Jasmine, who specializes in corporate—"

I have to stop him.

"Eli and I were thinking, regarding the venue for the evening, we'd keep it close to the campground you've booked the picnic at. There's the old observatory ten minutes down the road which is used mostly for weddings. It's very pretty." I pick up the binder and hand it to Warren.

He studies the pictures slowly, nodding. "I like it. It's the right size too?"

"Holds three hundred and twenty people," I report.

"And we have some sway with the owners, so booking it last minute shouldn't be a problem," Eli adds then side-eyes me. "Or rather, *Hil* has some sway with the owners. They just love her. Everyone just loves her."

"We were thinking tulips and china mums flushed with ferns and lemongrass for the centerpieces." I motion at the binder Warren holds. "Or stargazer lilies and dahlias with green vines on the table would work too. The pictures of the floral arrangements are on the next page. We might be able to add some silver glitter to the leaves to keep in theme with the colors of your company logo. Are you considering gift bags?"

Warren looks up at me, and his brows slowly knit together. "Do you think I should?"

My stomach flops, and I feel goosebumps race up my back. I clear my throat and brush some hair behind my ears. "Oh, um, well, it's really up to you."

"Most people do them," Eli says. "We could compile a list of items we think should go into each bag and see what you say?"

"That works." Warren gives Eli a quick smile, and a second later, his phone rings. He shuts the binder and takes the phone from his suit pocket. "Damn, I have to take this. Give me five minutes."

"Of course." I smile as Warren gets up and hands me the binder, stepping away from the table to take the call.

Once he's across the room, Eli slaps me on the arm. "What," he says sharply, "is wrong with you? Don't you know how to flirt?"

"I'm not trying to flirt with him!" I hiss back.

"You're certainly not," he smirks. "You're bumbling like a two-year-old."

"What about you?" I snap back. "Could you *be* overselling me any more?"

Eli jerks back a bit. "Okay there, Chandler Bing. If I don't oversell you, he won't consider you at all when this event is over. He probably already thinks you aren't interested!"

I'm about to snap back again when Warren suddenly appears. He runs a hand through his shiny hair. "I'm so sorry, but I have to go. There's been an emergency with a product."

"Oh, okay, that's all right." I hate the way my heart deflates a little bit.

"Email me the rest of the information," Warren tells me, "and I will see you Monday at one p.m. Please, stay and eat. It's on me."

Eli's smile is the biggest yet. "Thank you, of course we will."

"Great." Warren's smile reappears, and he looks from Eli to me. "Have a good weekend." As he walks away, he gives me a pat on the shoulder, and my pulse quickens.

Eli's mouth drops open, but he doesn't speak until Warren has left the restaurant. "Oh. My. God," he whispers. "I knew he was into you!"

"That meant nothing," I tell him, and maybe myself too.

A pat on the shoulder could have been just that. It's important that I don't overthink it, for my own sanity and my career.

"He didn't pat *my* shoulder when he left," Eli says.

"You're sitting across the table," I sigh.

Eli reaches for his water-filled wine glass and raises his eyebrows. "If he touches you on Monday, then he's into you, and I don't care what you say. I'm making it happen for you."

I roll my eyes and reach for my own water, allowing that giddy feeling that he may touch me again on Monday to rush through me.

🙰

I'm barely into the condo when Luna flings the door open wider and yanks me inside. I drop my purse and almost slide out of my heels. "What's wrong?"

She slams the door shut behind me, and as I look at her, I notice that Paulette, Bryson, and Mr. Tweed are sitting in our living room. There's a big box on the coffee table, a stack of flyers with my face printed on them sitting next to it. Behind Paulette is an enormous stack of plastic cups and lids.

"Okay, before you freak out, I want you to know that we are on it," Luna exclaims, her hands gripping my shoulders. "We saw it a few hours ago, and we've formulated a plan." She blows a few strands of curly blonde hair from her face.

"Saw *what*?" I frown.

"You didn't see it?" Paulette hoists herself up from the ground and exchanges a look with Bryson before playing with a strand of her blue hair.

"See what?"

"Oh, dear." Mr. Tweed leans back into the couch and fiddles with his fingers.

Bryson picks up a folded piece of paper from the coffee table and walks over to me and Luna. "Glover posted these all over the building a few hours ago. And slid them into mailboxes."

I take the paper from him and unfold it.

My gasp echoes around the room.

It's a picture of my face plastered over a photo of the shop I bought the washer and dryer from. In bold red letters, like droplets of blood, it says, "Supports Crime Lords? Mafia Princess?"

"What the hell is this?" I demand.

"The start of a smear campaign is my guess," Paulette says.

"That store is rumored to buy products off the back of trucks," Bryson explains. "Nothing's been proven, but that's the rumor. A building rumor, really."

Luna lets go of my shoulders. "She's making it seem like you support crime."

I fling the flyer at her. "Obviously! I had no idea about this rumor!"

Luna picks up the fallen flyer. "We've managed to take most of them down."

"Mr. Dorst says there are new ones in the elevator and lobby," Bryson announces as he looks up from his cell phone. "His wife is tearing down the ones in the laundry room, and he's removing the ones in the parking garage."

"Oh my God." I grimace. "How many are there?"

Nobody in the room answers me, and I let out a groan.

"Don't worry yet," Luna says. "It's really a ridiculous thing to have done. Nobody is going to believe that you're a mafia princess. I mean, you don't even look Italian."

Paulette snorts from across the room, and we all look at her. "I don't know… With that big hair and push-up bra, she kind of does."

"It's a regular bra!" I cry as I stomp both feet.

I reach for the door and pull it back open.

Luna backs away so it doesn't hit her. "Where are you going?"

"Where do you think?" I huff. "To take down the stupid posters!"

I ride the elevator down, ripping the posters from the walls. Once in the lobby, I stuff them into the trash can across from the elevator and look around the room. I can see ten of them right away. There are even some taped on the security desk.

"Unbelievable," I grunt as I head to the posters on the wall in front of me.

I have a bunch crumpled under my arm as I make my way toward the mailbox nook. I freeze when I see how many she's taped in that small corner.

The entire cork board for building events is covered in the posters.

I drop the crumpled papers on the ground and begin removing the posters from the cork board.

After a few seconds, a familiar voice asks, "I thought you were Greek?"

I pause for a second. "I'm not Greek. And I'm not Italian."

From the corner of my eye, I see Neal step up to his mailbox. I watch as he smirks at the poster taped on the box before he yanks it down. "Heard you're running against Glover."

"What gave it away?" I can't help the sarcasm.

I get annoyed when I see him smirk again. He scratches the light stubble along his jawline as he reaches into his mailbox. "You better be prepared to fight dirty. She's pissed."

"Really? I had *no* idea."

He shuts his mailbox, but instead of leaving, he leans his shoulder against it, facing me. "You think you have what it takes to be condo board president?" He stares at me with half a smile.

I frown at him, more than irritated. "I guess we'll see, won't we?"

"It's a big job," he adds.

I stand on my toes to reach the last poster on the top of the cork board. The downside to only being five-two is that even in heels, I still can't reach most things.

"I *know*."

He watches as I swing on my toes again. "It's not an easy job."

"I know."

I grab the bottom of the poster and pull. It rips in half, and I fall back onto my heels defeated.

He pushes off his mailbox and walks over to me. I say nothing as he reaches up and easily tugs the other half off the cork board. He hands it to me with a brassy smile, leans closer, and says, "You're welcome."

I snatch the paper from his hand and get a whiff of his cologne. It's the same woodsy, sweet scent from our first date. Our *only* date. My eyes drop slightly down to the chest hair that escapes his V-neck T-shirt, and I have to look away before he notices.

I hate the way my chest feels around him, all tight and warm.

I kneel down and pick up the crumpled papers at my feet.

"Want some help?"

"No," I answer quickly like I was anticipating his question.

Above me, he clears his throat. "Listen, Hilary, I wanted to talk to you about something."

"And what would that be?"

"About what happened three months ago."

I snatch the last crumpled poster up and hobble to my feet, arms full. "There really isn't anything to talk about."

"Oh, I think there is," he says, crossing his arms over his chest. "You seem upset at me, and I don't like it because—"

My chuckle cuts him off.

He doesn't like it? Well, *I* didn't like being blown off without a word!

"Like I told you, there isn't anything to talk about. Now, excuse me." I turn to my side, glance back at him, and add, "I have a busy day ahead of me. Have a good night, Mr. Turner."

The corner of his mouth lifts, and he scratches the back of his head again. "So we're back on a last-name basis?"

"As far as I'm concerned, yes," I reply sternly, moving around him.

He nods his head. "All right. Have a good night, *Ms. Brandt*."

I pretend to remain unaffected by the flirtatious way he says my name by snatching another poster off the wall.

Chapter Five

"Have a latte! Vote for Hilary!"

Luna and Paulette set up the latte station right in the lobby near the front doors so we wouldn't be missed. They stayed up late making signs on Bristol board to tape to the grey folding table. Mrs. Dorst set up boxes of her freshly baked cookies and muffins, and Mr. Tweed laid out the ridiculous blue and red pins Bryson had made.

Paulette and Bryson are in charge of actually making the lattes while Luna and I stand at the front table. So far, in the three hours we've been here, we've given out ten lattes and a bunch of cookies and muffins.

I handled the situation yesterday quite well, I think. After we set up, I wrote a letter to the tenants of the building, making sure to send it to Glover too. To show her how a mature person should handle a condo board election.

I'm quite proud of myself for it as well.

It's like all the letters I have to write to everyone at work when there's a rumor floating around. It's always better to squish the gossip the moment you hear it.

"Have a latte! Vote for Hilary!" Luna announces again with pep.

Behind us, Bryson reads out loud from his phone. "Dear Tenants of Fairway Towers. Good morning. I'm writing to explain the situation that arose last evening. My opponent is misinformed as to the reasoning I purchased the appliances for my condo. I certainly had no intention of purchasing appliances from a store that is rumored to have connections to the mob. I simply purchased them as the salesman gave me a fine deal. I am in no way connected to the mob (or to any deviant persons or behavior. I.E., thugs, thieves, drug dealers, illegal puppy breeders, etc.). I sincerely hope this clears things up for everyone, including our sitting board president, who I look forward to running against. Please join me downstairs for free lattes and cookies this morning!"

"Why puppy breeders?" Paulette asks. She leans against the latte table, a pair of paint-stained overalls taking over her look.

"Because there are a lot of dog owners in this building," I say.

"What's the point of this letter?" Bryson asks.

I turn to look at him. "To show everyone that I am above what Glover did, that there is a reasonable explanation to me shopping at that store, to end the gossip mill from turning."

"I don't think that's going to work to stop her…" Paulette locks eyes with me.

"I've dealt with people like her at work many times, and these letters always help. They end up making the other person look stupid and feel small."

At least, that's what I hope they make Jasmine feel like.

I smile at Bryson and Paulette who still don't look convinced by my move.

"Good morning, Mr. and Mrs. Zheng!" Luna greets.

I turn back around to see Mr. and Mrs. Zheng from the second floor approach the table. They both smile as Luna motions for them to take a muffin or cookie. Mrs. Zheng requests a latte, and Mr. Zheng pats down his black hair as he looks at me. "So, Hilary, why should we vote for you?"

"Er, sorry?" I smile at him slowly.

"What are your promises? Your values?" he clarifies gesturing with his hands.

I look over at Luna who looks as thrown as I do.

We never talked about this part of the election!

Behind Mr. Zheng, Eli enters the building, distracting me for a second. He takes off his super-sized black sunglasses and looks at me with a sympathetic but entertained grin. He's in checkered shorts and a denim-colored linen button-up shirt. When he spots the pins, he lets out a silent giggle into his hand.

"Ms. Brandt?"

I whip my gaze toward Mr. Zheng and smile. "Sorry. Um, well, obviously, my promise is that I will… I'll be—"

"She plans to have free lattes and baked goods monthly." Eli steps up so quickly that Mr. Zheng jumps a little.

What?

"Oh, that's nice," Mrs. Zheng smiles my way as she picks up two cookies. "I like that."

"Or maybe bake sales!" Eli adds looking at me with a big smile.

Luna takes the latte from Bryson and hands it to Mrs. Zheng. "And less meetings. One meeting a month."

Bryson steps up between me and Luna. "Maybe even less."

"What about the parking?" Mr. Zheng asks, looking squarely at me. "We don't have enough spaces anymore."

"Oh." I nod. "Okay, well, I suppose I can figure that out then."

"What about the courtyard?" Mrs. Zheng asks. "It's so ugly. It ruins the view from our bedroom. Mrs. Glover says we don't have it in the budget, but I think we could—"

"Actually, Hilary has been making plans to redesign it herself," Eli chimes in. He looks down at the baked goods and picks up the smallest chocolate chip muffin. "Yup, every day at the office, she doodles her plans."

I glare at him, but this only makes him smirk.

The elevator doors open, and I watch as Neal Turner walks out, setting his sunglasses on top of his head.

Eli's mouth drops open.

Neal chuckles at the sight in the lobby as he slowly walks toward us.

Luna slides an arm around my shoulders and pulls me close. "Hilary wants to start working on it right away, Mrs. Zheng. Her plans are really great. She has all these amazing flowers she wants to plant, and she wants to build a beautiful gazebo."

What is she saying?!

"We could do so much with the courtyard." Mrs. Zheng smiles approvingly. "Maybe even have a small garden?"

"Done!" Luna exclaims.

Hold on a second here. What are they doing?

"And what about the temperature of the building?" Mr. Zheng asks. "I hate that we have to keep it at seventy degrees. That's too cold for me! We should be able to heat our condos at whatever temperature we like."

"Okay, well, I would allow that," I say.

Behind him, Neal frowns.

I look back at Eli, his eyebrows high as he side-eyes Neal.

"Morning, Neal!" Luna greets with a smile. "Latte? Cookie? Muffin?"

Eli opens his mouth, no doubt to unleash a snarky comment, but backs down when he sees my glare.

The Zhengs move out of the way as Neal approaches the table.

"I'll take a coffee. Just black."

"Sure." Luna grins and turns around to get one from Paulette and Bryson.

Neal looks over at the Zhengs for a moment then turns to me. "You know he can't raise the temperature in his condo, right?"

"If I win, he can do whatever he wants." I shrug. "It's his condo."

"If he raises the temperature, it's going to affect the condo above him. Heat rises," Neal explains. "All condo buildings have a regulated temperature for that reason. It's all about the HVAC system."

Eli picks at his muffin as he looks from Neal to me.

"It's not exactly something for *you* to worry about, is it?" I shrug. "You won't be the president. I will."

Luna hands Neal a latte and a lid.

"That courtyard is going to cost a few grand to get done properly too. You need landscapers. You have to pull the dead—"

"Thank you. I know." I plaster on a wide, fake smile.

I actually *don't* know, but I can't have him telling Glover that.

Neal looks over at Eli. "Hi. Eli, right?"

Eli nods. "Yup, hi. Hi there. Welcome back."

"Thanks," Neal answers as he looks at me again. He raises his cup. "Thanks for the coffee, Ms. Brandt."

"You're welcome." My smile isn't so cordial. "Don't burn yourself."

I hear him chuckle as he heads toward the front doors.

Once he's gone, Eli slams his hands on the table. "He's back? You never said he was back!"

I shrug. "Who cares?"

"Who cares?" Eli repeats. "Who *cares*? I care, you care. I know you care."

"She cares," Luna agrees.

"I don't care!"

"Is that why you're being all weird with the Warren thing?" Eli questions.

"Warren?" Luna looks over at me.

"I'm not being weird about anything," I tell Eli.

"Who are you being weird about?" Luna pries eagerly.

"She has a thing for her new client." Eli gives Luna a quick glance. "He likes her too."

"You do?" Luna smiles at me. "He does?"

"No, no he does not," I tell Luna with a sigh. "He's just super nice." I turn to Eli. "And I do not have a thing for him. He's cute and sweet—"

"He's hot," Eli corrects, fluttering his eyelids. "He's hot and sweet and rich and—"

"And a client," I cut in.

"Stop saying that!" Eli orders. "In a few weeks, he won't be a client!"

"Hil, I'm proud of you." Luna nudges me in the side. "It's been a while since you liked anyone as much as you liked Neal."

"I didn't like him that much," I declare. "It was just a tiny crush. And it's gone."

Eli and Luna are both silent for a few seconds, then as Luna rearranges the muffin and cookie box, Eli looks at the front doors of the building. "He looked good."

I send Eli a warning look. "What are you doing here anyway? You don't live in this building."

"Jacob's at the farmers market down the block. Thought I'd pop by and be supportive." Eli plucks a pin up off the table. "Go, team Hilary!"

I grab the pin from him. "Give me that."

A few other tenants leave the elevators, and I look their way, immediately spotting Mrs. James bringing up the rear. She's looking through her big black purse, and I rush around the table and past Eli to meet her halfway. "Hi, Mrs. James!"

She looks up and smiles when she sees me. "Oh, good morning, Ms. Brandt! I meant to tell you how exciting it is to see you running for condo board president."

A coy smile appears on my lips as I shrug. "Oh, well, I thought we needed a change. Being an event planner at LaBeau and Gilde gives me a good advantage. I know how to make things better for people. To get people what they want."

Mrs. James gives me a small smile. "You know, a few other ladies on the board have worked with LaBeau and Gilde for some personal events and just raved about the service."

"That's great." I smile. "My boss will be very pleased to hear that."

Mrs. James looks at me with a straight face. "We, the museum I mean, has a new exhibit set to open in the fall. It's a rather big deal for us and the city. I've been considering looking into a planning company to help us with the big gala event for opening night. We expect quite a few big names to attend. You just might be the person I'm looking for to plan it."

I beam and clasp my hands together. "I promise you, Mrs. James, you will not be disappointed if you go with me and LaBeau and Gilde."

She chuckles. "Well then, I better make my decision quickly so as to not leave you hanging." She begins to make her way past me, and I follow her, motioning at the lattes and muffins.

"Have a latte or muffin, Mrs. James," I suggest.

She slowly approaches Luna and looks down at the treats on the table.

We spent the better part of the afternoon giving away the lattes, cookies, and muffins until we ran out. We got rid of most of the pins too, which surprised me. Then Luna and Paulette sat down with me over some wine to make a list of promises I should be promoting.

Mrs. James put me in the greatest mood, and I haven't been able to stop smiling since. I filled Eli in, and he was ready to go on a shopping spree in lieu of the bonus we would split.

"Okay, so other than the garden and the temperature changes, what else should we promise?" Paulette sits cross-legged at the coffee table with a pen and pad of paper.

"More parking spaces, less meetings," Luna calls from the kitchen.

"Mrs. Zheng also liked the idea of free lattes once a month," Paulette says as she adds that to the list.

I wonder if the event at the museum has something to do with art. Is there a traveling art show going on? Isn't one of Picasso's pieces part of some moving exhibit?

"Hil?" Luna pokes her head out from the kitchen. "Are you listening?"

"Yes, of course," I lie. I pull myself from my daydream of hosting an event for Picasso's great, great, great grandchildren at the museum—and becoming BFFs with said great, great, great granddaughter. Wait, does he even have great, great, great grandchildren?

"So free lattes for sure then..." Paulette checks it off on her list.

"Wait, how are we going to afford to do all this?" I ask her.

"We don't have to do most of it," Paulette says. "We just need to get you elected."

"But that means I lied to get elected?" I shift in my seat.

"So did Glover." Paulette looks up at me. "She promised monthly movies in one of the event rooms. She also promised a better laundry room in the basement. And a lot of other things she hasn't done."

There's a loud bang above us then the sound of

furniture scraping against the floor. Pax, who's sleeping on the couch, looks up at the ceiling, meowing his annoyance.

"What does he do up there?" Paulette wonders as she looks toward Neal's apartment.

"Who cares?" I grumble.

"Know what we could do?" Luna exits the kitchen with three glasses in one hand and a bottle of red wine in the other. "We could go door to door tomorrow and ask people what's important to them. What they want."

"Canvassing," Paulette nods. "I like it!"

"You, Bryson, and the Dorsts can do that," Luna suggests, "and Hil and I can start plans for the courtyard."

"Wait. We're actually doing that?" I ask.

She sets down the glasses and wine on the coffee table and smirks at me. "We have to at least show them that you're serious about this. So we can start something down there, even just plucking out the weeds or something. Paulette can you make flyers announcing the courtyard idea? Plaster them everywhere so people know Hilary is on it. Last thing we need is Glover taking the credit."

My eyes drop to the wine bottle. "Give it to me."

We ended up going through three bottles of wine that night. Judging from the way I felt when I woke up on Sunday, I had a feeling *I* went through most of it. As Paulette joined Bryson and the Dorsts in canvassing our neighbors, I took the empty bottles down to the recycling area in the basement. I spotted the Tempermans in the laundry room, bickering among each other. I knew better than to say hi though. They are as loyal to Glover as Neal is.

Paulette's courtyard flyers are already hanging up in the elevators and lobby. An image of the dead courtyard above, and a picture of what we want it to look like beneath. Paulette took it off Pinterest.

I meet Luna in the courtyard after my trek to the basement, and in the late morning light, I realize we *so* have our work cut out for us. Neal was right. We probably do need landscapers.

The broken stone table and bench in the center definitely aren't salvageable, and half of the yard is overgrown with dead weeds and thistles. All the tenants with windows facing the courtyard have their blinds pulled down. Not that I blame them.

Luna's in a pair of rubber boots, jean shorts, and an oversized T-shirt. Her short curly hair is pulled up high, and she has garden gloves over her hands. She hands me a pair of faded red gloves, and I exhale as I slip them on.

"So, we just pull everything out?" I ask.

"Yup, pull everything out," she orders and then points near the broken stone table. "Throw it all there, and we'll bag it when we're done."

She moves over to a patch of dead flowers to her left, and I do the same. "Can't believe I'm doing this."

"Stop being so negative," Luna remarks. "And get to work!"

Hours later, we've pulled out all the dead plants and thrown them into the paper garden bags Luna had purchased. There are ten and a half tall bags full. The courtyard still looks abysmal. Now there's dirt and holes everywhere, but I'm too tired and sore to really care.

"What do we do with all these bags?" I ask.

"I'll ask Bryson and Mr. Dorst to put them on the curb." Luna rubs her forehead and smudges a trail of dirt across it. "Tomorrow, I'll bring some plants from the shop home and plant them."

I rest a hand on her shoulder. "Thanks. Now let's go home. I need a bath."

Chapter Six

"This is the grilled coconut and pineapple sweet chili shrimp. One of my favorites, personally. Sprinkled with a bit of cilantro and light cheese. It's a big one with guests."

Eli shoves the tray of shrimp on skewers toward Warren, and I watch the CEO slowly pick up a skewer. He gives it a look then bites into the first mini shrimp.

It's Monday, and we're at Louis Girault's restaurant. We're in the back tasting room—a plain white room with a gorgeous dark harvest table in the center and matching antique wooden stools.

Since Eli called me out about my outfit on Friday, I went a bit more modest today in a pair of black trousers and red blazer, a white silk blouse beneath, and my hair a little less curly and big.

Warren, on the other hand, looks suave and classy in a tight grey vest, a navy-blue tie tucked beneath it.

"What do you think?" I ask Warren after he's chewed and swallowed.

"Good, a small kick to it, but it works." He nods approvingly and pushes the skewer my way. "Try it."

Across the table, Eli grins as I take the skewer from him and slowly pull a shrimp off with my teeth.

I've tried this dish hundreds of times before, and I've never been a fan of it.

"Hmmm." I nod as I chew into the shrimp and force myself to swallow it down. "Delish, yup."

Eli pulls another tray over to Warren. This one holds a large piece of homemade flatbread that's been cut in six pieces. It's layered with thin prosciutto and sprinkled with white cheese. "This is the grilled flatbread with prosciutto, arugula, balsamic vinegar, and a bit of goat cheese. Another guest favorite."

We watch as Warren tries a piece. As he chews, he smirks and sets his piece down on the plate. His smirk turns into a light laugh that causes Eli and I to frown at each other.

"I'm sorry, guys, but this is weird. You two watching me eat…" He pushes the tray of flatbread toward me and motions at it. "Let's just eat together and talk about it after we're done with the tasting."

"Oh, okay, we can do that," I say.

Eli nods and then pushes a plate of pear brie balsamic crostini toward Warren, "Okay. Then this is the pear brie—"

"No," Warren shakes his head and looks over at him. "Don't tell me what it is. I don't want to know what it's called. I just want to eat and then decide. If you tell me the name and fancy ingredients, I'll pick it based on that, and I want to pick it based on how I feel. Make sense?"

I attempt to hide my smile as I look from Eli to Warren. "Makes perfect sense."

"Okay," Eli says, pulling his hands from the table, "so then we just all, what, dig in?"

Warren laughs and gestures at the table again. "Dig in, yes!"

Twenty minutes later, most of the dishes are empty, and all three of us are satiated.

Warren sets his hands on the table and sighs. "Okay, what did you guys like? Hate?"

"I loved the coconut cream tarts," Eli declares.

"That we know. You ate like four," I joke.

Eli frowns.

Warren chuckles loudly and pats Eli's arm. "I liked them too. I also loved the crab imperial pastry tart things and the cheese puff things…"

"The pesto parmesan gougères," I tell him. "I liked those too."

"I think we'll go with him for the party at night," Warren says, beaming. "What about the dessert? Or the food for the picnic?"

I reach down for my bag and search for my phone. I've missed two calls and three texts from Luna, but I ignore them and open the email confirming the cake appointment. "For dessert, we have a meeting with a very well-known cake baker on Wednesday. She's very popular with weddings and anniversaries."

"Her name is Pepper Lauren. She's not just a cake baker but a cake *specialist*," Eli explains with a bright smile. "She's been on a bunch of cooking shows and is going to be a host on an upcoming bake-off competition. She's the real deal, and she's already been designing mockups of the cake for the event. You'll taste an assortment of flavors at the appointment."

Warren nods, smiling, and then looks across at me. "And who do we have for the picnic food?"

"Right, the barbeque theme." I recall his email last week. "So we've had a bit of a problem finding a caterer who will do the whole basic hamburger and hotdog over a grill type thing since you specified no frills for that portion of the day."

"Most of the caterers you know are high end?" Warren laughs as he runs a hand through his hair.

I slink back a smidge. "Kind of, yeah."

He gives me a warm, easy smile. "I have someone who could do the food that day. I'll email you his info, and you can set up a tasting. He's exactly what I want—salt and pepper burgers, ballpark hot dogs kind of guy."

Eli's face twists a bit in aversion, but as Warren glances at him, he smiles.

I clear my throat and slide off my stool. "Sounds good. Let me just tell Louis that we are definitely using him for the—"

"I'll do it!" Eli practically screams his offer as he jumps off his stool. He adjusts his black dress shirt, avoiding my eyes. "I have to use the bathroom anyway."

He *so* does not.

Warren and I slowly gather our things and head toward the exit.

"That was fun," Warren says when he notices me following him. "Not to mention delicious. Can't wait for the cake tasting."

"If you have a sweet tooth, you'll be blown away," I say as we reach the back door. "Pepper's such a natural, so gifted at baking. I think she's booked a year in advance for weddings."

Warren reaches for the door handle and throws me a

smile over his broad shoulder. "She must be really something."

I swallow a lump down and muster a small smile. "I think you'll be pleased. Most of my clients are."

He laughs, pulling the heavy door open, allowing the bright sun to rush over us. "Are you talking about the cake still or your approval rating?"

The giggle that escapes my throat isn't my own. At least, I don't recognize it. It's so high pitched.

Is he...flirting?

I feel my face flush and hide it quickly by setting my hand over my eyes, pretending the sun's rays are blinding me. "Oh, well, I was talking about the cake, but take it any which way you like."

Annnd great...

Now *I'm* the one flirting.

The corners of his mouth lift into another bright smile, and he laughs as we step out into the alley behind the restaurant. "How long have you been an event planner?"

"About four years. I started out as Sydney's secretary," I answer.

The door slams shut behind us, and we're just a few feet from the main sidewalk. Sirens and car horns fill the air between us, and we keep to the side so we're not in anyone's rushed way.

"Worked your way up. That's impressive," Warren says.

"It was definitely work." I recall all the horrendous clients I had to stop from harassing Sydney during my secretary days, and later when I was an intern. Or the bad reviews when I first started out. Or the several clients who took *years* to pay for their service even though they bought car after car. "Working in the service industry can be…difficult."

"I can imagine," Warren says. "I know people can be horrible, especially people of certain…class or status." I catch the hesitation in his voice and realize he must know these kinds of people too.

"Sometimes I think they assume they should be that way," I add, "because it's so cliché."

He laughs a bit and nods. "I agree with you there."

Now it's quiet, except for a trio of giggling girls that pass us.

"So, what about you? How'd you get into games and stuff?"

He smiles, looking away from me to the busy street. "I wish I could say that I worked for it as hard as you did, but it kind of fell into my lap after university. And then with the company, I got the money from my parents. Kind of a handout."

The dip in his voice and posture as he reaches for the phone in his pocket throws me off a little bit.

"But now you're one of the leading gaming companies in this country. You clearly worked hard to get up to that level." I rush to change the fallen ambience. "Doesn't matter if you were given a handout to start, it's still something to be proud of."

He smirks as he looks down at his phone. "So they say…"

I don't know what else to say, so after a few seconds of standing awkwardly together, him on his phone, I reach into my bag and pull out mine. I read Luna's text messages, the first sent this morning.

GLOVER CALLED A CANDIDATES' MEETING
WEDNESDAY NIGHT IN THE EVENT ROOM. WORKING
ON YOUR SPEECH NOW.

An hour later, after two attempted phone calls, she sent another text.

OKAY, DON'T PANIC. I DON'T THINK EVERYONE IN
THE BUILDING REALLY SUBSCRIBES TO HER
NEWSLETTER...

Another missed phone call then the last text.

PAULETTE AND MR. DORST SAY WE SHOULD TAKE
THE GLOVES OFF, TOLD THEM IT'S NOT REALLY
YOUR STYLE.

What the hell is going on?

Now I have to give a damn speech? What newsletter?

I check my email, and sure enough, there's Glover's monthly newsletter sitting in my inbox. When I took over my grandfather's condo, she made me sign a contract with terms, and there was a section requesting my email. I didn't know it was so she could send out monthly newsletters to all the tenants. I thought it was for emergency purposes.

I open the newsletter and wait for it to load.

Right there, in bold red letters, it says, *Is This Who You Want As Your President?* Beneath that is a picture of me looking quite disheveled as I carried our box of recycling downstairs. My hair is up in a messy bun, and I'm in the middle of a yawn. You can also clearly make out the few wine bottles sticking out from the bin, as that part of the picture has been blown up.

Stamped over the bin it says, *Raging Alcoholic.*

My body inflames.

"What?" I scream.

Warren looks at me, startled. "Are you all right?"

"Er, fine, yes." I give him a quick smile before I look back down on my phone. I'm trying to control my breathing, but I can already feel the wheezing.

She's unbelievable. Completely insane and mean and rude and— It was a few bottles of wine! Collected over a few weeks—not drank in *one night*!

A black town car pulls up in front of us, and Warren puts his phone away. "Would you and Eli like a ride back to the office?"

I'm tempted, especially as his relaxed demeanor and soft smile have returned, but then his phone rings again, and he looks down. "Damn, I have to take this."

"Go ahead," I say. "Thanks for the offer, but Eli may be a while, so you go on ahead."

"Warren here," he greets as his phone goes against his ear. But he looks at me as he moves the phone from his mouth. "You sure?"

I smile. "Positive. We'll see you Wednesday."

I don't know what's worse—sharing the elevator on the way up to my unit with three very loud, strange women dressed in tight workout wear, or that Glover's latest move actually has me really wanting a drink.

But when I get inside my condo, even though half my

team is drinking, I refrain from actually pouring myself a glass of wine.

Bryson nurses the beer in his hand and looks from Luna to me. "I say we fight fire with fire! If we don't, she's only going to come after you harder. Her tactic is to fight dirty. If we hit now, she may back off."

He sounds like Eli. On the way back to the office, and for the rest of the day, Eli told me the same thing. When I told him my idea about drafting another letter, he faked ripping his hair out.

"I agree," Paulette nods. She plays with one of her pigtails, searching for split ends. "She clearly doesn't think you're serious about running. Undermining you is her game."

"Maybe we can sue her for slander..." Mr. Dorst mutters from near the cookie tray on the dining room table. His wife sits next to him, rolling her eyes at his remark, arms folded across her chest.

"It isn't the worst idea in the world to fight back," Mr. Tweed agrees. He's sitting on the couch, his cane resting on his knees. "We could give her a taste of her own medicine."

Luna looks at me. She must catch my apprehension because she clears her throat. "That isn't Hilary's style."

All eyes are on me, and I shift in my place a bit. "I'd rather not fight dirty..."

"That's politics, my dear," Mrs. Dorst tells me, her eyes narrowing. "It's always dirty."

"This isn't politics!" I scoff. "It's a stupid condo board election! And speeches? Now I have to make a speech? That was never in the cards."

"It's not really a speech. It's more of an introduction,"

Luna jumps in, her smile kind. "A few bullet points as to what you stand for…"

"Maybe we should have a rally," Paulette says, "in the courtyard?"

"A rally?" I gawk. "Like, me standing on a podium?"

"We'll have a better idea of the number of people who are voting for her tomorrow after we're done canvassing," Bryson tells Paulette. "Maybe we can have it this weekend?"

Before I can protest, something scrapes across the floor above us so loudly that we all cringe and glance up at the ceiling. Pax meows as he leaves my bedroom and swings his tail lazily, passing through the living room to the kitchen.

Paulette draws in a breath as she looks down from the ceiling to Luna, eyebrows high. "Maybe we can use him to get to her…"

"Unlikely," Bryson chuckles. "He's her lapdog."

"Probably had a good laugh at the newsletter picture," Mr. Dorst says as he finally decides on a chocolate chip cookie. He bites into it and chews loudly.

I think about Neal for a second. He probably does find this entire thing entertaining. I bet he smirked his stupid smirk when he saw that god-awful picture of me.

"I'll bet the Tempermans were the ones who took that picture of me," I grumble. "I saw them arguing in the basement when I carried the recycling down."

"We could do the same thing." Bryson takes a good swig of his beer. "Glover walks her dog every morning. I could take a picture of her and claim she doesn't pick up after him?"

"No, it has to be much worse." Paulette brings her

knees to her chest. "She called Hilary a mafia princess and alcoholic. We have to hit below the belt."

The idea is tempting, and for a fleeting moment, I find my mind drifting to a few scenarios, but my sanity reins it all in.

"No, we're not doing that. I won't stoop to her level. I won't act so childish."

"It's not acting childish," Paulette sighs. "It's fighting fire with fire. She's going to keep coming after you if you don't do something about it."

"I *plan* to do something about it," I tell Paulette. "I've drafted a letter…"

The exchanging of glances among them immediately annoys me.

"What?"

"A letter? You plan to send her a letter?" Mrs. Dorst frowns.

I clear my throat, tugging down at my shirt. "No, I plan to send a letter to everyone in the building."

Paulette drops her chin into her knees, mumbling, "Because it worked so well the last time…"

"People have to know I'm not an alcoholic!"

Luna grabs my arm and gives me a smile. "Let's just take a breather and focus on your speech for Wednesday. Bryson and I already started it. You get five minutes to talk before people ask you questions."

"We need a snazzy opening," Bryson says. "You have to stand out."

"Tell a nice joke." Mr. Tweed smiles as he sits up. "I know a good beaver joke." None of us say anything so Mr. Tweed goes on, smiles and all. "What did the fish say when he swam into a wall?"

Again, we're all silent.

"Dam," Mr. Tweed finishes. He chuckles to himself as the rest of us frown at him. I'm the only one who can muster a small smile.

Supportively, I tell him, "I'll keep that joke in mind."

"Keep it in your back pocket, yes." Mr. Tweed nods. "It'll get you some laughs."

"What have you got for the speech?" Mrs. Dorst asks Luna.

Luna gestures toward her bedroom. "It's in my room. I'll go get it."

As she paddles away, we all look at each other, the silence a tad awkward.

"How has canvassing been going?" Mr. Dorst bites into another cookie and stands over his wife. "Any slammed doors?"

"Only from Mr. Novak in 5B," Paulette answers. "He says he isn't voting in this damn election because it's a damn waste of time. And damn us for interrupting his supper."

I've only met Mr. Novak once in all the years I've lived here. He yelled at me when a piece of my mail wound up in his mailbox. I cried. From then on, I avoid him at all costs.

"What about everyone else?" I look at Bryson as he takes a long drink of his beer.

"Uh, we've hit a few bumps."

"What does that mean?"

"It means out of the twenty-five doors we've knocked on so far, only about seven will vote for you," Paulette explains. "Three tenants are on the fence, and the rest are voting for Glover no matter what."

My shoulders drop, and I stare at Paulette. "Did you tell them my promises?"

"They don't care," Paulette says.

Mrs. Dorst sighs from across the room. "I bet they're worried about what Glover will do if she wins and finds out they didn't vote for her."

"It's enough to make me jump ship." Her husband chuckles. We all look at him, and he raises both hands in the air. "I'm kidding."

"Mr. Rossi said he'd consider voting for you though," Bryson tells me, "if you would consider changing the rules of booking the event room. Right now, each unit is allowed to book the event room only three times a year, and he hosts a book club once a month. He'd like to move it down there."

Paulette spits out a strand of her blue hair. "Personally, I'd like to see us rejoining the yearly neighborhood garage sale. She canceled it five years ago, and a lot of people were upset about it."

"I guess we could do that." I shrug. "No harm in having a garage sale."

"It's next weekend," Paulette announces. "I'll figure out if there is still time for us to join. It could be a good opportunity to showcase our fundraising skills to everyone too. Every table used to donate twenty-five percent of their earnings to the building's budget."

Luna returns, waving a yellow pad of paper at us. "Okay, here it is!"

She takes a seat next to Mr. Tweed, dropping the pad on her. "Good evening, everyone. Thank you very much for joining us tonight. I'm proud to be running for condo board president. If elected, I hope to do this building—and all of you—justice by serving to the best of my abilities. You deserve a president who is more than just a president, a president who is also your friend. Someone who truly cares about your needs, your problems. And I am that candidate."

She pauses and looks up at me.

"I like it." I smile. "It sounds like something I'd say."

"You should add a joke in there," Mr. Tweed suggests. "Tell the beaver one."

"Er, maybe we can close with that." Bryson looks at Luna, who struggles to hide a small smirk.

"Keep going," I tell Luna eagerly.

She gives me a smile and looks back down at the pad. "For those of you who don't know me very well, my name is Hilary Brandt, and I live in 603. I'm an event planner at LaBeau and Gilde and have excellent relations with all my clients, who return to me regularly to help with important events in their life. I'm very organized and work extremely hard to get my clients exactly what they want. You can rest assured I will bring the same kind of work ethic to the job as president if elected."

I find myself grinning like a fool, and when Mrs. Dorst gives me a frown, I clear my throat to unravel my giddy appearance. "That's pretty good, Luna. Go on."

"That's all we have right now," she tells me, "but we'll have it done by tomorrow night so you can practice it."

"Don't forget the joke." Mr. Tweed elbows Luna in the side. "Jokes are very important."

Chapter Seven

Dear Tenants of Fairway Towers,

Regarding my opponent's newsletter and accusation the other day, I only have this to say:

Those bottles were an accumulation of several months of girls' nights and dinner parties. I did not—could not—drink that much wine in one evening, or even over one weekend. I appreciate the concern from several of you and thank you for reaching out to me with offers of help to the nearest rehab center. But I repeat, I am not an alcoholic. I also appreciate and thank the tenant(s) who placed flyers to the nearest AA meeting in my mailbox. Your concern is warming.

Hope to see you at the meeting this evening!

Hilary Brandt

There. That should do it.

I hit send just as I step into the elevator and smile proudly to myself.

Luna told me not to bother with the letter, but honestly, after twenty-four hours, I was still itching to send it. Even more so after Mrs. Zheng emailed me the address to the nearest rehab center with a paragraph addressing her concern about my problem at such a young age. I checked our mailbox last night and found not one but *two* flyers to the nearest AA meetings in our neighborhood.

Still, I feel confident. Last night Luna and Bryson read me my speech, and it's really good! Best of all, no beaver jokes.

Bryson also said canvassing went really well. The last twenty tenants they talked to were more receptive, and out of those, nine said they would definitely vote for me.

Since the election is in a few weeks, I still have plenty of time to win people over.

Once the elevator hits the ground floor and the door opens, I hurry out.

I'm not only confident but excited too.

And it has nothing to do with the fact that I'm seeing Warren for cake tasting in a few hours. Obviously. Although, when I think back on the light flirting between us, I get all smiley and—

I stop in my tracks when I see the new additions to the lobby.

Glover stands in the middle of the commotion, wearing a bright yellow dress, rather expensive looking, and holds a clipboard in her hands. She's standing between four massage tables, each one occupied with a tenant from the building. The therapists are silently doing their work as a few other tenants stand around Glover.

She's laughing with them, her free hand pointing at the masseuses.

The scent of something delicious fills the air, crispy and heavy. I recognize it instantly. Bacon.

That's when I spot the buffet table near the concierge desk. Five chafing dishes sit covered with metal lids, a tower of takeout containers at the end of the table. There's also a small table with two large Starbucks thermal coffee towers.

"Ms. Brandt."

I pull my eyes off the food to see Glover looking over at me. Her smile, though big, is anything but cordial. She looks proud, knowing she bested me.

"Good morning," she goes on, looking over at the buffet table and slowly motioning with her hand. "Would like you some breakfast? Perhaps some coffee?"

I finally leave my place and walk further into the lobby. The Zhengs are on two of the massage tables, and Mrs. Toscano is on another, all three completely zenned out.

"I'm not very hungry," I lie as I look back at Glover. "But thank you."

I hope my mouth doesn't water.

"How about a massage?" She gestures at the fourth table, now empty. "They do fantastic work at Alora's Spa. I'm such a loyal customer, they jumped at the chance to give everyone in the building free massages for the whole day. How kind of them."

"Yes, super." I give her my own sharp smile then look past her to the doors. "Excuse me. I have to get going to work now."

Her steely smile widens, deepening her crow's feet and

laugh lines around her plumped lips. "Please, take some coffee."

She grabs my arm and ushers me toward the buffet table.

I watch as a fellow tenant picks up a tong full of bacon to throw in his takeout container. I have to look away before I cave and grab one for myself.

"This was a nice thing for you to do," I say as she pours me some coffee. She moves slowly, and I have a feeling it's on purpose.

"Well, I had to step it up when you gave away those tiny muffins, didn't I?"

"They weren't tiny," I object. "Mrs. Dorst made them."

"Just repeating what I heard, dear." She holds her smile as she lifts the lidless cup up to me. "Milk? Sugar? Cream?"

"Just milk," I say.

Glover adds the milk, wishing a few tenants a great day as they pass her, then hands me the coffee. "I must say, I was surprised you did that on Sunday."

I take a slow sip of the coffee. "Yes, well, I wanted to show people I was serious about running."

She laughs again, but it's loud and shrill. "With muffins and pins? That's so juvenile, my dear. It reminded me of what those girls used to do in my high school—the girls who always thought they could compete and win prom queen. But they always end up being, well, losers." Her smile turns sharp.

My mouth caves slightly, and my eyes narrow.

Then she looks over my shoulder and waves as the newest residents, whose names I don't know, approach the lobby, smiles on their faces when they see the free massage and breakfast signs.

Glover greets them with a bright smile. "Good morning! Have time for a quick massage? How about some breakfast?"

I watch as the husband hurries toward an open massage table while the wife stays near Glover, who's launched into a speech about her promises and strategy for the building.

Wait… Is she the prom queen? And I'm the loser? Is that what she means?!

"Good morning, Hilary!"

Mrs. Zheng pops up next to me, happily rubbing the back of her neck, her short black hair a slight mess from the scalp massage.

"Good morning, Mrs. Zheng. Did you enjoy your massage?"

She smiles at me, reaching down for a takeout container. "Oh, yes, it's been years since I had one. I should go more often. They gave me a punch card for two more free massages if I book a service with them!"

"That's great." I can't help but grumble as I sip my coffee.

I catch Mrs. Zheng looking me up and down as she slowly piles some bacon strips and home fries into the container. She smiles at me and pushes the container my way. "Here, have some breakfast. Maybe it will make you feel better."

"I feel fine," I tell her.

"Eat more," she winks, "drink less."

Oh, God.

"No, no, Mrs. Zheng, I don't drink. I'm not an

alcoholic," I proclaim, bringing my coffee from my lips. "I just wrote everyone a letter explaining that."

"Eat, eat, much better to eat than to drink." She pushes the container into my empty hand, and I almost drop it.

"Really," I say again, "I'm not a—"

"Hilary, pleased to see you grabbing some breakfast," Mrs. Glover calls my way. I look over and find her clenching her clipboard against her chest. "Let me know what you think, of course."

"You aren't having any?" I ask her.

"Oh, please, no." She lets out a laugh as she waves me off. But her eyes quickly drop to my legs and stomach. "I'm watching my figure…"

§

"Here." I drop the takeout container on Eli's desk.

He makes a face at it. "What is that?"

"Breakfast, courtesy of Glover," I huff as I walk toward my desk.

I take a seat, setting my purse at my feet.

Eli slowly opens the container, treating it as if it's a bomb. He looks inside, makes another face, and shuts the lid. "I don't eat this kind of stuff. It's literally a heart attack waiting to happen. Why did you take it from her?"

"Mrs. Zheng shoved it into my hands." I groan. "Says it's better to eat than drink."

Eli smirks. "They all still think you're queen of the winos, eh?"

"I found two flyers for AA meetings in my mailbox last night."

He lets out a laugh and leans back into his chair, examining my outfit.

I follow his gaze to my black dress pants and white short-sleeved wrap blouse. My hair is curled and pulled halfway back. "What?"

"I see we nixed the heels today." He points at my wedges. "We're dressing a bit more conservatively again, aren't we?"

"Eli." I roll my eyes and pull myself closer to my desk to turn my computer screen on. "Knock it off."

"I'm just saying what I notice."

From the corner of my eye, I see him watching me. I sigh. "What now?"

"Is this because of Neal?"

I snap my head his way. "*What*?"

"I'm just asking," he claims innocently.

"Please don't even bring him up."

"This is the first time I'm bringing him up," he declares. "I wanted to Monday and yesterday, but I was good and didn't. You can't expect me to let it hang in the air forever, can you?" He wheels his chair toward my desk.

I pull up my work email as Eli leans on my desk, setting an elbow down and resting his chin on the palm of his hand. "So, have you talked to him since he got back? What was it like? Is there still chemistry? I thought I felt, like, mad sexual chemistry between you two on Sunday."

"There was nothing!" I gawk at him. "And we didn't talk. At all. We will never talk."

"He looks good though." Eli ignores my annoyance. "The whole rough, scruffy thing works really well with him. Did you find out why he left?"

"What did I just say?" I ask him angrily. "I just told

you we didn't talk. And that I don't plan on talking to him —*ever*."

"Okay!" Eli pushes himself off my desk and widens his eyes. "I was just asking. I thought maybe he was the reason you dressed so…boring the last couple of days. Maybe you don't want anything to do with Warren anymore. In which case, I can kind of understand even though I think Warren—"

"I dressed boring Monday and today because you made fun of me last time!"

"I knew you dressed like that on purpose." He points a finger in my face. "I knew it!"

"Shut up," I snap, turning to my computer. "I'm already in a bad mood, and you're going to make it worse."

Eli rolls his eyes as he wheels back to his desk. "Christ. Maybe you *should* drink a bit more…"

"Eli."

I watch Sherry, a junior planner, and Debra from HR glance my way as they pass my desk on their way to Sydney's office. Debra whispers something to Sherry, and they both let out small laughs.

"What was that about?" I ask Eli.

"The saffron thing still seems to be the giggle of the office," Eli explains.

Two hours later, we're on our way to Pepper Lauren's cake shop near Harbor Front. Eli has fussed over my hair several times, and each time, I've had to swat him away. The cake shop is located right between the marina and a quaint indie village that is booming with farmers markets and tourists in the summer.

The cab pulls up alongside the curb, and I pay for our fare, stepping out first.

I look back at Eli and see him frowning at his phone. "Eli?"

"Oh, darn, there's some kind of emergency at the office," he says, keeping his eyes on his phone. He doesn't even bother to sound convincing.

"What kind of emergency?" I demand to know.

"Don't know." His answer comes quick as he reaches for the door. He pulls it so hard from my grasp, it slams shut between us. "I'll deal with it. Have a good time!"

"Eli!"

He slaps the back of the cab driver's seat. "Onward, good sir."

I gawk as the cab disappears into traffic.

Sometimes I wonder why I even bother putting up with Eli. I'll have to yell at him later. I can't be late meeting Warren.

I hustle from the curb toward the tiny sweet shop.

It's busy, which doesn't surprise me. There isn't a time of day that the shop isn't full of people wanting to place an order, grab a sweet treat, or catch a glimpse of Pepper herself. Once at the front counter, I'm led straight to the main tasting room.

Warren is already there, head down, phone in hands. He's seated behind a long metal table, which is already covered in cake slices of different shapes made in every color of the rainbow, from bright orange to dark grey. A pitcher of water and two glasses sit on the table as well.

Warren looks up when I walk into the room. He smiles and slips his phone into the pocket of his suit vest. "Morning. No Eli?"

"There was an emergency at the office," I tell him. "He had to go back. But he sends his best wishes for the tasting."

"More for us, I suppose." He smiles as I sit down in the chair next to him.

"Did you meet Pepper yet?" I ask him.

"I did, yes." He clasps his hands together. His bright eyes rest upon mine, and he smiles again. "She seems very nice, very proud of her work."

"Oh, definitely," I nod. "She works really hard."

"Says you're one of her favorite planners," he informs me.

"Really?" This makes me blush, and I push my hair behind my ears. "I didn't know that."

He sets his hands on the table near me. "I can see why. You're very impressionable. It's been a delight to work with you so far."

As if blushing from the earlier compliment hadn't warmed me up already, his sudden flirtatious tone makes my hands go all clammy again.

"Well, thank you," I say, aware that my voice has turned rather mousy. "You've been a great client so far."

"I hope so." He laughs. "I'm known to be the more easy-going one in my family."

"Do you have a big family?"

He lifts up two fingers. "One brother, one sister, both younger. My mother and father—"

The door swings open, and he stops talking. We watch Pepper Lauren enter. She's wearing her baker's smock, a bright orange dress beneath it. Her wavy blonde hair is tossed up in a messy bun, but her makeup is immaculate, her smile instantly warm when she sees me. "Hilary! You're here!"

"Sorry I'm late," I apologize as she walks toward us.

"Barely." She laughs. "Gave me a chance to chat with Warren about what I did and what he's looking for." She puts her hands on her hips. "Okay, are we ready to begin?"

Warren sends a grin my way. "Let's do it."

For the next hour, we try each tiny cake Pepper has made, from an almond amaretto pound cake to a chocolate bourbon cake with pecans and brown sugar. Warren is finishing off the vanilla bean pistachio cake, and I can't get enough of the Boston cream cake with creamy chocolate frosting.

"So, which flavor did you like the best?" Piper looks at Warren, and we watch as he looks at the ceiling. "Remember that I can dye the icing into any color you want if you still want to go with a specific theme."

"Can I have them all?" he jokes.

Pepper and I both laugh.

He sighs and puts one more forkful of the vanilla bean cake into his mouth, swallowing quickly. "Okay, in all honesty though, if I had to pick just one…which by the way is extremely difficult Pepper, well done…"

"Thank you." She beams.

"…I would have to pick…" He trails off as he looks over at my slice of Boston cream cake, briefly glancing at me before he sticks his fork into it one more time. He puts it into his mouth, chews slowly, and swallows.

"I can't decide," he finally states. "I honestly can't do it." He looks back at me, pointing his fork my way. "You do it."

"What? No," I object quickly, shaking my head. "No, this is your event. You have to do it."

"But I can't decide." He frowns for the first time, and even that is charming. A few wrinkles line his eyes, which darken a shade as they narrow. "Pick one."

I look down at the half-eaten cakes and bite my bottom lip.

No wonder he can't decide. They're all heaven.

Suddenly, his phone breaks the silence. He retrieves it from his pocket and places it against his chest as he looks at me. "I have to take this. Give me five minutes."

"Okay." I nod.

He throws Pepper a quick smile and hops off his chair, walking toward the furthest corner of the room to take his call.

Pepper watches him for a second then leans over the table and smiles at me. "You two are very cute, by the way."

Her comment brings me down from my high. "What?"

"How long have you guys been dating?" She keeps her voice at a whisper. "Can't be that long if he just became your client."

"Oh, no. No. We're not dating," I tell her with a nervous laugh. "He's just a client."

She raises an eyebrow at me. "Really? I thought maybe…" She gives him a brief glance. "I just assumed… You seem happier than most couples I bake for."

"Yeah, no, we are not a couple." I shake my head. "This is for his company's anniversary party. Didn't you get that in the email?"

"All Eli said was that I should stick to all my sexy flavors," she replies. "I don't even know what he meant by that, so I ended up going with my top fifteen flavors for wedding cakes."

I roll my eyes.

Sexy flavors? Where does he get this stuff?

"Well, if it's any consolation, you guys would make a cute couple," Pepper tells me with a shrug.

"I don't date clients," I tell her. "It's a rule I have."

Pepper smirks as she looks over at Warren again. "If I had a client that looked like *that*, and was as sweet as that too, I'd throw that rule out the window."

I follow her gaze and see Warren laugh. It makes me smile, and I look away quickly.

A few seconds later, Warren rejoins us. "Okay, sorry again. Did we decide on a flavor?"

"How about the vanilla bean one?" I suggest as I point to his half-eaten piece. "You seemed to be really into that one."

"One of our top flavors. Good choice," Pepper says to Warren. "It's rare to find someone who isn't a fan of it."

"Let's do it then." Warren nods, smiling at Pepper. "It really was one of the most incredible cakes I've ever tasted."

"Thank you." Pepper smiles and her cheeks flush a little bit. "I appreciate that."

We say goodbye to Pepper and make our way out of the shop toward Warren's town car. This time, when he offers to give me a ride back to the office, I take it. After we're settled in the car, I check my phone and find a text from Luna.

MR. DORST WAS ROPED INTO GETTING A FREE

massage from Glover's therapist this morning.

Traitor.

"So, what's the next step?" Warren asks.

"Well, we arrange a walk-through at the venues. That way you can plan where you want to set picnic tables or tents for the barbeque. And we can decide how to set the tables and band for the evening cocktail party. We'll need you to confirm numbers for that part."

"I can get my secretary to send them to you by Friday." As he puts his seat belt on, he turns to look at me. "Are you and Eli going to be joining us for the day?"

"We'll be there for setup, yes. Usually just one of us stays for the entire event. For this big of an event, we'll split up the duties."

"I see." He turns away from me and looks to the windshield. "In that case, I hope you stay for the evening events."

I hold back my girlish smile, but it's difficult, and a small grin appears. "That shouldn't be a problem."

"Eli won't mind?"

I snort as I think ahead to Eli's reaction upon learning he's in charge of the family event in the middle of the woods. "I'll tell him to bring extra bug spray."

Chapter Eight

"There are quite a lot of people here…"

"Looks like almost everyone in the building showed up for this," Bryson shares.

Luna and I stand with him in the front of the room. We're off to the left, and Glover stands with the Tempermans toward the right. They're a rather striking couple, middle aged, always on the go.

Miranda Temperman runs a small investment firm, and Charlie Temperman works for the mayor—or something like that. He's a tall, thin man with wire-framed glasses, and ironically, a loud booming voice, which I guess makes him perfect for politics. Miranda wears her dark hair in a low bun for the evening, and she's in a muted-yellow pant suit, no doubt an attempt to match Glover's bright dress.

There are several seats set out. The Dorsts, Mr. Tweed, Paulette sit in the front row on the left side of the room. Two empty chairs waiting next to them for Luna and Bryson, all six wearing their "Vote for Hilary" pins. They're the only ones though. We gave away quite a bit, but I don't see anybody else wearing them.

A few more people lag into the room, one of them Neal Turner. He looks over at Glover as the door shuts behind him and then over at me. A half smile appears on his face, but I frown back at him, quickly turning my attention to Luna and Bryson. "Are you guys going to introduce me?"

"No, Glover's doing the opening statement." Luna looks over my shoulder at the woman. "She's also making you go first."

"She's got something up her sleeve," Bryson guesses. "Today, I got a citation for blasting my music," he raises his hands to air-quote, "apparently."

"The Dorsts got citations for their barbeque this afternoon too," Luna tells him. "Even though they have a permit. Smoke complaint or something."

"Your speech is on the podium, the one on top of Glover's," Bryson lets me know. "Remember to look out into the crowd a few times. And don't read straight off the paper."

I stare back at the crowd and am suddenly overcome with nerves. There doesn't seem to be a single seat left, and several tenants are standing in the back or along the sides. Neal among them.

Somebody waves at me, and I realize it's Mrs. James sitting in the very back of the room. I smile and wave back at her, making a mental note to catch her before she leaves.

I feel Luna's gentle hand on my shoulder. "Hey, Hil. You'll be okay. You'll do great."

I swallow down a dry lump.

"The speech we wrote is killer," Bryson adds, giving me a small, crooked smile. "And hey, if all else fails, you have Mr. Tweed's joke."

I chuckle a bit but mostly for show. The nerves are still jumping in my gut.

"People, people! We're about to start. Please take your seats and put away your cell phones!"

Glover stands near the podium, both arms up in the air. She's smiling at everyone as she waves them to be seated. Once the room falls to a hush, her smile softens, and she clasps her hands together at her waist. "Good evening, welcome! I hope everyone enjoyed their breakfast and massages today."

Luna rolls her eyes as the room explodes in a chorus of gratitude.

Glover laughs and nods at them all. "Wonderful, wonderful. Now, let me thank you for taking the time out of your busy schedules to join us this evening. I promise you we will keep this under an hour so you can all quickly be on your way."

She glances my direction. "According to the election policy, whenever there is more than one candidate, there must be an introductory rally, which essentially is a chance for the candidates to outline their promises and goals, and then we open the floor to any questions. Let's keep the questions short but precise if we can. Nobody wants to be here past eight p.m." She chuckles to herself, and a few people in the crowd also laugh.

I frown. How was that funny?

"So, without further ado, let me introduce you all to Hilary Brandt. She's been a tenant in Fairway Towers for the past three years. Her grandfather was Herb Brandt and lived in the condo before her." Glover lets out a muffled giggle then cautiously looks out into the crowd. "Those who have been here longer than three years might remember old Herb *well*."

What exactly is that supposed to mean?

I cross my arms over my chest and look at her. When a few giggles ripple through the crowd, Miranda Temperman's the loudest, I don't feel surprised.

"Hilary?" Glover throws a smile at me, gesturing toward the podium behind her.

I give her my own steely smile and cross over to the podium as she walks off to the side. I step up onto the wooden box and smile at everyone. "Good evening, everyone. Thank you again for taking the time to join us tonight. It really is appreciated."

A few people in the crowd smile my way, but most stay somber. Clearing my throat, I glance down at the paper before me.

Except, this isn't my speech.

It's Glover's.

I lift the stapled papers up, but there isn't anything beneath it.

Okay. It's important not to panic.

I pull back to see if my speech is in the small compartment underneath, but it's empty. I scan the ground around me then look back over at Luna and Bryson. They both frown at me.

The door to the event room opens, and I look over as everyone turns to see Eli hurry into the room with Jacob behind him. As the door shuts behind them, Eli mutters a quiet, *Sorry*, to the room and looks over at me with an apologetic shrug. Next to him, in a smart Armani suit, Jacob throws me a tight smile.

"Everything all right, dear?" Glover shimmies closer.

"Er, fine." I step back to the podium. "Thank you."

Where the hell is my speech?

I look at Glover and find that she's smiling kindly at the crowd.

She took it.

She took my speech.

Okay. I just have to remember it the best I can. It's all I can do.

Looking into the crowd, I see a slew of confused expressions, whispers moving through the room. I give them a big smile and grip the podium with my hands. "So, let me just start by saying that I am very proud to be running for condo board president. If I am elected, I will do this building and all the tenants justice by serving to the best of my abilities. You know, and I know, that you deserve a president who is more than just a president, someone who is also your friend. A friend who cares about your needs and your problems. I am that candidate."

I take a quick breath as Luna gives me a thumbs up and a smile. Eli has taken a place with Jacob right next to Neal. He whispers something to Neal, and Neal looks down at him, frowning a bit.

What is he doing?

I clear my throat as I look away from the three and back into the crowd. "As some of you may know, my name is Hilary Brandt, and I live in 603. I'm an event planner at LaBeau and Gilde. My job relies on good communication with my clients and making sure the needs they express are met in a timely and structured fashion. I have clients who return to me regularly because I'm organized and work *very* hard to get them exactly what they want. Rest assured, I will be like this if elected. Representation of our building is very important. The building's reputation is held in high regard in this neighborhood, and I'd like to see it stay that way."

I'm mildly distracted when I see Mrs. Dorst whisper something Luna's ear, causing Luna to bite her bottom lip. I then realize I can't remember what comes next.

Shit.

What comes next? What did they write?

I look over at Bryson as he mouths something my way. What is he saying?

Carpet?

Arson?

Marvin?

What the hell is he saying?

"Um, I'm going to move on to a few of the policies I plan to put in place if elected." I look away from my team. "As some of you know, I've already started work on the courtyard, and I plan to turn it into a luscious green oasis so that we may all enjoy it. My team and I are currently researching a way to add extra parking spaces as well since that's something that many of you have expressed the need for."

I gesture at the ceiling. "This event room will be used more frequently to host free monthly movie nights, and tenants will be able to book the room whenever they need to. There will no longer be a limit to how many times a tenant can rent out the room per year. We'll be involved in the neighborhood garage sale again also. In fact, I'm planning to get a few tables for this year's sale that is happening next week. Some of you have expressed the need to redo the laundry room in the basement—that's at the top of my list. New washing machines, dryers, a complete renovation of the room. There's no need for a building such as ours to have a dingy, out-of-date laundry room."

From the corner of my eye, I see Glover narrow her eyes, but I remain focused on the nods of approval I'm getting from a few tenants.

I smile.

It seems like I'm doing quite well for having to wing it.

I decide to leave it at that, mostly because I can't remember the rest of the policies Bryson and Luna came up for me. "I'm going to end my speech right here, for fear of boring you if I go any longer. Thank you for listening so well to me, and let's welcome our standing president, Arlene Glover."

There are a few claps as I step off to the side of the room and Glover takes the podium. She smiles out everyone. "Thank you for the introduction, Hilary. And well done with the speech. Most people would prepare, but you did a satisfactory job just winging it. Let's hope *if* elected, you won't be as unprepared."

My jaw clenches. I glance back at the crowd and see that a few people smile or chuckle quietly at her dig, but my team looks vastly annoyed.

"I believe everyone knows quite a bit about who I am, and what I stand for, as I've been the longest-standing condo board president this building has ever had." Glover grins. "So let me just go into the policies I plan to make happen if re-elected, and remind everyone of the policies I have already placed. All of which have worked out positively, may I add."

The Tempermans are the only ones that clap.

"Lights, please," Glover calls out, signaling to someone in the back of the room.

Someone shuts the lights off, and behind Glover, a projection screen slowly comes down. A light shines on it, and I follow it to a projector hanging from the ceiling. Then a picture appears on the screen—a picture of our rooftop, which has two hot tubs and a patio section full of cute wicker furniture.

"Our rooftop patio has been a tremendous success. I know most of you have enjoyed entertaining guests and family up there for your anniversaries, birthdays, what have you." She smiles out at everyone as they nod or mutter in response. Another picture appears, this one of our lobby. "And our newly-renovated lobby was featured in *InStyle Magazine's* 'most trendy condos' last year."

It was?

"That alone grew interest in our building by forty percent. We have several realtors with buyers waiting to nab the next condo that goes up for sale. At my last count, the number is now in the high two hundreds," she boasts to the room. She motions back at the projection screen as a picture of a man in handcuffs with a red X pasted overtop appears. "We have the best security in the entire neighborhood. There hasn't been a theft, or even solicitation, in this building since I've been president." She lets out a small giggle as she side-eyes me. "Well, until recently, but we shouldn't be counting canvassing for votes as solicitation."

"I would," Mrs. Temperman declares, glaring my way.

I throw her my own scowl.

"Now I could go on and on with all my accomplishments," Glover says, "but I'm not much of a bragger."

Luna rolls her eyes and crosses her arms over her chest.

"What I plan to do, if re-elected," Glover goes on, "is rehash our entire budget. We're spending money in places we shouldn't be spending it in. In addition to giving our budget a huge overlook, I plan to establish a way we can grow it. Without much personal sacrifice from any of us." Her tone has taken a serious, but resolute turn.

"Condo fees? They can be lower if you want." She wags a finger in the air. "I will work at bringing them down by at least twenty-five dollars a unit. This I can promise you."

A few tenants begin to clap.

Someone shouts, "Hear, hear!"

I don't like the anxious frown that has appeared on Luna's face. She's crossed her legs, and her left foot bounces against the floor.

"I've heard your cry for more parking spaces." Glover nods sharply, glaring around the room. The picture behind her becomes that of a parking lot. "I'm currently in negotiations with the business next door for us to use their spaces, and here's the kicker… Free of charge."

Mr. Zheng nods and claps loudly.

Damnit.

"I know Ms. Brandt already has her own ideas for the courtyard that sound very…*endearing*." She gives the room a stiff smile. "But let's face it, when the courtyard is turned into her luscious paradise, will we use it as often as she thinks? I mean, we *do* have a winter here. Four, maybe even five months of the year, the area won't be used. What about the upkeep? Having to plant and replant every year, add new soil. It could take a good chunk out of our budget that would best be used in different areas. What if we, instead, work at turning our courtyard into a…."

The picture behind her turns into a modern oval-shaped pool with hanging pool lights and luxury loungers surrounding the crisp waters.

I stiffen in my place as the room explodes into a wave of applause.

"How cool! I would love a pool here!" someone exclaims.

"We could have pool parties!" a woman cries out from the back.

Luna jumps up from her seat and waves her hands in the air at everyone. "Hold on a second here. Hold on a second!" It takes a few seconds, but everyone simmers down enough so Luna can speak. "A pool is going to cost a lot more than a beautiful courtyard and will end up costing more to maintain in the end. How is that going to help reduce condo fees?"

"I don't mind adding a few extra dollars to my fees if we get a pool," Mr. Temperman states loudly.

"Me neither," someone else agrees.

"How much extra are we talking?" Neal asks.

I look over at him.

His eyes are glued onto Glover, who smiles softly at him before she answers. "Five extra dollars a month, maybe ten."

For a pool like that? Where is she getting it from? The appliance store around the corner?

"That's nothing!" someone declares.

"Let's do it!" another tenant shouts out.

Glover laughs and motions for everyone to settle down. "I know you're all excited, but we still have the question and answer portion of the event to get to. Lights, please."

As the lights come on, I drop against the wall behind me, defeated.

Everyone looks so excited about the pool idea. They can't stop smiling or whispering to one another.

"The floor is now open to questions," Glover announces as the room falls silent again.

Nobody raises their hand or stands from their seats.

I won't lie, that makes me feel a bit better. After Glover's pool promise, I don't think I can field any questions as great as that idea.

"No questions? Are you sure?" Glover pries, frowning a bit. "Not a one?"

Mrs. Temperman stands up, her hand half in the air. "I have one. For Ms. Brandt."

Of course she does.

"All right." I walk closer to the podium where Glover stands.

She's gripping the stand with both hands, and I realize there isn't a chance in hell she's letting me up there again.

"How do you expect to fund your laundry room renovation? I don't think that's in the budget."

"Well, I haven't looked into the budget yet—"

"Shouldn't you have done that before making such a promise to everyone?"

What a cow.

"I, uh, well, I have a backup plan if we don't have the money in the budget," I say, wishing my voice didn't drip with uncertainty.

"What plan?" Mrs. Temperman eggs on, crossing her arms over her chest.

"Oh, well, I was planning, hoping really, that…" I look over at my team for support, but they all shrug at me. "Well…that maybe we could raise the money together."

Glover chuckles into her hand as she fakes a cough.

"Raise the money?" Mrs. Temperman scowls at me. "How in the world would we—"

"Like a bake sale!" Eli calls out.

Everyone looks over at him, and he nods. "Bake sales could easily rack in two or three grand. Imagine if you had one twice a month, or if you rented out tables to local bakeries and made it a big thing. People love that kind of cute stuff. A mini café in your lobby."

"Exactly," I exclaim as I point to him. "Everyone loves baked goods!"

Someone from the crowd says, "Seems like a lot of work, though…"

"Well, sure, it can be," I agree, "but we—"

"Let's move on," Glover cuts me off quickly. "Any more questions?"

"Ms. Brandt, would we all get to use the courtyard if you made it into a big garden?" a woman asks me.

"Of course." I nod. "It's for everyone to—"

"But what if we *all* want to plant stuff? Are you going to divide it up evenly?" the same woman asks.

"She can't do that," a man barks next to her. "There wouldn't be enough room."

A few people agree with him.

"How much would it cost to maintain it?" Mr. Temperman asks. "Or do you expect all of us to take turns maintaining it?"

"We would get a gardener, of course."

"Another maintenance worker?" He frowns at me.

"How much would *they* cost? That would definitely raise our condo fees more than ten dollars a month!"

Before I can object, a young woman at the back of the room calls out to Glover, "If we do the pool, we could get *House and Garden* to feature it in their summer spread!"

That's not a question!

"Excellent idea, Tina!" Glover beams. "I'll make note of that…if elected, of course."

Suddenly, the room explodes with ideas of what kind of lanterns to get for the pool, or what color the tiles should be, even what the guest policy should be. With a sigh, I glance over to my team, who sit quietly and look as frustrated as I feel.

❧

"I think," Eli smiles supportively at me and pats my arm, "that went really well."

I shake him off. "It did not go well!" I hiss.

"Okay," he snaps, wiping a finger against his cheek. "There isn't a reason to spit!"

"Sorry, but… Luna, this went horribly!" I whine.

Next to me, she sighs and pushes her hair off her face. "I know, I'm sorry. I really didn't think she had this kind of stuff up her sleeve. I mean, a pool? It's so unlike her to want a pool in this building! When the idea came up two elections ago, she laughed."

"She's lying." Mrs. Dorst shakes a finger at us. "We'll never see a pool."

The room is almost empty now. A few tenants are still at the front of the room with Glover and the Tempermans, someone laughing every few seconds.

Mrs. James had disappeared before the event was over.

Jacob clears his throat as he stands next to Eli. He's at least six feet tall, and his dark Armani suit hugs his thin frame elegantly. His hair is trimmed short on the sides but long in the front. He's rather striking, even if he's rather dull. "I think your speech went well, Hilary. You kept it serious, to the point. You didn't need to use any gimmicks or jokes."

Mr. Dorst shrugs. "I mean, you could have made it livelier if you told a joke or two…"

"You should have used my beaver joke!" Mr. Tweed pokes me in the leg with his cane.

I blink at the old man, and after a second, I let out a long breath. "This was a nightmare…"

There's a burst of laughter behind me again, and as I glance over my shoulder, I see Glover and some tenants bent over in side-splitting laughter.

"She took a few pot shots at you tonight." Mrs. Dorst looks at me. "I really think you should reconsider throwing a bit of shade her way."

"I'm sure another letter will suffice," Eli murmurs, only loud enough for me to hear.

I throw him a look.

He takes a step back with Jacob. "Sorry. We're about to go get some dinner and drinks. Would you all like to come? It looks like everyone here needs a drink, or two. Or three, maybe four…"

I watch them all agree, Mrs. and Mr. Dorst more enthusiastically than the rest.

"I think I'll skip out on drinks, actually," I say, "I don't feel like drowning my sorrows in booze."

"It's probably not a good idea anyway," Bryson says as he slides his hands into his pants pockets.

Eli leaves Jacob and ropes an arm through mine, leading me toward the doors. "I think you should really reconsider coming out with us. Reason one… How long has it been since you've just had a fun night out with food and drinks? And reason two? I don't want to be stuck with your weirdo election team."

"They aren't weird," I protest.

Eli pulls his arm from mine and turns to face me, raising one eyebrow. "One of them has been telling Jacob and I groundhog jokes the entire night. I have never fake laughed so much in my *entire* life."

I smirk. "Beaver jokes. They're beaver jokes."

Eli frowns and shakes his head. "Wait, what? They're actually vagina jokes? If so, he's a pervy old man."

"No!" I cry. "They're about beavers! Beavers, the animals. Jesus, Eli."

He's about to snap back at me, I can tell from the way his face twists up, but something over my shoulder catches his eye. Instantly, he looks back at me and struggles to hold back a smile. "Well, anyway, I'll leave you be then. I have to get back to Jacob, the pervy old man, and your weirdo team." He points off to the side. "And you obviously have to deal with that…"

I glance over my shoulder and see Neal leaning against the wall near the door, tapping away at his phone.

Great. Just perfect.

In horror, I watch Eli back toward the room. He mouths something at me and motions at Neal. I shake my head at him, my jaw clenching.

He waves me off, and once he's at the door he looks over at Neal again and screams, "Neal!"

Startled, Neal looks Eli's way.

Eli smiles at him. "Just wanted to say good night. Great to see you again."

"Uh, yeah, you too." Neal smiles back.

Eli then waves at me, and I wonder if he knows how ridiculous he looks. "Have a great night, Hil. Enjoy your quiet evening at home. *Alone*."

I'm going to kill him.

I don't even hide my disdain as Eli disappears into the room with a smirk. Embarrassed, I turn back without looking at Neal and head down the hallway. To my relief, I don't hear Neal following me as I exit the long hallway. I'm even more relieved to see that the lobby is empty.

I head to the elevators and push the up button then take a step back to see where the elevator is.

Top floor.

I sigh to myself. "Figures."

As I cross my arms over my chest, someone comes around the corner.

Neal.

Damnit.

I pretend not to notice that he seems surprised to see me waiting for the elevator.

Guess his plan was to avoid me too.

He says nothing as he stands next to me and looks up at the numbers above the doors. The elevator is still on the top floor.

"Getting a faster elevator should have been one of her promises," he says.

"Yeah."

I keep my eyes down, my gaze focused. I do my best to ignore the palpitations in my chest that still flares up when I know he's looking at me.

"You could promise it," he suggests.

"What?" I glance over at him.

He shrugs and scratches the stubble on his cheek. "Just a thought."

Scoffing again, I trace the tiles under my feet with the toe of my shoe. "Right. Maybe we could raise the money by doing a bottle drive…"

He slides his hands into the pockets of his dark jeans. "The bake sales are a good idea. You could throw one together next week just to show everyone that raising money through one is doable—"

"Thanks," I interrupt, "but I'm good."

He chuckles. It's rough and full of amusement, which annoys me more. "Look, I'm just trying to give you a few pointers."

"I don't need any advice from you."

"Well, it doesn't look like your election team knows what the hell they're doing," he replies with just as much snark as I threw his way.

I place my hands on my hips as I turn to face him. "They know exactly what they're doing."

"Oh, okay, is the letters to the tenants thing your idea? Or theirs?"

"There's nothing wrong with my letters."

"They certainly bring a smile to my face." He smirks.

Now he's making fun of me.

"I'm just saying," he goes on when he sees my frown, "Glover's coming after you with knives, and you're hitting back with flower petals."

"What the hell is that analogy?" I retort. "It doesn't even make sense!"

Except that it does.

"Well, unless you want the entire building to think you're a bobblehead, I'd step up your game."

I realize my hands are now balled into fists, and my palms are sweating. "I never asked for your opinion or *suggestions*. I especially wouldn't consider them from a man who is the opponent's loyal little lapdog."

He frowns and opens his mouth to respond, but I throw up my hand to stop him. "Excuse me, I'm taking the stairs. Have a great evening, Mr. Turner. And please, do try to remain quiet in your unit. All the scraping across the floor is starting to piss off your neighbors."

Chapter Nine

Thursday morning went by much better than Wednesday. By last night, I had softened from my sharp interaction with Neal.

Ugh, I hate that he makes me so mad. That he jokes with me and then smirks and thinks he's being all cute and… and… and I hate the way my heart flutters whenever he comes near me. Or the way the flutter cascades down into my stomach.

All we had was one date—*one stinkin' date*—and my body's betraying me. Acting as if we had some kind of tremendous breakup when all he did was cut our date short and shove me out of his condo without a word. Then he disappeared for three months without bothering to tell me what was happening.

But yeah. Still not a breakup.

I shouldn't be as broken up about this as I am.

I need to focus on something else—work, my friends, this election.

Warren's event.

Eli and I received an email from Warren this morning confirming the number of employees for the evening portion of his event. Two hundred and seventy-five people.

We confirmed our viewing of the old observatory for Monday afternoon.

He signed off his last email with a winky face.

"I'm sure he hit the semicolon on accident. Why would he wink at me?"

"It was on purpose," Eli insists. "Nobody makes that mistake. Trust me."

"I have made that mistake once or twice."

"Yes, well, you are a grandmother trapped in a thirty-year-old woman's body, so that doesn't surprise me." Eli smirks as he drops down into the chair behind his desk, leaning back, his hands coming together behind his head. "I see we are in a much better mood today than yesterday. Gotten over the bobblehead thing, have we?"

I grimace. "I told you not to bring it up again." I bend over and grab my purse on the ground then heave it onto my desk.

"And I told you, based on your story, it doesn't sound like he called you an actual bobblehead. He implied everyone may *think* you're a bobblehead—"

"It's the same thing!" I exclaim. "He's just a stupid jerk." I sigh as I catch the time on my computer screen, and the virtual Post-it that reminds me I have a meeting at two thirty. "Do you have everything ready for our meeting with Mrs. Sarris? We have to leave soon."

"I don't really get the jerk vibe from him, though." Eli frowns, eyes on the ceiling. "I mean, the way he left your date—way back when—was kind of jerky, sure, and then disappearing for a while was too, but I bet there's a good explanation. I really think he's just teasing and trying to get on your good side, but you're all caught up in the past—"

"You've met him like, what, three times now?" I throw back. "Which of the three short times that you conversed with him gave you the idea he isn't a jerk?"

Eli blinks at me for a few seconds, clearly irritated by my tone. "All three times, but mostly Wednesday night. He said that he thinks you have a good chance to win this thing. And no offense, but out of the two of us, I'd say I'm more in tune to men than you are. You're practically a nun!"

I stop loading up my purse and slowly look up at him. "He said that?"

"Yup." Eli nods. "He seemed pretty confident in your abilities."

"Well, for someone who seems pretty confident in my abilities, he sure was a jerk about it," I mutter.

Eli scoffs. "Was he though? Because sometimes you can be a tad defensive…"

"I'm not defensive!"

Eli points a finger at me. "What was *that* then?"

"Are you ready for the meeting with Mrs. Sarris?"

"Of course I'm ready." He sits up in his chair and gestures at the folders on his desk. "It's a yearly Bingo auction, again. The easiest kind of thing to organize. I could do it in my sleep. I hate that we have to meet her at her office. It smells stiff in there."

"It's her perfume. She likes lavender."

"Lavender does not smell like a funeral home."

"Hilary. And Eli…interesting outfit, as usual."

We both look up to see Jasmine standing over Eli's desk. She points at his pleather pants and then moves up to his white T-shirt with a Rorschach symbol on the front. She holds her cell phone in the hand resting on her hip.

"And what were *you* going for?" Eli shoots back as he looks at her short plaid skirt and tight black blouse. Her glossy hair is pulled back into two curly pigtails. "*Enquirer's* spread for desperate pop star wannabes?"

"What can I do for you, Jasmine?" I interrupt their banter before Sydney can hear it.

"I'm just stopping by to chit chat." She smiles sweetly at me, turning her back on Eli as she approaches my desk. "Just wanting to check in, see how my gal pal Hilary is doing."

I raise an eyebrow at her.

"Where's my holy water?" Eli pretends to frantically search his messy desk.

"So," Jasmine continues, smiling my way, "how is it going?"

"If you mean with the Redler account, then it's going great," I smile back. "Super."

"He's very satisfied," Eli calls out. "*Very.*"

Jasmine waves off Eli's comment and shrugs, looking at her nail beds. "Please, I made my peace with that days ago. I've got much more important clients to worry about."

"So, why don't you hop on over to your desk and bother them then?" Eli suggests.

Jasmine's tone suddenly turns, and she looks from her nails down to me. "Although, Hil, I hear you're going to have your work cut out for you at this event…"

I pull my purse on my lap and let out a breath as I look at Jasmine. "What are you talking about?"

"Haven't you heard?" Jasmine blinks woefully at me.

I wonder if she's acting badly on purpose or just has no idea how poorly she plays the naive, mean girl. I watch as she works on her phone, swiping at the screen then turning it so I can have a look. The smile expanding from her plump lips is one of pity. Sharp pity. "I'm *so* sorry, Hil."

Eli wheels himself so quickly to my side, he bumps my shoulder with his as he strives to glance at the phone with me.

We're looking at a picture of Warren leaving some kind of building downtown with a gorgeous, tall, thin Asian woman. She's dressed in a pale bodycon dress, a chic black mini backpack hanging off her shoulder. He has a hand on her back, leading her through reporters with a wide smile on his face.

I pretend the picture doesn't sting. I mean, it's not that I would ever seriously consider Warren but, I don't know, it was kind of a rush to think he liked me.

I casually clear my throat and muster a small smile, glancing up at Jasmine. "So?"

Jasmine pulls her phone against her chest. "I know how you much you had your sights set on him. I can only imagine the disappointment after looking so nice for him…"

She's talking about the push-up bra day. Inconspicuous push-up bra my ass.

I can't let her think…

Okay, I have to play this well.

"Oh, Jasmine." I chuckle and shrug. "I know."

"What?" She frowns, looking from Eli to me. "You know?"

"Yes, I know he's seeing her."

I ignore Eli's stare and watch as Jasmine narrows her eyes. "You know he's seeing Rosamie Tomas?"

"Of course," I reply. "He's my client. He told me the other day. She's, um, his plus one to his event."

Jasmine looks down at her phone and then back at me, scoffing. "Well, good luck. I'm surprised she hasn't inserted herself with the planning already. I hear she's an awful mean cow."

"If you'll excuse us, we have a meeting to get to." I slowly stand from my desk and give Jasmine a small smile. "I'll see you later."

"Yeah, great. Fine." Jasmine shrugs, her attention returning to her phone as she swipes at the screen, not bothering to glance up at us as we walk away.

Eli says nothing until we get inside the elevators. When the doors shut, he hits me with the Sarris folders. "Who the hell is Rosamie?! And why didn't you tell me he's dating someone while he's flirting with you?!"

I push the folders away. "I didn't know! I was just saving face in front of Jasmine!"

"Oh." Eli calms himself and clenches the folders. "Oh, well then. Good... But who the hell is this Rosamie Tomas?"

"I don't know. He's never mentioned her." I run a hand through my hair. "And this just proves my point. He was never flirting. He was just being nice."

Eli jerks his head back at me. "It was not just being nice, stop saying that!"

"Whatever it was, it obviously meant nothing." I shrug, clasping the strap of my purse on my shoulder. "Just as I suspected all along. He's just naturally flirty, I guess. He's a client, nothing more."

Thank God I never let my hopes get up because, well, then this would just make me feel stupid. Really, really stupid.

The rest of the elevator ride is quiet. Once we hit the

lobby, my phone begins to ring. I slow down, letting Eli go ahead of me as I fish my phone out of my bag.

"Hey, Luna, I can't talk right now. I'm on my way to a meeting—"

"Someone sold you out!"

"What?"

"Someone sold you out. There was an email circulated from Glover, a CC'd email from a client of yours that Glover must have contacted somehow. It basically said that the tenants would be morons to elect you as you are unimaginative, the worst planner they've ever worked with, and that you ruined their party! Glover's printed the email out and posted it everywhere in the building, adding a section in which she accuses you of being a liar. She says, 'Is this an example of Ms. Brandt's hard work and dedication to her clients?' Then lists some Sarah person as the client, a quote from her, and—"

"Nooooo!" I exclaim as I stomp both feet. "No, Sarah's a menace! She's awful!"

"I know!" Luna screams back. "The Zhengs came to the door an hour ago demanding answers, and Bryson's been fielding emails from other tenants. This is a mess. Can you come home? Paulette says you should have a small meeting downstairs and explain the situation to the tenants."

"Are you serious?" I gape. "Luna, I'm at work. I have a meeting!"

"Well, can't Eli cover it? I mean, this looks really bad, Hil. This could cost you the election…"

"Can't you handle it?" I groan as I move out of the way of a group of men in suits.

"No one wants to hear from me! The Zhengs said they

wanted to talk to you, not me. And the other tenants are asking Bryson why he's answering for you. Why you can't speak for yourself…"

"Because I work! Because I have a career!"

"You can't say that when you're in an election! They're going to definitely think you don't care about the position at all!"

"I don't care!"

Eli slides up next to me. "What's happening now?"

"Hil, this is important. Really, really important for your image. Your reputation. Some of these people mingle with your client type, and if they start gossiping, well, it could affect your career."

Unbelievable. I cannot believe I'm actually going to—

I sigh, pulling my phone away from my mouth and looking at Eli. "Can you handle Mrs. Sarris on your own again?"

"Uh, yeah," he answers slowly, "you know I can."

"Okay, 'cause there's been an emergency with the election, and I need to go home."

Eli sucks in a breath. "Oh my God, did she do it? Did that old bat finally crack and kill someone?"

"No!" I exclaim. "No, God, what would make you think she would ever—"

"She's got Belle Guinness eyes," Eli tells me matter of factly. He points at his own eyes. "Exactly the same. Compare when you have the time."

I blink at him. "Who the hell is Belle Gu— Never mind. Just go to the meeting, okay?" I bring my phone back to my ear as he responds with a dragged out *Fiiiine* and tell Luna, "I'm on my way."

Mrs. Dorst shakes her head slowly, the wine glass close to her pink lips. "I mean, what's this obsession with the flyers and pamphlets anyway? It's not very normal if you ask me."

"Quite right," her husband agrees. He checks his watch for the third time in the last ten minutes. Both of them look dressed to kill, him in a fitted grey suit and her in a long black and gold cocktail dress.

I haven't moved from my place near the door since I got here ten minutes ago. I'm holding one of the flyers with Sarah's quote saying I was difficult to work with and that the slightest request she had was met with a dramatic excuse. Then she says I spitefully ruined her party by destroying her guests' clothing. Glover's words, in bold red, say "Is this an example of her work ethic? Is this an example of how dedicated she claims to be?"

"How did she even get to Sarah Graham?" I frown at the flyer. "I mean, *how*?"

Luna stands in the doorway of the kitchen, an apron over her yellow dress and her short hair pulled away from her face with a headband. "I don't know. Maybe they know each other?"

Mrs. Dorst points a finger at Luna. "That'd be my guess. They must be in the same social circle."

Paulette taps away on her laptop and gives me a quick look. "I have an idea…"

There's a knock behind me, and I turn around to answer it.

Mr. Tweed and Bryson enter together, stacks of crumpled flyers in their hands. Mr. Tweed's cane rocks unsteadily underneath his arm as he hands me two stacks of flyers.

"We got most of them down." Bryson sighs. "But the few tenants we ran into weren't super happy about this one…"

"Ah, fools," Mr. Tweed exclaims as he places his cane on the ground near his foot. "Only fools focus on one side of the story."

"Great, well, there goes that then." I throw my hands up in the air as I turn to face Luna. "We might as well admit defeat. Everybody is going to vote for Glover."

Luna points at me. "You don't know that."

"Yeah." Bryson elbows me softly as he passes me. "Mrs. James was nice about it."

"Mrs. James?" Dropping the flyers, letting them scatter around me, I grab Bryson's arm. "You saw Mrs. James?"

"Yeah." He nods, frowning at me. "Downstairs in the lobby. She said she's coming up to see you now. I think she feels bad for you."

I let him go and peer into the round mirror hanging near the door. I pat down my hair and give myself a once-over. I look okay, a bit disheveled, but I can calm myself down.

This is my chance. If she isn't coming up to offer me the event, I'll just have to convince her.

Paulette beckons us to her, spinning her laptop computer to face the small group. "I say we hit back with this…"

It's a poster. Glover's face is front and center with a big red line through it. The words "User" and "Abuser" run around the page with a slogan at the bottom that says, "If she already abuses the rights of the tenants, what makes you think she will stop after elected for a fifth term?"

"Ohhh… That's good." Luna smiles at Paulette and wags a finger at her. "That's really good."

"Who hasn't been a victim of her rule breaking?" Mrs. Dorst sashays closer in her gown, her smoky eyes focused on Paulette. "My husband and I pay for two parking spaces. It's our right to park our vehicles, whatever they may be, in that spot. We have the right to do so without being harassed."

"And Hilary?" Luna points at me. "She has the right to eat Indian food in the building if she wants! She can't take away that right."

"I happen to know that the Zhengs want a Siamese cat, and she's turned them down but approved several other tenants who wanted cats," Bryson declares, arms over his chest now.

Mr. Tweed stomps his cane on the ground, and we look over at him. "She doesn't let me hang my clothes out the window to dry, but she lets Mrs. Clemens above me hang her clothes out!"

"Er, right, yes." Paulette nods as she looks from him to me. "See? She bends the rules only when it suits *her*, and she's harsher to people who she isn't fond of. It's an abuse of power. Everyone in the building knows she does it. If we call her out on it and list everything she's done, maybe people will actually do something about it. Like vote for *you*, not her."

Luna points at the laptop with a bright smile. "Yes! Put that on the flyer and make pamphlets. Make sure to add that Hil would never stop someone from getting a cat or take away their parking spaces or—"

"Hold on a minute here," I shout over her. "I didn't say I wanted to do this."

I hate the rush of guilt already simmering through me as I think of Glover's awe-stricken face when she sees the flyers. It just seems so, so mean.

"Oh, so what's your plan then? Another letter to the building?" Mr. Dorst asks, smirking at his wife.

I scowl at him. "No. One to her, asking her to act maturely and to stop—"

Luna lets out an exasperated sigh, her hands dropping to her hands. "She's not going to stop, don't you understand? She has to make you look bad because it's the only way she'll win. She knows people love the allure of a fresh new face. So her plan is to make you look like a crude, lazy airhead."

"Your letters haven't been doing much, my dear." Mr. Tweed gives me a sympathetic smile. "It wouldn't hurt to give her back just a small dose of her own medicine."

"I just think it's mean."

The Dorsts roll their eyes in unison, and Bryson mutters something under his breath that I can't make out.

Luna lets out another sigh before stepping up to me and grabbing my arms. "Look, Hil. I know you think you don't have a mean bone in your body, but you do. It just needs a little push. Remember the washing machine incident? Or when you got drenched eating dinner outside in the rain? Just think about how angry you were then. Use that anger. Because deep down, you know she deserves this."

I bite my bottom lip. Why do I have such a shaky feeling about all this? Why can't I be even just a mean little?

Someone knocks at the door before I can answer Luna.

Mrs. James!

"Hold that thought!" I tell Luna.

I rush to the door and make sure my blouse is tucked into my skirt before I open the door, grinning.

Mrs. James takes a step back from the door as I swing it open. She's in a pair of beige pants and a bright yellow bowling league T-shirt, her name sewn over her left breast. *Sophie.*

"Mrs. James! Hello, how are you?"

"I'm all right, dear."

She looks past me into my apartment and sees everyone else. "Hello."

They greet her in a series of mumbles, and I motion to the hall. "Let's chat out here. They're all busy with election stuff in there. I don't want to bore you with all that…"

I hurry outside and slowly shut the door behind me. She smiles at me, and I return the same warm grin. "What can I do for you tonight, Mrs. James?"

"Well…" Her hands come together, and she eyes me carefully. "Well, it's just that I saw the poster downstairs—"

Shit.

"Don't worry about that," I interrupt her anxiously. "Nothing to worry about. Just some friendly, political jargon between two candidates."

"Friendly, political jargon?" She frowns, her light eyebrows coming together as one. "It seemed very *un*friendly to me."

"I appreciate your concern." I smile at her again. "It means a lot to me, but rest assured, I will be handling it."

"The problem is, Ms. Brandt, that poster was *very* concerning to me. As someone who is interested in hiring you and the firm you work for, I was quite alarmed."

No…

"It's a bunch of lies!" I panic, and my hands fly out. "A smear tactic by Mrs. Glover."

One of her eyebrows rises, the look not very reassuring. "But I made a call before coming up here. You see, Sarah Graham's husband is the brother of a friend of mine who also serves on the museum board. She said she was at that event, and her dress was, in fact, ruined by a blunder from LaBeau and Gilde. Sarah Graham was very distraught afterwards and unhappy with the way it was dealt with by your boss."

No, no, no…

"Mrs. James, I can assure you that what really happened was—"

Mrs. James cuts me and my hysteria off with a lift of her hand. "Now, I'm not usually one to listen to gossip, but this is a very big event. The second most important event next to our Christmas gala. I can't have any kind of negative—"

"But if you would just let me—"

"I'm sorry, my dear," Mrs. James' words slice through mine, and she shakes her head. "But I will be withdrawing you from consideration. I simply cannot risk it."

"But what if you hear my ideas?" I throw out pleadingly. "I could have them ready for you by tomorrow morning, and—"

"I'm sorry, dear." She sighs and takes a step away from me. "I do wish you don't hold this decision against me, and of course, I wish you luck in this election. Now, I have to move along, or I'll be late for ladies' bowling."

I can't believe this. Did that actually just happen?

I'm frozen in place. After a moment, the heaviness in my chest drops to my feet as I look down the hall at Mrs. James. She's at the elevators already, and before I can make one last-ditch effort, the elevator doors open, and she hurries inside without a word.

The condo door slowly opens behind me, and I hear the squeak from the hinges. I breathe in the wispy vanilla that fills the air around me, and I know its Luna.

"Ohhh, Hil. I'm really sorry," she whispers a second later.

Great. Everybody heard that. Humiliated *again*.

I look at the mirror across from our door and see my pathetic, defeated expression.

Luna whispers behind me again, "Hil?"

"Print the damn posters."

Chapter Ten

It's now Saturday morning, and I woke feeling good about my decision to print the posters. Late last night, Bryson and Luna plastered them all over the building, stuffing some into as many mailboxes as they could. We're in the courtyard, and Paulette texted an hour ago to say we have an inbox overflowing with tenants emailing us their stories of how Glover stepped on their rights.

One tenant complained that she'd forbidden them to buy their real Christmas tree from a different lot than the "approved seller" for the building. Another tenant said she locked the event room door on the night they had booked to use it because "the music was in poor taste." Another tenant, who is a therapist, was forbidden from doing work with her clients because she didn't have a special business permit issued by the condo board, but when she tried to get one, Glover denied her. It didn't matter that she had a permit from the province.

"Some of these are really good, guys," Bryson says. He's sitting on the broken bench, his laptop gently resting on the broken stone table. A baseball cap covers his hair, and he's in overalls, yet he's hardly done any work.

"They aren't good!" I frown and look up from the dirt pile I'm digging with a small shovel. "They're awful."

Bryson nods without looking at me. "I mean, they're good for us. A few of the emails end with, 'Voting for you, Hil!' or 'You've got my vote, Hilary!'"

"I knew people would see reason!" Luna gleams. She stands next to me, a carton of bright purple flowers in her hands. She's got dirt on her cheeks and all over her gardening pants.

Today's mission is to make headway with the garden. Luna brought in a bunch of annual spring flowers to plant, just for looks, and managed to pull in two flowering dogwood trees, both already in bloom. I've planted a few of the blue annuals and am now working on digging holes for Luna to plant the purple and yellow ones.

After yesterday's mess with Mrs. James, Luna suggested I throw my frustration into gardening with her and Bryson today.

I wish I could say it's working.

I feel defeated, *lost*, after the interaction with Mrs. James yesterday.

I *need* to fix it somehow.

"Maybe I'll send her a basket of muffins," I think out loud, pushing the small gardening shovel into the ground near my knees. "Some of those mini muffins. Everyone likes mini muffins."

I look up at Luna for reassurance, but she's looking at Bryson. Neither of them responds.

Fine. Axe the basket of mini muffins idea.

I keep digging holes, and Luna fills them in with flowers.

Then another idea pops up.

"How about a nice big bouquet of rare orchids? I sent that to a possible client once, and she called to sign with me immediately."

"Umm, I don't think Mrs. James is like your regular clients," Luna tells me.

"She doesn't seem like the kind that can be easily wooed with gifts or grand gestures," Bryson adds, looking up from the laptop again.

"She's old fashioned," Luna agrees as she looks up at him.

He gives her a smile that lingers *just* longer than normal. When he sees me looking, he shifts his attention back to the laptop screen.

An array of applause interrupts us, and we all look over at the closed glass door. It takes a few minutes for the clapping to stop, and when it does, Bryson gets up to see what's going on. We watch as he opens the courtyard door and enters the building, disappearing down the hallway toward the lobby.

I glance at Luna and go back to digging the hole. "He's cute, you know."

She shrugs as she packs a purple flower into the ground. "He's all right."

"I think he likes you."

"No he doesn't." Luna smirks, but she doesn't sound convinced.

"He's always smiling at you, looking at you," I share as I think back on the last few times we were all together.

"I don't notice that at all."

I laugh a little. "Well, I notice these things very well. I work with people every day. I've learned how to read faces."

"Do you now?" Luna finishes patting the dirt around a flower and rests her hands on her thighs, quirking her eyebrows at me. "You can read someone's face when they like someone, can you?"

I'm about to answer with a resounding "Yes!" when I realize her tone is sarcastic. "What do you mean?"

Bryson swings the door open before she can reply, heaving a sigh as he looks between us. "Uh, guys, you better come see this…"

We hurry from the courtyard and follow Bryson to the lobby where we find a large group of people, all tenants of the building. They stand around Glover, who stands on the small podium we used on Wednesday evening, addressing the tenants, immaculate in her white pant suit.

We watch from near the elevators.

"And so you see, that is exactly why I bend the rules occasionally," Glover goes on, her voice shaky and strained, but I have a hard time believing it's genuine. "Why, if I allowed the dear Zhengs to have the cat, we would have a major issue with their next-door neighbor who is *deathly* allergic to cats. It could result in their hospitalization."

A few tenants mumble agreeably with each other.

"Per contracts, pets are approved on a case by case basis."

I don't remember that in the contract!

"Also," Glover continues, "I just could not in my right mind allow a tenant to hang his undergarments out the window to dry. Hanging towels and pants or T-shirts is one thing, but briefs?" She slowly shakes her head. "I'm sure most of you would agree with me on that matter."

Almost everyone nods.

"Damnit," Bryson mutters. "Mr. Tweed…"

Glover puts a hand over her heart and smiles sweetly at the crowd. "And so, I greatly apologize to those I have offended. I wish I had been more clear in my explanations to you, and I plan to work on that starting this very moment. It is never my intention to make anyone think I enjoy abusing the system—or people who voted me in." She pauses dramatically, and everyone starts to clap, the Tempermans at the front of the crowd clapping the loudest.

Oh, give me a break.

I cross my arms over my chest as Glover steps down into the crowd and is warmly embraced by the twenty or so people that watched her speech.

"I did not see that poster backfiring," Luna admits, looking just as surprised as I feel.

We scan the crowd of tenants.

"So… What's the plan now?" Bryson asks us.

"Let's quickly finish with the flowers, leave the trees 'til tomorrow, and meet with everyone upstairs," Luna suggests, motioning for us to sneak back down the hallway.

Before I turn away, I spot Neal coming through the front doors. He pushes his sunglasses up from his eyes and looks at me, his wave awkward and barely there. I frown then follow Luna and Bryson to the courtyard.

We spent the rest of Saturday plotting and planning, but our ideas were far and in between. Each plan of attack we came up with, we figured out a way that Glover could spin it to come out looking like the hero. If we attacked her promise of a new laundry room, she'd say she used the money for the new venting system instead so we could all breathe cleaner air. If we attacked the movie night idea, she'd probably just say that nobody came to the first few and she thought it better to leave it vacant for tenants to use as they wish.

So we decided to focus on the upcoming neighborhood garage sale next Sunday. We slipped forms into every mailbox so people could sign up for a table.

"People love this building. If we put tables out front, in the lobby, and in the courtyard, they'll be more excited to shop because they'll want to see inside," I told my team.

"Such a brilliant idea, Hil!" Luna had exclaimed.

Monday morning came quickly, and I had almost put the whole Mrs. James thing out of mind—until I stepped into the elevator and found Neal. He was leaning against the back wall, but when he saw me, he stood up and gave me an awkward smile. "Morning."

"Morning," I reply as I enter. I clench the straps of my purse in my hands as it hangs in front of me.

He's wearing a pair of jeans and a plain white T-shirt, slightly see-through and smudged with dirt or grease.

Meanwhile, I'm in a black skirt and tight red blouse, my hair in a ponytail.

I look like a million bucks while he looks like…a penny.

It makes me smile.

The doors shut in front of me, and I pretend to be focused on watching the numbers at the top—and not on the feeling that he has his eyes on my back.

"Listen, there might be a lot of banging upstairs today.

I'm installing a new shower. I'm hoping to have it done before six o'clock."

"That's fine. I'll be at work anyway."

"You always work late?"

"When my clients require it, yes."

In the reflection of the elevator doors, I see him slowly nod his head. "Heard Mrs. James was considering you for the big Elnor exhibit."

Immediately, my shoulders drop, and my eyes flutter shut. I don't know who Elnor is, but they're probably bigger than I know. "She *was*, yes."

"Ah, I take it Glover's poster Friday ruined that bit for you, eh?"

I clear my throat as we reach the ground floor. "It's nothing I can't handle."

I won't have him going back to Glover and telling him how she ruined me.

The doors open, and I step out, noticing he's walking right next to me.

"What are you going to do? Send her a letter?" He smirks at his jab.

I refrain from clenching my jaw. I don't want him to see how he annoys me. "I'm thinking a basket of mini muffins," I reply sarcastically.

We both say "hi" to Mateo as we pass the concierge desk.

Neal opens the front door for me, and I squeak out a "thank you."

"You know," he says as we step outside, "she likes wine."

I stop. "Wine?"

He nods and slips his sunglasses down over his eyes.

"There's this Cali wine she buys all the time. It's her favorite. Coast Valley Vineyards."

"How do you know that?"

He takes a step back. "Every time I fix her damn washing machine, she gets me a bottle and gushes about it."

"Oh, well, thanks." I don't mean to sound so awkward.

He turns his back to me and makes his way down the sidewalk. "Don't worry about it."

***

"I need you to get me four bottles of Coast Valley wine, two white and two red. And a fancy gift basket. Maybe pick up some Godiva chocolates and a blank card."

I bark the order at Eli so fast, he sits up in his chair and frowns.

"And good morning to you too, Hilary. Why yes, I had a great weekend, thank you for asking. How was yours?"

I throw him a look as I drop my purse on my desk. "I'm sorry, but this is important."

"Who's the wine for?"

I tell him about losing my chance with Mrs. James and my ever-growing plan to win her back.

"Hmm, okay so we're wooing then." Eli nods. "If the wine and chocolates don't work, what's the backup plan?"

"Uh, I don't know." Damnit. "I'm kind of counting on that working."

"How did you find out that's her favorite wine?"

"Oh, uh, I just knew," I lie, making my shrug look as casual as I can while I sit down in my chair. "She mentioned it once in passing. So! Any messages?"

Eli shakes his head. "None."

"How'd it go with Mrs. Sarris on Friday?"

"As it always goes," Eli sighs, "long and boring. She approved the list of vendors but was skeptical about your newsletter idea. I convinced her to take a chance with it."

"Perfect."

"Oh, do we need a photographer for Warren's event?"

"I don't think so. Why?"

"Just wondering…"

I glance over at him and find him staring. "Eli."

He pushes away from his computer and glances around our desk as if checking to make sure the coast is clear. He then wheels himself over and leans an elbow on my desk. "She's a photographer."

"Who?" I ask.

"Rosamie Tomas," Eli whispers. "I did heavy recon on her over the weekend. To see what you're up against."

Of course he did.

"I'm not up against anything!" I exclaim, horrified.

"You most certainly are not," Eli agrees with a nod. "That one is apparently a first-class diva. *Very* difficult to work with according to a few sources that—"

"Eli—"

Eli ignores my tone. "I don't know what Warren could possibly see in someone so stingy and cold. All in all, Jacob and I think you can take her. Easily." He glances down at my shirt. "Run home and get that push-up bra."

I clasp my hands over my breasts. "I will not."

His dark trimmed eyebrows lift so high, his forehead crinkles. "I'm just trying to get you your knight in shining armor. Even for one damn night."

"Hey-oh!"

A bundle of letters drops down on my desk, and we look from them up to Marco. He stands with his hands on his hips, grinning at me, his muscles bulging under his tight grey T-shirt. "Someone need a knight in shining armor?"

"Ew, God no, not ever—never," Eli gasps quickly. He grabs my mail and holds it tightly against him. "Thank you, Marco, bye-bye now."

"Thanks, Marco," I say, motioning at the mail in Eli's hands.

He gives me a wink. "You got it, babe."

Eli and I watch as he spins and walks away.

Eli makes a face. "I swear he squeezes his butt as he walks."

I let out a chuckle and push him away from me. "Get to work. We have to leave in an hour."

"I love it! This place is fantastic, very impressive. You two have really outdone yourselves."

Eli and I smile proudly, exchanging a quick look as we watch Warren turn around in a full circle as he looks up at the ceiling of the observatory. Its rounded ceiling is stark white, beautiful twinkle lights hanging down to light up the room now that it's not used for stargazing. The walls in the round room are painted a dark grey with wooden accents to give the room a modern, elegant feel.

"So glad you like it." I smile.

"We're thinking round tables," Eli reports as he steps away from me, "white table cloths, and a big space in the middle for dancing."

"What about that?" Warren asks as he points to the ceiling above. "Can we open it?"

"If it's a clear night, yes, we can definitely open it," I say.

Eli points near the doors across the room. "The bar will be over there, away from the bathrooms and dance floor but not too far away from the tables."

Warren nods his approval. He looks positively ecstatic, a smile from ear to ear. He claps his hands and looks over at me. "This is perfect. I'm really very happy."

I can't help but smile at him again. "All that's left to do are the last-minute details."

Eli snaps his fingers at Warren and takes a breath. "Oh, darn, you know, that reminds me. Are you having a plus one, Warren? I forgot to mention that we need to know if you are bringing anyone." Eli ignores my eyes as they laser into him. "For seating numbers, of course."

Warren falls quiet for a moment as he slides his hands into the pockets of his dress pants. "I may need an extra seat at my table, yes. For a business associate."

"A business associate," Eli repeats, casting me a quick, but quite obvious, glance. "Of course."

He's *so* fired.

"Okay," I break the tension quickly, motioning to the doors of the observatory. "If we're all done here, we should get going." I look at Warren. "I'm sure you have to get back to work, and I know we have to meet with your barbeque man in a few hours."

Warren's face brightens again. "So you did contact Barbeque Joe?"

"We meet with him at two o'clock to finalize the menu." I nod.

Warren chuckles. "There isn't much to finalize, Hilary. It's all pork or beef on skewers or buns, barbequed to a fine charcoal finish."

Eli's face twists a bit, which makes me smile. "I know Eli is super excited to try his food."

I'm sure he would have thrown me one of his signature death glares, but because Warren gives him a smile, Eli only nods. "I'm just *super* excited, yes. Love, um, barbeque meat."

I smirk and motion for them to follow me out the door.

Eli clears his throat as we walk together. "So, Warren, I was wondering if you wanted us to hire a photographer for the event?"

Yeah, he's definitely fired.

Eli ignores my glare and leans over so he can see Warren on my left side. "It's just that some clients of ours prefer to capture the event with a photographer or videographer, and if it's something you would like to do, we should get that dealt with this week."

"Actually, I have someone who will do that for us, free of charge," Warren says. "She's very good. A friend of mine. She doesn't usually work events, but she owes me a favor."

"Oh, well then, how nice," Eli says, and I take the opportunity to elbow him hard in the side. He jumps a bit and elbows me back just as furiously.

I'm more than thrilled when my phone rings in my bag a second later. "Excuse me, I have to take this."

I hurry past Warren and Eli, through the front doors as my hand finds my phone. I'm briefly blinded by the sun as I step outside, but I can still see that it's Sydney calling.

"Sydney? Hi. I'm just finishing up with Warren.

Heading back to the office in a few."

"Hilary, I've heard something really unnerving just now."

I frown. "What is it?"

"I just had brunch with Amanda Corners from Corner's Catering, you know the woman, she's the best vegan caterer in the city."

I can't place her. "Okay, sure."

"Well, she just told me that she was contacted by the Royal Museum to possibly cater their upcoming Elnor event."

Shit! Did Mrs. James already hire someone else? Please no…

"And I thought to myself," Sydney goes on, "well, that can't be true because Hilary was going after that account, and she was very sure that it was hers. If she got it, she would tell me, and I would know about the catering…"

"I'm working on it, Sydney, don't worry."

I can't tell her the truth. I just can't.

"If you're still up for the contract then why are they calling caterers themselves?"

"It's, uh, a strategy Mrs. James told me about," I stumble a bit as I lie and hope Sydney misses it. "It's being handled though, don't you worry."

"Are you sure?"

I pause. "Absolutely, yes. I'll see you at the office later."

"I'm taking a personal day, but I'll see you tomorrow."

The call ends, and in frustration, I slam my hand against my forehead.

The wine and chocolates better work.

They *need* to work.

Chapter Eleven

The wine didn't work.

I delivered it to her door on Monday evening after work, and by Tuesday morning, I found it in front of my door. Unopened.

I was in a rotten mood all day. It didn't pick up when I got home on Wednesday either as Paulette, Luna, and I went through the twelve applications for the garage sale.

"I honestly thought we'd get more people than this." Luna sighs.

We're sitting at the dining room table, plates of freshly baked vegan cookies between us that Paulette hasn't been able to stop eating. While the two of them have the garage sale applications in front of them, I have a yellow notepad filled with ideas on how to woo back Mrs. James. My other hand strokes Pax's soft fur as he purrs on my lap.

So far, I have two ideas in addition to the two I've already set into play.

- ~~Wine and chocolate basket~~
- ~~Theater tickets~~
- *A bouquet of rare orchids*
- *A basket of mini muffins*

Okay, so the muffin idea is back because I have no other ideas.

Paulette bites into another cookie and looks at me and Luna. She slowly swallows then says, "I think I know why we only got twelve applications…"

Luna and I stiffen.

"Why?" I ask.

"Mrs. Temperman has been telling everyone that you're trying to bribe tenants to vote for you," Paulette explains. "She saw you with the wine basket for Mrs. James."

I drop my head into my hands. "Just perfect…"

"But I fired back with this," Paulette taps on the screen with one of her bright pink nails then pushes her cell phone across the table toward me and Luna, "per your suggestion the other day…"

It's a picture of Neal, one of the Tempermans below him. Between both pictures it says, "Tired of Glover's spies? So are we! Vote them, and her, out of office! Vote for Hilary!"

I feel my chest flare up, ominous with the feeling of guilt.

The poster is a good idea, but Neal did try to help me with Mrs. James.

"I sent it to all the tenants a few hours ago." Paulette smiles as she pulls her phone back over.

"I can just picture Glover fuming in her penthouse." Luna laughs. "Good job, Paulette."

Paulette looks over at me, probably for the same kind of approval.

I bite my lip.

She frowns. "What's wrong?"

"It's just… Neal is the one who helped me with the idea for the wine for Mrs. James," I explain. "And now we're calling him a spy…"

"*You* said he was her little lapdog," Luna reminds me.

"Yeah," Paulette agrees and then motions to the wine basket sitting near us on the floor. "And how do you know he didn't give you that suggestion just so they could say it was a bribery attempt for votes?" She shrugs as she grabs another cookie. "I mean, if he's her lapdog, then maybe it was part of the plan."

I never thought of that. I mean, that's probably what it was all about.

Wasn't it?

"He just seemed to be so genuine with the suggestion, that's all."

Luna puts a hand on my arm. "Uh, what happened to you hating Jerky McJerkface?"

"I still do!" I proclaim. "I just… I don't know…" I shake my head. "Never mind, forget it. I'm probably overthinking it all because I've had a crappy week."

Luna throws a hand on my shoulder and pulls me in for a squeeze. "Don't worry, there are only two and a half weeks left until this election is over. Then you'll win—"

"And a whole new slew of problems will greet you," Paulette interrupts, smiling. "None of which include Glover."

A series of thumps erupt overhead, and we glance up to the ceiling.

Seriously, what the hell does he do up there that he needs to make *that* much noise?

"Did you send her the tickets?"

"Yes. For the hundredth time since Tuesday, yes. I sent the woman two tickets for the premiere of *Phantom of the Opera* tomorrow night. Now stop asking."

Eli and I are in a cab on our way to meet Mrs. Sarris for lunch. He leans back in the seat, his big black sunglasses over his eyes. "I swear, Hil, you're giving me a damn headache."

"Sorry." I adjust my grey skirt at my knees. "It's just that I haven't heard anything from her or—"

"Why don't you just ask her if she got the tickets then?" He whips his head at me again. "She lives right below you."

"I don't want to seem too eager."

His eyebrows rise over his sunglasses. "You sent her a two-hundred-dollar basket of goodies on Monday. Then front row seats to a loved, be it overrated, musical. But you're worried knocking on her door is going to be too eager?"

I cross my arms and drop back into the seat.

Eli snorts loudly. "And now we are going to pout?"

"I'm not pouting," I retort, looking out the window. "I'm just…forget it."

"I have something that will cheer you up," Eli claims, fully turning to face me now. A smile spreads over his lips, and his sudden glee has me on high alert.

"What?"

"Warren emailed this morning. Says he wants to meet with us tomorrow if we have time. Asked if we had the whole afternoon free. I said I was busy, but you would be *thrilled* to join him for the afternoon. Naturally, I moved your appointment with Christina Kovacs to Monday."

"Eli!"

"What?" He shrugs. "Christina doesn't care. She just needs us for some athletic banquet for the private school next month. Lots of time to plan that."

"No, Eli, you have to stop pushing me at Warren," I order. "It's getting a bit ridiculous."

"I do it because he's such a great guy!"

"Huh, I seem to remember you saying that about Neal six months ago," I quip.

"He is!"

I roll my eyes and swat him away from me.

He sighs at me and lightly hits my knee. "Look, you can have more than one perfect match. If nothing happened with Neal, then it wasn't meant to be. Maybe that means Warren could be a good match. The most dangerous thing anybody can think is that there is only one person for everyone."

"Listen to me very closely, Eli," I turn to him and look into his big sunglasses. "I am not interested in dating anyone at the moment. Not Warren and not Neal. Even if I was the slightest bit interested in Warren, it wouldn't matter as he's seeing that world-renowned photographer."

Eli sighs and turns back to look out the window, swinging one leg over the other. "Nobody knows if he and that photographer are even serious—" He stops midsentence and frowns then sits up. I watch him push his glasses to the tip of his nose and slowly point out the window of the cab. "Um, Hil? Does your— Does your building have *bugs*?"

I crawl over him to look out the window. I see Fairway Towers half a block away from us. There's a big white truck parked out front, a giant beetle on the roof, held up with a giant silver spring.

"Um, could you please stop at that building?" I say to the cab driver.

He nods and slows down as he nears the building, pulling against the curb across the street.

I hand him a ten before bolting from the cab.

As I wait for the traffic to slow so I can sprint across, Eli appears at my side, his sunglasses pushed atop his head now. He slowly shakes his head at the truck. "That is so gross."

When there's finally a break, we dash across the street, reaching the front doors together. Eli pulls it open, and I enter first.

Mateo gives me a stare as I enter, and it's not a very nice one. "Ms. Brandt."

"What's going on?" I ask him, panic clear in my voice.

"Why don't you head to the courtyard and find out?" His tone is sharp, and he drops back into his chair without another word. I exchange a look with Eli before we hurry through the lobby and past the elevator.

As we turn the corner, we find the door to the courtyard propped open. Slowly, I enter, Eli trailing closely behind me.

There are two men in white zipped-up suits standing in the middle of the courtyard with Glover, who has a handkerchief over her mouth and nose.

She's pointing at the two dogwood trees that Luna planted the other day. Both of which are wrapped up in clear wrapping, a gentle fog blowing around in the bag that encases them.

"What's going on here?" I ask out loud.

The men and Glover turn around. Immediately, she puts her hands on the waistline of her black high-waisted skirt. Her short blonde hair rests in a bob at her jawline, and she slowly shakes her head at me. "What exactly do you *think* is going on, Ms. Brandt? We've got bugs!"

"Termites, to be exact," says one of the men. He smacks a wad of gum as he gestures at the trees. "Came in with those trees over there. We're foggin' them and killin' as much as we can."

Oh. God.

How in the hell did that happen? Didn't Luna see the bugs before she planted them?

The horror must show on my face because Glover gives me a small, tight smile as she slowly walks over to me and Eli. "Now, now, Ms. Brandt, I'm sure you had *no* intention of planting trees full of carnivorous bugs in our courtyard. An oversight on your part."

"How bad is the damage?" I look past her to ask the two men in suits, and they both shrug.

"Won't know 'til this evening," says the man with a mouth full of gum. "We'll have people here over the weekend and next week to check the units, make sure they didn't spread."

"Seeing as they've been planted for almost four days, we have reason to believe they may have spread to a floor," Glover side-eyes me, "or two."

Next to me, Eli swats twice at his arm and begins to back away from me. "Okay, well, I'm just going to go wait in the lobby then…"

"Go get Luna now," I tell him.

He gives me half of a nod and hurries from the courtyard.

I watch the two exterminators approach the trees together.

"Going to be a big cost," one of the exterminators calls out to me and Glover, "depending on if the bugs spread…"

Glover sighs loudly and shakes her head. "This will take a large chunk out of the budget. People will not be happy."

"I'll pay for it." I couldn't even stop myself if I wanted to. "I'll pay for it all."

She raises a thin eyebrow and steps up to me. It makes me want to back away from her. Her face is so constricted, unmoved as her light eyes scan my face. "You know, Ms. Brandt, I can't imagine anyone in the building being pleased by this turn of events. Can you?"

I swallow a lump down my throat. "No…"

"Now I don't have to tell anyone. I can call it a false alarm if someone mentions the truck," she lets me know.

"Y-you would do that?" I eye her suspiciously.

"Of course," she says, "only if…you throw in the towel."

Figures.

"Oh, come now, Ms. Brandt." Glover shrugs. "You know you can't win this thing. It's been a downhill spiral for you since the first day you put your name on the ballot. You're the loser in this competition."

That's the second time she's used the word "loser" to describe me and this entire situation.

"Yeah, no thanks to you and your smear campaign," I counter, my jaw grinding a bit.

Her face is that of a wide-eyed innocent. "That's politics, my dear. You should know it's a nasty game."

"It's a position for president of a condo board! Not Parliament."

"Ms. Brandt, I'm giving you the chance to back down gracefully. You can even give the excuse of a heavy work schedule," Glover suggests. "Whatever. There isn't any shame in admitting defeat and stepping down. It can be very admirable."

The nerve.

"You don't want this job." Glover smirks. "You aren't fit for it, and you know it."

I suppose the frustration from the last week is what causes me to heat up and angrily ball my fists at my side. I step closer to her.

"I'm not stepping down. And you're not going to bully me into stepping down either."

"Who's bullying?" Glover asks innocently. She doesn't give me the chance to respond. She turns on her heels and walks back over to the exterminators, pulling her phone out from her blouse pocket.

I had to send Eli to the meeting with Mrs. Sarris alone again, not that he minded. He ran from the building as fast as he could. I left to get Luna at her store.

The Green Room is less than a block away from our building, and when I enter, I find Luna behind the counter ringing up a customer. She gives me a small wave and bright smile as she takes the payment. She obviously misses my vibe.

I wander around the small store, looking at all the freshly delivered flowers in their metal holders, smelling the ones I think might be pleasing. I peer through the glass of the fridge door to my left and see even more flowers, herbs, and weird viney plants. The right wall is full of tiny potted herbs and rows of seed packets. It really is a nice little shop and being the only one in this neighborhood means it makes quite a bit of money.

I look back at Luna.

"Thank you so much for shopping at The Green Room." She smiles and hands the couple their bag. "Have a great day."

I give them a smile as they pass me, then I meet Luna in the middle of the room.

"What are you doing here, Hil? Why aren't you at work?"

"Luna, where did you get those trees?" I ask quickly.

"Trees?" She glances toward the front door. "Oh, the lilacs out front? They aren't really trees—"

"No, the trees for the courtyard," I interrupt, feeling my chest puff up a bit. I put a hand to my forehead, and her face falls.

"Why? What's wrong?"

"They have termites!"

Her small eyes bug out, and she starts to shake her head so fast I feel like her headband is about to fly out at me. "No. No way. I checked when they first came into the store."

"Well, they caught the bugs sometime between the time they were here and when you brought them into the building!"

Luna's hands go to her hips. "That doesn't make sense. If that were true, we would have termites here in this building, or in the plants and trees out front, but we don't.

I checked everything this morning because we just got a shipment of Dwarf Japanese Maple—"

"They had to bring exterminators into the building, Luna, so obviously they snuck in somehow!"

"Okay!" she screams back at me. "Calm down! Just take a breath. We can figure this out. I mean, when I planted them on Sunday, I didn't see one bug. Usually, you can spot one or two on the bark of the…" She trails off and looks up at me, eyes focused.

And then it hits me the same time it hits her because we both gasp out loud and shriek, "Glover!"

Luna clenches her jaw. "That sneaky, evil bit—"

"Where the hell would she get termites? You can't just walk into a store and buy a container of them like worms."

Luna points a stiff finger at me. "God, if we could only prove that she brought in termites, that'd be the end of her. I'm sure of it. There's a clause in the bylaws that states she has to step down if she brings harm to another or to the building."

"She's busy trying to get *me* to step down from running," I sigh. "She told me she wouldn't tell everyone that I brought in termites if I stopped running against her. She'd tell everyone it was a false alarm."

Luna frowns. "I hope you didn't agree?"

"No, I got all fired up and stuff."

"Good." She nods and grips my shoulders. "Go back to the condo. I'll text Bryson and the others and tell them we need to have an emergency meeting tonight. We'll figure out a way to get back at her."

I agree and say goodbye then make the slow trek back up the block to our building. The exterminator truck is still parked in front of the doors, and my stomach lurches a little bit. To make things worse, I almost smash into Neal.

He steps up to the doors at the same time I do. When he sees me, he raises his eyebrows but keeps his sunglasses on, frowning when he sees the exterminator's truck.

"Luna brought termites in the building by accident, from the trees she planted."

He barely gives me a passing glance before cutting ahead of me to open the door. He doesn't hold it open for me, so I shimmy in right after him. He heads toward the mailboxes, and I hurry toward the elevators.

I guess the spy poster really got to him.

Ugh, why is it bothering me so much?

I hit the button for the elevators and wait, leaning back on my heels to see what floor it's on. After a few seconds, I see Neal approaching the elevator. I pray he walks right past and uses the stairs.

When he looks up from his mail and sees me, he exhales a frustrated sigh. But he doesn't pass me. He just stands next to me, mail tucked under his armpit, eyes on the elevator numbers.

My foot begins to tap against the marble floor.

Jesus, he's right, this elevator needs maintenance pronto.

"You know, that poster was a pretty low blow."

There's a sharp tone to his voice that keeps me from actually looking at him. I feel my face redden, and my stomach turns. This is why I can't be mean. It just makes me sick.

"I went out on a limb to help you score with Mrs. James, and you made me look like an idiot."

"Okay, I'm sorry but, but…" I glance at him to find his blue eyes pouring into me. "I send the basket and it gets returned, and then there's a rumor in the building that I'm bribing people for votes!"

"So, what? You thought I set you up or somethin'?" he asks, his voice riddled with rough annoyance.

"Not me… Someone on my team…"

He scoffs and looks back at the elevator, angrily reaching past me and pushing the button twice. "Unbelievable."

"Well, you're so chummy with her. Everyone in the building thinks so anyway!"

"Clearly, because nobody's said a word to me since that stupid poster went up. Everyone is avoiding me."

I want to tell him I'm surprised he even cares, but I keep quiet.

"What makes you think I'm so chummy with her?" he snaps, glaring back at me. "Did you ever think maybe I hate her as much as you do? That I just tolerate her so she doesn't mess with me?"

I honestly never thought of that.

My eyes scan his face and draw over his rugged jawline and stubble. I can feel my heart flutter a bit and, though I hate it, I'm interrupted but a sudden, restless thought.

Paulette's idea from last week.

I grab his arm, trying to ignore the muscle under my hand.

He looks down at my hand.

"Then help me."

"What?" He frowns.

"Help me take her down."

He blinks once. "Are you crazy? After what you did, why would I want to help you, again? I tried to get back on your good side, and it blew up in my face."

"Okay! I'm sorry. But come on! If you don't want her in power, help me beat her! You know her as well as the Tempermans and—"

He shakes his head and pulls his arm from my grasp. "I don't think so. If you lose, she'll be hounding everyone who helped you for the rest of our days, and I don't need the attention." The elevator doors open, and he takes the opportunity to stride in quickly, turning to face me. "Besides, why would I want to help someone who thinks I'm a lapdog anyway?"

"I said I'm sorry," I protest.

He smirks when I stomp my foot. "By the way, thanks for the termites, bobblehead."

The elevator doors shut just as my mouth drops open at his insult.

I hit the elevator with my fist and let out a cry. "Argh!"

"No hitting the elevator!" Mateo calls from his desk.

I look over at him, and he throws me a deep glare.

"Sorry, he's just…really annoying."

Mateo sits back down behind his chair. "His lady clients don't think so."

I slowly glance over at Mateo. "What lady clients?"

"They come to see him every Monday and Wednesday. And on the occasional Friday and Saturday."

I bite the inside of my cheek as I turn and walk over to the concierge desk. "Mateo, what exactly does Neal do?"

He looks up from his crossword and frowns. "I'm not saying anything."

Interesting.

"Come on, Mateo," I plead, flashing him a coy smile as I lean against the desk. "I give you a good tip every Christmas. You can tell me, can't you?"

"You give me fifty dollars," he grumbles. "Mr. Turner gives me two hundred."

"Two hundred!" I exclaim. "What the hell does he do? Work on the black market?"

Mateo mimics a zipper across his lips. "I'm saying nothing."

"Okay, this Christmas, I'll give you two hundred if you tell me."

He squints his eyes at me. "I don't believe you."

"Ugh, fine." I fling open my purse, pull out my wallet, and sift through the bills. I have fifty-five dollars. I throw it down at the crossword puzzle book. "Here's an advance."

"This only covers half the information I know," Mateo claims as he picks up my cash.

I roll my eyes and wait as he leans over the desk.

"You want to know what he does? Check out 1282 Morton Avenue."

What the hell is on Morton Avenue?

Chapter Twelve

"I think it's brilliant, Hilary!"

"I think so too," I tell Luna. "He must be doing something illegal, or at least shady, if he's paying Mateo two hundred dollars to keep quiet."

"I'm still so shocked. I mean, when you told us last night, I think we all thought you were a bit crazy, but this morning, I rode the elevator down with Mrs. Dorst, and she remembered how she frequently sees groups of strange women riding the elevator up to his floor. Dressed in revealing activewear, she told me. Must be the lady clients Mateo told you about."

"I rode with them once too!" I recall.

"I wish I could spy with you," Luna whines. "If my boss wasn't away on vacation, I would so be there."

"I'm all right with Paulette. It won't take long. I should be back at work before I have to meet Eli and Warren."

Paulette and I are across the street from our building, coffees in our hands as we wait, hidden in a small alleyway, for Neal to come out. Paulette is dressed in her usual edgy hipster wear with her laptop bag hanging off her shoulder. I play the spy in a pair of black skinny jeans and a black T-shirt.

Paulette elbows me, and I follow her gaze to see Neal finally leaving our building. He's in jeans and a black T-shirt, sunglasses on top of his head as he makes his way westward.

"I gotta go, Luna, he just left the building!"

"Eek, good luck!"

I hang up on her and slide my phone into the pocket of my jeans. Paulette and I slink out of the alleyway and walk west, keeping to our side of the street so he won't see us. A minute later, we watch him head down into the subway, and we hurry across the street so we don't lose him.

Beneath the street, we find him waiting for the next train heading uptown. We stand among a group of loud teenagers as we wait. Once it arrives, we hop in and make sure to keep watch as he stands half a train away. He's busy on his phone, lucky for us.

The ride is only about fifteen minutes, and four stops later, we follow him out of the subway to Morton Ave. The street stretches out as far as we can see, all of the buildings only one story or two stories high, storefronts, pawn shops, an antique dealer here or there.

I've been here a few times before when Luna wanted to go antiquing or to a flea market.

"There he is." Paulette points across the street to Neal heading toward a hot dog vendor. He briefly stops to talk to him and then continues on, putting a good amount of distance between us. We cross the street, careful to stay near one of the storefronts. Finally, he disappears through a glass door that's propped open by a cinder block.

"What does the door say?" Paulette asks from behind me.

We stand fifty or so feet away from the open door, and

I don't want to get closer, just in case. A woman with arms full of groceries walks toward us, and I step in front of her, pointing to the propped door behind her. "Excuse me, do you know what that place is?"

She frowns and glances over her shoulder. "Self-defense place."

Paulette and I look at each other as the woman quickly passes us.

"Self-defense?" Paulette repeats, looking over at the door. "He teaches self-defense?"

Nothing about that is shady or illegal. Everything about it is honorable.

Damnit.

Honestly though, what did I really think I was going to find? Neal pushing drugs on some kids? Taking bets for a bookie?

Paulette must sense my dismay because she points across the street. "There's a Starbucks. Let's get some more coffee and something to eat and stake him out for a bit."

I wonder what the point of that is, but Paulette walks away from me before I can get the words out.

We watch Neal for over an hour. Or rather, I should say that *I* watch Neal for an hour. Paulette sits next to me messing around on her laptop. I'm almost finished with my latte and banana loaf. I've watched him with a group of older women, instructing them with moves against their individual punching bags and then against him. He is quite good, at least from where I watch.

"Are you going to eat that?" Paulette asks as she taps the bit left over of my banana loaf.

I push it at her.

"Check it out," Paulette says, motioning at her laptop screen.

I find myself staring at a page on our condo building's website. In bright yellow letters it says, "Condo Board Elections Happening Now!" and there's a short profile of both me and Mrs. Glover, along with our pictures. At the bottom of the page are two bars. One in black and one in green.

Paulette bites into the banana loaf and chews. "You're the green bar, Glover's the black one."

The black bar is significantly higher than the green bar.

"I'm losing, surprise, surprise," I mutter, setting my elbow on the table and resting my chin in the palm of my hand.

"We're still two weeks away from the election," Paulette says. "A lot could happen by then."

I finish off the rest of my latte. "I need a miracle after the termite thing."

Paulette gives me a smile. "The garage sale could be that miracle."

"Right…"

I lazily bring my gaze back across the street and notice that most of the women have left the class. Neal stands at the very back with another guy as the rest of the women slowly file out. Two of them head our way, wiping sweat off their foreheads with the backs of their hands, laughing to each other.

"Let's go," I tell Paulette with a sigh. "This is a waste of time."

"Okay." She shrugs, slamming her laptop shut and setting down the rest of the banana loaf. "Let me just get a water for the road."

She puts her laptop away and grabs her bag, hopping into line as I head toward the nearest garbage can. I toss my empty cup into the recycling bin by the door just as the two women from Neal's class enter.

"Are you going again tonight?" the blonde asks the brunette.

"Are you kidding?" She laughs, pulling her hair out of her ponytail. "I'm so sore. I'll be barely able to lift my arms by seven p.m."

"I may tag along with Tiffany," the blonde says as they approach the line. "His Friday classes are usually smaller numbers. He gives each attendee an extra one-on-one fight."

The brunette laughs and shakes her head.

Good grief.

I click my tongue and turn back around to see Paulette next up to the register. I glance back at the two women from Neal's class, all sweaty and red. I can't believe the blonde is going back to another one of his classes. She looks completely wiped, and she's going to spend Friday night getting thrown around by a—

Wait a second.

Mateo said his lady clients show up on the occasional Friday night. I think back on the noises that come from his apartment and glance back across the street. I can't see Neal, but I watch a new group of women, much older than the first group, slowly begin to fill the studio.

The first group he taught moved around a lot, jumping from spot to spot. That's the noise we hear coming from his place. He's teaching them in his condo!

And if he doesn't have a business license or approval from Glover, that is definitely against the rules.

If you lose, she'll be hounding everyone who helped you for the rest of our days, and I don't need the attention, Neal had said last night.

He didn't need the attention because that means she'd find out his secret.

If my theory is correct…

I hurry toward the two women who came from his class and tap the blonde's shoulder. "Er, excuse me?"

She looks over at me with her friend. "Yeah?"

"Did you come from the studio across the street?" I ask them.

"Yeah." The blonde's eyes narrow.

"I heard it's a great place. Are there any other classes today?"

"Sorry, no. Not for our age group anyway. It's a full studio," she claims after giving me a once-over.

Oh, for the love…

"It's just that my girlfriend and I were recently robbed and decided we needed to take some classes. I heard that the one instructor is really good."

For effect, I wave at Paulette in the front of the line who gives me a small smile as she mouths, *Almost done,* before turning to pay the barista.

The blonde sets a soft hand on my shoulder. "Oh my God! I'm so sorry to hear. I totally get it. My neighbor was robbed six months ago. That's why I signed up. You just missed Neal's class, but he has one that he runs from his place every second Friday of the month. Tonight, in fact. It's usually a light class and better if you bring a partner. I'm sure he wouldn't turn away the extra cash. It's thirty for the hour, starts at seven. Want the address?"

"That would be so great, thank you!"

I smile at her, and all I can think is, *Bingo.*

I sent Eli a big apology explaining why I couldn't meet up with him and Warren for the afternoon. He didn't reply until well after five, calling me a colossal moron. He wouldn't explain why except to say he deserved a massive raise after this afternoon.

I was too wired to go into work after Paulette and I got back to the condo. She got straight to work, trying to figure out if Neal had approval from the board. Turns out, he does not. Which means the chances of Glover knowing what he is doing is slim to none.

My plan is to intrude, er, *join* his class and somehow take a picture or two while pretending to reply to a text. That way I have evidence.

I suppose it's quite juvenile what I'm doing, bribing the man to help me, and I do see the irony, but I'm desperate at this point.

When Paulette and I walk into the building, the Zhengs barely say a word to me as we cross paths.

At six forty-five, I ride the elevator down to the lobby and leave the building. The blonde I met from his earlier class told me she was going to be there at ten to seven. I'm going to "run into" her and her friend outside the building so we could all ride up together. I'd shimmy in behind them so he couldn't slam the door shut in my face.

Not even two minutes pass before the blonde and her dark-haired friend walk up to the building. I slink out from behind the hedges saunter up to them. "Hi!"

"Hey, you made it." The blonde smiles at me as I fall

in line. "Where's your girlfriend?"

"She'll be here, just a bit late."

"Cool, well, let's go."

We walk inside, and I'm grateful that all Mateo does is frown at me. As we get to the elevators, I find myself getting nervous.

Why the hell am I nervous? I've basically got him now.

The blonde tells me how she's been taking his class for the last six months, heartbroken when he took a break for three months. Her friend remains on her phone the entire ride up to Neal's floor. Once the doors open, I follow both of them out and down the hallway.

We get to his door, and my nerves have now started to cramp my fingers. The last time I was here was a little over three months ago. The nerves were different then, definitely more the excited kind.

I expect the blonde to knock, but she brazenly opens the door and shouts a "Hello!" that echoes behind her. Her friend shuffles in after her, and before I can change my mind, I hurry in, shutting the door quietly. Slowly, I kick off my shoes.

With an anxious breath, I turn to the room but don't see Neal anywhere. Two other women are in the center of his living room. His black couches have been pushed up against the wall, and the glass coffee table we once had wine over is set against the dining room to the far right. I never knew his living room was big enough to do this.

I hear a set of footsteps to my right and look over to see Neal come out of the kitchen, looking at his phone as he speaks to the room. "All right ladies, unfortunately, tonight's class may end a little bit earlier than usual."

Finally, he looks up, and his eyes fall right on me. He stops in his tracks, his face unreadable.

"Oh, I told her it would be okay if she tagged along." The blonde comes to my rescue almost instantly. "I met her after class today. She and her girlfriend were robbed and wanted to learn some self-defense. I didn't think you'd mind, Neal." She bats her eyes at him.

I can't help but scrunch my face up before looking back at Neal.

"Robbed, eh?" Something—amusement, maybe?—flashes across his face. He slips his cell phone into the back pocket of his jeans while keeping his eyes on me. "I need you to sign a waiver."

"Her girlfriend is coming too," the blonde tells Neal, giving me a smile.

"Can't wait to meet her," Neal proclaims, his sudden closed-lip smile causing me to frown. Then he motions for me to follow him into the kitchen. "Forms are in here."

I approach the furthest counter and turn around to face him, hands on my hips. Any hilarity he may have showcased is now gone. He runs a hand across his scruff and steps toward his fridge, yanking a paper from the top. He walks over to me, slams it down on the counter, then flicks a pen toward me. "Sign it."

I slowly pick the pen up and glance down at the form. "So, *this* is what all that noise is."

Neal watches me fill out the top and sign the required space in the middle of the form. He smells freshly showered—that's how close he's standing next to me. When I pull the pen back, he puts a finger down on a line at the bottom of the page. "And here."

I do what he says, and before I can take my pen off the

page, he pulls the sheet out from underneath it. I feel the victorious tug in my lips as they form a cocky smile. He walks back to the fridge and tosses the paper on top, then he looks over at me again. "No cell phones."

"I'm expecting an important work call or text," I lie.

"Yeah," he rolls his eyes, "I'm sure you are."

I follow him out of the kitchen and into the living room. The blonde waves me over, and I cross the room to join her and her friend.

"Okay," Neal stands in the center of the group, looking at each of us, "since we have a new face tonight, I'm going to take the opportunity to do a brush-up on what we've been doing the last few months. We're going to focus on those quick and easy moves that you can use in almost any situation. Most of the time, your attacker is going to be bigger and stronger than you, so it's helpful to know some of the basic ways you can protect yourself. I'm going to show you the moves, then you'll partner up." He snaps his fingers toward me. "New girl, I'm going to demonstrate on you."

Like hell he is.

"I'll do it!" The blonde next to me must sense my apprehension—or she's into him.

Neal shakes his head at her. "Let's give the new girl a try first, Jane."

If Neal's expression is anything to go by, he's not going to let me out of this so easily. I push off the wall and drag myself to where he stands. He motions for me to move in front of him, so I do, my back to him. I look at the other women who watch us as Neal speaks behind me.

"Okay, so these are the pretty basic, attacked from behind kind of moves. There are several ways you can disengage someone who attacks you from behind. We're going to start with three before we move to the floor."

Move to the floor? To the floor for what?

I'm caught off guard when he swings his right arm over my head and rests it tightly over my collarbone. He pulls me up against him, and my hands fly to his forearms. I feel his chest against my back, and my breath catches.

"When someone grabs you from behind, they'll usually keep one hand free in anticipation of you attacking them with your own hands. In this case, you would keep your hands on your attacker's arm like the new girl is doing." He pauses, and I look up at him to find him looking down at me. "You'd lift your knee really high and kick back as far as you could."

Does he— Does he actually want me to do it?

"Go ahead," he tells me.

I suddenly feel very on the spot, and I have to shut my eyes tightly as I do what he says. I let out a breath of relief when his arm disappears from my collarbone and my leg hits nothing but air.

"Chances are your attacker will jump back before you can land the hit to his groin," Neal claims, hands in front of him. "No guy wants to be hit there—ever. It's what we imagine childbirth feels like."

The women laugh, and I even smirk a little bit before Neal steps up behind me again. Both of his arms come over my head and across my collarbone just as tightly as before. My hands grip his triceps, my chest caving under the weight of his arm. I have to keep my eyes forward in case my cheeks become as red as they feel.

Why is my damn body responding this way?

"Now, if your attacker throws both arms over you, it's

a sure sign he's going to choke you unconscious. In that case, you'd put your hands over his… Put your hands over mine, new girl."

I move my hands down from his triceps to his wrists.

"Then you would squat and turn your head to the left." He waits for me to do what he says. The squatting almost tips us, but his hold on me is tight. Once my head is turned, I realize we're inches apart, and his eyes sweep over my face before they lock with mine. "Then you'd elbow your attacker roughly in the side, and he'll definitely release a little at the hit in his ribs, giving you enough space to duck under his grasp and pull out."

"I don't want to do that," I admit, my voice barely more than a hoarse whisper.

The corner of his mouth jerks a bit as his tone matches mine. "You don't want to elbow me, or you don't want to leave my hold?" His eyes flash with…something…and a small smile appears on his lips.

I roll my eyes and loudly say, "I don't want to elbow you."

"Don't worry, you won't hurt me."

I shut my eyes, draw in a breath, and thrust my elbow back. I feel it slide into Neal's side, but he pulls away before I could really hit him, his arms loosening enough on my collarbone that I can duck under and jump away from him. "I did it!"

The women smile and laugh a little as Neal stands back up into perfect posture. "Okay, but what happens if neither of those moves work and he manages to take you to the ground?"

The blonde, Jane, throws up her hand. "You control the elbows!"

"Right." Neal nods then looks over at me and points to the floor. "Get down on your back."

I swallow. "For real?"

"Yup."

I exhale and sit down then lower the rest of my body to the floor.

Neal stands over me, looking at everyone else. "So if he does get you to the ground, he's going to try to choke you. You need to control his elbows…"

My pulse beats in my ears as Neal bends down between my legs and hovers over me. My legs rest against his sides, and he slides both hands near my neck, keeping them pressed around my collarbone. His hands spark something on my bare skin, and I do my best to pretend I feel nothing.

The urge to grab the collar of his shirt and pull him down on top of me hits hard, throwing my thoughts out the window for a moment.

"Cross your arms over my elbows," he tells me.

I do as he says, the feeling of more skin on skin contact sending a thrill up my spine that almost jerks me upwards.

"Okay, now press down as hard as you can."

I want to hesitate but don't.

"Good, now lift your legs in the air and wrap them around my shoulders."

Okay, he's suggesting that on purpose now.

"What?" I gawk.

"Trust me," he says, "just do it."

I bit the inside of my mouth and let out a breath as I heave my legs up into the air, I wrap them against his head, resting them on his shoulders. "Now, bring your hips up."

Is he kidding?

I manage to hoist my hips up just a little bit, and it loosens Neal's touch on my collarbone, hunching him forward a little bit. Then he lets go completely, and my legs drop onto the ground, my knees bent. He looks from me to the other women. "Looks complicated but it's really easy to do. You could break your attacker's elbows with that move. So, get partnered up and let's practice. Ten minutes then we'll move on…"

I'm starting to think this wasn't such a good idea.

Neal looks down at me, his hands resting on the waistline of his jeans. His smile is anything but kind. It's mischievous, and I realize he's enjoying the sudden reversal of torture.

By the time this whole thing is over, my legs are shaking, and my left shoulder aches down into my bicep from all the times I use it to swing away from Neal's "attacks." When we moved to the ground halfway through to incorporate some easy Jiu Jitsu takedowns, I almost walked out the door. That's when I learned Jiu Jitsu is no joke. You could seriously hurt someone with those moves.

By eight fifteen, we're done, and all I want to do is soak in the bath for hours.

I also realize I never took pictures as proof to use against Neal.

Damnit.

As the women file out, I take longer than usual to put my runners back on, and Jane keeps Neal at the door. I only glance up at them once, but I can see that he's getting impatient with her, maybe fearful I'll slip out before he can confront me.

I tie up the last of my left runner and watch Neal grab

Jane's shoulder lightly and smile at her, nudging her out the door. "That's great, Jane. You have a good weekend. I'll see you Monday."

"For sure!" She grins. "I'll bring you a coffee before class!"

"Great," he nods as she steps out, "thank you."

I take the chance to step toward the door, and after one last wave to the blonde, Neal slams the door shut right in front of me. The sheer force of it blows a light gust across my sweaty face.

"First off, you owe me thirty bucks," he declares, his eyes serious as they lock with mine. "And second of all, you spied on me today? Isn't that ironic."

I reach into my pocket and yank out two crumpled bills, shoving them into his chest.

His hand brushes mine when he takes them.

"Yeah, well, I think you got your revenge tonight, so call it even."

He leans against the closed door. "What's your game here?"

"You," I point at him, "don't have a business license to do this. You also don't have permission from Glover, do you?"

He clears his throat but says nothing as he crosses his arms over his sweaty T-shirt.

Ah ha. Got him!

"I knew it!" I smile proudly. "So what would happen if Glover were to find out you're *illegally* running a business out of your unit? Lapdog or not, she's in the middle of an election, she'd *have* to make an example out of you."

"What do you want?" he asks.

"I want you to help me," I say. "Win the election."

"How do you actually think I can do that?" He raises both eyebrows at me.

"You know everyone in this building better than I do, and you also know Glover."

"So what? You want me to help you use her weaknesses against her, is that it? You want me to tell you how to get people in the building to vote for you?"

"Yes," I exclaim, "exactly."

His blue eyes drop down to my mouth for only a second. When they meet mine again, he smirks. "Nah, I don't think so."

I frown. "Didn't you hear what I said? If I tell her, she'll make an example out of you. You'll probably be kicked out, or worse, fined. A lot."

He shrugs but doesn't say anything.

"I'm not bluffing," I claim.

Again, he shrugs, pushing off the door with his shoulder. "I think you are."

Grrr…

I shove him away from the door and grab the handle to open it. "Fine. We'll see. I know Glover is home tonight because she's probably planning a way to ruin our involvement in the garage sale. Telling her what you're doing may actually work in my favor. She'll be so busy trying to figure out how to reprimand you that she'll leave me alone this weekend."

I pull the door open and march down the hallway toward the elevator. I slam my finger on the button and tap my foot as I wait for the doors to open.

Finally, they do, and I rush inside, glancing over at the small tower of numbers. I hesitate for a moment, really just wanting to press six and go home. But my finger hovers over the number ten, and with a sigh, I push down on it before I can chicken out.

The doors start to close but a hand shoots through them, and they part again. I watch as Neal appears, standing between the doors, and after looking at me, he glances at the buttons.

"That's right, I'm not bluffing," I tell him, crossing my arms over my chest.

He sighs and looks back at me, lifting a finger. "Fine. But you keep your mouth shut about what I do in my condo."

Yes!

An ecstatic smile appears, and I uncross my arms. "Thank you! I really think I can win this thing with your help."

"Yeah," he says unconvincingly before reaching over and grabbing my wrist. He yanks me from the elevator before the doors begin to slide shut again. "Wait for the next one."

"Wait!"

He stops and looks at me.

"Give me something now."

"What?" He frowns.

"Give me something I can use right now. I need it," I say. "The termite thing hit me bad. Nobody is talking to me. Not even Mrs. Zheng, and she talks to *everyone*."

Neal sighs, rubbing the back of his neck as he stares at me. "She's the one who killed the trees in the lobby, forgot to water them. She's been blaming the cats in the building because she hates cats."

"Okay," I take a long breath in, "I think I can make that work…"

Chapter Thirteen

"When's his next class? Monday night? I can sneak across the street and take pictures from that apartment building. I've been in there. The window at the end of the eighth-floor hallway looks across to our building. I'll bet there's a good view of Neal's place from it. You just have to make sure he keeps the blinds open."

I give Bryson's offer some consideration, especially since Luna sent Neal a text last night telling him to meet us for garage sale setup at seven thirty. It's now almost eleven, and he's nowhere to be seen.

Our table is right outside the building, in direct sunlight, unfortunately. I don't have anything to sell, but Luna has loads, including some plants she bought from work. Bryson's table is right next to ours, and it's loaded with books, magazines, and a few board games.

Inside the lobby, there are five other tables, and because the courtyard is now closed due to the bugs, they're all kind of jammed packed, but nobody seems to mind. We've had steady traffic into the lobby and at the tables. Mrs. Dorst even set up a table next to Mateo so she could sell some baked goods, and Mr. Dorst is handling coffee and lemonade purchases.

Mr. Tweed's table is on the other side of the doors underneath the awning, providing him ample shade. His table seems to draw quite a bit of attention with an assortment of books, some of his wife's old jewelry, a collection of chess sets, and his late wife's lemon squares. He's almost sold out already, and he made four trays of them. Everyone stays at his table the longest, and he's loving the attention.

Despite all the traffic, we have barely broken two hundred dollars between all of the tables, and Paulette said the tenants inside are mumbling how this is a waste of time.

"That would require Hilary going to the class again." Luna laughs from her yard chair. "You should have seen her last night. She took a two-hour bath."

"You may have to go if he closes the blinds during his classes," Bryson says. "Does he close the blinds?"

I scrunch my face up as I think back on last night. "I'm not sure…"

Honestly, all I've thought about since last night is the way my skin felt whenever he touched me. I couldn't get it off my mind, and at each thought, my heart did that slow beating thing. Which is ridiculous because from his off-putting attitude, I know he felt absolutely nothing—

"Hey."

We look to our left and see Neal approaching our table. He has a box of donuts in one hand and a tray of four coffees in the other. My eyes rush over the long-sleeved grey shirt he wears. It hugs his shoulders well and dips low enough that a few chest hairs escape just above where his sunglasses hang.

I've never been more grateful that the sunglasses Luna

lent me cover half my face. Nobody can see where I'm staring.

"You're late," Luna tells Neal as she gets up from her chair.

"I have a class Saturday morning." He stops in front of our table. "But I brought donuts and coffee."

Bryson reaches for the box of donuts. "We accept your apology."

Neal sets the tray of coffee down in front of me, and I pick up a cup. "Thanks."

"How do you feel this morning?" he asks me.

I shrug. "Fine, why?"

He grabs his sunglasses and places them over his eyes. "Most people are sore the day after their first class."

"She took a two-hour bath last night," Luna tells him as she reaches for a coffee. I kick her foot, and she smirks before sitting back down in her chair.

I can see him snicker a bit, and I frown. "What do you expect? You used me to demonstrate the *entire* time."

He crosses his arms over his chest and shrugs. "Next time bring a partner."

"Nobody is ever going to want to come to a class like that with me." I scoff as I bring the coffee to my lips.

"Well, then I guess you're stuck with me."

"Who says I'm returning to the class?" I jest back, flipping my hair over my shoulder. "I got what I came for."

The corner of Neal's mouth lifts a little, and he asks, "Did you?"

Immediately, I flush. But I manage to pass it off as an annoyed sigh before I look away from him toward Mr. Tweed's table. Several older women in tight workout wear surround his table. One of the women, with brightly-dyed red hair, waves over at us. From the corner of my eye, I see Neal lazily wave back.

"My morning class," he says. "I teach at the retirement village a few blocks down."

"So what'd you do? Bribe them to shop?"

"No." Neal shakes his head then smirks as he walks away. "I wrote them a letter…"

I set my coffee down on the table and glare at his back. "Most people like my letters…"

"They do, yes," Luna's voice drips with sympathy as she stands back up, her shoulder brushing mine. She brings her voice down to a whisper, "What was that all about?"

"What was what all about?"

Luna tosses her head toward Neal. "The flirting."

"There was no flirting." I chuckle as I reach down and fiddle with the leaves of the nearest plant.

"There most *definitely* was flirting." She laughs but keeps it low so Bryson doesn't overhear.

I glance over at Neal through my sunglasses, hoping Luna doesn't see me looking. He stands with the group of older women, pointing at something on Mr. Tweed's table. After a moment, Mr. Tweeds laughs and shakes a finger.

He was flirting, wasn't he? Did that mean he felt the same thing I did last night?

No. I can't think about that. I have to remember what happened on our first—and only—date. How I felt afterwards, humiliated and rejected, and not the wishy-washy feelings that led me to that first date.

"Luna. Do you forget how he shoved me out of his apartment mid date without an explanation?" I sigh.

"Except to say 'Uh, yeah, I'll call you later.' And then three days later, he's gone."

"I know, but maybe you should ask him why he left?" Luna suggests.

I have been wondering, even more so since last night.

Luna softly flicks my arm. "Oh, hey, I shot off an email to Mina this morning about the cat thing. She said she's going to tell Mrs. Toscano, and by tomorrow, she predicts the whole building will be thinking Glover killed the trees on purpose to get rid of all the cats in the building."

Ha. Good.

"I also stuffed print outs of PETA flyers in her mailbox, and I taped some on the outside too." Luna snickers as she side-eyes me.

I laugh. "Luna!"

Someone slams a black Prada bag down on our table, and we both jump.

It's Eli. He's in a pair of black shorts, a white belt, and a faded grey ACDC T-shirt. His designer sunglasses rest on top of his head, and he stares at me with a single raised eyebrow and tightly closed mouth.

"Eli!" Luna smiles next to me. "Nice bag!"

"It's all right," Eli shrugs. "From the whiny boyfriend."

Luna's look says it all, and we both smirk a bit. "Thanks for coming by to support us. Maybe you'll find something cute!"

"Oh, God, no," He shakes his head quickly and makes a face at her. "I would never buy anything from a garage sale. You never know what you're bringing home with you."

"Then what are you doing here?" I ask him.

He locks eyes with me. "I'm here so I can yell at you for leaving me in the lurch with your gorgeous future husband. Do you know what I had to do yesterday? I had to test games. Awful, *awful* games for the picnic. I had to throw bean bags into a colorful box, something they call 'corn hole?' *Corn hole*, Hilary. Then I had to throw these heavy balls attached to strings at these poles, all connected. Each section of the pole is a certain slew of points… I don't even know what that game is called."

"It doesn't sound that bad, Eli," I say.

"Catch the tone of my voice," he retorts. Then he lifts a finger and begins to ruffle through his black bag on the table. He pulls out a bundled up bright blue shirt and throws it at me. "Here's your shirt. For picnic pride!"

I unbunch the shirt and stare down at the company logo. Other than that, it's very plain.

"We have to wear that at the picnic, per Warren's request," Eli reports. Then he throws his head back in a sharp laugh. "What am I saying? Not you. Me. Just *me*. Because I'm apparently helping out at the day event while you get to put on a cocktail dress and sip champagne under the stars."

Right. I forgot to tell him that tidbit.

"That wasn't my idea!" I protest. "I told Warren we usually split the duties when it comes to events that run all day, and he insisted that you take the picnic."

"Bug, Hilary, *bugs*," Eli barks. He stomps a foot angrily. "I don't do bugs or mud or—"

"You wanted me to go to the night event anyway, remember? Cause it would be all romantic—"

"But I wanted to go with you! I wanted to watch the magic of love unfold," Eli explains with big hand gestures.

"Well, I'm sorry. But if you go, I'll give you your Christmas bonus early this year," I offer.

He folds his arms over his chest. "I'll think about it." He glances around the table then through the lobby windows behind us. "Cute little setup you have here."

"Except we've barely made over two hundred as a building," Luna sighs.

"We've made two hundred and three," Bryson tells us as he looks down at his phone. "Paulette sold one of her Backstreet Boys CDs for five bucks. It looks like Mr. Tweed sold more of his lemon squares too, so maybe we're up to two twenty…"

Eli reaches over and hits my arm gently. "So why'd you take the day yesterday, anyway?"

"She had to spy on Neal," Luna says.

"Oh *really*?"

I roll my eyes. "Relax. I just needed to bribe him into helping me win the election."

Luna elbows me in the side. "They were flirting this morning."

Eli laughs. "I knew you still—"

"Nobody was flirting!" I practically scream. I throw Luna a look, and she just drops down into her chair, whispering something in Bryson's ear. He smiles and nods his head in agreement.

"Oh my, and there he is." Eli looks down toward Mr. Tweed's table. He snatches his bag off the table and clears his throat. "Perhaps I'll just hop on over and say hi…"

"Eli," I warn.

But he swats me off and rushes over to Neal and Mr.

Tweed. I watch them until a small navy-blue bus pulls up alongside the curb. It says "Green Acres Retirement Community" on the side in white cursive letters. I expect a crowd of older women to emerge the moment the door swings open, but older men slowly descend, one by one, with their canes and walkers.

They approach Neal, and he greets them as warmly as he did the women.

"He has a lot of clients," Luna remarks.

"I hope he asked more than that to come." Bryson sighs. "If we want to make the slightest mark for the building, we need to take it near thousand."

"A thousand?" I gasp. "Nobody said we had to make a thousand!"

Bryson gives me a small shrug. "When your grandpa was still around, we'd make five or six hundred dollars when we did this. But over the years, until our involvement was canceled, we were lucky if we made three hundred. One year, we only made eighty-five dollars."

I march past the two of them and peek inside the lobby. "There's barely any traffic inside!"

Our tenants look bored, some of their tables with barely any sale items and some completely overflowing but untouched. Paulette's table is at the far end, and she sits behind it with her laptop on her lap.

"We're at a disadvantage without the courtyard," Luna says. "People are only able to see the lobby, and it's pretty, but it looks like every other lobby in every other condo building."

Damnit. How long 'til Glover comes down, snickers, and shakes her head at my failure?

Luna said when she approved the building's involvement last week, she chuckled and shook her head, muttering something about wasting our time. I *don't* want her to be right on this.

"What's the matter?"

I glance over as Neal steps up to me. He bites into a piece of Mr. Tweed's lemon square. It crumbles from his hands a bit, and the lemon custard squeezes out from the side. My mouth waters a little.

"We need to make more money," I say looking up from the square, "otherwise this'll be another thing Glover will throw in my face. She'll say, 'How can she run a building if she can't run a successful garage sale for six hours?'"

"It's a garage sale," Neal says. "How much money do you actually think you'll pull in?" He offers me the rest of the lemon square.

I take it, slowly ripping a piece off. "Bryson said when my grandpa was alive, they'd make, like, five hundred dollars."

Neal pushes his sunglasses up from his eyes. "That was back in the day. Garage sales aren't as hot as they used to be."

"Thanks for the help," I retort, looking back into the lobby. I shove the piece of lemon square into my mouth, and the custard instantly melts on my tongue, the sweet, zingy texture making me sigh happily. "This is ah-mazing…"

Neal lets out a breath and runs a hand through the scruff on his chin. "Okay, well, we have barbeques on the rooftop, and it's done up pretty nicely up there. And it's a nice day."

"So, what?" I swallow the lemon square down quickly. "We throw ourselves a roof party?"

"People gotta eat," Neal states, ignoring my sarcastic quip. He puts his hands on his hips as our eyes lock. "Get a ton of hotdogs and hamburgers, drinks, and charge people. They're going to want to eat with a nice view."

It's not a bad idea. Our rooftop is beautiful. The view on the east side is of a park. The west side is of the rest of the city. North side shows off a bit of the lake and marina.

"That could work," I admit.

"It *will* work," Neal shoots back. "Go get the food. I'll head upstairs to light the barbeque. Bryson can help me grill."

ॐ

"This is such a great idea, Hil! Look at this!"

I rush around Mr. Tweed and Bryson to where Luna stands at the door to the rooftop. A trio of women have just handed her payment for hot dogs and drinks. Luna set up a table and is guarding the cash box with Mrs. Dorst, who has been counting the number of guests to make sure we don't exceed the rooftop's capacity.

Luna beams down at the cash box in her hands. "We're almost at four hundred dollars!"

It's only been an hour since Luna, the Dorsts, and I rushed off to the nearest grocery store, buying as many hot dogs, buns, and drinks as we could carry. It still isn't enough though. We're running out of water and sodas, so Mr. Dorst went back down to get more.

"After only two hours?"

Luna glances behind her at the line of people waiting

for their barbequed meats. "Two dollars a hotdog and two dollars a drink. Most people are giving fives and saying, 'Keep the change!'"

"How long 'til we have to close up shop?" I ask her.

She glances down at her cell phone on the table. "About two and a half hours."

"Do you think we'll make it to a thousand?"

Luna looks through the empty doorway to the roof. "We could. Paulette's doing a good job at sending people up."

Mr. Tweed pops up next to me, a closed-mouth smile on his pink lips. He leans on his cane as he looks from Luna to me. "Perhaps we could have a raffle?"

"We only have two and a half hours, Mr. Tweed," Luna says.

"What about an auction?" he suggests.

I exchange a look with Luna. "What would we auction off?"

"Ourselves! We can do that thing where people bid on you for dinner and a dance," Mr. Tweed smiles. "I just saw them do it on an episode of *Golden Girls* the other day…or was it *Frasier*…"

"We can't do that," I tell him. "I can just see Glover now, blasting me for hosting a slave sex auction or something."

"What's going on here?" Eli asks. He's popped up between Luna and Mr. Tweed, a water bottle in his hand. He frowns as he points at me. "Why do you look like that? This rooftop thing is a success."

"Only if we make a thousand dollars within two hours," I tell him, "and I don't think the hot dogs and sodas will cut it."

"We're thinking a raffle," Mr. Tweed tells Eli proudly.

Eli wags a finger at the old man, then shifts his gaze to me. "People do love raffles."

"We don't have the time to find anything or even get it properly together."

Eli folds his arms across his chest, his Prada tote bag sliding to his elbow. "Hil, you're in this business. Just take a minute and think about what can be done. You must have something in your place you don't use, or maybe even a service of some kind." We watch as he gestures toward Neal. "What about Neal? Ask him to take his shirt off and auction off a few private lessons."

I gape at him. "I will not!"

"I had the same idea," Mr. Tweed tells him. "She said it's slavery."

"No! I said that Glover would think it's— Ugh, never mind," I huff.

Eli shakes his head at me as he puts his hands on his hips, his bag falling back to his wrist.

I stare at the tiny silver upside down triangle then bite my lip.

I wonder if…

No. He'd never go for it…

"Your bag."

He gasps and clutches it to his chest. "You're out of your mind."

"You don't even like it!" I remind him with a whine. "You said it's blasé and not you and that Jacob is making you use it—"

"It is! But it's also worth seven hundred dollars!"

"You said he got it for a good price!"

He pushes his sunglasses from his eyes and frowns at

me. "Because his sister works at corporate! No way, Hil, I'm not giving you my Prada bag."

"Come on," I beg. "Please? If it gets over five hundred, you can keep the rest."

"No!"

"I will give you your Christmas bonus early," I beg, "next week even."

He scoffs at me and rolls his eyes. "You already promised that if I go to the picnic."

I lunge at him and grasp his right arm. "I'll go to the picnic instead!"

Eli slowly raises his eyebrows. "Really?"

"Yes." I grip his arm. "I'll go to the picnic, and you can go to the reception."

He bites his lips. "Picnic *and* early Christmas bonus."

"Eli."

He shrugs and pulls from my reach. "No Prada for you."

"Okay! Fine. It's a deal." I extend my hand and wait for him to shake it.

He takes a dramatic breath and grabs it firmly.

"But *I* will be running the auction," Eli insists. "If you do it, it'll barely rake in two hundred."

We make our way toward the patio furniture underneath the large metal gazebo. It really is an impressive area to sit underneath. Glover had Edison patio lights hung through the walls of the gazebo, and there were several wine bottles filled with tiny lights hanging from the ceiling. There's an outdoor straw area rug beneath the wicker and glass coffee table, and the matching wicker sectionals face each other. The rooftop is buzzing, and Eli pushes through the crowd, motioning for them to give him room.

I stand by the barbeque with Neal and Bryson, the smell of the grilling hot dogs hitting me within a second. They're perfectly lined up next to each other, plump and juicy. I watch the grease slowly escape the casings and hit the small flames through the grate.

I look back at Eli who's stepped up onto the glass wicker table.

"Attention," he screams, "attention, everybody! If I could have your attention, please…" It takes a few seconds and a whistle from Bryson to officially quiet everyone down. "Thank you so much for taking part in this neighborhood garage sale, and we hope you are having a fantastic time at our impromptu little rooftop patio party! Let's give a round of applause to our handsome grill masters." He claps and smiles at Neal and Bryson, most of the crowd following his lead. Once silent, Eli speaks again.

"Our gracious host, Hilary Brandt, has a special treat for everyone attending. In light of this impromptu party, we decided to have an impromptu auction!" He thrusts his bag up to the sky like it's the Holy Grail. "Behold, new this season from Prada's men's line. A stunning, versatile man bag with compartments for a man's every need. This trendy, sporty bag can even fit a man's laptop or work, err, things. And it can go to one lucky person today! At a starting bid of a hundred dollars."

"A hundred dollars? That's pretty steep," Neal says.

"It's worth seven hundred," I tell him.

He steps up next to me and motions at the crowd. "But these people don't know that. Half of them look like college students…"

"Everyone knows what Prada is," I say.

"But not everyone can afford it."

Maybe he's right…

He *is* right. Seconds pass, and nobody's thrown out a bid yet.

Next to me, Neal exhales then uncrosses his arms and throws a hand in the air. "A hundred dollars."

I glance over at him, his bid surprising me.

"Wonderful." Eli gives a half clap as he smiles at Neal. "Our first bid! One hundred dollars to our handsome grill master. Come on, folks, don't let this fantastic bag go for only a hundred!"

"One twenty!" someone yells in the crowd.

"One twenty from the lady in the Gucci T-shirt." Eli points at her.

"One forty!" Mrs. Dorst shouts from the door. She's looking down at her phone.

I'm guessing she's looked up its true value.

"One forty from the lovely lady in the blue workout suit." Eli smiles. "Do I have one seventy from anyone?"

"Two hundred," Neal declares. I look back at him, and he shrugs, "Upping the value."

Someone else calls out, "Two fifty."

I recognize the voice and look past Neal to the door. Standing in khaki shorts and a black button-up golf shirt with his dark hair blowing lightly in the breeze is Warren.

What is he doing here?

"Two fifty from the handsome gentleman at the door." Eli beams. He also throws Warren a wave. I see Eli side-eye me, the corner of his mouth lifting in a smirk, and I realize Eli had obviously told Warren about this yesterday.

"Two seventy-five!" Mrs. Dorst calls out to counter Warren's bid.

"Three hundred," Warren opposes. He opens his wallet and hands Luna a bill and then looks over at me. He gives me a smile and a wave.

I smile and return the wave. As I look back at Eli, I see Neal quickly glance from Warren to me.

Mrs. Dorst throws a hand in the air, elbowing Mr. Dorst in the side as he tries to pull it down. "Three twenty!"

"My, my," Eli laughs loudly. "We have ourselves a bidding war! Will the man at the door go to three fifty?"

Warren slides his hands into his pockets and smirks. He drops his head for a moment then looks back at Eli. "Three fifty."

"Three fifty!" Eli claps. "Wonderful! Anybody for three seventy-five? How about the lady in the workout suit?" He motions at Mrs. Dorst, and everyone glances at her. Mr. Dorst is whispering in her ear, and after a moment, she sighs and shakes her head at Eli.

"I'm out!" She states, her arms crossing in annoyance as she glares at Mr. Dorst.

"Anyone else then?" Eli asks the crowd.

It's silent.

I don't believe it! Warren's going to get it for three hundred and fifty dollars. He looks so confident, almost happy that he won. I watch him start to walk toward the crowd and Eli, lost to the fact that Mrs. Dorst's eyes graze over him almost adoringly once she sees who outbid her. But next to me, I hear Neal scoff.

"Three seventy-five!"

Warren stops and looks at Neal, frowning.

A hushed whisper runs through the crowd.

"What are you doing?" I hiss and pull on Neal's arm.

"I told you. You want to make money, don't you?" His tone is anything but serious though, and his scruff fails to hide a smile.

"That's a client," I let him know. "He's being supportive. Take back your bid. Three fifty is enough."

"Bet he'll go higher." Neal shrugs, looking away from me.

"Four hundred," Warren suddenly exclaims. His hands go to his hips as he looks from Neal to Eli, repeating his bid. "Four hundred."

Eli opens his mouth to accept the bid when Neal calls out, "Four twenty!"

I gasp and throw a hand over his mouth.

Everyone looks at us, and I see Luna smirk from the door.

"He's kidding," I tell Eli loudly. "It's not a bid."

Neal pushes my hand off his mouth as he frowns at me.

Mr. Dorst grunts loudly. "If he said it, it should be a standing bid."

"I agree," someone says in the crowd.

I grab Neal's arm to get his attention, and he looks at me with a small frown. "Neal, take back that bid. It's not your style, and you don't even like it."

"If you didn't want your client bidding, why'd you invite him?" Neal asks me quietly.

My jaw clenches. "I didn't invite him! It was Eli, and it doesn't matter. He's a big client. Don't make him look like a fool."

I can't see because he's still wearing his sunglasses,

but I'm pretty sure Neal rolls his eyes at me before turning to Eli. "My bid stands."

Arghhhh…

"Er, great." Eli's smile is shaky as he looks over at Warren. "Do we have four fifty?"

Warren is silent.

Uh oh.

"Four fifty," he suddenly agrees.

I move fast, swiping my fingers across my neck.

Eli takes my cue just as quickly. He points at Warren and shouts, "Sold! Four fifty to the handsome man in the khakis."

Chapter Fourteen

"I should fire you right here and now."

"On what grounds? I simply invited a friend of mine to come support another friend of mine."

"Eli, he's a client, *not* your friend."

"He calls me 'buddy.' In my book, that means friend."

I throw him a glare.

He just smiles then lets out a frustrated sigh. "I don't get you. The entire thing was a success! Why are you so crabby this morning?"

"We only made eight hundred and forty-five dollars. We missed our target," I remind him.

Eli's mouth twists into a frown. "If it's that big of a deal, why don't you just throw in the last hundred and sixty and call it a day?"

"Glover will accuse me of cheating." I drop my chin into the palm of my hand, my elbow resting on a pile of unopened mail from last week.

"Well, just put that all out of your mind," Eli orders, "because the event is on the nineteenth, and that's less than two weeks away. We have a bunch of last-minute things to talk about with Warren today." He sits back in his chair and eyes my outfit. "Nice outfit by the way."

I sit up and tug at my black dress. There's a slight swoop at the neckline, but it's a classy dress. Simple, tasteful. I'm wearing gold kitten heels and have thrown my hair into a ponytail. "What's wrong with it?"

"Nothing," Eli shrugs. "It's very…Jackie O. Sexy but mature."

"Mature as in old?" I gape.

"No! God, relax. I just mean not sleazy. Not like the push-up bra outfit you wore…" He shakes his head and goes back to his computer, muttering something under his breath.

I don't hear it and decide I probably don't want to know.

I am in a crabby mood after yesterday. We didn't hit our target, and I didn't even get to thank Warren for coming by. I was bombarded with cleaning up and congratulations from a few tenants who then wanted to talk more about my election platform.

I think I may have promised someone something to do with puppies and kittens…

"Oh, before I forget, Mrs. Sarris wants you to call her today. She said it's important." Eli waves a Post-it in his hand, but his eyes remain on his computer screen. "She's working from home."

I wheel myself from my desk and snatch the Post-it from his hand then slide back to my place. I grab my cell phone and am just starting to dial my client's number when Sydney calls out my name. I turn my head and see her standing in the doorway. She curls a finger and motions for me to come into her office.

Immediately, I set down my phone and hurry after her,

slowly shutting the glass door behind me. "What's going on?"

She stands in front of her desk, brightening up the space in a bright yellow skirt and white blouse with puffy sleeves, a yellow ascot tied neatly around her neck. "My niece is having her sweet sixteen birthday party next month, and I'm hoping you could squeeze the event into your schedule. She's coming in with Marco today."

"Sure, okay," I nod. "Is that all?"

"Any headway with Mrs. James?" Sydney's face is emotionless, and her tone is so smooth. I don't know if she's suspicious of something or nervous or…

"It's going great!" I lie under the pressure of her stare.

"Really?" Finally, she cracks a small smile.

"Yup! We, uh, discussed more caterers…"

Why am I lying?!

Sydney's hands come together. "Oh, Hilary, that's wonderful to hear! I was a bit nervous after hearing that rumor that she's still shopping for an agency, I'll be honest. I don't know why…" She lets out a small laugh. "I should have known you'd snag that account easily. I don't know why my faith in you weaned. It's not like you're Jasmine."

She glances past me then sighs, looking back at me with a smile.

I feel like sinking into the ground and melting away.

What the hell am I going to do now?

Sydney shoos me away with that bright smile. "Well, I won't keep you. I know you have work to do. I'll send my niece over as soon as she arrives."

"Great." I force a smile as I hurry from her office.

I shut the door and look over my shoulder to watch

Sydney sit down behind her desk and pick up the latest copy of *CityDaily*.

Okay, I have no choice now. I have to get Mrs. James to sign me as her planner at any cost.

"Eli," I say sharply, "you still know that secretary at Elite Planners?"

"Brittany? Yes, why?"

"Do me a favor and call her. Ask her if she's heard anything about Mrs. James shopping around for an event planner, and if she has, ask her if Mrs. James had contacted them."

Eli's eyes widen a bit. "Do you think she has? Hil, they're the only company that gives us a run for our money…"

"I'm aware, Eli. Make the call, please."

Fifteen minutes later, I'm in the meeting room with Warren.

Eli's been busy trying to get a hold of Brittany. He's also shot off a few emails to other planners we know to see if they've heard the rumors.

"Thank you so much for yesterday. It really did mean a lot that you stopped by to support us. Thank you, honestly."

"Happy to do it. I had the day free, and Eli said it was going to be entertaining." Warren leans back in his chair and laughs, his grey vest bunching up a bit. "Entertaining it was. I never expected to get into a bidding war over a Prada bag. I've never paid that much for a bag in my entire life…"

I feel myself flush as Neal's face pops into my head. "Sorry about that. I don't know what got into him…"

After the auction ended, I tried hard to avoid Neal

during the cleanup. Somehow, we always found a way to be next to each other, either stuffing discarded napkins into trash bags or recycling the soda cans.

Warren sits back up and puts a hand over mine.

My grip on my pen loosens enough for it to drop on the notepad in front of me.

"It's okay. I gave it to my assistant. I think he'll quit asking about a raise for at least six months."

I return a smile, and that's when I notice we've had eye contact for the entire conversation. Suddenly feeling awkward, I clear my throat and slip my hand out from under his. "Okay, well, let's get back to the schedule for the day. So your guests arrive at the campground around nine a.m., and Barbeque Joe serves his famous sausages, beans, and egg breakfast until ten thirty. Then you start a few games, right?"

"Potato sack race and the corn hole tournament. Oh! I was thinking about having a bubble station for the kids? My secretary said they had one at her husband's company picnic last year, and it was a big hit. Maybe a candy station as well? Unless it all seems a bit impossible to do last minute?"

What the hell is a bubble station?

"I can definitely do a candy station," I make a note in the binder, "and a bubble station…" I write 'Google' next to that and look up with a smile. "Okay, so after the games, Barbeque Joe will serve his lunch at one, his hamburger and hotdogs, smoked meats, all that. Is that when you will be thanking everyone? Or will you wait for the barbeque to end?"

He nods. "That's when I plan to do it, yes. I figure it will take about ten minutes, then everyone can hurry off into the lake for a swim before we end the day at four, four thirty."

"Fantastic." I check off the schedule notes I already made.

As I glance up at Warren, who's now focused on his cell phone, I see Marco through the glass doors. He's standing at the elevator, playing with the golden chain around his neck, his muscles bulging out of his tight white shirt. The girl standing with him could be his twin. There is barely any fat on her, her arms pop with tanned muscles, and her dark shiny hair falls around her firm shoulders in a bundle of curls. She's wearing far too much make up for her age, however, and looks about twenty-five instead of sixteen.

Marco catches me staring, and his crooked smile flashes through as he winks at me.

I grimace.

Suddenly, Eli appears in my view, pushing the door to the conference room open, his face stricken with shock. "Um, Hilary? Could I steal you for just a moment? It's an emergency."

Warren looks from Eli to me. "Uh oh."

"Give me five minutes," I tell Warren as I rise from my seat.

I hurry from the room, meeting Eli near his desk.

He's already holding my purse and cell phone in his hands.

"What is it, Eli?"

He pushes my purse and phone at me. "Luna called. She needs you to head home right now."

"Why?"

Eli leans closer after noticing Marco and his sister heading our way. "Apparently, your building was robbed."

I stiffen. "When?"

He loops my purse strap around my arm and tosses my cell phone into it. "She says sometime late last night, and Glover is blaming you. She says you let bandits and thieves in, and several tenants were robbed."

"Several?!" I exclaim.

No, no, no! How did that even happen? Everything is so secure in the building!

My heart races, and my chest tightens. I drop my head into my hands as I squeal. "Oh my God. I can't believe this!"

"Relax," Eli tells me, though his tone is far from comforting. "We don't know if it was someone who came in during the garage sale—"

"Of course it was!" I cry. "It was an open house!"

"Well… Well…" He shakes his head at me as he tries to find something to say. Then he flicks my arm. "Well, I found out that Mrs. James has not hired someone for the gala yet. She's still shopping around. I took the liberty of organizing a day of pampering for her at Haven Salon and Spa, on you of course. She should be getting the package in the mail by Friday. That usually seals the deal."

I sigh, my hands coming down from my face.

He's right. It usually does, but I can't get my hopes up. She did return the wine basket, and I heard nothing after the musical tickets were sent last week.

Eli collides into me as Marco appears on his side.

Marco points to me and then to his sister, who looks up from her phone, slowly chewing her gum. "Yo, Hil, this is my sister Jewel. She's the one who needs help with her party."

"Right, hi, great to meet you," I say.

"How old are you?" Jewel asks, raising a thin eyebrow. "'Cause I need my party planner to be *in the know* with what's in right now. I can't have some old person telling me that balloons and streamers are still cool. Tash Morrow had a planner like that for her eighteenth birthday party, and it was a mess. She's practically been in hiding ever since."

Next to me, Eli squirms, and I notice the wide-eyed tension come over him.

"I'll sit in on the meeting too," Marco states.

I'm not sure what offends me more, the fact that he didn't even ask to or the smile he's giving me that I'm sure he thinks turns me on. Seriously, *what* was I thinking?

"Shouldn't you be working?" Eli asks Marco, motioning at his tiny desk across the room.

"Unfortunately, there's been a bit of an emergency, and I have to run," I tell the brother and sister. When Jewel frowns, I add, "But Eli here will sit you down, and you can tell him what ideas you have brewing. In a couple of days, after I get things together, we will meet again. Sound good?"

"I can't meet on Mondays, Wednesdays, or Fridays because those are my training days," Jewel informs me, flipping her hair back a bit. "I'm training to be the next VJ on VibeMusic. You know, the TV channel that plays music videos?"

"Yup, no, we are aware of what VibeMusic is." Eli's offensive tone has Jewel rolling her eyes.

"Okay, well, I'm sorry, but I have to run." I take a step

away from them all, giving Eli a tight smile as his eyes beg me not to go. "Have a great meeting. I'll be in touch soon, Jewel. Eli, can you tell Warren I'm so sorry and will get in touch tomorrow?"

I run out of the office.

When I pull up to Fairway Towers, there aren't any police cruisers out front. I pay the cab driver and rush inside, heading straight past the mailboxes and elevators. I know Glover's having an emergency meeting in the event room right now.

As I get there, the doors are propped open, and the room is very full. I scan it, recognizing almost every single tenant. Glover is at the front of the room behind her little podium. She's answering someone's question with poise and grace, looking like an angel in her white skirt and matching white blazer. She even has a golden headband woven through her highlighted golden hair.

I see Neal to my far right, standing in the corner, leaning against the wall. He's listening to what Glover is saying somewhat intensely, arms crossed over his chest. Just as I'm about to look away, he spots me, and his arms uncross.

Glover's voice booms around the room, and anxiously, I glance toward the front. "I can assure you, Mrs. Tisman, we are absolutely one hundred percent safe. The police searched every inch of the building this morning. Nobody is lurking anywhere. That section of the basement is sealed off until further notice, of course, and tenants will not be permitted past the laundry room until the police have finished cataloging the stolen items."

Something brushes against my right arm, and I glance up at Neal. As he opens his mouth to speak, I lean in closer to him. "The Tempermans went into the basement this morning and found their bikes missing. Almost every locker in their row was busted open, a few things were stolen."

I feel only a little bit of relief when he informs me it was only one row. Our locker is toward the back and is loaded with my grandfather's belongings. Nothing worth a whole lot, but if someone stole his records, I'd be pretty upset.

"God, this is a nightmare," I whisper back as I look to Glover. "I can't believe I let this happen."

"Any tenants who have not yet reported their missing items to the police are urged to head down to the station tonight, no later than noon tomorrow," Glover states, glancing around the room then smiling softly. "I know this is a frightening situation, but we must all remember that we are still one of the safest buildings in the neighborhood. This was our very first robbery in nearly three decades."

"It's not your fault." Neal's voice remains low as he looks from Glover back to me. "Anybody could have let the guy in, open house or not."

"Sure," I say to him, "but it happened during *my* open house. Not Glover's, and not some random Sunday either. The front doors were open. I invited the guy inside to rob us blind."

He doesn't say anything as his eyes slowly scan my face.

I feel as if the room around us is closing in. I'm standing way too close to him, but I can't make myself step away.

"Ah, there's Ms. Brandt," Glover's tone becomes edgy as she shifts her attention to me, throwing a snarky, wide grin my direction. "Would you like to come up here and address everyone? After all, you are a possible candidate for this position. You could be our future president…" She doesn't give me a chance to respond. She steps off the podium and gestures at it, holding her creepy smile. "Come on, dear. Come, come…"

I bite the inside of my mouth as my eyes race around the room. Almost everyone is frowning at me. I can't spot a friendly face in the crowd.

"Don't do it," Neal mutters, a hand over his mouth like he's about to cough.

"I don't have a choice," I answer, unclenching my jaw as I walk away from him. Somehow, as I walk through the rows of chairs, I manage to smile at everyone even though they all scowl at me. All of them except Mrs. Glover, whose piercing smile greets me at the podium.

As I step up to the podium, I drop my purse onto it and exhale wearily as I look around the room. Everybody is silent, watching me with their narrow, angry eyes. I finally spot Luna and the Dorsts to my right, wedged between furious tenants, but only Luna smiles.

"Um, good afternoon, everyone—"

"Speak up, dear," Glover orders.

I try to brush off her sneering grin.

Clearing my throat, I begin again, "Good afternoon, everyone. I'd like to start off by saying I am truly very sorry for what happened here. It was obviously never my intention to bring any danger to our building by having the open house—"

"Why didn't you have a security plan in motion?" someone shouts out.

"To be honest, I never thought someone would slink in

and steal from us," I answer, my hands gripping the sides of the podium.

"A good president should be prepared for anything," Mrs. Temperman remarks from the front row. She looks over at Glover. "Don't you agree?"

"I do," Mrs. Glover nods, "but please, let Ms. Brandt continue."

Ugh, she's good. She knows there is no way I can come out looking good after what happened. She knows I could bury myself.

"That open house garage sale thing was a terrible idea," Mr. Temperman states as he gets up from his chair in a huff. His arms cross over his blue blazer. "We never should have started doing it again. It was a big mistake."

"Now just hold on a minute," Luna stands from her seat and looks over at him. "We raised over eight hundred dollars for the building yesterday—"

"Twelve hundred," Mrs. Dorst corrects loudly.

Twelve hundred?

Luna looks from Mrs. Dorst back to Mr. Temperman. "That's right, actually. We raised over twelve hundred dollars yesterday. That hasn't been done in years, not since Mrs. Glover became president. In fact, her fundraising efforts for the building have nearly disappeared."

"And for good reason," Mrs. Glover chuckles lightly. "Fundraising requires strangers into the building, and that puts our safety in danger. Yesterday was the perfect example of that."

"We let strangers into the building all the time. For deliveries, for maintenance," Neal speaks up. "Hell, our landscapers change monthly."

Glovers eyes harden at his voice.

Neal ignores her, casually continuing his thought, "I'm just saying, everyone here wants a bigger budget for the building, but the only way to do that is to fundraise for it. I mean, unless the Tempermans would like to make a sizeable charitable donation toward the budget?"

Mr. Temperman slinks into his seat, muttering something to his wife, who then throws daggers my way.

"The point is, what happened yesterday could have happened at any point during the year," Neal tells everyone. "Who went down to the storage room yesterday morning? Or yesterday afternoon during the open house?"

The room is silent.

I realize where Neal is going with his rant.

"That's right. Who was in the storage room yesterday?"

Again, nobody says anything. They all just look at each other.

"Okay, what about Saturday? Was anybody down there Saturday?"

Silence.

Slowly, someone's hand rises up on the left side of the room. "I was down there Wednesday night getting my waffle maker, and everything was okay."

I point at the hand in the air. "Okay, great. Was anybody else down there between Wednesday and Sunday night?"

Nobody says anything.

"So, really, the robbery could have happened on Thursday or Friday night—or even Saturday," Luna gathers. "It could have even happened during the day!"

"It also could have been a tenant," Mr. Dorst suggests with a smirk. Though I know he means it as a joke, I watch as everyone glances at each other, a few people beginning to whisper.

"I doubt it was anyone in the building," I quickly exclaim. The last thing I need is everyone accusing a neighbor. "The point is, until the police are done with their investigation, we won't know when it occurred. We shouldn't be jumping to conclusions."

"We should be focusing on what to do with the extra twelve hundred Hilary brought in for the building." Mrs. Dorst leans back into her chair, an arm draped on top of Luna's empty seat. "I personally think we should invest it into the courtyard now that the building's been deemed safe from termites."

"What about the laundry room?" someone calls out. "It's so dark and dingy down there."

"We could do that," I agree.

"If we do the courtyard, we can have an opening ceremony for it!" Mrs. Zheng, who up until five minutes ago was one of the people giving me the stink eye, is suddenly smiling widely at me.

"Sure," I smile back.

I cast a quick glance at Glover, who's struggling to maintain an emotionless composure, her eyebrows tense with each passing moment as she glances around the room.

"Something like that has to be put up to a vote," Mrs. Temperman practically shouts. She motions at Mrs. Glover. "And the president has to make the decision on what to do with the money in the end anyway."

"That's not fair!" Luna proclaims angrily.

"Those are the rules," Neal tells Luna. He motions at Glover with a nod. "President calls a vote and then makes the final decision whether or not to go with the majority."

With his sudden support, Glover throws him an eminent grin before nodding herself.

"We will have a vote Wednesday evening," Glover declares to the room. She makes her move up toward the podium and shoos me down from it. After she claims her place, she smiles at everyone again. "Now if I could have the victims of the robberies please stay behind so we may have a word, I would be ever so grateful."

"Wait, what about the rumor going around?" a woman in the back calls out.

Glover and I exchange a look with each other.

"Rumor?" She frowns.

The same woman stands and points at her. "I heard you're trying to get rid of all the cats in the building because you hate them! What about all the dogs?"

"It's not fair that dog owners get better treatment," someone shouts in agreement.

Glover shifts uneasily in her place. She tugs at her blazer and forces a small smile on her mouth as her gaze locks with mine. "I will definitely be willing to address that rumor right now to anyone concerned."

I throw her back a smirk and back away.

And just like that, the meeting ends.

As people begin to file out of the room, or toward Glover, I meet Luna and the Dorsts outside the room. Luna stands with a scowl, arms crossed over her chest.

"Luna, I thought we only raised eight hundred and forty dollars on Sunday?" I keep my voice to a whisper as I lean toward her.

"Neal sold off some passes to his class," she explains. "Some blonde girl bought like twelve."

Bet it was what's her name… Jane?

Not that I care, really.

I pull my purse straps up my arm as the four of us fall into a comfortable silence for a few seconds. "I think it went okay in there."

"Neal saved the day." Mrs. Dorst looks past me into the room. "I would have never thought about bringing up the budget stuff."

"Yes, and he may have blown his cover by doing so," Mr. Dorst grumbles. "There goes that plan."

"No, I think he fixed it with what he said at the end," I counter. "Glover looked pleased with him."

"Except that we could have all agreed on how to spend the money right then and there," Luna replies. Her eyes move from me into the room.

I follow her gaze to where Neal stands near Glover. She's saying something to him, hands gesturing, and he just listens.

"Now Glover gets the final say."

"I'm not sure I like that either," Mrs. Dorst sighs.

I watch Glover and Neal for a few seconds. He says something that makes her laugh, and she touches his arm gently.

My forehead crinkles, and I look away. My stomach feels heavy, and I'm suddenly feeling agitated all over again.

"Are you okay?" Luna asks me.

"I'm fine," I reply, my face scrunched as I ruffle through my purse. "I just can't believe we were robbed…"

"*We* weren't," Luna tells me. "I went downstairs and checked. I brought up some of your grandfather's crates, the ones with the records to double check. I couldn't count them downstairs because Glover was barking orders at everyone until the police arrived."

"Thank you." I let out a sigh of relief as I take my phone from my bag, glancing again at Neal and Glover, who still stand close together. "Uh, I need to head back to the office if we're done here. I'll see you guys later."

I stalk away from them, barely hearing their farewell.

I don't know what throws me more, seeing Neal being all chummy with Glover or the nasty feeling that just washed over me.

Jealousy.

Chapter Fifteen

What's that saying?

Take one step forward and three steps back?

Well, that's exactly what happened after Monday's meeting.

On Wednesday morning, there was an email circling in the building about Luna's past. Her small misdemeanor about getting caught smoking pot when she was eighteen. A tenant called for her eviction, citing a clause in the contract that states a tenant can be evicted if they prove a danger to others. That tenant was none other than Mr. Temperman. He CC'd his suggestion to half the building, including Glover.

How Glover found out about that is anybody's guess. Luna must have told a few people in the building.

Bryson and I both had to block our condo door to stop Luna from crashing the vote. She still managed to pull me away.

"This is just another stupid tactic to ruin your chances!" Luna shouted for the hundredth time in the last hour. Bryson stayed against the door because Luna had tried to make a run for it while we were distracted, twice.

Luna paces in the middle of the room. Her short hair is

sticking up at her temples, her forehead sweaty from the rage. "I mean, she's pathetic. She's so friggin' pathetic to use a person's past like that! It's one thing for her to accuse me once or twice of *growing* pot, but it's another to actually say that I was arrested for it!"

I'm sitting on the couch with Pax purring next to me. "I agree."

She stops pacing and looks at me. "There was never a charge! It was one joint! The cop gave me a break, and it's been years since I've smoked any of it."

I raise my eyebrows, expressing my disbelief.

She exhales. "Fine. It's been a few weeks, but it's legal now, so it's not a crime!" She lets out another frustrated sigh and places her hands on her hips. "The whole point of getting Neal in on this is to use his knowledge about Glover. He needs to give us something bigger than her hatred of cats."

"It worked though," Bryson tells her. "A few tenants, including your neighbor down the hall that throws up when she smells Indian food, have said they're voting for Hil because she loves animals."

I smile at Luna.

"We still need something bigger, a nail in the coffin, so to speak."

"I'll talk to him after the vote," I assure her. "Just calm down. You're wearing out the rug."

She drops down onto her knees. "This better not hurt us in the polls. We've finally been doing well."

"She's got that pants party Saturday," Bryson tells Luna. His eyes stay focused on her as he motions toward me. "She can convince Mrs. Toscano to vote for her easily.

The woman hates Glover as much as we do. If Toscano votes for Hil, so will her minions."

"Right," I agree, "I'll just buy a pair of leggings or something."

Luna raises an eyebrow. "You think she'll let you get away with buying only one pair?"

Oh, God. I hope so. I know how expensive those leggings can be, and in truth, I don't even like their styles.

I begin stroking Pax again as Bryson's phone pings in his hand. He looks down and reads the text message. "They've voted, and Glover says we can all go back down to the storage lockers. She requests that we go down and tidy things up."

"I'll tidy up her stupid storage locker all right," Luna mutters.

Bryson smirks.

I motion at the green crates of my grandfather's belongings Luna had brought up. "Bring those back down with you."

"I haven't finished looking through them." She sighs.

"They aren't very valuable, and we don't play records," I tell her.

Luna just shrugs as she crawls over to the two crates and begins to shuffle through them.

A few minutes later, there's a knock at the door. I stand at the same time as Luna, and Bryson slowly opens the front door. He peers out and then opens it wider when he sees who's on the other side of the door.

Mr. Tweed, Neal, and Mr. Dorst.

The door isn't even shut behind them when Luna asks, "And? What did they decide?"

"Courtyard," Mr. Dorst answers, a hand sliding into his

pants pocket. He takes out his cell phone and is lost to us now.

"It was between the laundry room, courtyard, and replacing the stolen items," Mr. Tweed explains. "Glover was really pushing for replacing the stolen items."

"Yeah." Neal smirks. He stands next to Bryson, his hands tucked into the back of his jeans. "She made it clear several times that it's what *you* would have wanted, you know, based on your guilt."

Luna claps her hands together loudly, almost all aggravation has evaporated from her face. "Okay, so courtyard it is. We could have it all done by Sunday, I bet, and have a small ceremony that night."

"That's in three days," I say. "We can't do that in three days!"

"The election is on the nineteenth," Luna reminds me, "next Saturday. We have to have it done before then. Maybe, if we're careful with our spending, we can show everyone we have a good chunk left over to help with maintenance for the rest of the year..."

"You're going to replant everything in that yard in three days?" Neal frowns at her. "You're aware that most landscaping companies would need a week for something like that, right?"

"We don't have a week," she replies. "We have three days." She reaches over and grabs hold of Bryson's arm. "Tonight, let's get rid of all the flowers those exterminators trampled on. I can take Friday off work, and tomorrow, I'll bring over a whole bunch of fresh flowers."

"What about the gazebo?" Mr. Tweed asks her. "Didn't you two promise a gazebo to everyone?"

I look at Luna whose face suddenly falls. "Oh my God, we did, didn't we?"

"*You* did." I shoot her a glare. "You promised that stupid gazebo."

"Okay, well, we can still do it…" Luna assures us, but her tone is less than confident.

"How?" I cry. "Those things cost thousands of dollars, and even if we had the time to build one, that still would cost us about two grand, Luna!"

"All right!" she shouts back at me. "Just…give me the night to think about what to do, okay?" She swats a hand against Bryson's shoulder. "Come on, let's get to ripping everything out downstairs." As they head to the door, Mr. Tweed and Mr. Dorst follow them. Luna turns back at me when she opens it and motions at Neal. "Don't forget to ask him for some dirt."

I nod my head at Luna as I push them further out of the door. "Yes, I will."

Leaving the door open a bit, I turn back to Neal.

He has his hands on his hips as he waits for me to explain.

"I need some more dirt on Glover."

"Is this about the pot thing?" he asks.

"I don't know how she found out about Luna's past but… I think she did it because we managed to turn the tables on her Monday."

"Yeah," Neal agrees slowly, "she wasn't too happy about that."

I think back on the flirting between the two of them but push through the pit growing in my stomach. "Anyway, what else do you have on her?"

"Look, about that…" Neal walks closer until he's

standing directly in front of me. He extends an arm and plants his left hand on the wall near my face. I back into the door until it shuts, the pit in my stomach fluttering away any jealousy. "I don't know what you think I have to tell you about her. She's pretty straight-laced, other than hating cats."

"There has to be something. Everybody has things they don't want people knowing."

He scratches the back of his head as he looks from my mouth to my eyes. He's shaved the rough stubble off his cheeks, and there's more of an outline of a goatee going on now. Focusing on anything but his jawline is hard.

"She gambles," he says.

My eyes nearly bulge from their sockets.

"She gambles?" I repeat, aghast.

"Roulette. And horses," Neal explains. "She goes every Thursday morning. To the Woodland Casino, an hour up from here. She does pretty well on the horses."

"Does she use money from the budget?"

He frowns. "No, why would you think that?"

I shrug as I cross my arms over my chest. "I guess it would kind of help me out more if she did, that's all."

"People knowing the president has a possible gambling addiction and is in charge of a lump sum of money isn't going to work for you though?"

I roll my eyes. "Point taken. I just have to find some way to start the rumor…"

"Why don't you follow her?" Neal suggests sarcastically.

I grin. "Tomorrow is Thursday." I point a finger in his face. "I could get Bryson to follow her and take pictures."

"I was kidding," Neal claims, frowning again.

"Well, it was a good idea."

We stare at each other for a few awkward seconds, then I pull my eyes away, pretending to pick at the nail bed on my thumb. "Oh, thanks for selling a few of your passes Sunday."

"Sure."

I can feel his eyes burrowing down at me, and I look back up at him. "So, who bought them?"

"A regular student."

"The blonde? Jane or whatever?"

Why am I asking him this?

His eyebrows lift slightly, and he seems amused, which makes me automatically feel stupid.

"Maybe," he answers, the corners of his mouth twitching a bit. "Jealous?"

I let out a forced chuckle. "Hardly."

"How'd your client enjoy the bag?"

"He gave it to his assistant if you must know." I cross my arms over my chest again. Sarcastically, I add, "Thanks for that, by the way."

A small smile, that I could only describe as sly, comes over him. "Hey, why not milk your rich clients? If he wants your attention, you should make him work for it."

"I can't believe you just— He doesn't want m-my attention," I stutter as I brush the hair behind my ears. "That's so, ugh, it's not even—"

I have no words.

"Then how come none of your other clients showed up?" Neal asks, his smile holding, clearly enjoying the teasing.

"Because, because— I don't have to explain anything to you," I reply firmly.

"Is he the reason you've been dressing up for work?"

I gasp. "I would never… I don't date clients. It's a personal rule of mine. And I *always* dress nice for work." I watch him chuckle and run a hand across his mouth. Annoyed, I throw my hands on my hips and frown at him. "What's it to you anyway? Jealous?"

He bunches his face up and shrugs before his eyes meet mine again. There's a glimmer about them that melts away my annoyance almost instantly. "You never wore a push-up bra for our date."

Even though I know he's joking, I throw my hands over my chest. "That wasn't a push-up bra!"

His eyebrows rise above his jovial eyes, a clear sign that he, like Eli and Luna, doesn't believe me.

"Fine, it was a push-up bra, but the lady at the store told me it was one of the natural looking ones and that no one would be able to notice. Clearly, she was wrong, she just wanted the damn sale."

"Clearly," he repeats with a chuckle.

I shake my head and relax as my hands drop to my sides. "I'm getting rid of that stupid bra."

"I don't know, you could always cosplay Wonder Woman with it," he jokes.

"Oh, ha ha," I retort, "very funny. Yes, because it's a push-up bra, I get it."

He frowns. "No… Because it's red and gold."

My hands fly to my chest, and my mouth drops open. After a second, I manage to spit out, "How do you know what colors my bra is?"

"You wore it with a tight white T-shirt. Not exactly concealing."

Oh my God… Why didn't Eli tell me?! I sat in a meeting with Warren looking like that?!

I'm so mortified. I cover my face with my hands, my cheeks instantly on fire.

"You didn't know it was see-through, did you?" Neal asks in almost a whisper.

"Not exactly," I mumble into my palms.

"Had an important meeting that day, did you?"

"I may have."

Is that why Warren became all flirty with me? Because of that see-through bra thing? Jesus, did I come off as all… all…Jasmine like? Is that why he—

Just *wonderful*.

"Why didn't you look at yourself in the mirror before you left the house?" Neal asks.

I drop my hands from my face and glare at him. "I threw the shirt on after I did my hair and makeup! Then I rushed out so I wouldn't be late. I forgot to look into the mirror."

He nods, still smirking.

A surge of annoyance rushes through my bones. "Yes, it's all very funny. I feel like such a loser, but everyone else finds it so hilarious—"

"Okay, okay, relax," he tells me. The smirk slips off his face. "I'm sorry. Nobody thinks you're a loser."

My laugh is high as I think about Jasmine and Glover. "Oh, there are people all right."

"Glover?" he guesses, dropping his head for a moment. "She calls everyone a loser. I think it's because she can't swear. Or she finds swearing unladylike. Not sure which… In any case, she probably only called you a loser because you're running against her."

"She hasn't liked me since I moved in here three years ago," I remind him. "From the moment she set eyes on me, even when I sent her the gift basket of macaroons as a peace offering, she's been nothing but nasty to me."

Neal's mouth opens slightly, but then he closes it and sighs. His eyes slowly sweep over my face. As they rest on mine, I have to swallow, almost nervously, before dropping my eyes from his.

My breathing slows, and I can feel my chest tighten as a flutter of thrill sends the hair on my arms upright. I realize, somewhere in the middle of our conversation, I've pushed my back off the door so were almost as close as we were for his class. And his hand left the wall. I wonder, just for a moment, if I were to touch his arm, would I feel that spark that I felt when his arms were over my chest?

He steps closer to me, the space between us almost gone. Just as I think he's going to lean down, he reaches up and brushes a piece of my hair behind my ear. His fingers lightly graze my skin, and my entire body weakens. I look up from his grey T-shirt to his face, and that's when his hand rests beneath my ear, his fingers combing through my hair.

He dips his head, bringing his lips down onto mine as my eyes shut. I grasp his sides, allowing him to deepen the kiss as his other hand comes across my back. I can't help but slide my hands up his chest and around his neck before my hands cup the sides of his face.

My legs wobble a bit beneath me, or rather I think they do, but I manage to stay in place.

Suddenly, the door slams so hard into my back that our kiss breaks, and Neal stumbles back, pulling me with him.

"Hey!" Luna calls. "What's in front of the door?"

I jump away from Neal as the door opens wider.

Luna's confused expression greets us, and she slowly looks from Neal to me. "You guys all right?"

My cheeks burn. My entire body feels hot, and I'm sure it shows on my face. I can't glance at Neal to see if he looks as flustered as I do.

"Fine, yup," I tell my roommate. "I thought you guys were going to pull everything out downstairs?"

"We are," Luna says, slowly entering the condo. "I just needed to grab some of my gardening stuff." Again, her eyes fly from me to Neal, and she smiles. "What were *you* guys doing?"

"Nothing. Just figuring out a way to get back at Glover," I hope my voice comes out as casual as the statement does, "from what Neal told me."

Luna's clever grin slides off her face, and she looks over me to Neal. "What is it?"

"Uh, she gambles."

I give him a quick glance over my shoulder and find him standing directly behind me, his hands in the pockets of his jeans. Nothing about him looks suspicious.

I really need to work on my facial expressions.

"No way!" Luna exclaims. "Gambling? I can't believe it. You're sure of it?"

"Yeah," Neal replies. "She's put down a few bets for me." Suddenly, his sarcasm is ignited again. "Hilary had the *great* idea of having her followed tomorrow."

"Yes," Luna beams, "that's brilliant! This is so perfect. She's a gambling addict? How ironic too…"

Neal's phone goes off, and we both watch as he answers it, his eyes on the floor. "Hey." A moment later he looks up at me but answers the voice on the other end.

"Uh, yeah I can. Hold on a second…" He puts the phone to his chest. "I gotta take this call."

"Sure." I nod, my hands slipping into the pockets of my jeans. "Whatever."

I hope the shrug I add is convincing.

"It may be a while, so I'll see you guys later?" Neal's eyes bounce from me to Luna then back to me.

My insides churn at the disappointment, but I make no show of it, just nodding again. "Okay, have a good night."

He says goodbye and places the phone to his ear as he rushes past me and Luna. "Hey. I'm here…"

Luna waits until he's gone then kicks the door shut with her foot before turning back to face me, her smile bright and wide. "What exactly were you guys doing?"

"Talking! I told you. Glover gambles."

"Yeah, sure." Luna wags a finger at me, her smile not fading. "But when I got to the door, I didn't *hear* any talking. I heard…nothing. So, what were you guys doing in all that silence? Where you perhaps doing a little bit of…" She purses her lips together and makes kissing noises.

I cover my face with my hands.

Luna lets out a laugh then sings, "I knew it! I knew it!"

"Luna, stop!" I mumble into my palms.

"You guys were making out!" She giggles.

The heat from my cheeks burns into my palms.

After a second, I hear Luna step up to me and pull my hands from my face. "Hil, relax, I'm only being a goof. I'm happy for you, really. I'm excited to hear you guys were locking lips."

"I don't want to talk about it," I quickly shout, taking my arms away from her. I walk into the hallway.

"Oh, come on! Was it at least a good kiss?" she asks, following me. "I feel like he'd be a good kisser."

I say nothing as I reach my bedroom.

"Hilary!"

I turn around to face her and find her pouting a few feet away from me.

"Just tell me."

I sigh loudly, and though I want her to know I'm annoyed, I'm also elated as I think about what just happened. "It was…good." I glance down at my feet and have to bite my bottom lip to stop from smiling.

Luna lets out a snort. "Oh ho, it was so much better than good, wasn't it?"

I step back into my dark room and say, "Good night, Luna," then slam the door.

"I knew you were still into him!"

Chapter Sixteen

I didn't see Neal at all on Thursday, and now that it's Friday, I was expecting my giggly, school-girl behavior to completely dissipate. But it hasn't. I've managed to stop smiling as much, but my heart starts drumming in my chest whenever I think about that unexpected kiss.

Bryson followed Glover yesterday and managed to take two pictures of her placing her bets on the horses. Paulette had Bryson post the pictures on our campaign website instead of sending them through email or hanging posters around the building. Within an hour of them being posted, our hits had skyrocketed, and my green bar had gone up by ten percent. Glover was only leading me by five points now.

Suffice it to say, yesterday had been a great day. Right now, even though it's well past lunch and I'm starving, sitting in this meeting with Jewel and Marco can't even get me down. It certainly has Eli frustrated though. His foot taps on the floor, and his hands grip the armrests of his chair. Whenever I gaze over at him, his eyes squint at the brother and sister. Occasionally, he bares his teeth.

"I do like the movie theme night," Jewel says to me, uneasily glancing around the room. Today's she's in a yellow romper, her hair tied back in two neat fishtail braids. "I just feel like it will be super juvenile."

"There are lots of ways we can make it posh," I inform her with a smile. "We could have—"

"Could you hire paparazzi?" she asks, her eyebrows squeezing together.

"What?" Eli blurts, frowning. "Again with the paparazzi?"

"Yeah…to take pictures of me and my friends walking down a red carpet," she answers slowly as if he is unaware of what paparazzi do.

Eli looks at me, his face reddening.

I can see his neck stiffen. I try not to laugh.

"Paparazzi, Hil, she wants paparazzi…"

"We could hire fake paparazzi for the party," I inform her as I look away from him. I hope she didn't catch his cold sarcasm. The last thing I need is for her to go cry to Sydney.

"I don't want fake," Jewel pouts as she leans back into her chair. "I want real ones."

"You aren't a celebrity!" Eli cries. He hits the armrests with his hands. "I told you that yesterday. And Wednesday!"

"But I will be!" Jewel snaps back at him. "I told *you* that."

My hands come out between them. "Okay, Jewel, I don't think I can get real paparazzi to come out to your party, but I can hire fake ones. Your friends won't know the difference."

"And what happens when they ask about the pictures the paparazzi took that night, huh?" Jewel throws back at me.

"I can— *We* can," I correct, pointing at Eli, "throw them up on some blogs. We know a few bloggers that post about events this company does. It's good free press for us, and the bloggers get traffic to their website, which means more money for them."

Jewel raises her eyebrows, clearly unimpressed, "Bloggers? That's it?"

"Yo, don't diss bloggers." Marco finally looks up from his phone. "If a blogger doesn't like your biz-ness these days, you may as well kiss your product goodbye. If a blogger doesn't like you as an asset," he waves his hand over his sister's head, "then you're old news. Bloggers can make or break you."

Eli looks horrified, but he keeps quiet, for which I'm grateful.

"Er, right, yes," I reluctantly agree with Marco, and the sound of my voice produces an impish glimmer in his eyes that I look away from quickly. I smile at Jewel. "So, do you like the idea?"

She sighs, swatting her hand at me. "Whatever, the fake paparazzi and bloggers are fine."

I grin back at her. "What are we thinking for food? Eli says," I look back on the notepad with Eli's chicken scratch covering the page, "he says you want fancy… fancy…*what is that*?" I ask as I point down with my pen.

"Oh!" Eli's sarcasm whips into high gear as he gives me a tight, horrified smile. "Shit. She wants fancy shit."

I laugh.

"Okay." I look up at Jewel and Marco. "So, what exactly were you thinking of?"

"I know I want waiters carrying around silver plates

with fancy crap," Jewel interjects. "Like super fancy foods. Crab things and snail stuff…"

I'm about to respond with the actual name for both foods when I spot Warren stepping out of the elevator. He looks toward my desk, and when he finds it empty, he looks around the room. I see Jasmine at her desk. She's on her phone, but the moment she sees him, she hangs up on her caller and stands up, adjusting her mini skirt and playing with her glossy hair before hurrying toward him.

"Would you excuse me for a moment?" I ask as I get up from my seat. "I'll be right back."

I rush around the table and out of the room just as Jasmine shakes Warren's hand. She gently touches his arm and lets out a soft giggle.

Honestly, she has no tact.

"Warren," I call as I head their way, moving faster as I get closer.

They both look over at me, but only Warren smiles. "This is a surprise. What can I do for you?"

"I was just in the neighborhood, actually. I'm hoping you and Eli are free for a late lunch maybe?" He rolls up the sleeves of his dress shirt and smiles at me again. "A token of appreciation for doing a good job on the event."

"Aww, too bad you have a meeting, eh, Hil?" Jasmine's pout couldn't look faker if she tried.

She's not wrong. I can't leave a client meeting for lunch with another.

And besides, I don't think I want to.

"Dinner then? A friend of mine just opened up his own bistro by the waterfront, and I have yet to check it out."

I see Jasmine's lips part. "Sounds great, sure. What time?"

Anything to keep Warren away from Jasmine.

"How's seven o'clock for you?" he asks. His eyes shift to the meeting room. "And Eli, of course." The elevator opens behind him, and as two women hurry out, he takes the opportunity to step back toward it.

"I'm sure that will be fine, yes." I nod as our eyes meet. "I'll confirm with you as soon as our meeting is over."

"Fantastic," he smiles as he steps back into the elevator, "looking forward to it."

Neither of us say anything as we watch elevator doors shut, both waving Warren goodbye. After he's out of sight, I look over at her. She's already turned herself to face me, her hands on her tiny waist, golden bangles clanging together as she raises an eyebrow at me. "You know, Hilary, I'm surprised. Flirting with a client? Very unlike you."

"I wasn't flirting with him," I insist. She doesn't have to know about the last few weeks. "I make it a personal rule never to date a client, unlike some people I know."

"A personal rule?" she repeats, ignoring my digs. She lets a hollow laugh escape her glossy lips. "It's a company rule. We *all* have to stick to it. Clients, future and past, are off limits. Conflict of interest and all that."

I refrain from scoffing. If it *is* a rule, then she's broken it several times. That I'm sure of.

"Dinner with Warren probably wouldn't be appropriate." Jasmine sighs, now examining the pink polish on her left hand. "We wouldn't want Sydney to catch wind of you wooing a client in a, well, sexual manner, would we?" Her lips spread into an evil smile.

"Anyway! Have a great weekend. I'm off to the family cottage. Need to brush up on my sailing skills…"

We turn away from each other at the same time, and again, I wonder how a woman like her can truly exist. Sometimes I think she watches too much TV and that's why she's adopted that obnoxious, mean-girl behavior.

As I get back into the meeting room, I find Jewel on her phone near the windows and Marco lecturing Eli about something. "Dude, you need a base tan before you hit the beach. I guarantee you it will stop you from burning. Look, I can hook you up. My roommate Flash works at Tan and Dive on Bleaker street—"

"Your roommate's name is Flash?" Eli frowns.

"Yeah," Marco nods, "we call him Flash because he—"

Eli quickly lifts a hand and shakes his head at Marco. "I don't know why I asked because I truly do not care." He sighs as he looks over at me. "So, what did our client, who can only be described as a reincarnation of Adonis himself, want?

"Your client's name is Adonis?" Marco laughs at me. "What a stupid name."

Eli's eyes widen. "As opposed to Flash?"

"His name is Warren," I tell Marco, and then I frown, realizing it's none of his business. I turn to Eli. "He just wanted to take us out to dinner tonight. At some bistro near Harbor Front to thank us—"

"I hope you screamed yes," Eli interrupts, his smile huge.

Before I can reply, Marco exhales and stretches in his chair. Eli has to swing his head back before Marco's hand accidentally slaps him in the head. "I've seen that place. Right around Club Eleven, which is where I will be tonight. I can swing by that bistro place around nine. You guys can come with me to the club—"

"No!" Eli screams.

Jewel throws him a nasty glare before turning her back on us and returning to her call.

Eli points a finger at Marco. "You are not to come anywhere near us this evening. I won't have your lubed-up, pineapple-smelling abs ruining dinner with us and Hil's future husband. No thank you."

My jaw clenches. "Eli."

"Future husband?" Marco swings his dark eyes from Eli to me then leans into his chair, smiling as if satisfied with himself. "So that's why you've been giving me the stink eye the last few—"

"Meeting's over," I declare loudly.

I motion for Eli to grab the notes on the table.

He squints at me.

Jewel turns, still on her call, and I give her a smile. "I have everything I need and will get the ball rolling on the venues. We'll meet up next week, okay? I'll have Eli call or email you. Have a great weekend!"

I back through the open doorway before she can respond.

I thought about bailing on dinner with Warren and Eli, but Eli made it known that if I did, he would show up with Warren at my place with takeout anyway. Still, as I got dressed, I felt, well, wrong agreeing to go to dinner.

Which I know is ridiculous seeing as all Neal and I had was half a first date and one kiss… But I still feel guilty.

I'll just eat quickly and come home. No flirting with Warren whatsoever, maybe even mention how we are not allowed to date our clients once or twice. Maybe I'll say I'm a bad kisser. Or I'm really mean outside of work.

As I ride the elevator down, it clunks every few seconds. I don't see Neal in the lobby as I begin to cross it. I do, however, see Mrs. James in the mailbox area, and she's stuffing something into my mailbox.

"Mrs. James?" I call out.

She stops and looks over at me, her posture straightening as she comes toward me, holding a letter in her hands.

"What can I do for you?" I ask, smiling.

"I am returning this to you."

She extends the letter to me, and I notice it's unlabeled. Inside, I find the spa certificate Eli sent her. "I must make this clear, Ms. Brandt. I am not one for bribes, and I—"

"It's not a bribe," I interject, a forced smile on my lips now. "It's just a gift."

"As was the wine basket and the musical tickets, I'm sure." Mrs. James' lips come together in a thin line, and she crosses her arms over her grey blazer. "Ms. Brandt, I appreciate it all, but I have to tell you that I still won't be considering you for the museum. Please stop sending gifts my way. Have a fine evening." She makes her way around me, and I bounce back to stop her from leaving. She isn't amused.

"Mrs. James, maybe I could give you a list of my clients to call for referrals? Or you could even call my employer? She'd tell you just how high my approval rating is and—"

"My dear, she's your employer, and I'm sure she wants

you to nab this event as much as you do. What makes you think she won't lie to me?"

"Because she's Sydney LaBeau! She's known for her honesty and hard work, and she would never employ someone who was lazy or mean to their clients," I proclaim. "If you don't believe me, ask your board members. I bet they've heard of her, of *us*. I bet they'd tell you just how great we are."

She pauses, her eyes locked onto mine. "I have several interviews tomorrow with event agencies. I'm very sorry, Ms. Brandt, but the answer is *still* no. Now, please excuse me."

I move out of her way as she passes me and heads toward the elevator. When she pushes the button, the doors open immediately, and she enters silently. I'm about to turn around and head out the door to wait for Eli outside when Neal comes around the corner, giving me a quick nod as he heads toward me. He says hello to Mrs. James before the elevators shut.

"Hey, I was just coming up to get you," he says as he reaches me. His pants are stained with dirt, and there are a few rips in his T-shirt. His forehead is damp with sweat, a few beads dripping down near his sideburns. "I need you to come to the courtyard quick."

I freeze. "Why? What happened?"

He doesn't say anything, only motioning for me to follow.

What now? More termites?

"What is it?" I ask Neal as I walk next to him. "Did Glover sneak in a beaver? Or a woodpecker? Did she plant some pot plants and tell the building they belong to Luna?"

Neal smirks and shakes his head. "I think she's got

enough problems explaining her gambling habits to the building."

I almost forgot about that. I grab his arm.

He stops, turning to face me.

"What is everyone saying?"

He shrugs, wiping the back of his hand against his forehead. "I don't know. Some people think she's playing with the condo board's budget, other people sympathize with her, and someone pushed a gamblers anonymous pamphlet under her door. She's having a meeting in her condo at eight for any concerned tenants."

"Are you going?" I ask.

"Are you?" he counters almost playfully as he begins to walk again. I tag along beside him, and we fall into a comfortable silence. He beats me to the door of the courtyard and stands in front of it as he faces me again. "Ready?"

"Oh, God," my voice shakes a bit. "Okay, just open the door. Rip it off like a bandage…"

He grins and pulls the door open, allowing me to walk in.

I shut my eyes, preparing for the worst. I stretch my arms out as I feel my feet scrape against the pavement and feel the warm, stuffy air around me.

"Why are your eyes closed?" Neal asks, standing right behind me.

"I don't want to see the mess."

He squeezes my shoulder, quickly relaxing me. "Just open them."

I do and am stunned into silence.

There are tiny marigolds patched into the ground, surrounded by tiny white plastic garden fences so nobody steps on them, and blue hydrangeas planted alongside the stone walls. Beautiful green ferns and orange and red begonias are set in several planters around the courtyard. Tall rustic lanterns are planted into the ground, flameless candles lit inside the glass.

The broken stone gazebo is gone, now replaced by a beautiful cabana made from thin silver pipes. Its walls are made of sheer, white sheets that gracefully drape over the four pipes, coming together over the top and creating a sheer rooftop. Patio lights in the shape of Edison bulbs are strung throughout the cabana.

"This looks amazing!"

"Not too bad," Neal agrees.

I look over at him. "Did you do this?"

"Luna did the plants. Bryson found the lanterns and patio lights at the flea market uptown."

"What about the cabana?" I ask, stepping away from him.

"I did that. Wasn't too hard. I went to the scrap yard yesterday morning and picked up the pipes. I had a friend come by this morning and weld them together for me. A few burns here and there, but it's done. Luna put the sheets up. She's gone back to the shop to get some more potted plants."

I glance back at him.

His arms are crossed, relaxed, and he's nodding as he looks around at the courtyard.

"Thank you, for all of this," I say, the corners of my mouth pulling into a smile.

He shrugs. "Team effort."

I take in his appearance, noticing a few welts on his hands and the holes in his clothes. He catches me looking and glances down at his shirt. "Don't worry about it. This is my work shirt."

"Holy shit! This place looks insane!"

I step to the side as Neal turns, and we spot Eli in dark jeans and a dark blue dress shirt at the door of the courtyard. His mouth hangs open as his dark eyes scan the area. "I feel as if I've just stepped into a Nancy Meyers movie."

"Who?" Neal frowns.

"Never mind," I mutter. "Eli, I told you to wait out front."

"I was going to, but your doorman told me he saw you come here," Eli answers as he steps further into the courtyard. He gestures at the marigolds around him. "This is so midsummer night's dream. I just love it." He then gasps when he sees the cabana and rushes over to us, crying out, "How romantic! People could have dinner dates out here! It's like a secret garden. Where did you get it?"

"Neal made it," I say, exchanging a look with him before I grab Eli and try to usher him back to the door. "Okay, let's go."

"You made this?" Eli asks. "Seriously?"

"Wasn't too bad," Neal says. "Had a friend help."

"It's so modern and chic," Eli gushes as he looks back at the display. "I want one."

I finally manage to pull Eli away. "Time to go." As I push him toward the door, I look back at Neal. "I, uh, just have a dinner thing but I'll be back by nine if you could tell the team?"

"By nine?" Eli repeats. "I don't think so. I plan for you to be at this dinner late."

My nerves have reappeared, and my right leg starts to shake as I look at Neal.

"I have a party to go to tomorrow," I say, my eyes shooting fire at Eli.

"What party?"

"Mrs. Toscano's pants party."

Neal comes up to us, his hands in the pockets of his jeans.

I so don't want him to know Warren is who we're having dinner with.

"Leggings," I explain to Eli, "she sells those crazy designed leggings."

Eli nods slowly and asks, "When's the party?"

"At one, now let's go before we're late," I urge.

"Oh my God," Eli laughs, "you can stay out past nine tonight. Besides, I'm sure Warren will insist." He wiggles his eyebrows.

My stomach churns as I feel Neal look at me.

"Dinner with the client, eh?" he asks.

"A little thank you from him," Eli explains. There's a pep to his voice, and it makes my toes curl in my shoes. "Really a nice guy."

"Customary for your clients to take you guys out for dinner?" Neal's question isn't really a question but more of an accusation.

Eli frowns. "Um, sometimes."

"Great." Neal gives him a stiff, forced smile, and a light hit in the shoulder. "Well, you have a *great* time." He walks between the two of us, avoiding looking at me, and disappears around the corner.

Damnit.

"What," Eli's voice is sharp, "was that about?"

I rush after Neal and find him waiting for the elevator. When he sees me, he pushes the button twice.

"I can explain," I blurt, but he doesn't look at me.

He repeats my words from the other night back at me, his tone deep and brisk. "Make it a rule not to date your clients? Unbelievable. Can't believe I listened to a woman who outright stalked me."

"I did not— Okay, maybe I did a little. But look," I choose to drop that argument because I don't have much time before the elevator gets here, "tonight is not a date. I mean, come on! Eli is joining us. It's a work thing!"

He inhales, and his eyes narrow, but he says nothing. The elevator doors ping open, and he brushes past me into the small box. I watch as he reaches over to push the button to his floor.

I don't know what else to say. He looks so angry at me, arms crossed tightly over his chest, his eyes hard.

I brace myself. "Neal, I am not—"

"Forget it. And don't send me any crap."

What?

The doors close in my face, and I hear a shuffling next to me.

Eli clears his throat. "I think he means the baskets and stuff…"

I glare at him.

Eli mouths, *Sorry*, and takes a step back, hands in the air.

I hit the elevator button.

"What are you doing?"

"I'm going to go up and talk to him."

"Okay, what's happening here? What did I miss? Why

do you care if he's upset with you? You aren't dating. You said you don't even like him anymore!"

"I know that," I say.

He motions for me to go on.

I look at my feet. "But that may have been a lie, and we may have kissed the other night…"

Eli blinks. "You guys kissed? When?!"

"Wednesday," I reply.

He hits me hard on the arm, and I gasp. "Why didn't you tell me? I thought you've been all smiles and walking on cloud nine because you finally got that witch Glover. I didn't know it was because you guys kissed!"

"Well, it may not matter now," I grumble and run a hand through my loose curls. "I don't even know if he's going to talk to me now."

"Probably not tonight, no," Eli agrees. "He seemed really mad." He sighs as he watches me rub my temples. "Look, there's nothing you can do right now. Or *should* do just because he's angry. Let's go to dinner with Warren and have a few drinks. You can try tomorrow with a clear head, and when he's calmed down."

I don't want to do that.

"Come on," Eli pulls at my arm as the elevator doors slide open. "Come on, Hil."

"Okay."

Chapter Seventeen

It's hard for me to concentrate on what Warren is saying, but I'm trying. Our entrees were just set down, and I'm on my third glass of red wine. I'm lightheaded and relaxed, and my thoughts are filled with regret. I can tell Eli notices because he keeps giving me looks from across the table. He's even kicked me in the ankles a few times.

The bistro is a lovely place, right on Harbor Front, and of course Warren snagged a table for us on the patio overlooking the still, dark lake. It's a warm night, so the light breeze is insanely welcoming. Tiny lights run over the balcony walls, and there are trellises with beautiful vines bursting through them, leafy with bright yellow flowers.

"So you don't even game much yourself then?" Eli chomps down onto a piece of grilled chicken as he waits for Warren to answer.

"Uh, no, not really. Just solitaire." Warren chuckles. "But I used to when I was a teenager." He then looks over at me, and I feel Eli's shoe tap mine.

"I don't game either," I say to Warren. My bruschetta pizza oozes with feta cheese and tomatoes, the crust crispy and golden, but I can't bring myself to eat it.

I feel bad as I look back at Warren. He looks really good tonight in a pair of dark shorts and a denim shirt that's tight around his arms. The blue in his eyes shines brighter with that coloring. His dark hair flutters a bit in the wind, and he smells of a cinnamon aftershave.

"This would probably surprise you, but almost forty percent of our customers are women." Warren smiles at me.

"Really?"

"Oh yeah." Warren nods as he leans over the table. He picks up his fork and knife, gently setting the fork into the grilled salmon on his plate.

I circle my finger around the stem of my wine glass.

"Women gamers, girl gamers, they're slowly taking over the industry. Year by year, our numbers grow. I think it's fascinating watching a once male-dominated industry phase into becoming more dominated by women. To be honest, the last two games we released hit best-seller status within two weeks. I have a feeling it's because I had female leads, who in turn employed more female writers, designers, and— I'm sorry, this is boring you."

I lift my eyes from my wine glass, noticing the sharp look Eli throws me, and smile at Warren. "No, no it's not. I'm just tired. I think it's great that there are more women interested in the game industry. I don't know much about it, but girl power and all that."

Warren laughs as he puts a forkful of salmon to his mouth.

"This place is gorgeous." Eli lifts his glass of red wine. "And my grilled chicken is so juicy. The seasoning is on point."

"It's pretty nice," Warren agrees. "I'm guessing you

like the wine, Hilary?" He smirks as he watches me take a sip.

I quickly swallow and nod. "Yes, it's excellent."

"Hilary's had a long day," Eli jumps in. He reaches across the table and pushes my glass of water at me. "She should probably drink her water and eat a bit."

"Bad day?" Warren asks as I set down my wine glass. He looks at me so softly that I feel that ping of regret bubble up again.

I think of Neal, and that makes my chest ache a bit.

Get a grip, Hilary. You and Neal aren't dating. It was half a date and one kiss!

But it was a *good* kiss.

"Sort of," I mumble. I pick up my fork and knife and begin to cut through my pizza.

"Your co-worker seemed nice," Warren states, obviously referring to Jasmine.

Eli and I look at each other.

"She's…nice enough," Eli says before putting another piece of chicken in his mouth.

Warren looks from me to Eli then lets out a chuckle.

"She's a monster, isn't she?"

"The worst!" Eli exclaims, a sigh following. "She's awful. She's always trying to undermine Hilary's efforts, starting rumors about her."

"Eli," I caution.

"It's okay," Warren tells me. "I kind of caught that from her today. She offered her future services to me before you interrupted."

Unbelievable!

"I bet she did," Eli mumbles into his glass of wine.

I see the look Warren gives him, and although I'm

feeling tipsy, I'm sober enough to take my chance to tell him about the company rule.

"He just means that event planners at LaBeau and Gilde aren't allowed to date their clients," I explain, "present, future, or past."

Warren nods and looks down at his plate as he cuts into more of his salmon.

"Jasmine breaks the rules all the time," Eli adds loudly, giving me a sly smile. "It's one of those rules our boss overlooks as long as it doesn't cause drama." I bore my eyes into him, but he just looks back at Warren. "So, Warren, are you all set for next Saturday? I can't believe the nineteenth crept up on us so quickly."

I stop myself from putting the piece of bruschetta into my mouth as I stare at Eli.

What did he say? The nineteenth? The nineteenth is next Saturday?

"What?" Eli asks annoyingly when he catches me staring.

How…the *hell*…did I not realize?

I set my fork down on my plate without taking my eyes off him. "Next Saturday is the election."

"The what?" Warren asks.

"Are you sure?" Eli frowns as he gestures toward my half-empty wine glass. "You've had almost three glasses of wine. Maybe—"

"It's the nineteenth."

As if I couldn't feel anymore lower, all I have to do is picture Glover's reaction when she realizes I can't even make it to election night. It makes me slump back into the bistro chair.

"What election?" Warren pries as he raises another forkful of the salmon to his mouth.

"I'm, uh, running for condo board president," I tell him. "Or rather, I have been, and the election is next Saturday night."

"She's definitely going to win," Eli beams. "It's been a tough election, but she recently got a leg up over the competition."

"Good for you," Warren smiles at me as he chews. "I'm sure you will do great at it."

I *can't* miss the election. Glover will use it as a last-ditch effort to undermine me and swing the votes before anyone goes to the ballot boxes. But I can't exactly ditch the evening event of Warren's anniversary party. Not after I begged Eli to take the company picnic.

As Eli and Warren fall into another conversation, I reach for the rest of my wine and down it.

I just want to go home.

Two hours later, I stumble from the cab with Eli holding my arm to make sure I don't face plant onto the pavement in front of my building. My vision is blurry and spins as I wobble. My stomach lurches a bit, but I swallow a gulp of fresh air to stop myself from vomiting.

I hear Eli pay the cab driver, and as he appears next to me again, he grabs my purse and begins to fiddle through it.

"What'rrre you doin'?"

"I'm texting Luna to come get you," Eli mutters as he finds my phone.

I'm tired, and though well past tipsy, I can still process the scene around me well.

I think.

Sort of.

I exhale as I look up at all ten floors of Fairway Towers. "It's suuuch a pretty old school building. One of the prettiest old school buildingsss in the city, donchew think, Eliy?"

"Um, it's Eli," he corrects, visibly annoyed. "And stop talking. You sound like a drunken pirate."

I wheeze at him, shaking my head slowly. "What crawled up your butts?"

"You made a complete fool of yourself tonight," Eli cracks.

I look at him, feeling my face scrunch up, and watch as he throws my phone back into my bag.

He grabs my arm and begins to pull me toward the front doors. "I mean, thank God Warren is so sweet and understanding. He didn't take offense when you called him Adonis—or implied he has a porcelain butt."

"Oh, whateverr…"

He continues yanking me through the bright lobby of my building. So briiight. I have to shield my eyes with my arms. I hear Eli greet Mateo before we continue on toward the elevators. Eli lets me go as he hits the button, and I flop against the wall.

"Heyyy, didn't we have a club party tonight?" I remember as I squint my dry eyes at. I lean over and remove my heels.

"A what? Club party? What are you talking abo— Wait a second. Are you talking about Club Eleven?"

"Yes!" I exclaim with a small giggle. I stand back up and shake one of my heels at Eli. "That's the name."

"Why on earth would we ever go somewhere with that clown Marco?" Eli snaps. He shakes his head before hitting the elevator button a few more times. "Hurry up, stupid old metal box…"

"Oh yeah, Marco!" My laugh is so loud it echoes around the empty lobby, which only makes me giggle some more as Eli places a hand over his forehead. "Hey, Eli, want to know a secret?"

"Normally, yes," he replies, "but right now, I am so livid about your behavior that I can't—"

"Marco and I kissed!"

I throw my hands up, and my shoe flies out of my grip. It comes crashing down between me and Eli.

"You mean you and Neal kissed."

"Noooo," I snort, "no, I mean me and Marco, after Neal vanished!" I make a poof sound for emphasis.

Eli jerks his head back. "Hold on a second here. Are you telling me you and Marco made out?"

"Kind of, sort— Hey, my shoe!" I shriek as I bend forward to pick up my black heel. "How did it get down there?"

"Hey, focus!" Eli snaps his fingers in my face as I get back up, wrenching the shoe from my hands. "You and Marco kissed?"

"Yes, sir," I nod then scratch the back of my head. "Lonnnggg time ago."

"Oh. God." Eli's hand covers his mouth as he gasps. "Please tell me that's all you did."

"Duhh!" I punch him in the shoulder, and his eyebrows drop. "He's my boss's nephewww! It was like a one minnnute kissss at her birthday thingy."

The elevator *finally* pings signaling its arrival, and I let out my own 'ping!' as the doors swoosh open. Eli throws me a look as he shoves me into the elevator and pushes my purse into my hands. He then bends over and grabs my other shoe, throwing both of them into the elevator with me. "Luna's waiting for you on your floor. I'll call you tomorrow. You have so much explaining to do. Urgh! I can't even process all of this right now."

I click my tongue and shake my head at him. "Eliy, you have to stop being such a snobby baby. Reallyyy!"

His mouth drops open, but the elevator doors close between us before he can say anything else.

I nod to no one. "Good. Where's my shoes?"

❧

And sleep I did.

I wake to a dry mouth and taste metal, all sharp and grody. My head is pounding, a sharp zing of pain hovers behind my eyes and across my forehead. It makes me groan.

"Well, good morning, star shine," Luna's voice floats my way, her giddiness instantly making me cringe. "Or should I say, good afternoon…"

Afternoon?

Slowly, I peel my eyes open and find myself face up on our couch. The curtains are drawn over the balcony windows, keeping the living room as dark as possible.

A blue ceramic mug comes into view above my head. "It's a little after twelve if you're wondering."

I do my best to push myself up on my elbows, the pain reeling inside my scalp, and I hiss through my teeth. "I have never been this hungover *ever…*"

"Eli said you drank a bottle and a half of wine at dinner without even touching your food."

I moan and push myself up into a sitting position, slowly taking the mug Luna holds in front of me. I smell the earthy aroma, and my mouth suddenly craves it. I take a big gulp of the strong coffee, thankfully it's not too hot, then set it down on the coffee table.

"You better drink a bottle of water and get into the shower," Luna suggests.

I look up at her and try to focus.

She's in her gardening clothes and a green smock from her store.

"Why?"

"Mrs. Toscano's party starts in fifty minutes," Luna reminds me, pointing at the large wooden clock hanging on the wall over our TV. "You can't miss this one. You know she can get her groupies to vote for you, and those six votes could be all we need to win this."

"Right." I exhale. "Forgot about that."

I rub my hands through my hair and scalp, feeling Luna's eyes on me the entire time.

"Why'd you get so drunk last night?"

I'm about to say I don't know when everything comes to me in flashes. The courtyard, Neal's cabana, Eli, and then Neal again. My stomach drops then gurgles.

I think I'm going to be sick.

"Ohh, God, I got drunk at dinner with Warren." I slowly gaze up at my roommate. "Ohh nooo…"

"Yeah," Luna smirks, "you did. Eli said he was a gentleman though, and he helped you into a cab. He doesn't think Warren will say anything to anyone."

"How do you know?"

"Eli called you four times this morning. I picked up the

last one. He told me everything that happened last night." She laughs and runs a hand through her short blonde hair. "Did you really tell Warren you think he has a porcelain butt?"

I gasp and jump to my feet, panic setting in. "Noooo! NO! Did I say that?"

She laughs again and nods. "According to Eli, yes. You also called Eli a snobby baby or something…"

I grab my face, blood rushing to my head, the stabbing headache only getting worse. "I can't believe this. I can't believe I was such a loser!"

"Relax, Eli says Warren really didn't hold it against you. He said he understood that you're under a lot of stress and needed to let a load off." Luna's tone is soft, reassuring, and I look up to see her smiling at me. "Look, right now there's nothing you can do about last night. So just take an Advil and hop into the shower. I'm making French toast. After you shower and eat, you'll feel better." She pulls me from where I stand and pushes me slowly into the hallway, both of us stepping over my black heels. "Hop to it!"

God bless extra strength over-the-counter medications.

By the time I shower, eat the breakfast Luna made, dress, and leave my condo, my headache is down to a dull throb. Downing those two water bottles and two cups of coffee might have helped too.

I ride up to the eighth floor, stifling a yawn, which is ridiculous seeing as I slept for almost thirteen hours.

Mrs. Toscano lives in 801, the largest unit on the

eighth floor. As I knock on the door, I can hear the chatter of her groupies.

She opens the door with a wide smile made very visible by her super bright pink lipstick. Her curly black hair is pulled up in a chic bun, and she's in a white tunic and a pair of those Saucy Leggings, bright pink with red hearts all over.

"Hilary!" She throws her hands up and pulls me in for a quick hug. "So happy you could make it! Come in!"

"Happy to be here."

Her entire living room has been taken over by Saucy Leggings. They're in bin upon bin, and dozens of them are draped over the couches. Some even hang on the walls. Leopard print, cheetah print, some are tie-dyed, and a few are plain colors like red, black, and orange. I even see one with the faces of the Muppets.

In the middle of the room are eight chairs, six of which are already occupied. The glass coffee table is full of treats —fresh fruit, pastries, and a veggie platter. There are also three bottles of red wine.

I hold back a shudder.

"Please, have a seat." Mrs. Toscano ushers me to one of the nearest chairs. "Everyone, you know Hilary Brandt. She lives in 603. She's running against Mrs. Glover for president."

They all say hello, and I greet them back, recognizing all of them as tenants of the building.

Mrs. Toscano takes a seat next to me and smiles again. "We were just going to go through the new products, so you've made perfect timing. Have you ever worn Saucy Leggings?"

"Can't say that I have, no."

"They will change your life," she swears, a hand over her heart. "I literally wear nothing else but these leggings. For everything, *everywhere*."

That seems excessive.

"I gave away all of my *other* brands after I bought my first Saucy pair," the woman on the other side of me adds. She grabs her thighs, and I see she's wearing a pair of leggings that are grey camouflage. As I glance at all the women, I realize they all wear leggings in different designs.

There's a pair with skulls, a pair of flaming red and orange ones, there's even a pair with pineapples. I'm the only one in jeans.

"You'll get so addicted!" A young woman across from me laughs. She sits cross-legged on the chair and rubs her calves. Her pair of leggings are tie-dyed blue and yellow.

It's like a cult.

"The best thing about them is that they are one size fits all!" Mrs. Toscano smiles. "Size 1 is size 00 to 8, and size 2 is size 10 to 16 and size 3 is—"

How is that one size fits all?

"What size are you?" she suddenly asks, looking down at my waist and legs. They all do, and I feel anxious as they size me up.

"Er, a size 6, usually."

They all let out a laugh, and Mrs. Toscano places a hand on my shoulder. "Welcome to the size 1 club!"

This is weird.

"Okay, enough chit chat." Mrs. Toscano waves her hands so everyone settles down. She then gestures at me, her eyes on the other women. "Let's show Hilary some of the new leggings we have this season. Maybe we can pull her over to the dark side."

She begins to show me a whole bunch of different designs and even makes me stand. I hold my hands up as she holds pair after pair against me, motioning at my waist, my thighs, and even my butt, talking about tuck and seams and fabric bunches.

Within an hour, I have four different pairs of Saucy leggings sitting neatly in my lap. A black pair, a grey striped pair, a pair with hundreds of cat eyes, and a pair covered with red roses and thorns.

"There are so many benefits to selling these," Mrs. Toscano tells me. "You get thirty percent off, and when you hit your sales goals, you get a free pair of leggings. They even have cash awards for sellers who meet target. Once a year, they have a big competition where the five top sellers get to go away on a two-week cruise!"

Whoa.

"That sounds so fab," I say. "What a great company."

Mrs. Toscano smiles proudly.

This party isn't so bad. They're actually really nice. And okay, so they're obsessed with leggings, but there are far worse things to be obsessed with.

"It's so cool you came to our get together," says the blonde with the tie-dyed leggings. "Mrs. Glover never comes."

"Well, Saucy Leggings aren't her thing, Jenny," Mrs. Toscano replies with a smile.

"She just doesn't like the MLM organizations." Jenny rolls her eyes, leaning back into her chair. She looks at me again. "She thinks it's a cop-out to prevent tenants from getting business approval from her."

"She thinks the leggings are tacky!" someone else claims. "I overheard her telling Mrs. Temperman that once."

Perfect.

"I think they're cute," I remark as I look down at the pile on my lap. "Creative and certainly comfy."

And I'm only half lying. They are really comfy.

"You don't mind tenants selling products with an MLM organization?" asks the woman on the other side of Mrs. Toscano.

I shake my head. "No, I don't really see it as any of my business. Unless it directly affects me or the building, I wouldn't care who decided to sell stuff like this."

Mrs. Toscano exchanges a smile with the woman who asked me that question.

"Would you be opposed to people selling their products, say, at markets or the neighborhood garage sale?" the same woman asks me.

"No," I almost laugh at the question, "I wouldn't care."

"Mrs. Glover won't let us sell Saucy Leggings at the farmers market. Says it's against the rules to put Fairway Towers as our primary address for our business," Jenny tells me. "I think it's really because she hates them."

"Hilary," Mrs. Toscano turns to me, her hands clasped together on her lap, "I don't think I have to tell you that this group is very excited that you're running against Mrs. Glover. Most of us have never experienced another president in this building, and most of us are sick of Mrs. Glover's closed mind."

"Tenants should be able to sublet if they need to. I mean, the president can have a say on who the subletter is, but we shouldn't be denied that right," says the woman next to me. "Friends of mine are able to sublet anytime they need to at their condo building. They just need the president to approve the subletter."

"Right, okay." I nod.

A woman with wavy chestnut hair waves at me. "Ava Miller here, 306. How come we don't allow trick or treaters in the building anymore?"

"Some people find children annoying," Jenny says to Ava. "I don't want them knocking on my door nonstop."

"Fine, but we used to be able to give out candy downstairs," Ava says, looking back my way. "Then three years ago, Glover stopped me from sitting downstairs and handing out candy! Ridiculous."

"Apparently, the building used to have a yearly tenants' party," the woman next to me tells everyone. "One night in the summer, dinner and drinks, a nice party for everyone who lived here."

"I could do that," I say. "I work as an event planner."

"And the Halloween candy thing?" Ava asks.

"We can start up the lobby thing again," I answer. "Maybe we could get other tenants involved. I don't understand why she took that away. Seems unnecessary."

"Exactly." Ava nods once.

"Wonderful." Mrs. Toscano places a hand on the back of my shoulder as she looks at everyone. "Didn't I tell you all that Hilary would be a perfect addition to our little club? And as condo board president."

Club?

"We meet every second Saturday from one to three p.m." Jenny smiles my way. "We take turns bringing snacks, and we are each allowed to bring guests!"

"We decided on just you today." Ava reaches down for

a muffin. "Figured it would be best not to divide our attention with potential customers."

"I'll shoot you an email about the benefits of joining the team, more info on the discounts, and the conventions Saucy Leggings have for their sellers." Mrs. Toscano motions at the box at her feet full of leggings. "The styles you'll be able to start with, the selling manual, all that."

Wait, what?

They want me to sell these things?

Oh, no.

My lips part to politely decline the request, but Mrs. Toscano claps her hand loudly. "Well, I think our time is up today, ladies, we'll get together in two weeks." She raises her index and middle finger up in the air. "Everyone bring a guest or two. I need the final guest number emailed to me by the Wednesday before."

A ringing comes from the kitchen, and Mrs. Toscano stands, giving me a quick smile. "Let yourself out, Hilary, I have to get that." She rushes from me but then stops at the doorway to her kitchen and glances back. "You have our full support for this election, one hundred percent. As well as our spouses."

Yes!

I smile at her. "Thank you so much!"

I scurry from Mrs. Toscano's condo as fast as my feet can carry me, figuring I can politely deny the option to join her team of sellers after the election. It's not that I think she'll hold my refusal against me if I decline to her email before then... It's just... Well, it's better not to chance it.

With my leggings against my chest, I enter the elevator before any other tenants can join me and hit the close button. The ride down is short with the elevator stopping on floor seven.

Neal's floor.

I hold my breath as the doors open, but it isn't him. It's the couple who live down the hall. They enter quickly as I remember what happened last night. Taking the chance, I leave the elevator and walk down to his door.

I press an ear to the door and give it a listen.

Nothing.

Dropping the leggings at my feet, I kneel and fish out a pen from my purse. At the bottom of my bag are several crumpled receipts. I find the least crumpled one and begin to write my letter.

Dear ~~Mr. Turner~~ Neal,

I just wanted to thank you once again for the beautiful cabana you made for the building. I am very appreciative of it.

I also wanted to clarify a few things that may have confused you.

1. That dinner was a business dinner with a client. Strictly work related.

2. Eli was only joking about Warren and me! He doesn't really want him to be my husband...well, okay, he does, but I am so <u>not</u> into that idea.

3. I really hope you'll come to the courtyard

opening. It would give me a chance to explain everything if anything needs further explanation.

4. Unless you want to talk to me before the courtyard opening. In that case, I'll add my cell phone number below.

Thank you for taking the time to read my letter,
Hilary

There. Perfect.

I stuff it under the door as best as I can. Once it's gone, I let out a sigh and push myself off my feet.

Chapter Eighteen

I have to hand it to my team. The courtyard looks impeccable.

Garden lights are strung from wall to wall, white and gold paper lanterns hang from the cabana, and bunches of assorted flowers now live in metal pots that Luna brought over from the store. And it smells *fantastic*.

Luna had spent the better part of yesterday cooking with Mr. Tweed and Bryson. She made everything from vegan chili to chicken Alfredo. Mr. Tweed made his late wife's mini lemon tarts, and they were just as big of a hit as they were at the garage sale. Mrs. Dorst made dozens of cookies and brownies, laying them all out on neat little silver tea trays next to Mr. Tweed's lemon tarts. We had made two punches, one with alcohol and one without, orange slices and cherries floating in each punch bowl.

It seems like everyone in the building is down here.

Except for Glover, the Tempermans, and Neal.

I watch the Zhengs enter the courtyard. Mrs. Zheng's smile grows as she points at the tiny garden lights over our heads, making me grin a little. Her husband just nods.

"Hey, so I went through your grandfather's records." Luna gives me a quick glance as she pours some punch into a cup. "I found some pretty cool stuff in there. You should have a look at it tonight."

We're standing behind the punch bowls, Luna in a blue denim dress that hugs her curvy figure well, and me in a blue off-the-shoulder dress that flares out at the waist.

"I'm not an oldie music fan," I say.

"No, I know." She nods. "Buuut I found something in there I really think you'd like."

I laugh and glance back toward the door, watching a few more tenants wobble inside. "I don't think so—"

"Just look at it tonight! And will you stop looking over at the door every two seconds?" Luna snips. "You should be mingling, securing any last votes. The election is six days away."

"I'm not looking at the door every two seconds," I snap back as I cross my arms over my chest.

"Yes, you are. Who are you waiting for?"

I don't answer as she fills a few more cups full of the non-alcoholic punch. I help her by setting paper cups in rows.

After slipping Neal the crumpled note under the door, I expected to hear from him, but now it's eight o'clock on Sunday night, and there's been nothing. I haven't even heard any scraping across our ceiling.

I hear Luna sigh. "Hil, he's not coming."

We stare at each other, and she gives me a small smile, one of those "poor you" smiles that would make any person want to rip their hair out. "Neal. He's not coming. Bryson texted him yesterday morning, and he said he had an emergency and was going out of town."

"Oh." I hope my casual shrug hides the stab of

disappointment that hits me square in the middle of my chest. "Oh, I don't care. I wasn't even—"

"Hil, I know you like him, but the thing is… After what happened Friday, he kind of overreacted. Don't you think?"

I frown at her. "What do you mean?"

"You're not dating. You went on half a date and kissed once. You told him it wasn't a date with Warren, just a dinner with a client. It's his problem if he doesn't believe you. Furthermore, did you forget what happened on your half date? He pushed you out of his apartment without an explanation and then disappeared for three months without telling you what was going on. Has he even told you since he got back why he had to rush off in such a hurry?"

I glance down at the paper cups in my hands. "Well, no, but I never asked either."

"You shouldn't have to ask," Luna says. "He should have told you why he took off. He doesn't really have the right to be upset with you about a dinner with Warren, if you ask me."

"I one hundred percent agree!"

We both look up from the table to see Eli standing across from us, donning slacks and a checkered bow tie that stands out against his black short-sleeved dress shirt. His eyes are solely on me and less than jovial.

"I believe," he begins, "you owe me an apology."

"I'm sorry for calling you a snobby man baby."

"It was snobby baby." Eli frowns. "*Snobby baby.*"

I pick up one of the cups filled with the alcoholic punch and hand it to him. "Well, I'm sorry, and thanks for coming. Where's Jacob?"

He takes it and nods his thanks. "You're very welcome.

And he's at home. He's been so whiny lately, I needed to get away." I watch as he takes a sip of the punch, cringing as he swallows. "Whoa. This is strong. Who made it, and what is in it?"

"Mr. Dorst made it. I think its rum."

Eli nods and places a hand to his hip. "So, we're still upset about the whole Neal thing, are we?"

"Not *upset*," I say, "just, iffy about it is all…"

"He's left anyway," Luna tells Eli, "so it doesn't matter. We probably won't see him for another three months."

"He left again?" Eli shakes his head at me now. "Okay, no, that's it. I know I was all about you getting a man, and I know I was *all* about Neal and his return, but I have to tell you that it is now time to seriously begin entertaining thoughts about Warren. Hilary, he's kind and funny, wears the hell out of those suits, and he likes you. You should give him a chance. Even after that drunken stupor of yours Friday night, he emailed me Saturday asking if you were okay."

Oh.

"He did?"

"That's so sweet," Luna coos.

"Who cares if he's a client," Eli tells me. "Next week, he won't be. And if something does happen between you two, well, then he can always go to another event agency."

"That's a big account we would lose. You know Sydney won't be happy, and according to company rules, she could fire me over that."

Eli scoffs and takes another drink of his punch. "She would never fire you. She needs you. And if she does hint at it, I will just throw all of Jasmine's rendezvous in her face. I know she's been looking the other way for years because the clients keep coming back."

Luna elbows me in the ribs and motions to the doorway. "Don't worry about that right now. Look who's here."

I look to the door and see Mrs. James surveying one of the large fern plants against the wall. She smiles at it then glances around the room, stopping when she spots me. I give her a small wave, and to my surprise, she motions me over to her.

"I thought we lost that account," Eli whispers.

"We never had it." I sigh. "Excuse me." I hurry around the table and make my way toward Mrs. James. I do my best to smile, though it's hard to after that conversation with Luna and Eli.

Maybe they're right.

I should just cut my losses with Neal. I mean, he hasn't treated me that well. He ditched me on our first date, and I have yet to find out why. He wouldn't believe me on Friday when I told him it wasn't a date with Warren. Now he's disappeared again?

Last time, I stewed for three months. Then he came back, and after talking with him a few times, I stupidly let myself fall back into lust.

Meanwhile, Warren has been, well, kind of great.

As I get to Mrs. James, she slowly smiles, gesturing around the courtyard. "It turned out quite lovely, Hilary. Job well done."

"Thank you, Mrs. James. It was really more my team than me, if I'm going to be honest."

"A good boss is someone who can delegate well to their teammates," she says, "who can imply their vision easily and make sure the job gets done to everyone's satisfaction."

"Er, yes, right."

The silence that follows is immediately awkward, and we avoid each other's eyes. I look at the plants near the door, and Mrs. James' eyes drift to the sky. But after a moment, she clears her throat. "I had meetings yesterday with a few event planning agencies."

I had spent the weekend trying to forget that.

"How did they go?" I ask as I cross my hands over my chest.

Her eyes flutter back into mine. "Fine. Well enough."

This is agony.

"Who did you meet with?" I find myself asking, though Lord knows why. I must like the emotional torture.

"D.D. Events, Coral Planning, Elite Designs, and Wilson's Corporate Events."

I know a few planners from three of the four agencies she mentioned. Elite is one of our top competitors. We're always going after the same clients, sometimes they win and sometimes we do.

"You know them?" Mrs. James asks.

"I do. Elite Designs is right at the top. They've got some very talented planners with them, and they have some great connections, especially in the exotic plant world."

"What about Wilson Corporate?" she asks, her eyes narrowing.

"Uh," I bite the inside of my mouth as I think about them. "I worked a joint account with them a few years back when I was starting out. They specialize more in weddings, bridal showers, baby showers, but they've been trying to branch out to more corporate events. Alyssa, the woman who owns the company, works a lot of the events herself. She knows her stuff."

"And D.D.?"

"I haven't actually heard of them before. They must be new," I admit. "Coral Planning has their own flower department, which makes it easier for the planners and clients to nab flower arrangements at a discounted price. They work a lot with art galleries and festivals downtown."

The corners of Mrs. James' mouth tug back a bit, and I realize she's trying not to smile.

"What is it?"

"Very admirable, giving me such great reviews of your competitors."

"Well, I still think LaBeau and Gilde is better than any of them, but I might be biased."

She smirks. "Indeed."

It's silent and awkward again as we stare at each other.

I can't take it.

I motion at the courtyard behind me and take a step back. "Well, thank you for coming down. I really appreciate it. Please help yourself to some food and drinks."

"Hilary," her voice is suddenly very eager, "I know you have to mingle with the tenants so I'll be quick." I step closer again, and she goes on. "The meetings yesterday did not go well. D.D.'s planner was very pushy, and the planner from Wilson's Corporate seemed to be all over the place with her ideas. I found that Coral Planning and Elite Designs had no grasp on what the Elnor exhibit opening is supposed to convey."

"Do you want me to give you the names of some other agencies? Maybe some smaller ones?"

She frowns, crossing her arms over her chest. "No, dear girl, I'd like to take you up on your offer to meet with me."

My mouth explodes into a smile as I lurch forward and grab her arms. "Really? I would love to! You won't be disappointed, I promise."

She unfolds her arms and adjusts her posture, holding a small smile over her nude-colored lips. "I'm sure I won't be. How about Tuesday morning? Ten a.m.?"

"I can do that, yes!"

And if I can't, I'll make it possible somehow.

"Very good. You know the way to the museum?"

"I do, yes."

"I will see you on Tuesday morning then." She nods, her smile never leaving her face. "I look forward to it."

"Me too!" I squeal.

She smirks as she passes me, and I turn to watch her walk over to the cabana where a bunch of our neighbors have gathered.

I don't believe it!

I have a meeting!

I rush back to Eli and Luna. He's helping her fill punch cups and frowns when he sees my smile. "What happened to your sour puss attitude?"

"We have a meeting with Mrs. James!" I blurt, fanning myself as I realize how the sudden adrenaline has awakened me. I'm boiling.

Luna lets out a small shriek. "No! That's fantastic, Hilary!"

"Are you serious?" Eli gawks. His hands freeze mid air, cups hovering just above the table.

I nod over and over again. "Tuesday morning at ten."

"H-how? I thought she was dead set against hiring you."

"Her meetings yesterday were awful," I explain, "so she's giving me a chance."

Eli drops the cups on the table and grabs my hands. "Okay, you cannot blow this."

"I know," I let out a long breath, "I know, and I won't."

"We nab her, and we'll have a very good chance at nabbing every *single* event the museum throws," Eli reminds me. "And we get featured in *CityDaily*."

"You do?" Luna's eyes widen. "Even my boss reads that business magazine, and she's a hippy."

Eli squeezes my hand, and I squeeze back. "Hil, we have to know everything about this guy whose exhibit they're featuring."

"Right. Tomorrow, we spend all day researching."

"Good plan," Luna agrees. She then breaks me and Eli apart and gestures at the tenants in the courtyard. "But tonight, you have to mingle. There are a few undecided voters down here, and we're down to the wire. As of a few hours ago, you and Glover were neck and neck. She's leading by only three points now."

I pat down my hair. "Okay, I'll go mingle."

Eli sets out the last of the cups and hurries to me, looping his arm through mine and pulling me close against him. "Don't think I'm letting you off the hook after what happened Friday."

"Eli, now's not the time to talk about Warren," I

declare, a smile coming over my mouth as Mrs. Zheng waves at me.

"Not Warren, Marco. We need to talk about Marco." He squeezes my arm, perhaps in anticipation of me running away from him, which I definitely have the desire to do. "First of all… I cannot believe you."

"Okay, I can explain." I wave at a few tenants as we near them and ask how they're enjoying the food. As we move along, I hold a smile while explaining to Eli through a clenched jaw. "It was a few days after Neal went AWOL, and I was upset. I drank too much at Sydney's birthday party, and we made out in the closet in her front hall. It was only for a few seconds because I got a hold of myself."

"Lord, have mercy." Eli exhales sharply. "No wonder he's been acting so weird toward you. I thought it was just a random crush or something."

We stop talking as I get to the Zhengs and listen to Mr. Zheng's idea to charge guests of the building for parking.

As we move along, Eli hisses in my ear, "I can't believe you didn't tell me! That was three months ago, and you kept that a secret?"

"I'm sorry, all right? I was embarrassed! I felt like such a loser after that happened, so I didn't tell anyone, not even Luna."

"I'd feel like a loser too if I locked lips with that man," Eli admits. He then sighs at me. "I forgive you, one-time mistake on your end."

My faces bunches and the cloud of shame looms over me again, the one that makes my stomach turn. "Actually, it happened twice."

Before he can react, we reach another group of tenants,

and for five minutes, we listen to their praise for the courtyard, give ideas on how to expand next year's garage sale, and even fundraising tips on how to raise money for an indoor pool that could take over the laundry room.

"What is the *matter* with you?!" Eli exclaims as he pulls me to the side. He looks at the sky as he lets go of my arm. "I swear if you tell me it went beyond making out, I will scream."

"It didn't, no!" I shudder. "God, never. I stopped myself both times."

"You clearly can't stay away from the man."

"I was drunk both times, Eli!" I whine. "I was impaired. I wouldn't have done it sober!"

"Is that why you've been such a hermit?"

"Sort of. The last two times I had too much to drink, I made poor decisions."

"Honey, that's everyone."

I chuckle. "Too true."

"Well, when was the second time?"

"Last month after dinner at the Soko House when we all got drunk off sake. I was waiting for a cab, and he followed me out and kissed me."

Eli pretends to bless me with the sign of the cross. "You need to smudge yourself."

I push his hands away and roll my eyes. "Go help Luna with the punch. I need to mingle."

Chapter Nineteen

Eli and I spent Monday researching Elnor Haur. We found out he was the son of an immigrant investment banker that killed himself after Black Tuesday, which spiraled Elnor's mother to move the family back to Europe. After growing up rather poor, he turned his anguish into moving paintings and sculptures. He died in 2013, but his son and grandson have turned his art into a traveling exhibition. The Royal Museum is going to house his work for a full year.

Though his pieces are rather grim, people flock to see it, and he brings in millions of dollars wherever the pieces are showcased.

"And you have a detailed list of ideas for the event? What about ideas for events to bring people back to the museum when the hype dies down?" Sydney looms over her desk, elbows straight, hands together as she looks from Eli to me. She's in an orange and pink wrap dress, spiked bracelets on her thin wrists, looking like a work of art herself.

We're in her office, and it's nearing the end of the day. To say that Sydney is ecstatic for this meeting tomorrow is an understatement. She's been checking in on me and Eli all day, offering advice and a suggestion here or there. She even bought us lunch so we wouldn't have to leave our desks.

"The artist's birthday is six months from now. I have ideas for Mrs. James on how we could celebrate it." I nod, smiling. "Including a private event after the museum doors are closed for the evening, with only a limited number of guests able to purchase tickets. I'd have to work with their PR department, but I don't think it will be a problem."

"There's also the International Day of Painters," Eli adds, looking down at the notes on his lap. "We thought we could have an open house that day for the exhibit and work with caterers to create a menu with food named after his paintings that people can purchase."

Sydney smiles at him then gazes back at me. "It seems you have everything under control."

"I have it all printed out for her." I place a hand on the thin file folder on my lap. "I also pre-approved a slight price decrease for future museum events. I didn't think you'd mind…"

Sydney raises an eyebrow at me, but she smiles. "Ballsy of you. How much of a discount?"

"Ten percent."

Sydney nods. "Doable. If that doesn't appeal to her, raise it to fifteen."

"Discount was my idea," Eli reveals.

Sydney pulls her elbows off the desk and leans back into her chair. "And like I said, Corrine at *CityDaily* will be delighted to do a spread about the event as well. You should mention that to Mrs. James tomorrow just for good measure."

Eli's smile extends from ear to ear at the mention of *CityDaily*.

"Now, get home and finish preparing," Sydney says, her eyes falling to me. "I want you to call me the moment you've finished the meeting. The *exact* moment. You hear me, Hilary?"

I nod, a smile coming over me again, and get up from the chair. "I will call straight away."

❧

I fly home, my spirits soaring.

I know exactly what I'm going to say to Mrs. James tomorrow. I even told Eli that I'm going to the meeting alone. I want a meeting without any of Eli's pizazz. Everything about Mrs. James and the museum is still on such uneven ground, I need the meeting to go perfectly. Without a hitch. Without any of the drama and exuberance Eli can possess.

I take the elevator up, shaking my head at the clinks and clangs, deciding that if I win on Saturday, my first mission is to fix this bloody elevator.

With my folder of notes for the meeting against my chest, I walk to my condo and find the door propped open. I freeze, hearing a jumble of murmured voices on the other side, so I listen in.

"There is no way we can hide this from her. I don't see how."

Luna's voice.

"This is a low blow, even for Glover."

Bryson.

"What did you all think would happen?" Paulette. "Since we exposed Glover as a gambler, she's been in hiding. I knew when she didn't hit back right away, she was planning something major. I just didn't think *this* would be it…"

My mouth is suddenly dry, and my stomach drops.

I don't even know what happened, but I know it's worse than I can imagine.

I hear Luna grumble. "This is bullshit. This can't even be true. Hilary would never do this."

"Where did it go out?" Bryson asks. "Via email?"

"In every single mailbox," Paulette answers, "except all of ours."

Again, Luna groans. "Shit, shit, shit…"

"The election is five days away. Maybe if we can make her rally like crazy before then, she doesn't have to find out," Bryson suggests.

"It's going to be the first thing they'll ask," Paulette reports, "you know that."

I hear Luna swear again before demanding, "So, what should we do, then? Any ideas?"

My heart almost hurts against my chest as I take a shallow breath, lick my lips, and push the condo door open.

All three of them jump. Bryson's eyes drop to the floor, and Paulette looks away from me as she crosses her arms over her chest. Luna's smile is so forced, it makes me instantly irritable.

"You could just tell me what she did."

Luna exchanges a quick look with Bryson.

"Tell me. Just rip it off like a bandage. What'd she do? Did she accuse me of murder? Did she say I'm part of a massive cult? That I sell puppies to animal testing farms? *What* could she have possibly said about me that nobody wants me to know?"

Luna draws in a breath and walks up to me, her hands out in front of her. "Okay, don't panic but she put a flyer into everybody's mailbox—"

"Except ours," Bryson carelessly interrupts, nerves shaking his voice a little bit. "Like, nobody on the election team I mean…"

"What was it?" I ask looking from him to Luna.

"She said you had an affair with your boss's nephew to further your career."

I turn to stone.

This is worse than being accused of murder.

This is far, far worse.

I'd rather be accused and found guilty for a murder I didn't commit.

"Hil?" Luna's expression billows into one of worry, and she steps closer to me. "Are you okay?"

I blink.

"We know it's not true," Paulette declares as confidently as she can. "We know you would never mess around with someone to get a promotion or whatever."

"She's grasping at straws," Luna adds with a stern nod. "I mean, she has nothing. The gambling accusation and cat thing were too big, and she hasn't been able to handle it well. All she did was have an emergency meeting Friday night to try and convince tenants she didn't use any budget money and that going the day before was a one-off. I don't think many people believed her."

Somehow, though my legs are jelly, I manage to get myself to the couch before I drop down. The folder falls onto my lap, and my purse slides off my arm onto the floor, dropping with a thud next to my feet.

My shoulders lurch forward, and my elbows fall to my knees. I drop my face onto my palms.

"Give us the night," Bryson says, "and we'll figure out something to hit back with—"

"No, just...stop."

How the hell did she find that out? Nobody knows. I told nobody except Eli, and that was three days ago. How the hell did she find out about Marco?

"We have to come up with something," Luna says. "Telling people it's not true isn't—"

"It's not...not true," I blurt into my palms, my voice sharp and high. "Sort of..."

Silence fills the room.

"What do you mean it's *sort of* true?" Luna finally asks.

I peel my face off my palms and look at each of them. Paulette shakes her head, and Luna looks nervous, her brows coming together. When Pax jumps up on the couch next to me, I barely give him any notice.

I sigh. "I did kiss my boss's nephew, but it never went past that. I was upset about Neal, and I was drunk both times, but it never helped my career. My boss never found out—"

Luna groans loudly. "*Both* times?"

I don't hear what Paulette mutters to Bryson, but he shushes her.

"I swear," I tell them slowly, "nothing helped my career. It was just a stupid, stupid mistake, and I didn't tell anyone because I was embarrassed, I *am* embarrassed, and I don't even know how she found out!"

"You sure you didn't tell anyone?" Luna presses.

"I just told Eli Friday, that's all."

I drop against the couch, and the folder slides off my lap, hitting Pax in his fluffy side rolls.

The sight of it jolts me upright.

Mrs. James.

I snatch the folder up and get to my feet.

"Where are you going?" Luna cries as I hurry past her.

"I'll be right back!"

The short ride to floor eight has me swaying back and forth on my toes.

My blood runs cold as I pray Mrs. James hasn't seen whatever Glover put in the mailboxes.

Glancing up at the ceiling, I press my eyes shut and whisper. "Please, God, if you make it so she doesn't see it, I will start going to church, I will start donating and volunteering. I'll even get baptized."

Once the elevator doors swing open after a jerky stop, I rush out to the left, running down the hall until I get to Mrs. James' door. I pound on it with my fist and wait.

As the door cracks open, I take a step back and work at controlling my breath.

Mrs. James' high eyebrows greet me. Her stare gives me a slight shudder.

"I can explain," I begin.

"That seems to be your catchphrase, my dear," she cuts me off, arms coming across her chest. In her black robe and curlers, she looks like Minnie Castavet from *Rosemary's Baby*. "And truthfully," she goes on, "I really don't care to hear any more of it."

"But it's not true! Just like the other rumor about my work ethics, none of it is true!"

She rolls her eyes before staring into mine. "My dear, I called your place of employment, wishing to give you the benefit of the doubt. I asked for the nephew of your boss. When I asked him about you, he seemed very pleased with himself that he knew you. He even made some lewd comment about almost 'hitting that,' and I knew the rumor of your tryst had merit to it."

Ugh! I'm going to kill Marco!

I shake my head. "But it wasn't a tryst! I just kissed him twice by accident."

"By accident?" She frowns at me. "Did you fall onto his lips?"

"Mrs. James," my voice shakes as her name rolls off my tongue, "I would never sleep my way to the top. I was just in a very bad place, emotionally, and I did a stupid, stupid thing. I mean, haven't you ever done something incredibly dumb because you were angry or upset or—"

"No, my dear, I simply cannot risk it." Her head shakes quickly as a hand comes to the edge of the door. "If members of my board were to get wind of this, I'm afraid I could lose my placement, and that I will *not* toy with. Consider this my official word: I will not be hiring LaBeau and Gilde to help with the Elnor exhibit. Have a good evening."

I'm stunned into silence as she slams the door into my face.

As I force myself to walk back to the elevator, I feel a bit numb. Even pushing the button gives no feeling to my fingertips.

What am I going to tell Sydney?

I can't believe I screwed this up so badly.

My pulse slows.

I can hear the *thump thump* of my heart in my ears.

My eyes begin to burn.

Great, now I'm going to cry.

The doors to the elevator slide open, and I step inside, stopping when I see Neal. He's in black pants and a dark dress shirt beneath a blue blazer. I'm shocked by the lack of jeans and T-shirt. He hasn't shaved though, a five o'clock shadow coming in strongly.

He gives me a quick look, then his eyes drop down to the phone in his hands.

I step in as the doors come toward me and turn my back to him.

Never have I ever felt this awkward before. My toes are even clenched in my shoes.

Could this night get any worse?

There's a loud clinging, and the floor rumbles beneath my feet. The elevator jerks to a stop, and I almost go flying into the metal doors.

Perfect...

I reach over to the emergency call button on the panel and hit it quickly.

"It doesn't work," Neal says. "It hasn't worked in over a year."

"Of course," I mumble, but for some reason, I push it a few more times.

"I just said—"

"I heard you," I snap.

"Bad day?"

He sounds sincere, and for some reason, it gets my blood boiling. I can feel my face warm up. "It was fine."

I suddenly recall the note I slid under his door, and my eyes close.

"Aren't you supposed to be out of town?" I ask, my voice sharp.

"Back for a few days. You dropped something."

I turn back to see him bending over, picking up a sheet of paper. He gives it a quick glance before he hands it back to me. I assume it's part of the James file, and I stuff it into the folder I'm gripping.

"And you're welcome," he says, scoffing a bit.

I feel my body spring alive. Words whip out of my mouth, "I didn't ask you to pick it up, okay? But thank you. Thank you for picking up my stupid piece of paper. I don't know what I'd do if you didn't pick up that paper. Thank you *so* much."

He scowls at me. "Jesus, I'm guessing this is because of what was in everyone's mailbox today. Maybe you should be more careful—"

"I'm not asking for your advice," I hurl, "you gave up that right on Friday night, so just keep things to yourself from now on." He opens his mouth to reply, but I throw a hand into the air. "Conversation over."

"Hey," he snaps, "just because you did a stupid thing and got caught isn't a reason to—"

"A stupid thing?" I repeat. "You're right, I did a stupid thing. I did a really stupid thing because of *you*, which makes me feel even stupider." His eyebrows rise, but I'm on a roll now. "I'm not saying this is your fault, I'm just saying— You led me on. You made me think you really liked me, and I went on a date with you, which I thought was going great, and then you shoved me out in the middle of it. You up and leave for three months, and I'm left feeling like a huge loser and hating myself for liking someone so much that after half a date. I was heartbroken. And you didn't even have the decency to tell me why you disappeared!"

He runs a hand through his hair, avoiding my eyes.

"I did a stupid thing after a few drinks, but I never ever did any of that to further my career. I would *never* do something like that, and people who know me would know that."

I feel my grip on the folder loosen, and it drops, the papers scattering on the floor between us. "I would never sleep with anyone to get a promotion—not a client, not a relative to my boss, nobody! But hey, that doesn't matter because Mrs. James thinks I'm a tramp, and there goes my chance at a massive event." I have to blink as tears quickly fill my eyes. "Running in this stupid election has just ruined things for me over and over again, and I can't do this anymore. I'm not cut out for this, and I hate everything about the last few weeks, and I hate living here—"

The ground beneath my feet shakes, and the lights above us flicker, silencing me. A few piercing clanks break the silence, and the elevator begins to move again. Just as slowly as ever.

Neal stares at me, scratching the back of his head.

I can't bring myself to look at his face. It's then I realize my cheeks are damp, and my body has practically seized up. My shoulder blades ache from the tension.

I wipe the tears under my eyes as the doors pull open next to me. I don't even care that it's Neal floor, I hurry out. I can take the stairs down one flight.

Chapter Twenty

"Hil, exactly how long do you plan to stay in there?"

"Forever."

"Have you gotten up at all today?"

"To pee."

Luna drops down on the bed right next to my feet. "Your phone is flashing with over ten missed calls and text messages."

My head is buried between two pillows, my duvet wrapped around me like a burrito. "I don't care…it's all Eli, I checked. And my boss."

"Have you eaten at all today?"

"I'm not hungry," I lie.

The truth is, my stomach has been growling for hours, but I couldn't bring myself to roll out of bed and spend any time in the kitchen. After how I reacted in the elevator last night, how I spewed out a racket of unsteady emotions at Neal, I feel more humiliated than I have in years.

I can't believe I cried in front of him.

Not just cried… *Screamed.*

My shoulders move toward my ears as my body tenses from the memory. I can feel a jittery spasm forming in my left calf.

"Come out of there and let's talk," Luna whispers.

"I'm fine."

"Did you call your boss at least? To tell her you weren't coming in?"

"I emailed."

"Don't you think this is all a bit…melodramatic?"

"Yes, but I don't care."

Her sigh is laced with frustration. A second later, the duvet is pulled from around me, a gust of air sending goosebumps across my skin.

"You have to get up, Hilary. It's been ten hours since I left for work, and you're in the same spot. *Ten hours*."

"I don't care."

"Stop saying that," she snaps. "I know you. You care."

I smoosh my face into the mattress. "Not anymore."

"It's not the end of the world, Hilary."

"The entire building thinks I've slept my way to the top," I remind her as I finally lift my head up for a bit of air. "Glover has ruined me."

"So what? None of them are your clients!"

I roll onto my back, resting my head on a pillow. My eyes linger on the ceiling, but I can see Luna standing next to my bed. She's in jeans and a white T-shirt, her shop smock over her front. She's pointing at the crate against the wall, the one full of my grandfather's old records. "Did you look through those like I told you to?"

"No."

She walks over, pushing her short hair off her face, and pulls a stack of paper out from in between the records. "Hilary, I told you there is important information in this crate."

"I don't care," I sigh, very annoyed.

She throws the paper on my stomach, and I jerk my head up, my chin resting on my chest awkwardly. It's a stack of opened envelopes tied together with elastic. "Look at it. It involves Glover."

"I don't care anymore." I push the letters off me.

Luna bends over to retrieve them. She drops them onto my collarbone. "Stop saying that and just read them. Now."

I push myself into a seated position, my legs close to my chest. "Why?"

Luna scratches the top of her head, creating a mess of curls. "I told you how I was looking through our stuff after the robbery, right? Well, I found these. I know I shouldn't have started reading them, it was none of my business, but I saw a letter addressed from Glover to your grandfather postdated about three and a half years ago. So I opened it and… Okay, she had an affair with your grandfather while she was married."

I let out a croak of laughter. "Please, Luna."

"I'm serious, Hilary. It's right there in those letters," she points at the bed, "in her own handwriting. She talks about their secret rendezvous and says your grandfather reminded her of an older Jimmy Stewart, and she had never felt that kind of connection with anyone her entire life. Kind of nauseating if you ask me. But it's there. She goes into details about their late-night dinners while Harry, I assume that was her husband, was away. She writes to him about looking forward to their secret walks. She signed most of them 'Eternally yours.'"

That can't be true.

My grandfather would never get romantic with a married woman.

Glover would never do that.

I've blinked at Luna about seven times, my head tilted to the side. The confusion that roils inside me must show on my face.

Luna bends over, her hands landing on her knees, and she narrows her eyes at me. "Hil? Are you all right?"

"I don't… No." I shake my head as my legs straighten out. "No, there must be some mistake. It must be someone else you're confusing with Glover."

Luna stands back up, a haughty chuckle escaping her small mouth. "Oh, believe me, it's her. In one of the letters she writes to him she says she was considering having him off the board as people may get suspicious."

This— No.

No.

I feel my stomach tingle a bit, either from hunger or disbelief, I'm not sure. Maybe both.

I manage to swallow despite a dry mouth. "My grandfather would never do that."

"I know this must be hard for you." Luna sighs, her face softening. "I know how close you were to your grandfather. But everyone has secrets, and everyone does stupid things." She gives me a pointed look. "Our grandparents, our parents. We're all human." She shrugs before going on. "We've heard the rumors about Glover's husband, notorious workaholic, rarely home. Maybe she was lonely? And your grandfather was a handsome man, even at almost eighty." She motions at the picture of my grandparents hanging in the hallway outside my room. "Maybe they were in love like Glover says in her letters."

I recoil, my face twisting as if she had just forced lemon cubes into my mouth. "He would never love someone like Glover. She's mean and heartless and thrives on destroying people. My grandfather was loving and funny and kind. She'd be the yin to his yang. Mr. Tweed even said that while he was on the board, he and Glover never got along!"

"Opposites attract," Luna tells me. "Happens every day."

He wouldn't—

This is wrong.

Luna must be confused.

I snatch the letters from their place and rip off the elastic band keeping them in their bundle.

Luna backs away toward the door. "I'll leave you to it…make you something to eat."

"Uh huh," I mumble, yanking open the first letter.

She clearly misread things.

My dearest June Bug,
I cannot wait to be alone with you again…

I don't know how long it took me, but when I was finished, I just sat there staring down at the large pile of torn envelopes and colored papers around me, ever so thankful they kept these letters PG.

June bug. He called her his June Bug. She called him her Shining Knight.

I would have thrown up if my stomach had anything in it.

"Hey…" Luna stands in the doorway, a plate of what smells like scrambled eggs and toast in one hand, a glass of orange juice in the other. "I figured breakfast for dinner is in order tonight… Also, Eli's here. I paged him up."

I barely register what she says, my eyes still drawn down to the letters. "I can't believe this…"

"I know," Luna agrees, expelling a deep breath. "I was stunned for hours afterwards. I didn't know whether to tell you or leave it. I decided to let you find out yourself."

"It seems like they carried on for a while," I tell her as she sets the food down on the end table. "Do you think," I glance up at her, "do you think they were doing their thing when he died?"

"Maybe. Who knows."

We both stare at the letters, unable to move.

Luna finally breaks the silence, stepping up to the bed and picking up some of the scattered letters. "Okay, so, now that you've read them, what do you think we should do with them?"

"Burn them?" I'm half joking, of course, but as I think back on all the XOXOs and smoochie comments, I realize it's not a bad idea.

"I think we should use them," Luna says, looking straight into my eyes.

"What do you mean?"

"I think we should use them. Expose her. Let the whole building know about her affair." My eyes widen, and Luna nods her head. "It's only right, Hilary! Look what she did to you. You said yourself she's ruined you. The entire building thinks you slept your way to the top. Do you realize how this could work to our advantage? If we expose her as an adulterer, that means she's a liar. Then people will think she lied about you sleeping your way up the ladder."

"She *was* lying," I remind her, "I didn't do that."

"Yes, I know, but… You know what I mean." She waves a letter in her hand. "Let's photocopy these and distribute them. All over the building. Tonight. Right now!"

A heaviness pulls in my chest, and it makes me uncomfortable.

"I don't know…"

"Oh, come on! Hilary, she deserves this, and you know it."

I bite the inside of my cheek.

An affair like this is, well, it's life-ruining for someone like Glover.

I mean, it's *juicy* gossip. There are enough traditional people in this building who would demand her resignation —or who would definitely swing their vote my way.

What would her children say? Wait, does she even have children?

This is the big one, I can feel it, and deep in my bones, I know I could use this.

So why the hell is my entire body shaking?

"Let me think about it," I tell Luna.

"What's to think about?" Luna drops the letters on the bed.

"My grandfather. I mean, everyone here loved him. If people find out about this, what are they going to think about him then?"

"We could black out his name! Anything that gives a hint that it was him."

That would solve that problem, wouldn't it?

Still…

"I don't know, Luna."

Someone clears their throat, and we look to see Eli standing in the doorway. He's in a pair of skinny jeans, white dress shirt, and thin black tie. His hands are on his hips, his dark eyes fixed on me. "So you haven't been ravaged by the plague or hit with scarlet fever I see. It's just a case of the melodramatics."

"Pot calling the kettle black," I say.

Eli wanders into the room. "Eleven phone calls, Hil! I had to tell Sydney you got a terrible case of food poisoning! She's been wondering what happened with the meeting with Mrs. James."

"You didn't tell her?"

He points at me. "That's your bit to do. But you should know, Jasmine's started spinning her rumor mill again. Something about a nervous breakdown, jilted by a client..." He must see my face drop because he quickly adds, "Sydney didn't believe her though. I don't think anybody did but that tart in HR... Anyway, Sydney's just confused, says you not showing up and sending her such an obscure email at six a.m. is unlike you."

It is unlike me.

All I said was 'Can't come in today, so sorry, Sydney. Taking a personal day.'

Eli crosses his arms over his chest. "She wants to meet with you tomorrow morning, the second you get in. I told her you'd be there."

The thought of facing Sydney tomorrow is too much to bear. I had lied, said the event was basically mine. I said it was a for sure thing. Now I'm going to look like a complete failure, a liar, and a fraud. But I can't miss work again, and I can't prolong the inevitable.

Eli motions at the letters. "What's all this?"

"Letters between Hilary's grandfather and Glover," Luna replies, a snarky smile coming over her lips. "*Love* letters. They had an affair."

Eli's mouth drops open. "No. Shut up. No!"

I touch the letters with my fingertips.

"I'm trying to convince Hilary to use them against her before this Saturday."

Eli grabs my ankles tightly. "Yes! Hilary, you have to! You have to!"

I wiggle my ankles out of his grasp and swing my legs over the edge of the bed. Letters crumple beneath me as I slide off the bed. "I haven't decided if I will yet."

"What's to decide?" Eli throws back. "She has everyone in the building thinking you slept your way into your job! This is too good of information to pass up."

"I just need to think about it," I tell them both. "I'm going to go shower then come back and eat. No more talking about the letters."

Eli shrugs and drops down on my bed, turning on his stomach as he reaches for the letters. "Fine, but I'm reading them."

❧

I head into work early on Wednesday so I can get settled at my desk before anyone else arrives—including Eli and Sydney. I spend hours trying to find leads through my connections. Any prospective clients, big fish, who need a planner either now or in the very near future. I find nothing but a rumor from my go-to florist about the mayor's wife possibly needing a planner for a correspondence dinner.

By the time Eli arrives, I've exhausted myself and am slumped over my desk.

"When did you get here?" he asks.

"Seven thirty," I mutter, my head in my hands. "You didn't happen to bring me a coffee, did you?" I open my eyes and swing myself toward Eli's desk.

I spot a coffee tray in his hand with two paper cups in it. He's dressed as if he came off a runway, but there are visible bags under his eyes, no concealer.

"Thank you."

I wait until he gets situated and hands me my coffee before asking, "What's wrong? You look like you hardly slept."

"That's because I did hardly sleep," he reports, dropping down on his chair and letting out a quick yawn. "I broke up with Jacob last night."

I burn my throat as I swallow my coffee down too quickly. "What?"

"I should clarify… I *tried* to break up with him last night." Eli points a finger up as he reaches for his coffee with the other hand. "I tried for hours and hours and hours. He wouldn't let me off the phone. Kept giving me reasons why we should work out our issues, yadda, yadda." He takes a loud sip of his coffee and happily exhales after he swallows. "I'm going to need these on rotation every forty-five minutes today. He kept me on the phone 'til two thirty. And when I woke up, he'd texted," Eli reaches for his phone and reads out loud, "'We good, honey?' To which I replied, 'We broken up, honey.'"

I scowl. "That's harsh, Eli. He didn't deserve that."

"Really?" Eli raises his eyebrows at me. "Well, did you know when his sister asked him to find an event planner for an after party during Fashion Week that instead of using you, he went to Elite whatever? Even though he knew he would get a discount from us. He did it because he thought our last two events prior lacked spunk and courage."

"Jerk off!"

"My thoughts exactly." Eli nods as he takes a drink of his coffee.

"Why didn't you dump him back then? Why'd you wait 'til now?"

"He tried to tell me that I needed to tone down my style," Eli snorts, "coming from a man who doesn't know what socks to wear with dress shoes…"

"Hilary?"

Somehow, we both missed Sydney's arrival. She stands in the doorway of her office, wearing a bright yellow cardigan over a lavender patterned dress, a large Starbucks coffee in her hand.

I feel my wobbly smile as I start to talk. "Hi, Sydney, I—"

She shakes her head sharply to cut me off and raises a hand at me. "No, no. In my office, five minutes."

I feel myself relax a bit as a smile appears on her face, but something about it isn't as soft as it always is. It's stiff, forced.

Eli and I watch her disappear into her office.

"Uh, oh," Eli whispers.

"Hilary! How are you, darling? Feeling all right?"

The patronizing tone can only belong to one person.

I spin in my chair and find Jasmine standing in front of my desk, a large rose gold Kate Spade bag hanging off her arm. Her look is solemn as if she's genuinely concerned for me. "Feeling okay?"

Oh, riiight. Her "nervous breakdown" comments Eli told me about.

"I'm fine. Just a case of food poisoning."

Jasmine points a finger at my head. "Hmmm, I believe you. It shows on your face."

"Nothing shows on her face!" Eli exclaims. "Go to your desk, leave us alone."

But Jasmine ignores him, her eyes swooping toward Sydney's closed office door. "She was very upset yesterday before she left the office. I heard it's about you. Something about a possible nervous breakdown." She then laughs, pushing some hair off her face. "You know how the gossip mill runs here."

"You mean *your* gossip mill," Eli corrects.

Jasmine locks eyes with me. Her stare is so intense, I feel as if she's trying to read my mind. I crinkle my forehead as I slowly bring my coffee to my lips. "Nope. Not a nervous breakdown, just food poisoning."

"Well then," Jasmine's grin returns, but it's as unwelcoming as all the others, "glad to have you back." She shimmies away from us and drops her bag on her chair, immediately lifting the receiver to her desk phone.

"Who do you think she's calling?" Eli asks.

"Is the rumor about me having a nervous breakdown really that bad?" I ask him. "I mean, on a scale of one to ten? Should I write an email t—"

"No! For God's sake, no more emails, no more letters." Eli groans. Then he gestures to Sydney's closed office door. "Just get in there and beg forgiveness."

My legs feel like jelly as I push to my feet. They tingle from my toes to my calves.

I feel as if I'm walking into a sauna.

I knock on Sydney's door.

"Come in."

And I do before I lose my nerve. I push the door open, run inside, and slam it shut behind me. When I turn around, she's behind her desk, hands folded over her large desk planner.

"Have a seat," she tells me, and then she waits, watching as I sit down across from her. "Tell me, how is Mrs. Sarris's event going? It's tomorrow, isn't it?"

Mrs. Sarris?

"Um, it is, yes," I nod, "and it's going great. Eli is going to be going through the final checklist today."

She looks down briefly before locking eyes with me. "She's pleased with everything?"

Wait…why are we talking about Mrs. Sarris?

"I'm confused," I confess. "Aren't we here to talk about Mrs. James?"

"Among other things, yes," Sydney replies. Her shoulders then slump a little as she sighs. "Hilary, I received a rather distressing call from Mrs. Sarris yesterday before I left for the day. She's very upset. Says you've been ignoring her over the last few weeks, leaving everything to Eli, whom she has no problem with of course, but he's just a junior planner. She hired *you*, not him. You haven't shown up to the last few meetings or returned her phone calls. She informed me yesterday that this will be the very last event she does with LaBeau and Gilde. Now I know she isn't as big as the Redler account or the James', but her charity work does bring in a good number of referrals for us."

' What?

No, no, no!

"But she's been with us for almost three years!" I almost fall off my chair.

"Then I suggest you remedy the situation immediately," Sydney orders. "You have an excellent reputation in the planning community. You don't want something like this to change that." She dips her head, looking down at her phone, then says, "Okay. On to item number two…"

Item number two? How many items are there?

"Marco."

Oh, Christ.

My stomach knots, but I remain still because she looks up at me with both eyebrows raised.

"I heard a rumor a few months ago about the two of you but I dispelled it just as that—a rumor," Sydney explains, slowly leaning back into her chair. "But then I heard the rumor again last week, so I had to ask Marco. He denied it, and I warned him about starting rumors for attention, you know how he loves attention, of course." I nod, and she doesn't miss a beat. "Then on Monday, he tells me that he got a call about you and that this lady asked him if you had ever had any interoffice relationships. She never gave her name, and Marco foolishly thought it was a ruse of mine to catch him in a lie. Fearing he would get in trouble, he came to me right after the phone call and confessed. He said that you and he had, on more than one occasion, 'made out.'"

I throw my hands so hard over my face I actually slap myself.

"I'm so sorry!" I cry. "It was such a stupid thing to do. I hate myself for it—"

"Hilary—"

"I was just in a bad place! I was feeling rejected, and both times, I had too much to drink—"

"Hilary—"

"And I didn't mean to do that with him—"

"Hilary!"

I look up at her, parting my fingers so I can see through them. I'm sure I've smudged my eye makeup something fierce. I can't make out her expression though.

"You won't be getting in trouble for this," Sydney informs me. "Both times, it happened off company property, and Marco advised me you both knew it was happening. I thought about suspending you both, without pay, but then I'd have to suspend another well-liked planner, and I can't afford to do that right now." She glances past me, and I assume she's looking at Jasmine. As she brings her attention back to me, she points a finger my way. "But, let this serve as a warning to you if you should ever entertain a relationship with a fellow employee again..." She looks away from me, her voice dipping a bit as she adds, "It could get very messy, very fast. Trust me."

"I promise. I won't ever do anything like this with anyone again." I raise my hand and cross my index and middle finger.

"Good," Sydney smiles, "but do me a favor and speak to Marco about it when he gets back next week. He seemed pretty upset when he told me he realized there was nothing between the both of you. I gave him the rest of the week off to collect himself."

I hold back a scoff. I'm so sure he was *that* upset. He's probably laughing about his paid leave.

"My nephew," Sydney sighs, "can be a bonehead, but he has a heart of gold."

"Er, right," I hope I sound convincing as I agree with her, "yes."

"Now," Sydney pulls herself from her softened state and looks at her phone, "last item on the list. Mrs. James. Where are we with that? Did you manage to make it to the meeting yesterday or did you have to reschedule because of the food poisoning?"

She's giving me an out. I can tell her it was rescheduled and try again all week to get a meeting with Mrs. James. If nothing happens, well, then I can just tell Sydney next week that I— Oh, forget it. Mrs. James is lost.

"She won't hire us. Err, she won't hire *me*," I admit, and as the words roll off my tongue, my entire body feels like it could collapse into the chair.

Sydney's face falls. "What? Why? I thought it was a sure thing!"

I can't tell her that the final nail in the coffin was Mrs. James thinking I slept my way to the top. I just can't.

"She just…" But I have no lies left to tell, and I realize that I don't have the energy to come up with a new one either. "We never had the account, Sydney. I'm sorry. I should have told you the truth, I shouldn't have been so confident I'd get it. I tried to woo her—a bunch of times—but ever since this condo board election began, things have just popped up and driven her away…"

"Condo board election?" Sydney frowns. "Are you running?"

"Against this tyrant of a lady who rules with an iron fist. I'm still losing, so it's all been to shit."

Sydney is quiet, and I force myself to look up from my feet. She's looking at me, her eyes narrow. After a moment, she sighs and sits forward, setting her hands over her desk again. "Well, if we never had the James account and you have tried everything to get it—"

"I have, yes, everything."

"Then we just have to move on, don't we?" she concludes. "I'm very disappointed in this turn of events. I never expected it from you, my dear."

Ugh, just kill me.

"I know, I'm sorry," I say again. "I'm so disappointed in myself."

Sydney nods then motions for me to get up and be on my way. "Let's fix this mess with Mrs. Sarris and make sure the Redler event goes as smoothly as possible, shall we?"

"It's all I'm going to focus on this week," I tell her. "I promise."

"Good." She watches me turn and head to the door. "Oh, and Hilary? We should never hate ourselves for being confident. We just need to learn how to separate the ego from the confidence. It's the ego that blinds us."

Chapter Twenty-One

By Thursday morning, I have lined all my ducks in a row. I will attend Mrs. Sarris' event and stay from open to close today. I switched with Eli for Warren's anniversary party. He'll be attending the evening formal event, and I'll be at the barbeque. I'm hoping that would squash any of Warren's romantic ideals by ripping apart the holier-than-thou image Eli has painted of me. This whole ordeal with Mrs. Sarris and Mrs. James has thrown me a good reality check. I won't ever take my job for granted and will start treating it just as serious as I had before. I won't falter, not even for a rich, kind-hearted, good-looking man who most women would think I'd be an idiot for dropping.

Oh, God, please don't make me regret this decision.

I push all pleas to God aside and focus on what's in front of me—Mrs. Sarris, who I've been begging for forgiveness for the past three hours, but to no avail.

"I'm just asking for one more chance, one more, Mrs. Sarris. I know I dropped the ball during this event, and I promise not to do it again."

She doesn't look convinced. A single dark, bushy eyebrow rises above a wide blue eye. She's tied her black hair back into a bun on the top of her head and wears the signature bright-red smock embroidered with the words "Grecian Ladies Charity Bingo Luncheon" on the front.

We stand next to the bingo caller, the bingo cage loaded with small white balls.

I suddenly see the irony of what I just said.

"I've just had a lot of personal stuff pop up, and I foolishly let it affect my work. If, uh, if it makes you feel better, I also had it affect a few other jobs of mine…"

"It does not," she remarks, arms crossed over her chest.

I exhale.

To my left, I can see Eli fending off Mrs. Sarris' niece, Athena. She's in a tight yellow dress for the occasion, though it's more of a dress for a night out. After two years, she still hasn't realized that Eli is gay.

The Kaapo Greek Hall downtown has always been a go-to for charity events, Greek related or not. It easily fits three thousand people and has beautiful white marble pillars throughout. The bay windows overlook Trinity park, our city's version of Central Park, just a few miles smaller. Swarovski chandeliers light up the room, and marble statues pop out from the walls.

Today, it's filled with hundreds of long rectangular tables, and women of every nationality compete for some of the insane prizes offered. There are two big screen televisions, one weekend away in wine country, a week-long cruise, and a boatload of gift cards.

"It looks like you've had a fantastic turnout," I say, really grasping at straws now.

"More people than last year." Her voice is still flat.

"More people than last year?" I repeat, looking back at her. "Really?"

She eyes me suspiciously.

"So the newsletter giveaway worked then? That's the only thing we did differently this year."

"Yes…"

Maybe I should play this a different way. Pleading isn't exactly working.

I take a breath and stand directly in front of her. "Look, Mrs. Sarris, you've been with me for, what, three years, right?"

She holds her glare. "Yes…"

"In three years, we've done how many events together? About six events a year, so that's eighteen events. Eighteen events that have gone smoothly." Her arms uncross at my certainty, and I continue on. "Eighteen times I have been at your beck and call without fail. Eighteen times your events have had fantastic turnouts. Eighteen times I have never failed. *Eighteen times.* What happened here, this event, was one mistake—"

"Mistakes."

"Mistakes," I agree, "but, it's one time out of eighteen that I've made these mistakes. One time out of eighteen that I failed to be right by your side the entire time. I left most of it to Eli, who you have to agree knows his stuff when it comes to this industry. He has answered every email, every phone call, shown up promptly at every meeting in my place. When I knew I couldn't be there, I made sure to send the best, and the best is Eli. I made sure you were taken care of and everything you wanted was done. I should have been there more often, and I'm very sorry for that. I don't think it's fair you dump LaBeau and Gilde because of my one, tiny mistake. I let several personal problems get in the way, and I won't ever do that again."

Her eyes bore into me, and she stands so still, I think I may have stepped over the line. But she throws her hands up in the air and smiles at me. "Of course I won't dump you!"

Her strong hands pull me into such a tight embrace, it kind of hurts.

"Oh, well, thank you."

She pulls back but keeps her grasp on my shoulders as tight as before, and her entire stony face has melted back. "You are sorry. I can see it all over your tired face."

Mrs. Sarris pats the side of my face and smiles again. "You are too young to look so tired, child. Come. Tell me what problems you have…" Her arm slips around my shoulders, and she pulls me against her, walking me away from the BINGO table.

"Oh, uh, they're nothing, really," I say, "just little stuff…"

Her eyebrow rises at me. "Little stuff is what made you drop the ball?"

"No." I let out a hefty sigh. "I'm running for condo board president, and the woman I'm running against is really awful. She's been playing dirty this whole time."

"Ah, yes, I know how nasty those can get." Mrs. Sarris balls a hand into a fist. "You must fight back!"

I push her fist away from my face. "I have been, but it hasn't been working. Now she has the entire building thinking I slept my way into my career."

She breathes in sharply through clenched teeth and shakes her head. "Ah ya ya."

"And I do have something against her that my team thinks I could use to finally bring her down, but I'm unsure of whether I should use it."

Mrs. Sarris nods and removes her arm from my shoulders. "Drugs."

"What? No, not drugs."

She winks at me and taps the side of her nose with a finger. "Ah, mafia hit."

Good Lord.

"No! No drugs, no mafia, nothing illegal," I say quickly. "An affair, she had an affair with my grandfather, that's all."

"That's all?" Mrs. Sarris repeats aghast, her hands flying to her chest. "An affair is not 'that's all,' Hilary. They are like a spider web." She begins to intertwine her fingers as if she's about to knit or something. "They pick person by person apart, trickling down the line from the unsuspected to the children to the parents to the careers, even to the—"

I cut her off as my stomach spins. "I know that. It's why I haven't decided whether I should use it. Even if it could help me win."

I run a hand through my hair as I turn to look at the room. I see Athena wandering around, her head cocking left and right. Eli's nowhere in sight so I assume he's hiding from her.

"Now, now," Mrs. Sarris steps back up to me and pulls me against her encouragingly. "You don't want to win that way. Winning that way is the coward's way. You want to win honorably, and if you must lose, then you lose honorably. But at least you can keep your head high…" She wags a finger in my face. "Your head will not be held so high if you reveal her secret. Let it weigh heavily on her conscience, not yours. Now come, if you don't get some Moussaka now, there won't be any left!"

I decided not to use the letters.

I came home late Thursday night and tucked them back into the crate, which I shoved into the back of my closet. Then, knowing I'd be up before she would on Friday morning, I left a note on Luna's door. I warded off her phone calls the rest of the day as Eli and I checked and double checked everything for Warren's event the next day.

Eli would be at the hall at twelve on Saturday to oversee setup as everything was being delivered. Since the barbeque portion of the day is starting at eight a.m., I had to be up at five just to get to the campground and oversee the setup required there.

It's a hot morning, and I'm already sweating in my jean capris, the company barbeque T-shirt, and a black baseball cap. Having my hair up in a ponytail is doing nothing to cool me.

At seven thirty, Luna had already called me twice. By the third call, I decide to answer. I can't avoid her forever, and even if I could, the election is tonight. Throughout the day, tenants are able to come down and vote in the event room. The tally and results would be at six p.m.

"Hi."

"You know, you really have to stop ignoring phone calls. You have no idea how annoying that is."

"I'm sorry, but I've been busy. And I didn't really want to argue about not using the letters between Glover and my Grandpa again."

"Oh, believe me. I won't be arguing with you about

that. It's too late to do anything about it anyway. I just want to make sure you'll be here by five at the latest."

"I told you, Luna, I don't know if I'll be able to make that work," I remind her. "The event ends around four. By the time I get home and shower, I'll be lucky if I'm there by five forty-five."

"Leave early! Hil, you can't miss the vote! You can't do that to your voters—or to this team. It'd be really shitty of you. You're going to disappoint all these people who support you and worked hard—"

"Ha, I can just add them all to my growing list of those I've disappointed," I remark.

"I'm serious, Hilary. I know your job is important, but this is important too. People are counting on you to be here, to be present. The people who voted for you want to see you here. God, think about what will happen if you win and you aren't here? Glover will demand a recount, and people will be so mad they'll vote for her—"

"Okay!" I huff. "Look, I'll try really hard."

"Don't try, just be here," she snaps before hanging up on me.

I frown as I pull the phone from my ear.

"Bad news?" Warren sidles up next to me, setting his hands on his hips. He's in the male version of the picnic day shirt, which hugs his toned torso well. His suave hair is hidden underneath a blue baseball cap.

"Oh no, just, uh, my roommate." I smile then slide my phone into the pocket of my jeans.

"Where's Eli?" he asks, gracefully looking around the picnic area.

The park is surrounded by trees, short and tall, bushy and bare. The field of grass, though freshly cut, is spotted with burnouts from the sun's rays. There's a wooden stage beneath a bundle of pine trees, and it's decorated with streamers, balloons held down by weights, and a large grey and black banner that reads "Welcome Families!"

There are three large wooden pavilions in the area. Warren and I stand in the one designated for eating, dozens of long wooden tables that easily seat thirty to forty people are stacked up row by row. I can see the barbeque food truck parking about twenty feet away. It's long and black with red flames crawling up the sides. A pig holding a spatula with a chef's hat is painted above the flames.

"We switched," I tell him. "He just isn't a fan of the whole outdoors thing. He's going to oversee the dinner, and I'm here to manage the events of the day."

"Oh, well, that's all right, I suppose." Warren shrugs then turns away to look around the park. "Everything looks great. I love the bubble station over there." He points to the furthest pavilion where I've set up a candy station, a bubble station, and a few easy games for any children eager to play, including an hourly UNO tournament. Some bubbles are escaping the large bubble wands already, and the automatic bubble blowers I rented are warming up.

"Thank you. This was the first time I had a request for a bubble station."

"Hope it wasn't too much trouble," Warren says, looking at me with a small smile.

"Not at all. Eli was able to pull everything together for the kid's station quite easily."

"He's your right-hand man, isn't he?" Warren smirks as he steps closer to me.

"In work and in life it seems," I joke. "He keeps my life pretty interesting."

"He's an interesting man, that's for sure," Warren pauses, his hands still on his hips. "Always has the nicest things to say about you."

Oh no. Time to set my plan in motion.

"Oh, I'm not that nice." I scoff and wipe some sweat off my forehead. "I mean, I work a lot. *Huge* workaholic. I'm a big pushover. I make stupid decisions based on my emotions. I don't date. I'm a terrible kisser. I should have been a nun. I wear push-up bras for attention."

There. That should do it.

Warren blinks at me. Obviously thrown, he runs a hand across his mouth. "That's quite the image you have of yourself."

Damnit. Did I overdo it?

"But I'm one heck of a planner. One of the best in the business."

"That I believe." Warren nods as he gestures at the campground.

"I better do one last check to make sure everything is ready before the guests arrive," I tell Warren as I take a step back. "Give me a shout if you need me!"

I'm pretty sure I'm going to pass out from this heat.

My entire back is drenched. The fabric of the cheap shirt sticks to me like glue and itches every few minutes. I've wiped the sweat off my forehead onto my arm so many times that the hairs on my arm are sticking.

Oh, God. When is this bloody event over?

I manage to pull my phone from the back pocket of my jeans and check the time. It's almost three o'clock.

According to Eli, everything at the observatory is almost ready.

I have a little over two hours left here.

Except that I'm supposed to be out of here *right now*.

I look down at the spoon I'm holding, a bright white egg resting on top. For the last hour, I've been helping with the egg race, and broken egg is splattered all over my runners.

"How's it going?"

Warren pops up next to me, and for a moment, I realize I had completely forgotten about him. I'd spotted him mingling with his employees a few times, joining them for some games, but we hadn't spoken since I degraded myself this morning.

"Good, great!"

A little girl swipes the spoon and egg from my hand without a word. She then darts off to her waiting parents. I slip my phone back into my pocket and wipe my sweaty hands on the front of my jeans.

"You do look like you're enjoying yourself," Warren remarks. He, of course, has barely broken a sweat. If anything, the dampness on his cheeks just makes him glow. His smile is almost radiant.

I think back on the schedule for the day. "It's almost three o'clock. Are you getting ready for your speech?"

"Delivering in fifteen minutes," he tells me. "Everybody should be out of here by four thirty."

There's no way I'm going to make the election results.

Biting the inside of my mouth, I look around the campsite. It's so loud and busy. I think for a moment about sneaking out. Would Warren even notice?

Of course he'd notice, I scold myself.

Oh, who cares about making it? I've lost this by a landslide. Why should I even show up? So Glover can flaunt her win in my face? So people can throw disapproving looks my way?

"Is everything okay?" Warren's looking at me with a slight frown.

I unhinge myself and smile back. "Fine, yeah."

"You sure?" His eyes glide down to my feet, and I realize my foot has been tapping impatiently in the dirt. "You seem…agitated."

"I'm just…hot," I reply, freezing my foot in place. "Super hot day!"

But his frown only intensifies. "Are you sure you're all right?"

"I could be getting a bit dehydrated," I say as I notice the drink tent across the field. "Maybe I'll just go get a bottle of water."

"I'll join you," he offers. "I wanted to talk to you about something, anyway."

Oh no.

I don't have anything to say, so he just keeps going, his arm brushing against mine as we walk. "I want to thank you again for the great work you've done for me today. It's been a delight to work with you and Eli. I don't think I've ever had this much fun planning anything ever—"

"Oh please. No need to thank me," I say. "It's my job. My profession. I'm a professional and all."

He looks a bit confused, his eyebrows dropping a bit as he looks at me. "Right, well, I was hoping…if you have the time tomorrow night, and have the night free, not that I assume you d-do." He stammers a bit, and it throws me.

He's nervous? "Maybe I could make dinner reservations at—"

"Stop!" I don't mean to practically shout the word at him, but I'm one step away from erratically running away from him.

As he stops and turns to me, his hands go to his hips again, and his face twists into a baffled half frown.

I stare at him and let out a long breath. Even looking so confused, there's a soft aura about him that draws you in. "I'm sorry, I didn't mean to shout. I just— I just can't have dinner with you. I can't date you, even if I like you a little bit, and trust me, I do. I think you're very kind, handsome, and funny. You're totally a catch, but you're a client of mine." He opens his mouth to reply, but I slowly lift a hand. "And I'm kind of interested in someone else, even though," I snicker to myself, "even though we've just been crossing wires since the very first date, and it's most probably, definitely over after I screamed at him the other night, which maybe is a blessing because—"

Warren's boisterous laugh cuts through my words. Now it's my turn to frown as he continues laughing, shaking his head as he struggles to regain his composure. "Hilary, I'm not interested in dating you."

What?

"You're not?" I ask slowly.

He laughs again, removing his ball cap from his head. As he runs a hand through his soft, fluffy hair, his laugh dies off, and he smiles at me. "No, I'm not. I'm actually interested in someone else."

The photographer.

"Oh," I exhale, "the photographer, Tomas whatever her name is!"

He pulls back a bit. "Rosamie?"

"Yes, her. I know about you two."

His laugh returns, and he places his ball cap back onto his head. "No, God, I'm not romantically interested in her. She's just a very good friend…" He jerks his head back a little, and smile spreads over his lips. "Hilary, do you think I'm straight?"

"Wha— Aren't you?"

"No," he chuckles, "no, I'm not straight."

"You're gay?" I sound as if I'm repeating a foreign word.

"I am."

"But you've been flirting with me this entire time."

"No I haven't." He jerks back at my accusation.

"Yes you have! At the cake tasting. And at dinner, you were all touchy. You have always been so nice to me and asking Eli if I'm all right after—"

"I was just being nice! I'm a nice guy. Believe it or not, there are more of us out there than you think." He shrugs, his smile stuck in place.

I yank my hat off my sweaty head.

"Look, I'm sorry if you thought I was flirting with you. I didn't mean to give you mixed signals, I really was just being nice, in a friendly way."

"Right," I grumble as I avoid his eyes.

I'm so stupid! I knew he wasn't interested in me. I *knew* it. Why, oh why, did I let Eli convince me otherwise? I just want to run away.

Warren sighs and steps closer to me. "Haven't you ever been nice to someone for the sake of being kind and had them think it meant more?"

Marco, at least according to Sydney. I still think he lied about how upset he was to get a few paid days off work.

I almost explode with laughter at the irony of this all.

"I may have…" I admit, and after a second, I look back up at Warren. "Well, okay, but then why were you just going to ask me out for dinner tomorrow? And why did you ask me out for dinner on Friday?"

He scratches the back of his head, suddenly all awkward, and swaying a bit. "Well, I do like you, and I thought you and I could be friends."

I can't help but smile.

"And also," he clears his throat and shrugs as he looks up at me. "I was hoping you could put in a good word for me…with Eli. You're his best friend and all."

The laugh that escapes me is throaty and loud. I shake my head in disbelief.

"What?"

"I don't need to put in a good word for you with Eli," I smirk, "trust me."

Warren smiles shyly and looks down at his feet again.

"Why did you ask me to the formal event instead of Eli then? The formal event could be much more romantic."

"I'm all business during those types of things. My investors are coming as well as a few board members. I wanted Eli to come to the day event so he could see my fun side."

Damnit. Another smile escapes me.

This guy really is perfect.

"But I guess it doesn't matter," Warren states. "I mean, you said yourself, planners can't date clients—future, past, or present."

"There's a loophole. You're *my* client, not Eli's. He's

just a junior planner. He has no clients himself," I explain. "And he's *very* newly single. But I'm warning you, he can be a bit dramatic."

Warren laughs. "I've noticed."

A calming silence comes over us as we smile at each other.

"Don't you have your election tonight?" Warren suddenly asks.

"Yeah, in about three hours. But I'm down in the polls by quite a bit. I won't win," I tell him. "So it doesn't matter if I show up or not."

"Every hear of losing graciously?" he asks me.

"I recently have, yes." I nod as I think back on Mrs. Sarris.

Warren glances down at his wristwatch. "We're quite a ways away from downtown. I'd get going if I were you."

I admire his attempt. "I can't leave an event until it's over."

"I won't tell if you won't." Warren shrugs and smiles then takes a few steps back. "Do everyone a favor first and shower. You kind of smell like a teenage boy going through puberty."

Chapter Twenty-Two

I don't believe it!

I made it back to Fairway Towers by four thirty. Enough time to shower, get dressed, and even grab something to eat from the kitchen. At five twenty-five, I head out of my place, after a quick squeeze from Pax for luck, of course.

Even though my loss is inevitable, I still decided to dress the part. A pair of skinny black pants, white blouse, and red blazer. I even flipped out my hair and grabbed an empty black clutch, purely for show.

As I get to the elevator, I realize that if I did win through some crazy miracle, I didn't have an acceptance speech written. I didn't have a "Congrats, Mrs. Glover" speech either.

I push the down button and think.

Obviously, I'll have to thank the Dorsts, Mr. Tweed, Paulette, and Bryson, with a special thank you to Luna too. There's no way I'd thank Neal. No way *ever*. What'd he really help with? A few pieces of information here or there? Basically nothing.

I wonder if he'll be down there…

Doesn't matter. I won't be speaking to him.

What if he told Glover about my screaming fit in the elevator?

"Oh, God," I cry, pushing my clutch against my face as I shut my eyes. I'm jolted back to Sunday night, and my body begins to heat up as the humiliation sets in again.

The elevator pings open, and I exhale, forcing down the shame, and take a step toward it.

I stop when I see that I'm not alone.

Standing directly in the middle of the small elevator is Glover.

I take a moment to look at the appearance of my opposing candidate.

She's dressed in a pristine black suit, a skirt that ends at her knees, a matching black blazer, and white blouse beneath. A blue silk scarf is tied neatly around her neck. Her hair is in a wavy bob, pinned back with sleek black clips. She reminds me of a blonder Sophia Loren, and for a moment, I can see why my grandfather was drawn to her.

Despite her cool demeanor, she's stylish and attractive for a woman in her…whatever age she is.

"Well? Are you just going to stand there and delay my arrival, or will you be joining me in the elevator?" Her tone is strident. And so is her stare.

Grrr… I should just take the stairs.

But as I move to turn away, something stops me, and I hustle into the elevator with her.

I stand off to the side and keep my eyes forward, staying silent as the doors shut in front of us. Slowly, the gears begin to creak as we start to move down.

Her eyes are on me.

I can see her in the reflection of the elevator doors.

She's looking at the back of my head then her head tilts downward as she surveys my outfit.

The lights above us flicker off, and the elevator jerks to a rocky stop. I stumble a bit, grabbing the wall to my right so I don't completely fall over. A loud cranking sound echoes in the small space, and I hiss through my teeth at the shriek as it rings in my ears.

Once it's died off, a dim light flashes on at the back of the elevator. The smell of burning dust hits the air almost immediately.

Oh no. Oh no, please, please tell me this isn't happening.

I reach across and jam my finger against the Call button several times. Then I remember Neal saying how it hasn't been working in over a year. I push the Emergency button instead, but it doesn't light up either. I hit the Call button again.

Oh, God. I'm stuck in a small, dark space…with Glover.

"That button is out of service, Ms. Brandt."

Across from me, Glover attempts to examine her hair in the darkened reflection of the elevator doors. There's no emotion on her pale face, hardly a care in the world.

Meanwhile, my heart starts pounding in my chest.

"Whose fault is that?" I ask. "Certainly not mine."

Her eyes land on me, but she only says, "It will restart in a few seconds, if not minutes. It may be old, but it's reliable."

"It's not reliable!" I scoff as I stretch my arms out around me. "It's stopped working! Twice in one week for me. Who knows how many times for the other tenants in the building?"

She rolls her eyes and begins to retie her blue scarf.

I turn from her, arms folded over my chest. "This hunk of junk should have been fixed years ago."

Her laugh is so brittle, goosebumps cover my arms. "It isn't in the budget. You'd know that if you had come to a condo meeting or two in the last three years. We have to wait until the end of the year."

"I'm sure everyone in the building wouldn't mind fundraising for a new one," I retort, "or you could have spoken to the building's owner. Having an unstable elevator like this is an insurance issue. They could be sued."

"Could they now?" Her sarcasm jars me. "I had *no* idea."

I can't help but grind my teeth.

I wish I could just, just drop a house on her.

"Perhaps we should remain quiet until the elevator kick starts," I suggest, grumbling.

"Your first great idea in weeks."

Ugh.

I don't know how much time has gone by, but I know it has to be over ten minutes. I checked my clutch for my cell phone, but when I find it empty, I remember I chose this clutch just for show. To match my outfit.

I lean against the wall, arms hanging down at my sides, feet tapping silently on the carpet. Glover's looked at her watch several times since I suggested we keep quiet, but she hasn't moved from her spot.

When I see her glance down at her gold wristwatch again, I ask, "How long has it been?"

"Twenty minutes."

Twenty minutes!

"I thought you said this thing moves after a few minutes!"

"It usually does," she snaps back. "Perhaps there's too much weight in it..."

I clench my jaw. "There isn't. It stopped on Sunday when Neal and I were in it, and it restarted after a minute. There was more weight in it that day."

She shrugs. "If you say so."

God, she's...she's so infuriating.

"I don't know what the hell my grandpa ever saw in you," I mutter the steely words to myself, but when Glover spins to face me, I realize I hadn't whispered them like I thought I had.

"*What*," she demands, "did you say?"

Good God, I've angered it.

I swallow the lump down before I answer. "Nothing."

She steps closer to me, a finger in the air. "You said, 'I don't know what the hell my grandpa ever saw in you.' What did you mean by that? Tell me now."

"I, uh, I just meant because he thought you were such a nice lady," I lie, adding a small shrug. "That's all. Why? What did you think I meant?"

I don't know why I threw that last bit in, maybe to mess with her, but it works because she looks flushed. Her cheeks get red, and she looks away from me, folding her arms over her chest, saying nothing.

I can't stand to be in another fifteen minutes of silence with this woman.

"Do you have your cell phone on you?"

"No, I don't carry a cell phone," she replies. "Don't you have one?"

"I forgot it upstairs."

"It wouldn't have done any good anyhow." She sighs. "I hear from the tenants there is hardly any reception in this elevator."

I want to tell her that even with one bar, I could have sent a text to Luna asking to send help, but I decide against it.

"I cannot believe I will be missing this election." Glover grunts and stomps her foot against the carpet.

"I'm going to be missing it too," I remind her.

"Yes, but you're going to lose," she says, swatting at me. "So it doesn't matter if you show up or not."

Now I stomp my foot. My hands ball into fists and jam into my hip bones as I push myself off the wall. "And whose fault is that?"

She smirks at me. "I assume the individual who brought termites into the building hoping to woo tenants."

"There were no termites in those trees when Luna brought them in!" I exclaim. "You brought them in to sabotage me, I know it."

Glover rolls her eyes. "Oh yes, just like I brought in a robber to steal from everyone."

"You probably did," I accuse. "After all, you hated the idea of the open house and garage sale. You probably hated the fact that I smashed my fundraising goal."

"Don't be a child," she retorts.

"*You're* the child. Creating rumors and posting false stories about me around the building when I never intended to do any of that to you."

"That's politics, my dear," Glover claims, narrowing her eyes at me. "It's a dirty game. And what about your gambling accusation, hmm? Was that not dirty play? Or that blasted cat one?"

"It's not politics!" I scream. "It's a stupid condo board election! And I only outed you there because you kept coming after me! But what you did to me is far worse than me accusing you of being a gambling addict or a cat hater."

"You would think, wouldn't you?" Glover throws back. "Do you have any idea the number of calls or knocks on my door I have received over the last week? Tenants demanding to see records of budget spending throughout the last six years of my presidency! I've even had a few demand to see proof that their condo fees went into the right kind of spending! I've had PETA members contact me! My reputation is completely sour now because of you."

I shake my head at her. "Oh, big deal! So I tarnished your stupid presidential reputation of being a what? A boring, old, fuddy-duddy?" I point at her as she glares at the name calling. "You tarnished my reputation as an event planner by telling everyone I slept my way to the top! That's far worse. You don't get paid to be a tyrant of a president, and when you finally step down, nobody will remember you or your stupid reputation! But I get paid to plan. It's my livelihood. I need it to survive. And I'm damn good at it, I have the highest approval rating in the entire company, beating out my boss herself—"

"We've learned why, haven't we?" Glover sneers at me.

My ears pop as I scream back. "It's because I work my

butt off, that's why! I give up my weekends, my evenings. I work ten, sometimes twelve-hour days. I've put my entire personal life on hold, in aggravation to some friends. So I made out with my boss's nephew once or twice after a bad day. If you knew anything about my life or the company I work for, you'd know my boss would have sacked me had she found out at the time."

That's probably a lie, but who cares. I'm too angry right now.

My entire body feels like it's on fire. My legs shake a bit, my hands clenched at my sides.

All she does is sigh and roll her eyes up to the ceiling. "Are we finished with our tantrum?"

I gawk at her.

She turns to the side and plays with the sleeves on her blazer. "I'm not one of your friends. I won't be bothered to calm you down. Control yourself."

I turn my back on her and kick the wall before resting my palms on the cool metal and leaning into it. "You're just a bully. You have no real friends. All you have are people kissing your ass. If you had anybody who loved you, even a little bit, they'd tell you that the way you run things is psychotic."

I drop my forehead against the wall, and through a stiff jaw, I say, "I should have posted those stupid letters like Luna told me to. You deserved that humiliation. You deserved the building to demand your resignation." I grunt against myself as I shut my eyes. "I'm such a goddamn pushover…"

"Letters? What letters?"

I almost don't answer her.

"The letters from your *Shining Knight*."

I hear her gasp.

"H-he kept those?"

Something in her voice causes me to look over my shoulder. She stands facing me again, but her eyes focus off to the side, a few fingers resting on her bottom lip. Finally, she looks at me, realizing I'm looking at her. "You read them?"

"Unfortunately, yes," I admit, "so did Luna."

"I can't believe he kept those…" She frowns, looking away from me. "What was he thinking?"

I turn and stare at the wall again. "Maybe you should have emailed. Easier to delete the evidence."

"Your grandfather didn't have email. He hated anything electronic, and he liked the old way of doing things."

I say nothing as I drop my hands from the wall and lean my shoulder into it.

From the corner of my eye, I see her take a step toward me. "Can I have them back?"

I feel my body recoil into itself at her request, and I frown as I glance over at her. She catches my vibe instantly because she immediately says, "Never mind." She takes a step back then another one forward again. "It's just that… He said he was going to get rid of them all. So I gave him the ones he sent me too."

"I don't care."

I wait for her hurl of insults, but what comes next surprises me.

"W-why didn't you post them?"

"Because I'm stupid, that's why," I retort. "And because I didn't want people thinking less of my grandpa. It didn't have anything to do with you. I could care less about you." I chuckle. "Although I should have just said forget it and let everyone know. My grandpa's dead, so is your husband, so it may not have mattered much."

"I have a son and a daughter," she tells me. "It would have definitely mattered."

I'm quiet, arms crossed over my chest as I stare at the buttons in front of me. For whatever reason, I reach over and push the Call one again. Then I press the Emergency button.

"Well, thank you. For not revealing my secret to the entire building."

My ears must be buzzing.

Did she really just thank me? And sincerely?

"Ms. Brandt? Did you hear me?"

"I, uh, heard you." My eyes drift toward her. "And you're welcome. I guess."

We're both silent.

"How did you know about me and Marco?" I ask. "Nobody knew."

"I overheard you last Friday at the elevator with your friend," she says. "I was surveying the courtyard and came out to overhear your drunken slur."

Well, that's that.

I just nod and look forward again.

"The courtyard turned out," she pauses, and I glance her way, "nice."

I scoff. "Thanks."

"Very nice," she admits, letting out a small breath. "The cabana Neal built is a wonderful touch. It looks much cozier than any pool ever would."

She's baiting me.

"I'm being serious," she declares when she sees my stare. "It surprised me."

"Oh, well, thank you again then."

Glover catches a glimpse of her wristwatch and lets out a frustrated breath. "It's six o'clock now. They'll be reading the results."

"If we're both missing, won't they hold it off?"

She shakes her head and drops her hands to her hips. "No, I expect not. Everyone's anxious to find out who the winner is."

"It'll be you," I state. "You have me beat by over twenty points on the website."

"I wouldn't count yourself out," Glover mutters, "those polls are never accurate." She looks me up and down, clearing her throat softly. "You know I had to play dirty, don't you?"

"What do you mean?"

"When I saw your name on the nominee list, I knew I had no chance. You may be a pushover, but everyone in the building likes you, and everyone in the building *loved* your grandfather. You were a shoo-in. I had to find some skeletons in your closet."

"You could have played fair. You never know, you may have won easily that way. You have experience."

"Nobody cares about that except the Tempermans," she says. "People want fresh blood. Your job gives you an advantage as well. It requires good organizational skills, communication skills…" She slowly pulls the clips from her hair. "I instantly knew you'd make a good condo board president. Playing dirty was the only option for me. All I have is this stupid condo board…"

She throws the clips to the ground and massages her

temples with her fingers. "I gave up my career as a teacher over thirty years ago so I could raise my children, stay home and keep house, which I never really minded, of course. When they went off to school, my husband's law firm was such a great success that we didn't need two incomes. So I busied myself at PTA meetings, the country club, and later, with this condo board. It's so pathetic to think it's all I have left."

"You have kids."

She sighs and stops rubbing her temples as she looks at me. "My daughter runs a chain of yoga studios, and my son is a doctor. Neither married, neither have children. I'm lucky if I see them at the holidays." She smirks and shakes her head. "So maybe you're right. Maybe it wouldn't have mattered if you posted the letters. They probably wouldn't have ever found out about the affair."

I hate that the dip in her voice has my chest ping with regret for her. With pity.

I hate that I feel bad that she's so lonely.

Ugh.

"Why'd you have it? The affair, I mean."

She bites her lip, clearly unsure whether or not to tell me.

I let out a laugh. "It doesn't matter anymore what you tell me. The worst part is me knowing about it anyway."

"I suppose you're right." She hugs her chest as she exhales a long breath. "I was lonely. My husband had just confessed to a ten-year-old affair that produced an illegitimate son…" My eyes widen, and she nods her head at my acknowledgement then goes on. "My children called me once a month, if that. I was just elected as condo board president, but everyone was so, so rude to me because I was the first woman elected. Your grandfather was on the board as you know, and he told me I had to stop being so nice."

"You? Nice?"

"I am nice, or rather, I used to be. But nobody took me seriously. They'd vote over my head, make changes without consulting me, take money from the budget without permission, run businesses without licenses. Then when we got caught, they somehow got me to front the bill."

I think about Neal for a moment.

"So over the years, I implied tougher rules, hoping things would run smoothly. And for the most part, they did. They *do*. The only thing that's really aggravating are the ridiculous requests from some tenants," she tells me. "Do you know Mr. Gaines in 204 keeps sneaking in a mouse circus?"

I make a face, which Glover mirrors.

"Disgusting. And Mrs. Koch from 401 thinks the building is cursed, and every year, she badgers me to get a priest in here. I've had the place dosed with holy water about ten times! It angers our non-denominational tenants so much, they always threaten to sue. Mrs. Toscano's another story, her and her leggings. I don't mind people selling things for a side income, but when they badger other tenants, constantly pushing people to join their organization? The complaints I get are endless. Oh! And you know that newly married couple who moved in six months ago?"

I nod even though I've never met them.

"They want to exercise their right to use the event room once a month for swinger parties. *Swingers*!"

I let out a chuckle at the thought of semi-naked people dancing in the event room while Glover supervises. I see her crack half a smile, and when I stop laughing, she adjusts herself and goes on.

"Anyway, your grandfather was just very, very kind to me. And over the years, our friendship deepened to something more. My husband never noticed. He worked until he died."

"Were you still having the affair when my grandfather died?" I ask.

"Yes, but we were discussing ending things. He wanted me to leave my husband, but I was on the fence." She lets out a sharp chuckle. "I can't even remember why. I stopped loving Harry years ago. Maybe I was just scared… Lord knows."

I watch as she looks down at her heels, her face no longer visible. Her shoulders slump, and I can only guess the feelings overtaking her.

"I'll give you the letters tonight," I say, "after the election. Just meet me at my place."

She looks up at me, and I see the tears in her eyes. She tries hard to blink them away as she gives me a small smile. "I'm sorry I told everyone you slept your way to the top. I know it isn't true, and I know it ruined your chances to nab Mrs. James as a client."

"How did you know about that?"

"Child, you sent her gift after gift, I put two and two together." She reaches into her pocket and pulls out a Kleenex, blowing her nose loudly. "Also, Neal told me Tuesday. I know you were using him to get to me."

Why am I not surprised?

"He told you?"

She wipes her nose then stuffs the Kleenex into her pocket again. "No, he didn't. He didn't have to. He was one of the only people who knew I gambled. When you threw that out, I realized he must have told you. I was livid, but I knew why he did it, I could understand. I knew he'd help you if you asked."

"I did ask, but he turned me down. Although that may have had to do with the fact that I called him your lapdog. I had to bribe him in the end."

"Bribe him? With what?"

I don't know if I should say. I mean, I don't ever want to see Neal again after Sunday. I could care less if Glover found out he was running a business behind her back, but…

"Nothing, it's nothing."

Her brows come together as she stares at me. "It's hard to believe he has a secret… Oh, could you be talking about the self-defense classes?"

"You know about those?"

She rolls her eyes. "Of course I know! I get the noise complaints from the other tenants."

"So you know about it," I say, "and you let him do it without a business license?"

She shrugs. "I find the classes admirable. Every young woman, and man, should learn how to defend themselves. There are crazy people running around in this world. Besides, he's a very helpful man to anyone in the building. I decided to throw him a bone and forgot about the license."

"Does he know you know?" I ask.

She scrunches her face up then shakes her head. "I don't think so. Maybe?" Then she smiles a little. "I'm not surprised he let you bribe him. He's always been partial to you."

"Right." My sarcasm steals her attention from the floor. "So partial, he's blown me off twice."

"It's been a hard year for the boy," she tells me.

"I wouldn't know that now, would I? He disappeared after our first date. Correction, in the *middle* of our first date. And then wouldn't talk to me when he thought I was dating a client. Even though I wasn't, he wouldn't even let me explain. Then you spread that rumor about me sleeping around."

She grimaces. "I am sorry about that. If you like, I can speak with him—"

"No, no, don't bother, it's okay." I shake my head at her offer. "I'm over it all. I've given up on whatever he and I had." I lean against the wall. "Can I ask you something? Did you plant the termites?"

Her face twists a bit. "I may have."

I knew it.

"What about my speech that went missing?"

"I stuffed it under the podium, but," she raises a finger in the air, "before you ask, I never arranged the robbery. That was by chance. I do, however, have to congratulate you on the money raised that day. I was quite impressed."

I'm about to thank her, but all I can manage to do is smile because the floor shakes beneath our feet. We both grab at the walls as the lights flicker above our heads. There's a loud humming sound that echoes around us, and the lights stop flickering. Something bangs overhead causing the entire box to rumble. Just as quickly as it starts, it stops, and the humming noise goes with it.

Then, it moves.

Slowly but surely, it's moving down.

I look over at Glover, who, like me, has a hand planted over her heart as her other hand stays plastered to the wall.

"We're moving," she breathes out in relief.

"Thank God."

We push ourselves off the walls, and like she's suddenly remembered why we're in the elevator together, Glover gasps and glances down at her watch. "And we're late, very, very late…"

Chapter Twenty-Three

When we land and the doors swing open, we rush out together, almost out of breath. We watch the elevator doors close tightly behind us.

Glover points at it. "First thing Monday, I'm making a call to replace that damn elevator. Forget waiting 'til the end of the year." Then she catches herself and looks at me. "That is, unless you're the new president."

"It's going to be the first thing I do," I say, "I promise."

"Be careful with those promises," she warns, raising an eyebrow at me. "If elected, saying you promise to any tenant is just asking for trouble. Always say 'I'll do my best.'"

I smile. "I'll do my best."

She nods in approval, and our attention shifts when someone rushes around the corner.

Neal.

He spots us, and his shoulders drop. "Where the hell have you two been? They called the election already."

Back in jeans and a black T-shirt that hugs his arms nicely, he scratches his cheek, giving me a brief look.

I look away from him, avoiding eye contact.

It's key. Otherwise I'll remember my freak out, and—

Ugh, too late.

My cheeks are already burning.

"We were trapped in the elevator," Glover tells him as he reaches us. "For over thirty minutes."

He stands in front of us, looking from her to me then back to her. "You two were stuck in that elevator for thirty minutes...*together*? And you both came out without any broken limbs or bruises?"

"Don't be dramatic." She frowns at him. "We are quite capable of being in the same room with each other. Honestly." She shakes her head as she adjusts the blue scarf at her neck. "Sometimes, I think this building and its tenants thrive on drama." She turns to me. "Now, excuse me. I will meet you in there, Ms. Brandt."

She gives my arm a small pat then turns to walk away from us.

I move to follow her, but Neal calls out to me. "Can I talk to you for a second?"

"I'm late."

"It'll only take a minute," he tells me, raising two fingers in a peace sign, "maybe two."

"Maybe after everything is over in there," I motion to the hall behind me. "I'm really late."

"I just want to say I'm sorry," he hurries on. He runs a hand through his hair and slips the other into the front pocket of his dark jeans. "For last Friday. I didn't mean to act like such a dick." He pauses and looks down at his feet for a moment. "I should have believed you about the client dinner. I was upset at something else that happened, and I took it out on you. Which was wrong. I'm sorry."

I shrug. "Forget about it."

He runs a hand over his mouth and five o'clock

shadow. "And, uh, look, I'm sorry for what I did three months ago. I did have a great time with you, but something popped up, and I didn't have a choice. I had to—"

"It's fine." I wave my hand. "It doesn't matter anymore."

"No," he frowns, "it matters. It bothered you then, and it still bothers you, and you're right, I should have told you what happened. Though in my defense, I tried to tell you at the mailboxes after that mafia princess poster went up. You kind of blew me off before I could explain—"

"You don't owe anyone an explanation," I say.

"I know I don't." He lets out a quick, sharp sigh. "Jesus, will you just stop interrupting and let me talk?"

"Ironic, isn't it?" I shoot back. "How frustrating it is trying to get someone to listen to you?"

"Okay, point taken." He points at me. "And now I'm going to go on."

I fold my arms over my chest, standing perfectly still as I take him in. His dark T-shirt is tucked into his jeans but only at the front, and as he rubs the back of his neck, I realize he's nervous. The deep lines across his forehead a dead giveaway.

"I'm not from the city. I'm from Fort Kent. It's about three hours north of here. It's where I grew up. My dad, brothers, grandparents still all live up there. Two years ago, my mother died, and my dad's been fine on his own. But eight months ago, he broke his leg pretty bad, and then three months ago, he had another accident. My brothers want him to sell the house and move in with one of them."

He smirks and softly shakes his head. "My dad's a real stubborn ass, and he won't leave the house we grew up in.

It's a nice house, I don't blame him. Right off the main drive, half an acre of land… Anyway, the night we had our date, the call I took was from my brother Patrick. My dad had another fall, and they were trying to get power of attorney. So I went home. I honestly didn't think I'd be coming back. I thought I'd have to move back in to help my dad."

"Why can't your brothers help him?"

His story has sucked me in, and I feel less…guarded.

"Patrick runs his own construction company. He's divorced…got two kids…trying to make the payments. He just doesn't have the time to take care of him," Neal explains. "Troy, he's in New York, works at some stock market firm. He does his best to communicate via text." He sighs and slips both hands into the pockets of his jeans. "Anyway, I managed to get a live-in aide for my dad. That way he has help when his leg gets too bad, and he doesn't have to leave the house. Or give my brothers power of attorney."

I nod but don't have anything to say. I simply give him a soft smile, which he returns.

"I did think about you up there. I felt like absolute shit at how I left things. I didn't think I'd be coming back so I didn't think there would be a reason to tell you—" He sees me take my eyes off him, and his words fall short.

There's no way I can be angry at him after this story.

In fact, it just makes me want to throw my arms around his neck and kiss him.

God, I'm a basket case.

After a silent second, he goes on. "Anyway, I'm sorry. I didn't mean to hurt you. I didn't know you liked me… like that. I thought I was the only one who felt…

something. Then you crashed my class, and I realized that maybe I still had a chance. I didn't think I was your type."

"My type?" I repeat his words as if they're foreign.

"You know, the Ken doll look-alike." He's joking, but it hits me that he's talking about Warren.

I draw in a slow breath. "Oh my God. He does look like a Ken doll! I can't believe I never noticed before…" I see Neal smirk and casually shrug. I uncross my arms and clear my throat to break the silence. "I, uh, no, that's not my type."

"So Luna says."

"You talked to Luna?"

He nods once. "She explained some things. She's a good friend to you."

"She is. An annoying campaign manager, but a good friend."

I see him smile at me, and for some reason, I think back on his return. "If you— If you still liked me when you got back, why were you bugging me so much with your smirking and your—"

"Teasing? I don't know. It was clear you were angry at me. I guess I thought joking with you and flirting a bit would make you hate me less…soften you up?"

I trace the outline of the tile with my foot. "Well, I didn't *hate* you. Not really." I look up to see him smile and remove his hands from his pockets.

"So, do you think we could have a do-over on that first date?"

"No, but we could have a second date."

My suggestion makes him smirk, and he nods his head at me. "Okay, how about tonight?"

"I could have a late dinner."

We smile at each other, but there's something still so off about this moment.

Why's it so…so weird?

"Little bit awkward, I'm feeling," Neal suddenly says, motioning at the space between us.

"Yes!" I cry out. "Why is it so awkward?"

"Probably because it's real life, not a movie," he guesses, shrugging. "I mean, if this were a movie, after my declaration of adoration, there'd be some sweep-you-off-your-feet kind of kiss that'd have all the people watching shriek happily."

I laugh at his choice of the words *declaration* and *adoration* and cover my face with my hands. When I part my fingers, I find that he's stepped closer to me. His smile is small but spritely as he wraps a hand around my waist, the other reaching up to cup the side of my face.

My stomach flutters and I grab hold of Neal's shirt, pulling him toward me.

The kiss is exactly as it was the first time. Enough to make my knees wobble a bit, and my mouth to part a little more. I can feel his heart pounding inside his chest this time, and as my hands run from his chest to his neck, his grasp tightens on me.

As the kiss ends and we pull back, whatever awkwardness we felt earlier is definitely gone.

"Okay." The word escapes my lips rather mousy sounding, and I have to clear my throat as I look from his mouth to his eyes. "Um, now I'm definitely really, really late."

He smirks at me. "Then let's go."

We leave the elevator area and hurry down the hall. As we near the event room, both of us practically speed walking, we can hear the celebration through the large closed doors. There's dance music blaring and waves of loud laughter every few seconds.

Neal reaches the door before me and grabs the handle. "Ready?"

I'm nervous. My fingers begin to twitch at my sides. "No, but just open the door."

I don't know why I should feel this way.

I know I've lost.

He pulls the door open, and the music rushes toward us. We step through the doorway together, Neal holding the door back, but nobody seems to have noticed that we've arrived. They're all sipping on champagne in plastic champagne flutes.

The room is decorated with black, white, and gold balloons. Some have fallen from the ceiling and glide around the legs of the tenants. There are gold and black streamers from corner to corner. The chairs are positioned erratically instead of in their usual perfect rows. I don't see any of my teammates, but I do see Mrs. James and the Zhengs near the door. I also spot Glover shaking hands with Mr. Tweed. She's smiling at him, and whatever he says to her makes her nod and laugh.

So she's won.

I expected to feel a bit upset, but all I feel is a smile coming over my lips as I watch her talk with Mr. Tweed. She looks very happy.

"I guess I better do the right thing," I say to Neal, "and congratulate the winner."

He puts a hand on my back, ushering me into the room with him and shutting the door behind him. I leave his side and walk over to Mrs. Glover.

Mr. Tweed spots me first. He raises his cane in the air. "There you are! We were wondering what happened to you! Arlene told us you two had been stuck in the elevator for half an hour."

"We were," I tell him, and then I look over to Glover. I let out a short breath and extend my hand to her, my smile anything but fake. "Well, congratulations. The better woman won."

Her brows come together, and she looks over at Mr. Tweed.

He lets out a laugh and shakes his head before tapping my foot with his cane. "You mean the better *man*."

Er, what?

"Mr. Tweed is the new president," Glover clarifies when she sees my expression. "The people voted for him."

How can— How can that be?

"Hilly!"

Luna pushes through Mrs. Glover and Mr. Tweed, obviously flustered, her face red and hair frizzy. Based on her blue dress and white belt, I assumed she had been done up nicely before the results were called. "They all staged a coup!"

"Who did?"

She elbows Mr. Tweed in the shoulder and glares down at him. "Our team. Everybody but me and Bryson and Neal. They all went behind our backs, had secret meetings, and worked to vote in Mr. Tweed!"

As Neal steps up behind me, I can't help but let out a laugh.

Luna's eyes shoot to me. "It's not funny!"

Except that it is.

It's hilarious.

After all this work, all this backstabbing, all this…this *drama*, neither one of us walked away with the crown. Neither one of us has the power now. It's been handed to a man in a blue and yellow checkered vest.

My shoulders rock a bit as my laughter subsides. "Oh, Luna. It's fine. Really, it's better this way. There was no way I was going to have won."

"Yes, you could have!" Luna exclaims. "If you had done what I told you to do this week—"

"Your goal was to have me overthrown," Glover interrupts. She takes a slow drink of her champagne as she looks at Luna. "It's done now. What does it matter who did it?"

Luna ignores her, motioning at the Dorsts who stand in a group not too far from us. They haven't even noticed that I've arrived. Luna's eyes turn fierce. "They don't even have a good reason as to why they betrayed us."

Paulette appears next to me and Mr. Tweed, her hair now highlighted with pink and orange streaks. Her small eyes are on Luna. "For goodness' sake, Luna, I told you why we did it!" She points at me. "After the first week, we knew Hilary wouldn't be the president this building needs. She's too busy with her job. So we started entertaining another idea behind your back because we knew you'd throw the biggest fit if we mentioned Mr. Tweed as a new candidate."

Luna raises a hand in Paulette's face.

Paulette looks at me with annoyance. "I'm sorry, Hil, but you didn't even really want to do this. You didn't really want to be president. You said it many times."

"I guess I did, yeah," I admit, exchanging a look with Glover. Then something hits me, and I frown at Paulette.

"Wait a second, so you all knew that Mr. Tweed would most likely end up being the winner and you *still* let Glover and I go at it for *weeks*?"

"That's quite rude," Glover interjects. "Much of our time and resources were wasted on besting each other."

"Exactly!" Luna cries. "They just sat back and watched us all stress over nothing!"

"Hey." Paulette points a finger toward me and Glover. "First of all, we didn't know that Mr. Tweed would really win. It was a gamble. And second, it wasn't our fault you guys started battling it out."

I gawk at her. "Yes it was! You kept pushing me to do it!"

"But she started it!" Paulette motions at Glover in a huff.

Mr. Tweed shakes his cane between us.

"Now, now. What's done is done. There is no use in getting ourselves all worked up. We do have to exist in this building together, so let us all be civil. Let us all be neighborly. That said," Mr. Tweed smiles at me and Glover, "I would be greatly honored if you two would join me on the board." Mr. Tweed gives Paulette his cane. He then extends his hands, placing one on my shoulder and the other on Glover's. "We could make fantastic changes with the other three members."

I look at Glover, whose lips have come together tightly. I know that look well.

"I think we'll pass," I quickly say to Mr. Tweed. I give him a smile as he removes his hands from our shoulders. "I think people may not be very happy if Mrs. Glover or I sit on the board after this whole mess."

"Oh." He frowns a bit, his thin white brows looking

almost nonexistent. Then he smiles brightly at me and chuckles a bit. "Well, maybe you're right. You two did come off as crazies the last few weeks."

Glover and Luna are the only ones who don't join in on our chuckling.

Paulette hands Mr. Tweed his cane and smiles. "Come on, Mr. Tweed, you have to make your winning speech in five minutes."

He takes his cane back and nods at her. "Yes, of course. Well, I'll see you all after my speech. We've ordered some pizzas, and Bryson has run out for more drinks. It will be a fine celebration!" He raises his cane excitingly, and Paulette ushers him toward the front of the room.

"Ms. Brandt? May I have a word?"

As I turn from everyone, I find Mrs. James standing a few feet behind me.

I walk over to her and motion at her shimmering dress. "That dress is gorgeous."

"Thank you. I have a museum benefit tonight, so I have to be quick here." She opens the black purse hanging off her white gloves and retrieves a bundle of crumpled paper. "I believe these are yours."

I take the papers from her, frowning as I unfold them.

It's my notes for our meeting.

"Mr. Turner was kind enough to drop them by my unit Tuesday evening," she informs me, her chin high. "I took a look at them after he told me how good they were. He's right, they are quite interesting. I'm intrigued. He was also brazen enough to tell me that I had you pegged completely wrong. And I just spoke with Mrs. Glover, who also sang your praises and explained to me how it was an error on her part to spread a rumor about you that she had not fact-checked. When I told her I had investigated myself, she said that your boss's nephew is known to spin lies for attention."

She covered for me?

I look over my shoulder. Glover's shaking her head at Mrs. Temperman, who, if I'm going by her posture, is as upset at the election's turn of events as Luna is.

"She did?" I say.

"She did." Mrs. James nods as she shuts her purse. "So, if you are still interested or willing to meet—"

Oh my God!

"I'm willing!" I scream at her. She jumps a bit, startled, and I pull my voice and energy back down a bit. "I'm willing, yes."

She blinks at me. "Very well. How is your schedule this week upcoming?"

"I can do any day of the week. You name it. Monday or Tuesday or—"

Wait. I'm not going to risk waiting again.

"How about tomorrow?" I suggest, "I know it's a bit unconventional since it's Sunday, but we could meet for breakfast and get it out of the way. That way you could take it to your fellow board members on Monday and give them a week to decide?"

She raises an eyebrow. "All right, tomorrow at ten a.m. You know the Garden Cafe a few blocks from here?"

I pull the notes against my chest. "I will be there at ten a.m. sharp."

"I shall see you then." She adjusts the gloves at her elbows then turns away from me. "Have a good evening, Ms. Brandt."

"You too, Mrs. James."

I watch as she leaves the room, and it isn't until the door is shut behind her that I let myself detonate just a little. I jump in place and squeal with a toothy grin.

Eeekk! I got the meeting back! She was intrigued by my ideas!

I have to tell Eli.

Oh, damn. I forgot my phone upstairs.

Someone steps up next to me, loudly clearing their throat and thrusting a flute of champagne in front of me. I look up to find Neal watching me with both eyebrows raised.

"I don't care." I point a finger at him while my other hand fumbles with the papers and takes the champagne. "I don't care if I look stupid. I just got the meeting back with Mrs. James!"

"I don't think you look stupid." He takes a drink of his champagne and shrugs as he watches me do the same. "A little bit nutty maybe…"

I kick his foot as I swallow the cool, bubbly drink. It fizzes down my throat. "Thank you, by the way, for talking to her and giving her my notes."

"I wasn't able to convince her to speak with you," Neal admits, he then points back to where we stood earlier. "But she was."

I look at Glover. She must feel my eyes on her because she looks away from Mrs. Temperman.

I mouth, *thank you*, unsure if she can even tell, but when she winks back, I ease into a small smile.

"Looks like you two are best buds now," Neal says.

"Oh, I don't think so," I confess, looking up at him. "I think we'll always bump heads."

He finishes his champagne. "You want to stay for Mr. Tweed's speech, or do you want to sneak out for dinner?"

I grin, almost shyly, as I bring my champagne to my mouth. "I can sneak out."

I down the drink, and Neal sets our empty glasses on a nearby chair. Just as he takes hold of my hand, his phone rings. He pulls it out and checks the caller, making a face.

My heart sinks a little.

"Oh, is it an emergency?" I ask. "Do you have to go?"

He looks from the phone to me as he pushes the door open. He cancels the call and slides the phone back into his pocket. "It's Troy. It's fun to piss him off. And the only place I have to go is out to eat. With you."

The End

Acknowledgments

I promise I'll keep this short!

The biggest shout out needs to go to my wonderful editor/publisher Karan Eleni. Without her, this book wouldn't have come to life, and the title would have been much worse (not to mention boring!). Thanks for being my saving grace when I needed it.

To my wonderful sidekicks, Monica and Josemine. You keep my creative juices flowing, and I think you know there would be no writing career for me if it were not for the two of you.

To the fantastic bloggers who are always willing to read, review or feature my work: Breakfast at Shelby's, Book Lover in Florida, One Book at a Time/Books and Wine are Lovely, Chick Lit Central. And all the members of ChickLitChatHQ that are always willing to lend a hand with promotion. Sincerest thank yous!

And lastly, to all my delightful readers. Whether you beta read or ARC read for me, or just read for pleasure because you don't think my books sucks…thank you, thank you very much. Your reviews mean more than you know.

About the Publisher

Kindred Ink Press is an independent publisher of (almost) all things romance. From romantic comedy to cozy mystery, historical to contemporary real-life romance, we've got a bit of romance for just about everyone. Our books range from quick reads to those of epic length and can be found in digital and print formats with audiobooks coming soon.

Visit kindredinkpress.com to learn more about our books and to buy books online. You will also find features, author interviews, and news of any author events.

Sign up for the Kindred Insider email newsletter to receive new release and sales notifications in your inbox!

https://kindredinkpress.com/insider